Some of the 5 star reviews

Fast-paced near future dystopia set in the UK. Background ...

ByAlfon 19 May 2015

Fast-paced near future dystopia set in the UK. Background and setting all too plausible. I had to read the second half of the book in one go, as I could just not put it down.

Excellent contemporary political thriller

ByAmazon Customeron 25 April 2015

An excellent contemporary political thriller. Steve Grieves gets the different 'voices' of people in politics at all levels spot on. This is book well worth reading, with a plot that gathers pace, twisting and turning to the end of the book. Highly recommended.

Gripping thriller, well worth a read!

ByKaterina Popion 14 April 2015

Set some 20 years in the future, when the UK has become little more than a source of bonded labour for China, with the 'undeserving poor' forced into so-called New Towns which more closely resemble gulags, Steve Grieves' novel forces us to confront some hard truths indeed. Set in a run-down Mancunian housing estate, with a large cast of characters, he depicts a confrontation between the forces of power and ordinary people which is the result, I believe, of a logical extension of the policies of our most recent governments. I found my frustration with the devious tactics of the politicians in the story, and their servants the spin doctors, the private security companies, the police and mainstream media growing with every chapter. Mr Grieves clearly understands the way in which power can be abused, and how the consequences are frightening for our democracy. The residents of the Riverside

Estate, who appear to have few resources to fight their removal from their homes, find inspirational leadership, and decide that to come together as a community is their only hope. The tension ratchets up as the story proceeds to a taut climax, which leaves the reader with plenty to ponder on.
Some good, if complex, plotting, and a strong narrative thrust plus believable characters make this the one novel you really must read before you vote in the upcoming General Election.

A scary possibility!

ByM Neveon 26 March 2015

Interesting if somewhat scary view of the hopefully fictional future of the UK, well written especially for a first novel. Well done Steve

Thought provoking as well as thoroughly entertaining

ByGraehamon 14 March 2015

Very well researched. Three dimensional characters. Plenty of cliff hangers to keep you turning the pages. A great read that would readily convert to the silver screen.

Amazing fast - paced political thriller

ByAmazon Customeron 10 March 2015

Amazing fast - paced political thriller. Set in the not too distant future and very topical dealing with poverty, corrupt government and how people have to make very hard choices that affect everyone around them. Couldn't put it down. Can't wait for his next book.

This novel is a work of fiction. The names, characters and incidents portrayed in it are the work of the author's imagination. Any resemblance to actual persons, living or dead is entirely coincidental.

Edited by Sue Millar

THE GATES OF SEDITION

Original and modified cover art by Kevin Dooley and CoverDesignStudio.com"

ISBN-13: 978-1523642762

(CreateSpace-Assigned)

THE GATES OF SEDITION

By
Steve Grieves

For Ellie & Zee

& especially for

Mrs King
(AKA)
Maureen Twomey

She who makes me better than I would otherwise be.

Please Note this book was previously published under the title Alithiea

Alithiea (Greek: Η Αλήθεια, meaning "The Truth"

Chapter One

Downing Street London

Gregory Mablethorpe, British Prime Minister and Christopher Jennings' boss, was in trouble. Christopher could hear the tell-tale buzz running through the press pack which, he thought, had the kind of cacophonous musical quality when something bad was about to happen.

Mablethorpe, as usual these days, was oblivious to the mood in the room as he once again lectured them on the progress of the Government's 'Future Way Strategy'.

Christopher could see the UK section of the press core were simply bored with the topic, which was unsurprising, given how much it had been the main topic of every briefing for months now. Mablethorpe, however, was determined to remind them once again that, before the Future Way Strategy (or FWS as it was now known), and the partnership he had personally negotiated with the Chinese Government, the UK had been sliding into bankruptcy and potential social implosion.

That was true, Christopher had to admit. China had delivered on its end of the deal, pouring billions into the UK economy after it had seceded from the EU. They had also moved quickly to establish the first tranche of the so-called 'New Towns' on the windswept Northumbrian coast. New Towns were fast becoming the centres of China's manufacturing and distribution hub in Europe and, more importantly for China, they made a bold statement about its intention to dominate European trade. The New Towns were populated by volunteers who were given substantive relocation grants to move and work there. Mablethorpe's government of National Coalition had restricted applicants to people who lived in areas that had been classified as Zone 1. Fundamentally, that meant anywhere crime, unemployment and poverty, were rampant and out of control.

There were many who applauded the government's initiative and of course many who did not, though in the latter case most critics were merely the marginalised and disempowered, so had little impact on the debate. The vast majority of 'active' citizens still applauded a project which meant the long-term unemployed were found work, whilst at the same time the problematic Zone 1 areas were emptied out of undesirable social elements. The pilots had been deemed a success so far and Parliament had now gone as far as passing the 'Gating Act' which meant that Zone 1 areas were now being controlled in an unprecedented way.

Christopher suddenly zoned back in to the meeting as he noticed that the Prime Minister was becoming visibly irritated, at least to those who knew the signs, with the line of foreign press questions.

"Prime Minister Mablethorpe, Jenny Warburg International Free Press. What do you say to the charge that many of your government's critics make, both here and internationally, which is that what you are actually undertaking is a form of economic cleansing by forcing the poor and helpless into forced labour camps?'

Mablethorpe tipped his head to one side slightly, a gesture that he knew on camera made it look like he was listening attentively, but which Christopher knew meant something completely different. The PM's voice when he spoke was at its most reasonable.

"Well Jenny, I know that there are many who say that, though I'm sure you wouldn't expect me to agree!' He gave them his prize winning chuckle supported by the UK press who chuckled right along with him as he went on. "No, Jenny. What I and this government are interested in, is freeing our citizens from the yoke of poverty that successive governments both nationally and regionally have placed around their necks. That yoke, though well- intentioned is too often rooted in bureaucracy and regulation, and is of course one of the main reasons why we left the European Union. You know we British have a proud history of valuing our freedom, it runs through our veins, and is ingrained in every fibre of our being. Indeed, whenever we British have remembered our heritage and embraced the notion of individual freedom, of individual liberty; that is when we are at our strongest. This government of national coalition is determined that the United Kingdom will continue to champion the freedom of markets, and will continue to slash burdensome bureaucracy and regulation so all our citizens can enjoy their true birthright."

The woman from the International Free Press tried to come back but Christopher had already given the prearranged signal that the microphone should be moved along to the next foreign correspondent.

'Prime Minister, Jacque Lafferte, Paris Review. What is your response to the European President Giovanni Carlotti who just yesterday compared the UK's Zone 1 Gating Act to how the Nazis fenced in the Jewish quarters before the Second World War?'

Mablethorpe drew himself to his full height of six foot two inches, gripping the sides of the rostrum as he leaned forward, his green eyes staring into the camera that was broadcasting live around the capitals of the world. Christopher felt himself tense as he awaited Mablethorpe's reply.

"The President of the European Union shames himself by making such remarks. It was Great Britain who above all others stood against the Nazis; it was Great Britain who gave the countless lives of its sons and daughters to defend not only the Jewish people, but to defend the whole of Europe. This at a time I might add when President Carlotti's family along with their compatriots were applauding the love-in between Mussolini and Adolf Hitler!"

The room exploded in camera flashes, audible gasps coming not just from the foreign correspondents. The Italian reporter was on his feet shouting that Mablethorpe should apologise but was largely drowned out by the rest of the press core calling out questions.

Christopher leaned across and tapped Mablethorpe on the arm pointing to the note he had written and placed in front of him, 'GO NOW!' Mablethorpe looked at the note and then at Christopher, about to argue, but whatever he saw in his Communication Director's face, panic maybe, seemed to get through to him as he nodded tightly. Jennings switched on his microphone, and raised his voice.

"I'm sorry, Ladies and Gentlemen, but we have run over time and the Prime Minister has another important meeting to attend!"

As they left the room Mablethorpe smiled and waved to the cameras as if everything had gone rather well.

*

An hour later Christopher stood with the PM's press team behind the single camera of Sky News as Gregory Mablethorpe, after much ranting and railing, had finally accepted the inevitability that he would have to apologise. It had been agreed that the interview would be straightforward with agreed and scripted questioning, and would last for a maximum of ten minutes. Christopher was happy so far at how Mablethorpe was handling the interview. He had already delivered the apology in a graceful and sincere manner, as he explained that of course he had known that the Italian Prime Ministers family had fought against the fascist Mussolini, and that the President's own Grandfather had been executed by the fascists. He had smiled at the interviewer as he went on to say that it was just an honest 'misspeak'.

So far so good! Christopher thought, forcing himself to relax the tension in his neck.

"I have of course already spoken to Prime Minister Carlotti and did so immediately after this morning's briefing, and Giovanni accepts it was a simple misunderstanding."

The truth Christopher knew was that the President of the European Union had threatened to fly over and kick Mablethorpe's balls through the back of his head. The Italian press were already comparing Mablethorpe's own family history with Carlotti's - which was uncomfortable given that the Mablethorpe family had been active supporters of Oswald Moseley's fascist 'Black Shirts' in the thirties. In the end it had been agreed that Mablethorpe would go on air to apologise, though at least Mablethorpe had had the wit, Christopher acknowledged, to insist to Carlotti that the interview would be done by a British broadcaster of his choice. The interviewer Suzanne Gretch was seen by many TV anchors as a lightweight and eye candy for low-brow news junkies. Christopher knew differently. Even now he could see how the woman with a little toss of her hair here, the unconscious shift to settle her dress there, and the frequent sympathetic smiles were all working well on the master of charm himself, who had begun to lean unconsciously toward her aura of support and sympathy. Christopher ran his hand across the ache at the back of his neck as he felt the tension coming back. Instinct told him that this was going to be bad and, as usual, he was the one who would be blamed.

Chapter Two

Riverside Estate North Manchester

Berni's Bistro wasn't really a bistro and it didn't belong to Berni, at least it hadn't for the last ten years or so, if indeed it ever had. Katy, the café's current owner for the last ten years, had thought about changing the name on occasion, maybe 'Katy's Caff' or the 'Dockers Rest'. In the end though she'd decided she liked the irony of it. After that she'd even emphasised it with a cheap reprint of Van Gogh's 'Cafe Terrace' alongside other pictures of the glamorous cafes of Europe. They didn't exactly fit in with the chipped Formica tables, the plastic, bolted down orange chairs or the lino floor, which after years of use from Dockers boots had little left of its once gaudy pattern. But Katy kept the place spotless and Berni's was recognised as serving the best and cheapest fried breakfast in the area. Before Riverside had been 'gated- in', business was OK, not great, but good enough to feed her and the two kids she had mostly raised alone and who had long since departed the nest. The gates though had changed everything. Barton's Dockside, which ran behind the Riverside Estate on the banks of the Manchester Ship Canal, had been the hub that serviced an industrial estate that, in its heyday, employed over seventy five thousand people in numerous factories. Now it was largely home to warehouses and transit stations that dealt with the imported goods that, these days, arrived mostly by road rather than ship.

The canal which had once been the main route into the industrial north was now a ghost of its former self. Still, the few big ships that spewed out their cargoes of oil and grain on the opposite side of the canal once or twice a week had been enough to give her a steady trade. Merchant seamen used Riverside as their main access to the bright lights of the city of Manchester, which meant Katy usually got them mostly hung-over or sometimes still drunk as they made their way back to their ships in the early mornings. Now though Riverside Estate was classified as a Zone 1 area, and they had gated off all routes in and out including easy access to the City of Manchester. This meant the seamen, who seemed universally to have an almost pathological dislike of authority, preferred a less monitored location from which to take their shore leave. She knew if something didn't alter soon she had maybe five or six months before she'd be forced to close the business - and then what?

She leaned on the kitchen counter, only half watching the TV on the wall. Like the majority of her customers she didn't really give a stuff about politics and politicians, especially the 'Great Arse' himself Gregory Mablethorpe who was currently spouting off. Those people had nothing to do with ordinary people and anyway, as far as she was concerned, they all pissed in the same pot and were only there to line their own pockets. Today though was different as, out of the blue, Riverside and the other eight gated estates were once again back in the news. The only other time the small run down housing estate had been noticed by the great and the good was during the last riots. It was those riots that of course that had created support in the wider country for the draconian measures that were to come. At that time the estate had been crawling with camera crews from across the globe. Even the most hopeless residents of Riverside, and there were plenty of them, got their fifteen minutes of fame as the world's media rung its hands on how the new Coalition government was proposing to deal with the chaos in the rundown British estates.

Riverside had been buzzing for that brief moment as people had argued for and against the gating in of whole communities. The government argued that it would make the Zone 1 areas safer places for the people that lived in them. Katy had even bought into that for a little while. What was the difference between wealthy neighbourhoods being protected by gates and private security, and places like this? She and many others had actually thought that's what it was going to be like, that the government was actually trying to help people like her for a change, people who just wanted to live a decent safe life. Of course it had soon become very clear that Zone 1 gating was something new and nothing whatsoever to do with helping the likes of her. For the wealthy estates, the gates and guards surrounding them kept the criminals and troublemakers out, making for a safe environment where families could prosper. But for Riverside and the other Zone 1 areas, the gates weren't designed to keep trouble out but to keep it in. And it didn't matter if you happened to be a decent hard-working cafe owner. If you lived in a Zone 1 area you had effectively become a prisoner.

In theory of course you could go out of the estate whenever you wanted. You needed the right passes which everybody had, but the processes involved with leaving or entering were both laborious and intimidating. Still, most people who didn't live in Zone 1 areas seemed to think the system was working. The government said crime nationally had fallen dramatically and now with the New Towns, people from Zone 1 areas many of whom had never worked in their lives were being found work.

If she could choose she would have put MTV on instead of rolling news feeds, but for the last twelve months, since she had been with Doc she'd had to watch more news and listen to more political drivel than she had heard in her preceding forty three years. He had drifted into Riverside the same way as all the 'arty-farties' or 'bohemians', as Doc preferred to call them, had arrived in dribs and drabs and without creating much fuss. They were an odd bunch of intellectuals, artists, musicians and general off-the-wall types. A lot of them were a bit weird and had some strange ideas but, in the main she thought they were OK and mostly they kept to each other's company. Apart from Doc of course who, when Sunny had brought him into the bistro on that first day, had seemed to claim it as his own informal office space. It still amazed her that they were together, chalk and cheese, oil and water. Even physically they were total opposites. Katy, as her mother used to say was 'big-boned' - or a 'fat cow' as her delightful ex had frequently called her. Doc was taller than her but didn't have a pick on him, probably weighing no more than ten and a half stone wet through. Yet, with Doc, Katy had met, for the first time since she was a young girl, someone who made her feel attractive and even on occasion beautiful. She still savoured the day a year and one week ago tomorrow, when he had arrived and was sat in the same chair he sat in now. He had told her she had beautiful hair and asked if she was Irish. She had been tempted to give him a wallop, a 'Katy special' as the regulars called it. But something in his expression had stopped her. Instead she had smiled and touched her hair like some daft schoolgirl.

'No, but my Grandmother was from Dublin,' she had said sounding even to herself like a simpering idiot. Then she had walloped Old Lofty on the back of the head for sniggering, while the rest of them had quickly looked down at their plates in case they were next. Nobody who knew them sniggered now of course. Doc was as much a fixture in the bistro as the old boys who supped one mug of tea every three hours. She still didn't know why he had chosen her or even Riverside. She knew he had been a teacher at a big London university and that he had been blacklisted for supporting the protestors in 2018, but other than that he didn't talk much about it. He was also posh. Even though she teased him about how hard he tried not to be, it was obvious to her and the rest of them that he came from a very different world to theirs. But, they fit together so well, they made each other laugh and he had lit her up physically like no-one ever had. Before she met Doc an orgasm to Katy was eating a cream cake. The three of them, Doc and his two regular cronies Sunny and Jo, were sat glued to the TV now, Sunny throwing his head back and laughing at some crack Doc was making. Jo winked at her and rolled her eyes. She liked Jo, the woman was definitely not big-boned - 'dark and willowy 'like a Spanish queen' Doc had said to Katy one night whilst they lay in bed. She had squeezed his balls for that till he had squealed like a girl and they had both collapsed laughing in each other's arms. That Jo was in love with Sunny had been obvious to her for a long time, and that Sunny felt the same was equally obvious. Yet the two of them couldn't get it together and were always tiptoeing around each other. She had tried to talk to her about it. Sure Sunny had had his problems, but he had been sober for at least the year he had been in Riverside and that Katy had known him, and she'd told Jo on more than one occasion that she should give him a break.

Doc slapped Sunny on the back, "Well that's one nil to you, my happy friend," he said.

Sunny laughed as he replied, "Ah it was obvious he would have to come back on!"

"Nevertheless you called it Sunny, my man. Katy we owe Sunny a coffee on the house."

Katy gave him a look, "Oh yeah! And whose house would that be Doc?"

Doc grinned and pulled out his beat-up wallet looking for a coin, then scratched his chin.

"Forget it lover. I'll take it out of you later!" she said.

Mablethorpe was on the TV apologising over his gaffe as Sunny had predicted half an hour ago that he would have to. Suzanne Gretch, the Sky woman who Katy called 'Cruella', was drawing him out on the gated areas, even mentioning Riverside by name. The whole bistro was quiet now as she continued to push him. The bistro door opened and John Mallet went and sat at his usual corner table by the window; she tilted her head at him letting him know she would get his tea and bacon roll. He smiled in acknowledgement turning his own eyes to the TV.

Gretch was in her stride now as she had gotten Mablethorpe relaxed enough to let him wax eloquently on his government's massive achievements to date. She decided to step up the pace conscious that they only had five minutes of live feed left.

"Prime Minister, there are those who say that what you have done by gating in these estates is in effect internment, and that the only way out is for people to volunteer for the New Towns project."

Mablethorpe's eyes flicked briefly to the side as he could see Jennings frantically making cut the interview gestures, this hadn't been part of the pre-agreed questions - but it was a live broadcast and Mablethorpe knew if he tried to shut it down it wouldn't look good, not at all. He turned back to Gretch and took off his spectacles a sign that he was going to be his most sincere self, a man unafraid of the tough questions.

"You know, Suzanne, when this government came to power the people asked – no, they didn't ask, they demanded. They demanded of this government that we did two things, just two, Suzanne. The first was that we brought a halt to the escalating violence in our inner cities, the disorder on the very worst estates that so threatened the ordinary people of our country that they no longer felt safe in their own homes. The second demand they made was that we create the conditions that would lead to employment for all of our people. We have, I'm proud to say Suzanne, risen to those two challenges, and have in a very short time seen remarkable progress not least through the 'Future Way Project'. Now I know, Suzanne, that people are saying all sorts of things about the New Towns and that people have concerns, of course they do and I completely understand that. But the simple truth is that we are giving people the opportunity to leave what are broken and desolate areas and start a new life. An opportunity, incidentally, that has only been made possible because of the tough decisions that this government and this Prime Minister have taken."

"Yet the rumours persist, Prime minister, those rumours that insist the Chinese are effectively running work camps in the New Towns and that, though people have volunteered to go there in the first instance, your critics say that in effect it's a one-way ticket, and of course the Europeans are saying that….."

"I'm afraid that these rumours, these innuendos, are just nonsense, Suzanne, they really are. I have seen these camps first-hand……"

"Camps?"

"Towns, the New Towns are... well, they are transparent and open to scrutiny-"

"Then why aren't we allowed access to them despite our repeated requests? If you allowed unrestricted access, wouldn't that assure our viewers and the wider world that the criticisms aren't valid?"

Mablethorpe replaced his glasses. "As I have said on many occasions, Suzanne, there are proprietary technologies which means some limited restrictions are necessary. And of course we are trying to give people a new start without……"

"It's is also being reported that the gating-in strategy has actually had the opposite effect to that which you intended."

"I don't follow?"

"Well, many people believe that, far from the gating-in of Zone 1 areas leading to people moving out of deprived areas, such as Oakland's in the Midlands, the operation has actually led to an upsurge of sympathy for those left-wing political groups who have been organising against the policy."

"Please, Suzanne, let's call these people what they actually are which is Subversives, clear and simple, and no amount of propaganda from outside of these shores will change that. These Subversives that you describe as political groupings are no such thing, they are Subversives and they are terrorists whose sole agenda is the overthrow of our democratic traditions and beliefs."

"That is, if you'll forgive me saying, Prime Minister, a rather simplistic view-"

"No it isn't, not in the least! Now, you have asked me the question so please allow me to answer it. We have secured these troubled areas and we will continue to do so in order to protect the citizens of this country from subversive elements and terrorist groups. That policy will not change, not as long as I remain Prime Minister."

Gretch smiled, "Prime Minister, that is very clear, thank you. Finally, as I am afraid we are running out of time, do you foresee a time - or rather is it your hope- that these communities will agree to move voluntarily? That is that they take up the offer of relocation to the New Towns? And, if I may also add to that, what if they don't agree to move voluntarily. What is your message to them then?"

Mablethorpe stared at Suzanne Gretch for a moment that seemed to last much longer than it actually was on live television, before replying. "My message is very clear, Ms Gretch. This government will assist all those who wish to work and contribute to our society. We have offered them an opportunity, a chance of a new life in clean modern housing. We have offered them a not insubstantial grant to give them a good start in that new life. And of course we offer them a job that is guaranteed for life. For life! Now who else gets such guarantees?" Mablethorpe held up his hand forestalling her interruption. "To answer your specific question, frankly I cannot conceive of anyone not wanting to take up such opportunities when they are currently living in the type of squalid run-down places that we've been discussing. That is, of course, unless they have a different agenda, and by that I mean a subversive agenda. In that case, and in those circumstances, those people should be labelled for what they are, subversive enemies of the State, and we as a government will deal with them accordingly!"

When Doc turned the TV off there was silence in the bistro. Everyone still staring at the blank screen. Finally Sunny broke the silence.

"So if I understand what he's just said correctly, our government has just declared that anyone who won't work for the Chinese in their New Towns is a terrorist?"

Doc placed his hands flat on top of the table, still staring at the screen as he spoke, "I have told you before, my friend, they are coming for us. All you have to decide is what you are prepared to do about it?"

Before Sunny could answer, Katy said in a loud voice, "Sergeant Mallet, your tea and sandwich!"

Mallet smiled. Nicely done, Katy, he thought, admiring how she had shut down any discussion in front of him. "I think I'll have it 'to go' though!"

Sergeant John Mallet bit into the bacon sandwich whilst he leaned on the outside of the boarded-up post office opposite Katy's café. Sorry, Bistro, he thought, smiling to himself. It was true the place had seen better times like the rest of Riverside, but unlike most of the estate, Katy kept the place spotless, and in his view served the best bacon butties he had ever tasted. He was watching the latest two additions to his ever-decreasing thin blue line. They couldn't be more different, he thought. Hilary Lewins was the very model of the modern graduate police officer. Lewins was convinced she was destined for great things in the force. Sadly he thought she's probably right. Right now she was diligently checking IDs and any packages that hadn't gone through the baggage monitor. Smith on the other hand was as usual in his favourite spot, leaning on the graffiti-splattered street lamp chewing gum, his arms folded. Mallet still hadn't decided whether he should tell his young charge that some enterprising young spark, knowing how often Smith stood in the same spot, had written 'PC Dickhead' on the lamppost just above head height, with an arrow pointing down toward his helmet just in case it wasn't quite clear who their intended target was.
He noticed that a small group of males, maybe six or seven strong, were coming through the checkpoint. He spotted Schofield, or 'Rusty' to his mates, in the middle of them. He wasn't hard to spot with his carrot-coloured hair and the fact he was a foot taller than the rest of them. They had clearly been drinking and were fooling around with the private security guys who in turn were beginning to get hostile, fingering the grips of their holstered Tazers. Mallet stood up from the wall, reluctantly dropping his half-finished coffee and sandwich on top of the existing litter that overflowed from the bin, and groaned at the ache in his lower back. I really am getting too old for this bullshit!

He started off across the cracked and weed-crazed concrete paving of cenotaph square, trying not to notice the dilapidated condition of what had once been the civic centre of the estate. When he had first arrived here all those years ago, the estate's shopping precinct had been a thriving community all freshly painted, with even a few of the bigger chain stores opening satellite shops. Back then the place had been full of hope and a good place to live, with plenty of work across the canal. He tried to pinpoint exactly when it had changed to the rundown shit tip it now was. Probably when Greening's the last major employer pulled out and moved its manufacturing base to take advantage of China's cheaper labour costs. He grimaced at the irony of that, given what was happening now. Apart from the bookies, the loan company and a couple of charity shops, there was nothing left of the shop parade that once ringed the cenotaph's square. Even the grilled-in mini market only opened twice a week now, moving its main business to better premises beyond the gates just a month ago. He should feel some sense of satisfaction that he had at least managed to keep the druggies from gathering to shoot up in the abandoned shop doorways - but he didn't really. He knew they had just moved down to the canal-side warehouses to get away from his wrath. He had always held on to the hope that the place could be turned around again with not too much effort; just one new large employer moving into the area could change people's attitudes overnight. There had even been brief signs of hope a few years ago when the bohemians had started moving down here, taking advantage of cheap properties within commuting distance of the city and bringing new life to the place. But the gates had put an end to that, and an end to what little hope he had clung to. That brought him up short as he realised that for the first time in almost fifty years of policing the area he had finally given up on it. His eyes trailed across to the black steel meshed fencing and turnstile gates that blocked the one main route in and out of Riverside. The vehicle gate was as usual closed as very few people in Riverside had access to a car any more. He cursed the stupidity of those people who believed that this was any kind of solution. Anyone who really believed the damned gates would make things better was living in cloud cuckoo land. He forced himself to move away from such thoughts. He was already looked on as suspect by his superiors for expressing his opposition to the whole gating policy, and had been warned by his Superintendent Allan Jones (a good man) that he had best keep his radical views to himself.

The youths were making a song and dance about having to empty their pockets into the scanner tray, even though it happened every time they left or re-entered the estate so they were well used to it by now. He had lost count of how many times he'd told Pat Dixon, the private security Chief for Riverside, that it was a waste of time. No-one who used the Riverside gate on a regular basis would be stupid enough to carry in any drugs or weapons, or anything else that was prohibited. All these searches did was wind people up even more than they already were. Riverside had only been declared a gated area six months ago, the initial anger at the restriction of liberty quickly turning into sullen but reluctant acceptance, but it wouldn't take much for things to turn ugly again. Mallet believed it was only that most of Riverside's population were unemployed and totally dependent on the gated sustenance funding that provided them with food and clothing stamps that kept any kind of lid on things. But at some stage it's going to blow up in all our faces, he thought, unable to keep the contempt he felt from his face as he thought of the power that these private security companies had now been given.

He walked over to PC Lewins, sparing a brief glance for Smith who managed to straighten up from slouching on his accurately-named leaning post.

"Morning, Constable."

"Oh! Hello, Sergeant, finished your cuppa then?"

Mallet attempted a smile which came out as more of a grimace. Sarcastic cow, he thought, nodding in the direction of the gate.

"Is there a problem?" he asked her.

"Not really, Sergeant. The 'Tupperwares' have decided to frisk pockets today, and the animals are getting restive."

It was the first time he had heard her use any Riverside slang, and it sounded strange coming from her. She had been with him two months now and normally she only used academy-speak. 'Tupperwares' or 'Plastics' were street names for the private security forces. Two of the cleaner ones anyway, he thought.

"Constable Smith," he called over his shoulder, "if it's not too inconvenient, would you care to join myself and Officer Lewins?"

The three of them walked toward the gatehouse and stood just outside the chevrons which defined the security area - and the point where the British police ceded power to private corporations, Mallet thought, unable to keep the curl from forming on his upper lip. Mallet had told his superiors on numerous occasions, to no avail, how ridiculous it was that his jurisdiction over the area didn't include the three metre perimeter surrounding the gates. Schofield the ginger-haired kid was being frisked roughly by one of the guards and was beginning to act it up for his audience.

"Take it easy pal, you might damage the goods."

The guard, who matched Schofield in height and build, shoved him in the chest forcing him to step back a foot, and then began to check inside Schofield's waistband.

"Fuckin' 'ell...are you some kind of fuckin' queer then or what?"

The boys nearby whooped, then whooped some more as Schofield shouted

for their benefit.
"Jeez, watch yourself boys. This plastic's gettin' a fuckin' hard-on over here!"
The guard's neck began to redden as he stepped back and reached for his pistol.
"Hold it!" Mallet's command made them both start.
"Hey Sarge, this guys a woolly wooftah you should…."
"Shut your mouth, Schofield. Officer, a word please?"
Mallet watched the man's hunched back, his hand still flexing on the butt of the pistol. Mallet's own hand was resting lightly on his nightstick, his own weapon still fastened in its holster.
"Officer?" he said again, ready to throw the stick if the man went to draw the pistol. He felt his own unconscious tension slip away as he saw the guard's hand finally leave the gun as the guard turned toward him.
Mallet turned to Smith, "Officer Smith, escort the rest of these boys across the square and then make sure they head off to see their mommies in separate directions."
Smith pulled himself straighter as he spoke to the group of laughing boys, "Right, you heard the Sergeant. Move it!"
"Not you," Mallet said as he saw Schofield go to follow them. "You stand here next to Officer Lewins."
Schofield shrugged and started toward her smiling. "Yo Occifer Leeerings, how yer doin'?" he said. Mallet was about to speak but relaxed as Lewins replied.
'I'm good soft lad, now stand here and shut up."
Mallet suppressed a smile and turned back toward the guard just as the man who was still staring hard at Schofield drew a finger across his throat. Mallet made the two strides to reach the guard before the man could even raise an arm in defence. He shoved his forearm into the guard's chest, pushing him back against the side of the gatehouse cabin.
"What the fuck you old bastard!" the guard said while grabbing with his free arm for his Tazer. Mallet shoved him again, this time shoving his forearm up under the man's throat cutting off the air to his windpipe.
The voice that cracked across the square was a match for Mallet's own. "Sergeant Mallet, can I ask why you are asphyxiating one of my people?"
Mallet turned his head toward the speaker without relinquishing his pressure on the man's throat. "He's one of yours is he Pat? Sorry, for some reason I mistook him for some kind of vigilante."
Pat Dixon, Chief of Riverside Safeworld Security Corporation, smiled. "No, Sergeant Mallet, he is definitely SSC personnel so I would be grateful if you'd release him before he faints?."
Mallet let the man go and stepped back, his stance still ready if the man tried to retaliate.

Dixon spoke calmly. "Thank you Sergeant," then turned to the guard, who was rubbing his throat, his eyes locked on Mallet's.
"You, go inside."
The man began to protest, "This fucking…. "
"I said, inside now!" Dixon said, walking toward the man, who quickly turned away from Mallet with one last stare and marched off.
Both men smiled when they heard the gatehouse door slam from around the corner.
Dixon held the palms of both hands outward toward Mallet. "Want to tell me what's going down here, John?"
Mallet shrugged, shaking his head as he spoke, "Pat, how the hell did you end up working for these people?"
"We've had this discussion too many times already John. I know you don't understand it but, when you retire, and you're bored shitless all day and living on a shitty police pension...well, maybe then you'll get it. Which is when by the way? When do you finish?"
Mallet sighed, "Just short of four months."
"The big Seven O eh! Ah well it comes to us all John. Look, you and I are too alike, retirement will drive you nuts. I've told you before I can get you on at SSC, same rank as me, Chief of an area and you'll pull in triple what you make now."
"It's not for me Pat, we both know it. But thanks anyway."
"John, I was against all this," he waved vaguely at the fence behind him, "but even you have to admit that it's working. I mean when was the last riot?"
Dixon stared at Mallet waiting for him to respond for a moment, then shrugged. "OK, OK, I know we disagree. So what will you do, fish?" he said nodding toward the Ship Canal.
They both laughed. Though Riverside was named as it sat on the banks of the Ship Canal, it was a water course devoid of any life, unless you counted rotting bicycles and shopping trolleys.
"Oh I don't know, Pat, although I have been toying with the idea of putting some more time in here at Riverside. There are some good people here now, doing some good work around the community centre. I think I..." he broke off as he saw Dixon's troubled expression. "What is it Pat, what have you heard?"
Dixon looked across at Lewins and Schofield, making sure that they were out of earshot before speaking. "They'd have my arse on a plate, John, if they thought I had told you anything, and anyway there isn't really much to tell."
"That isn't what your face says. Come on Pat, we go back a long way. If something is going to happen on my patch I want to know about it."
"I need a smoke," Dixon said in a loud voice, looking pointedly at Lewins.

Everyone had heard of the incident at the back of Bernie's Bistro where, before Mallet intervened, she had been ready to arrest the illegal cigarette smokers who congregated there.
Mallet was about to speak when Lewins called across "Sergeant, is it OK if my friend soft lad here and I take a little stroll while you finish up?"
Mallet acknowledged her with a slight nod, surprised by her twice in one day now. Maybe she'll be alright after all, he thought.
The two men walked a little way down to the far end of the security cabins, and Dixon offered Mallet a cigarette.
"American." Mallet said. "You take out a bank loan for these?"
Dixon gave Mallet a light and took a deep drag, exhaling the smoke as he spoke. "I mean it, John. There isn't really much I can tell you."
He looked at Mallet's face, then across the square to check that Lewins had done as she said.
Mallet continued to stare at him.
Dixon sighed and scratched the back of his neck and looked around again. "This is just for your ears, right?"
Mallet nodded.
"Ok then. Well, an instruction came down last week that all leave is to be cancelled for the next six weeks; and I also heard that our senior guys at SSC have been summoned to meet the new Chief Commissioner - who has also been given direct governmental oversight for the Zone 1 areas including Riverside, of course." He looked at Mallet and frowned. "John, they've appointed Hawksworth."
"Richard Hawksworth?"
"Your friend and mine!"
Mallet looked at the tip of his cigarette then crushed it out on the asphalt with his boot heel. He looked back at Dixon. "When are they going to do it?"
"Jesus, John. I already said there isn't any……."
"Pat, if they have given the job to Hawksworth, then we both know what the agenda is."
"There are a lot of people who think relocation is a good idea, a chance for people to start over. A job, a house - is that really so bad?"
Mallet thought about it. When you put it like that it sounded OK of course. The Chinese government had invested billions into the new North East townships, making the UK the biggest manufacturing base in Europe. In return, the Government had accelerated its exit from the European Union and introduced a total deregulation of the jobs market. They had also promoted heavily the 'Future Way Project' and were now offering a hefty grant for people who agreed to relocate to the new towns. It was, he knew, to many people a good thing. The grants for now were only available to those who lived in a designated Zone 1 area, and a lot of people had moved

out already, including here in Riverside - which was part of the reason it was looking more and more like a ghost town. Under the policy, it was planned that once an area became completely empty, the government would completely flatten the run-down zones and allow private deregulated development - or 'Free Zones' as they would be called. Mallet thought the policy was a disastrous idea but even he knew that a few people were going to get very rich on the back of the whole business. The government had hit a major snag though, as the rumours that the new 'China-towns' were effectively work camps was gaining traction. The government wouldn't allow the Independent Press access to the New Towns due, they said, to commercially sensitive systems. That was bullshit Mallet knew, as did many others. The pseudo state-broadcaster Sky was given restricted access, but the so-called documentaries they had published were embarrassingly bad propaganda.

Mallet looked at Dixon, a man he had known and worked with for most of his adult life.

"Pat, you can't support these evacuations. It's against everything we ever stood for! If people volunteer to go, that's one thing - but to force people, surely that crosses some kind of line?"

Dixon remained silent looking across the square, avoiding Mallet's gaze.

He tried again. "Things are changing, Pat. People are talking and what they are saying isn't good. There are rumours that these New Towns are almost bonded labour camps."

"Rumours come on John, there are always rumours."

"Damn it man, I'm not talking about idle gossip. Some of the credible subversive groups have published covert footage from within the New Towns that show…."

"Whoa!' Dixon said, holding the palm of his hand out toward Mallet. "Don't even tell me you are talking to the bloody subs. Jesus, I didn't think you were that stupid. Christ, man, listen to yourself, 'credible subversive groups'. Jesus, they are fucking terrorists plain and simple!"

Mallet took off his police cap and brushed his hand through his bristled grey hair.

"Pat, you and I both know that isn't true. Most of them are just sick of the way the country is being run. Sure they are disruptive, but to call them all terrorists because a few extremists hijacked their cause… "

"They are fucking terrorists and you want your fucking head examined if you believe any differently."

Mallet shook his head, recognising that his next comment would likely as not determine the future of their long friendship.

"Pat, you're wrong. Look, there is something broken in our society - surely you can see that - and when people like you can support this...this internment…. "

'For Christ's sake, John, just listen to yourself will you? Riverside isn't the nice little estate we started out in all those years ago. This place is a shitheap, one that's full of druggies and wasters, and the sooner they demolish it the better for everyone!"
Mallet looked at Dixon trying to understand how they had come to grow so far apart. They had come up in the force together and he had always credited Dixon with having the same, or at least broadly similar views to his own. He tried again, "Pat, there are still a lot of good people here. You know people like Katy, for instance, or the Rev... Frank Johnson he's a friend, right? Are they wasters? Is he?"
Dixon ran his hand across his face and sighed, "No they're not, he's not but they chose to stay here, John, knowing what they know and they have to live with that decision. And anyway, we both know that people like Frank, and even Katy, will be able to afford the release bond and avoid the relocation, and then they can simply move on with their lives."
Mallet had heard of the so-called release bond but had thought it was just counter propaganda put out by the subversives. The subs said the bond would allow people who lived in Zone 1 areas, those who could afford it that was, to avoid forcible relocation to the New Towns. The current amount was rumoured to be ten grand. Mallet had dismissed it when he had read it on the blogging sites which he checked out frequently. Now Dixon had just confirmed it was true, and Mallet realised that Dixon thought he already knew about it.
"What if people refuse to move, Pat, what happens then?"
"Then I guess there will be a few broken heads, but you know as well as I do, John, that resistance won't come from the people you and I want to protect, the decent ones, but from the scumbags…."
"What clearance has the operation been given?" Mallet asked, cutting Dixon off.
"Level four."
They stared at each other both knowing that level four authorised deadly force. Worse, Mallet understood that it also authorised SSC, a private company, to use deadly force.
He placed his hand on Dixon's arm, "Pat, this is wrong, you know it's wrong, when a society starts killing its citizens …"
Dixon cut him off, "Enough. I don't want to hear any more of this leftist crap. Do you know, just for the conversation we are having, you could be dishonourably discharged? And that, my old friend, means no pension, no medical insurance, nothing! Now I respect you, John, You are one of the best coppers I have ever known. And I know you aren't some kind of sub, but I'm telling you now that when this thing starts to go off, you best keep out of the SSC's way."
"You threatening me, Pat?" Mallet said, a mirthless smile on his face.

“I am trying to tell you that this thing is going to happen, one way or another. The only thing you have to decide is whether you want to keep what you have worked for and, if that sounds like a threat to you my friend, then I guess it must be!”
Mallet nodded slowly before speaking.
“OK Pat. I think I know where we are now. You go easy, big man.” he said turning to leave.
“John, wait. Look, I have a responsibility. You have to understand...“
Mallet looked back over his shoulder. “Oh I do understand Pat, I really do. By the way, do me a favour. That boy of yours, explain to him for me, will you, that the next time he threatens violence or worse against a private citizen of Riverside, scrote or non scrote, I will bust his balls so hard that he won’t sit down again for a month. You understand, Pat, I have responsibilities as well.” He walked across the square to deal with Schofield, his hands clenching unconsciously into fists.

He could have, probably should have, he told himself, corrected Dixon’s assumption that he was somehow in contact with any subversives, as he wasn’t. He did know who they were though, at least those who were in Riverside, but even that was only educated guesswork based on months of observation. Doc, Katy’s unlikely new lover, he was definitely one; and maybe Frankie Johnson’s daughter Josephine, or Jo as everyone including her father called her. Quite a few others he thought could be activists, and then there were many who, if not active, were certainly sympathetic to the subversive cause - but that probably included most of Riverside’s population. There had also been quite a few new faces appearing in Riverside over the last year, and his guess was that at least some of them were part of the disparate group that the government and Pat Dixon would describe as ‘Subs’. He had been keeping a discreet eye on them even though they appeared to be artists or musicians - in other words, the usual bohemian crowd - and so far they seemed harmless enough. Dixon accusing him of collaboration was laughable really, as the simple truth was that he would be the last person they would talk to. Mallet knew, to anyone with subversive tendencies, he would be seen as the face of the establishment writ large, a tool of the oppressive police state. He knew locals called him ‘Old Hammer’ behind his back. He quite liked it if he was being honest with himself. The knowledge that he now had a huge decision to make weighed heavily on him and, despite himself, Dixon’s reminder that if he chose wrongly he could lose his pension and his reputation wasn’t enough on its own to keep him silent. Dixon was right, of course, all he had to do was step back when it happened, keep his head down and retire. No-one would think anything less of him. He would after all be carrying out his duties by upholding the law. His plan to put some time into the community centre would be gone though, and he had genuinely wanted to do that, to try and make a difference - especially to the kids he had watched for years wrapped in the ever-tightening ratchet of crime and hopelessness. He thought he had a chance to effect at least some positive change, especially if he was no longer in uniform. Some of them, the long-standing Riversider's especially, would never forgive him for simply standing back. For them he wouldn't be upholding the law but betraying the community he had always served - not that there would be anyone left to remind him of that as they would either be shipped off to the New Towns, or worse. He thought about people like Frankie and Katy looking at him if he stood to one side watching as they were herded away from their homes and livelihoods and shivered. For Mallet, though, worse than any local censure was the far greater internal critic that always seemed to hold him to account, his father Danny. Despite that the man had been dead almost fifty seven years, his memory of the father's moral certitude was never far from his mind. Even all these years later, his father's writings and speeches (which he still kept despite their current political sensitivity) caused him to question the morality of the choices he made. As a child, he had not only not listened to what his Father would say but actively ignored it. Danny Mallet had been a big Union man, eventually ending up leading the once formidable General Workers Union, the GWU. He was a powerful advocate for his members, passionate and as hard as nails. He was also completely unforgiving if ever crossed by friend or foe. But the young John Mallet thought all that mattered was his father was hardly ever there for him and his mother, forever away at this meeting or that conference. If there was a big dispute or strike going on in the days before striking was made illegal, he would only get to see his father at all on the television news channels, demanding justice for some dispute or other. The press had a field day calling him 'the enemy within' and 'anti-business', and the one that stuck of course, 'Red Dan'. Mallet got in more than a few fist fights at school defending his dad from the other kids who would parrot their parents' prejudices and taunt him with chants of 'Red Dan the Commie Man'. Mallet hadn't known then what a Commie was, and neither did the kids who taunted him with it, but all of them knew it wasn't a good thing to be. His father had been killed in a freak car accident one week before the planned general strike and on the day before his thirteenth birthday. It shamed him even now that he had been more upset because it meant his birthday party was cancelled, rather than that the remote figure that was his father had died. Mallet's mother fell into a depression that she never really recovered from, leaving him even more isolated and more resentful of his father. Mallet still wondered today if his decision to join the police force had been what he really wanted to do, or whether it was what he knew his father would have most hated. Yet many of the things his father had taught him had stuck with him throughout his life and shaped how he went about his job. More recently, after the death of his wife, he had spent some time going through his father's old archives. These weren't the speeches and reports that he had looked at occasionally over the years but the private journals of his late father, which finally led him to an empathy and even to a grudging liking for the man who he had never really known. That was ten years ago and Mallet had found it a transforming experience. He didn't think the child in him had yet quite forgiven the man for dying out on him, but at least he had come to let go some of the old pain. It was his father's voice he could hear now telling him that if good people did nothing, then evil would reign. He shook his head trying to clear his mind of old ghosts. It was crazy, he knew that. He wouldn't, couldn't speak to the subversives directly. He trusted them no more than they would trust him, probably less. And if he was truly honest with himself, he wasn't sure that he was prepared to risk all he had worked for, not for a bunch of people who in large part despised him just for being a police officer. Yet if he stood aside and did nothing, could he live with himself?

As he drew near to Schofield and Lewins, it suddenly struck him that he could risk a conversation with Charlie Taylor, or Sunny as he was known. Sunny played a regular spot in Frankie Johnson's blues club and knew most of what was going on at any one time. He was also, Mallet felt reasonably confident, not part of any group, subversive or otherwise. Sunny Taylor was like himself, an outsider. The difference was that people liked and trusted Sunny, and that might be all Mallet needed. He knew he couldn't stop any forced evacuation if it was sanctioned at the highest levels of government. But what he could do, he decided, was at least try and prepare people so that there would be minimal resistance - which would at least mean fewer people being hurt or even killed, he thought, remembering the incident with Dixon's gorilla. It wasn't much, he accepted, but it was as much as he could do, and at least his decision seemed to quieten the conscience monster that was his father, for a little while at least.

Chapter Three

London

Richard Hawksworth, the newly-appointed Chief Commissioner of Police and Head of the UK's internal security branch, felt calm and confident as he sat at the head of the table in the Cabinet Office briefing room. The banks of television and media screens behind him were blank, emphasising the cave-like atmosphere of the low -lit, wood-panelled and windowless room. Though the twenty-four seats of the conference table were occupied by the great and the good, the only sound was the low hum of the air conditioning, which kept the subterranean room supplied with fresh air even in the event of an external attack. They were all looking at him, waiting for him to begin the meeting. Even though Mablethorpe, the Prime Minister, was seated to his right, no-one was in any doubt that this was Hawksworth's meeting. He had spoken briefly with the Prime Minister earlier in the morning, mainly to make sure the man wasn't having one of his infamous wobbles. After yesterday's media debacle, the Prime Minister was in an extremely tetchy mood and that, as Hawksworth knew from past experience, made him less easy to control. He also knew that the PM was caught on a great big Chinese hook and, no matter how much he wriggled, he was stuck with the bargain he had made with them, which gave Hawksworth a little more wiggle room himself. Not that Mablethorpe realised how much Hawksworth actually knew of course. He knew Mablethorpe saw him as just one more functionary, someone who would carry out with minimal instruction the Prime Minister's wishes. The difference was that Hawksworth didn't have Mablethorpe's degenerative disease which plagued the current crop of populist politicians - the man itched to be liked. Even if the policy he was carrying out was shafting the people concerned, Mablethorpe still wanted those people to think well of him while he did it. It was one reason why Hawksworth had managed to negotiate an increase in his responsibility and authority when he had been appointed. Mablethorpe didn't like to be bothered with details, especially given that the operation Hawksworth had been tasked with could so very easily blow up in all of their faces. The less Mablethorpe knew about specific details, the more he could deny culpability if the operation went awry - so much so that he hadn't even wanted to attend today's briefing until Hawksworth had insisted on it.

"I don't know whether you want to say anything, Prime Minister?" Hawksworth said, adding quickly to forestall one of the man's interminable pep talks, "Though it's probably better if I just go through the briefing and then you can take over afterwards?"

Mablethorpe nodded curtly for him to continue, though Hawksworth could see he wasn't happy as the man would cheerfully give a speech to a dead cat if it was the only available audience. He smiled at Mablethorpe, then signalled to his aide to light up the screens and dim the room's lights still lower. A small halogen pencil light over each place allowed the participants to read documents or take notes.

The legend 'Operation Unify' appeared in large gold lettering on the screen. He had chosen the operational codename himself with no hint of irony. He truly believed that what they were about to undertake would help unify a society and nation that had been torn apart by social decay and moral decline. The gated areas were only one of the most overt responses to a society which had split between those who were prepared to work and contribute, and those who, despite repeated attempts at rehabilitation, chose to live in a chaotic and debauched way. Now, with the establishment and continued growth of the Chinese New Towns, society had found itself with a major opportunity to heal itself whilst, at the same time ridding itself of the wasters and scroungers by putting them to some productive use. He turned to Mablethorpe, "Prime Minister, with your permission?"
Mablethorpe inclined his head in assent.
Hawksworth hefted with some difficulty his nineteen stone frame out of the chair. He had instructed that the temperature in the room be lowered, but could already feel a bead of sweat begin to trickle down the back of his shirt.
"Gentlemen, this meeting and this operation as you know is security code four and, as such, all briefings pertaining to Operation Unify, all external requests for support, and any deviations from the strategy will be cleared directly through my office." He looked around the room to ensure everyone was paying full attention before continuing. "In ten days time we launch Operation Unify. There are as you know six areas which are," without any signal his aide brought up the next slide, "listed here. As you can see, we have four major locations that will utilise the main body of our resources. The two in Birmingham will be conducted under the control of Chief Constable Peter Davis; in London, Deputy Commissioner John Carpenter will take the lead. You have already received the extensive briefing pack that outlines both the timetable and actions required. But, and I must emphasise once again gentlemen, that these timelines are not, repeat not, flexible. They are not to be deviated from without my express permission. As most of you will be aware, last night's pilot operation in Wales was a resounding success. As you can see on this info graph, the Rhyl West Two area had been largely emptied through voluntary locations prior to our entering the estate. This left us with three hundred and sixty residents who had refused relocation. Included in that number were forty three children under the age of thirteen. This has been a useful factor to understand as we go forward, as clearly those with younger children in their charge were... less resistant. In the end, there were sixty three hostiles who refused to board the relocation transport. Of those, sixteen were deemed of significance including six known subversives. Eight people were tazered and have been detained for further questioning under the 2023 Zoning Act.

Three individuals received bullet wounds, with only one of those deemed as critical. The subversives were unable to communicate externally either by cell phone or internet, and therefore the operational parameters were completely fulfilled." Hawksworth paused to wipe his face with a crisp linen handkerchief and smiled at them. "In other words, gentlemen, the operation was a complete success! The media containment package will be released in," he looked at his watch, "a little over an hour, and will be broadcast exclusively by Sky who have assisted us in editing and providing a news anchor for the privilege. Now, as you are aware gentlemen, West Two was chosen for its size and remoteness and, given its complete success, we are now ready to begin phase two of Operation Unify by evacuating Manchester's Riverside estate. Whilst this is a proportionally larger proposition than last night, we believe it also should be relatively straightforward. It will once again be essential that the media blackout and the blocking of all electronic communications from Riverside be completed prior to the evacuation stage. I am confident, however, that the process of lock-down and evac will be relatively straightforward given the still relatively small population.

Malcolm will be leading the Riverside op." he nodded at Chief Constable Malcolm Dennings who, as ever, sat stiffly to attention.

Hawksworth clasped his hands across his ample stomach looking at Dennings, and smiled a smile that made everyone else grateful that they weren't its recipient.

"Malcolm is of course completely aware of the need for a swift and clean execution of Riverside, which the whole of Operation Unify now depends on in order that we can then move onto the more significant Midlands and East London estates." He smiled again as he saw the redness begin to creep up Dennings' neck as he merely nodded tightly. "Gentlemen, we know that the subversives have not been idle whilst Project Unify has been under development. They have been cranking up their propaganda machines against the New Towns, and quite frankly our Chinese partners have become extremely sensitive to the subversives wholly unfounded allegations, allegations that have unfortunately been promulgated by our international neighbours. The Prime Minister has made it very clear to me, therefore, that Project Unify must be carried out with the minimum fuss and zero media attention. It is possible of course, though highly unlikely, that some information on Project Unify has leaked. If that is the case, then it is also possible that some of the main agitators could already have relocated out of the targeted zones. We cannot, therefore, allow the possibility of the Riverside Estate, which we already know from intelligence to have minor subversive cells, to act as a media conduit that would, as they say, let the rabbit out of the hat. As I say, this is highly improbable as the plan I have devised, under Prime Minister Mablethorpe's guidance," he

added quickly, noticing how the prickly bastard had started to fidget, "is flawless, providing of course, it is carried out as per the operational plan."
Aden Walshaw CEO of the European arm of Safeworld Security Company SSC raised a hand. Hawksworth felt his temper begin to smoulder. He hated this smug folksy American shit-bag, and if he could have kept him out of this briefing he would have done so. Unfortunately, the Prime Minister had decided that Walshaw was going to be part of the inner control group of six. Hawksworth understood why of course. SSC were inputting huge resources and manpower into Project Unify and, in addition to servicing the Zone 1 operations, they were also contributing to the management of the wealthier voluntary gated communities. Mablethorpe knew only too well that SSC were a large part of the reason for his continued popularity. They were a main partner in ensuring affluent areas remained secure, whilst effectively locking down those areas that were degenerate crime riddled slums. Hawksworth wondered though whether, if people knew the full consequences of the detailed arrangements that had been made, and the authority that the UK had ceded to the SSC people and their Chinese paymasters, they would be quite so content. It was though a cost- effective solution that, as part of the New Towns agreement, the Chinese would fund the associated security costs from Zone 1 gating. Without such financial support, the whole strategy would be unviable, which would in turn mean the UK's crime rate would be off the scale, given the levels of unemployment the country was now experiencing. The Chinese had surprised all of them in opting for SSC as their private muscle; it was after all an American company. Although when Hawksworth had commissioned some private research, it became clear that it was Chinese intermediaries who were effectively in control of SSC. So we are stuck with them, Hawksworth acknowledged to himself, but he didn't like it. They were, on paper at least, under his command, but paper meant little when it came to command decisions. That was always down to the old adage that 'he who pays the piper picks the tune'. So, sucking in his irritation, he attempted to smile warmly at Walshaw,
"Aden, please don't stand on ceremony."
Aden Walshaw didn't return Hawksworth's smile, but removed his steel rimmed glasses and began to polish them with his tie as he spoke in his broad Texan accent.
"Thanks, Ricky, appreciate it. First let me say that I think the plan you have laid out in here," he picked up the briefing dossier and dropped it back on the table before continuing, "it's good, sure enough it is good, t'aint flawless of course, no plan ever is but…" he held up his hand forestalling Hawksworth who was about to object.
"Now, now, Ricky don't go gettin' all defensive on me, there's no need, the plan is good sure, but flawless, son, why that's the work of the Lord!"

Hawksworth folded his arms across his chest, his mouth a tight line of irritation.
"No, as I say, the plan here is fine, the thing I have a concern with though is this - and again I mean no disrespect here - but the main threat to this plan is whether the intelligence you have on the ground is sound. If it is then all's well and good... but if it aint?"
"If there is a point Aden?"
"Well, here's the thing, Ricky, one of my guys, Pat Dixon, think you might know him…?"
"Good man," Hawksworth said unconvincingly. "What about him?"
"Well you know he's running things for us down at Riverside?" He placed his glasses back on and looked directly at Hawksworth, who nodded. "Well, old Pat down there at Riverside tells me that one of your guys is in cahoots with the subs, the subversives that is, in the area." He looked down at his notes. "This fellah, one o' yours it seems, a man name of Sergeant John Mallet, who interestingly enough it turns out, had a father who was a radical leftie years ago. Now Pat says that it don't amount to a hill of….. "
"John Mallet! You are trying to tell me that John Mallet is colluding with subversive elements!" Hawksworth said looking round the room, the mockery in his voice clear.
Mablethorpe suddenly spoke up."Commissioner Hawksworth, who is this Mallet fellow? If we have a problem perhaps you should go down there and… "
"There is no prob…" Hawksworth stopped himself, suddenly aware he was raising his voice at Mablethorpe, the man whom however weak and pliable still held his future, at least for the time being, in his hands. "Sir, my apologies, but I do not believe that there is a problem. John Mallet is someone who I served with and who was under my command some years ago."
"Then you are saying that Aden is mistaken, that this man is a friend?"
"I am certainly saying that Mr Walshaw, or his source, Mr Dixon is mistaken. John Mallet is an old school copper, Mr Prime Minister, as straight as an iron rod," and about as flexible he thought. "As for being a friend, no, he isn't that Sir, simply a colleague officer, our personal relationship is...non-existent, and in truth irrelevant. Sir, this man Mallet is a dullard, a throwback if you like. But I can say without fear of contradiction that he would no more conspire with subversives than you or I. I know Dixon as well Sir, Mr Walshaw's source," he added to Mablethorpe's blank look. "Pat Dixon served with Mallet before he went working for Mr Walshaw's organisation. I suspect this is simply, in fact I'm certain that this will be some personal spat between the two of them, nothing more."
Mablethorpe looked relieved and turned to Walshaw. "Aden?"
Walshaw, smiled at the Prime minister. "Well, Sir, seems to me that Ricky

here is responsible for this whole kit 'n caboodle. An' where I come from you don't give a man a tin star then piss on his bullets. You know what I'm sayin' Prime Minister?"

Mablethorpe looked at him blankly for a moment then turned back toward Hawksworth "Commissioner?"

Hawksworth unfolded his arms and ignored both of them; instead he glared at his assistant who hastily brought up the next slide in the presentation.

*

As the room began to clear, Mablethorpe put his hand on Hawksworth's arm signalling that he should stay.

Hawksworth just managed to stop himself from looking at his watch; instead he called out to CC Dennings who was just leaving the room.

"Malcolm!" he shouted, watching as the man's shoulders tensed when he turned to face him, though there was no sign of concern in his expression.

"Check out this thing with Mallet, not you obviously, have it done discreetly. We both know this is bullshit, still I want everything battened down. Of course, if there is anything, then you know what to do?"

"Yes, Sir, I'm already on it," Dennings said holding his phone up.

"Of course you are, Malcolm. I never doubted it. Still, remember what I said discreetly, we both know what a pedantic soul our good friend Sergeant Mallet is!"

When the room was empty and the door resealed and activated, Mablethorpe turned his chair at an angle to face Hawksworth directly. His voice was low as if the room wasn't soundproofed and didn't have state of the art electronic screening.

"This fellow Mallet, is there anything I need… "

"Sir," Hawksworth held his hand up, forestalling him, "it's a minor detail and I can assure you there will be nothing to it."

"And if there is?"

"Then I will deal with it directly. Now, Sir, what's this really about? You seem, well, a little... apprehensive?"

Mablethorpe laughed, and drew his hand through the white mop of hair that was the subject of so much lampooning by political cartoonists.

"Apprehensive! Bloody hell, Richard, if this goes wrong it will be a disaster - and I do mean for both of us, by the way!"

Hawksworth decided to ignore the threat. "Sir, there really is no need to concern yourself. The operation has been planned to take account of all contingencies. We are after all dealing with a disparate group of ne'er-do-wells. Oh I know there is a lot of talk about the subversives and their threat to state security. But, sir, you and I both know that such a threat is in reality

non-existent, even if the idea of it is, well, helpful."
Mablethorpe started to protest then sighed and nodded.
"Within these walls, sir, you and I both know that the subversive groups, what are left of them that is, are a weak, non-violent bunch and are no threat to the UK's security."
"They are still capable of causing trouble, Richard…. "
"I agree Sir, and that's why the whole situation will be managed… "
"I have had a discussion with the Attorney General!"
"Indeed! Well it might have been helpful if you had invited me to that discussion," Hawksworth said leaning forward toward Mablethorpe, who unconsciously moved back before continuing.
"You have to realise, Richard that I have a responsibility to the State.. "
"What was the Attorney General's view, sir?" Hawksworth asked.
"Well, and I know you are concerned about leaks, but we are talking about the Attorney General for God's sake. He is after all the highest legal officer of the Crown, so I think he should be safe don't you?"
The man is a drunken old fool, Hawksworth thought, but nodded smiling as he spoke.
"Of course we can trust him, sir, he's one of us."
Mablethorpe looked relieved.
"Yes, yes he is. Anyway his analysis of our... of… "
"Operation Unify?"
"Yes, quite, well it's rather worrying actually; he has drafted advice that says we could be facing charges in the ICC, the International Criminal Court, if the full facts were ever to come out!"
Hawksworth looked up at the ceiling in disbelief.
"Richard, the Attorney General says that by forcibly removing a population against its will to the new towns it's, well in the AG's assessment, it could be termed as indentured labour, slavery, Richard!"
Hawksworth had heard enough. "Sir this is all well and good, but the facts of the matter are this." He counted them off on his fingers as he spoke, "Firstly, we are not forcing anybody anywhere. What we are doing is providing transportation and assistance to a group of our citizens who currently have very little, so they can start a new life. Anyone who says otherwise is merely a part of the whole subversive propaganda machine, 'the enemy within' that you talk so eloquently and so often about to the Press. And sir, the AG's advice is based on the idea that in some way Operation Unify will become public. You've just sat and listened to a three hour detailed briefing that ensures that it will not!"
Mablethorpe nodded slowly, "Yes...yes. Well, sometimes even I wonder whether what we are doing is actually the right thing. I know it will lead to better lives for these people, and that it will make the country more prosperous and safe, but... well, don't you ever have doubts, Richard,

doubts that maybe this is just one step too far?"
"I have no doubts whatsoever, sir. We, or rather you, sir, have tasked me with dealing with this situation. I believe in this project sir, and I believe that it is absolutely essential if the 'Future Way Project' is to be a success. And quite frankly, Prime Minister, if a few individuals' rights and freedoms are circumscribed to achieve that, then I believe that is a price worth paying for a safer world."
Hawksworth could see that Mablethorpe was still having doubts.
"Sir, you know as well as I do that the simple truth is that people have stopped moving out of the Zone 1 areas. The subversive propaganda is working, and if we don't supply the labour you have agreed to.... Well, have you considered the Chinese response if we cancel Operation Unify? Of course, that is a political matter and outside of my remit, but perhaps you should discuss your concerns with Ambassador Tan.. "
Mablethorpe suddenly sat up straighter and looked directly into Hawksworth's eyes.
"You're right, Chief Commissioner, that is indeed a political matter. The United Kingdom's relationship with the Chinese Government is not only way above your pay grade, but also I might suggest, way outside of your skill set!"
Hawksworth looked at his hands to hide how angry he felt, his voice when he spoke was contrite.
"Of course, sir, my apologies."
Mablethorpe stood up, "Well, make sure I am kept up-to-date with any issues." he said not offering his hand.

Hawksworth watched the Prime Minister walk stiffly out of the room, and looked at his watch; there was still time to contact the cultural attaché at the Chinese embassy. He needed someone to stiffen Mablethorpe's spine. The man was right about one thing - if the situation went wrong then it wasn't just the PM who would be facing disaster.

Chapter Four

London

Christopher Jennings had not had a good day. Mablethorpe was still blaming him for not stopping the press conference earlier. He was now being given the 'Mablethorpe Freeze', something the PM did quite often with those who displeased him. He didn't quite ignore you, in fact he was overly polite, but everyone in the room would know that you were out of favour. It was, Jennings admitted to himself, a bit like the sunshine of the man's aura being switched off, and it left him feeling chilly and morose. Technically, he was responsible to the Cabinet Secretary who was the head of the Civil Service, but he had only made the mistake once of complaining about the PM to Sir Alistair Cooke. Now when he was given the freeze, he would simply sink in to a dark depression and compose one of his self-pitying and never sent resignation letters.

In the 'good old days' when Press Secretaries had been politically appointed, he knew Mablethorpe would have sacked him by now. But various scandals had meant an end to political appointments both for the 'special advisors' and his own role of Communications Director. The Prime Minister these days was reduced to choosing his Communications Director from a candidates list of usually no more than five people, all of whom had to be career civil servants. Christopher had been chosen by Mablethorpe not for his political or communication skills, but because he happened to have been in the same house at Cambridge and was therefore seen by Mablethorpe as 'one of us'.

Tonight though, he was determined to put Mablethorpe and the rest of them out of his mind. He was sitting in the armchair of the Majestic Hotel, Streatham, and could feel the familiar tingling of anticipation that always accompanied the start of one of his increasingly infrequent rendezvous. Both he and Dominic who was 'preparing' himself in the locked bathroom, had less and less opportunity to meet these days. He unconsciously smoothed out the invisible creases of his short blue gym skirt, and checked that his white socks were pulled up to cover the ankles on his shaved legs, pleased with how the whiteness of the socks reflected onto his flat black patent leather shoes.

With an effort he finally forced the problems of the day from his mind and concentrated on where he was now. It had been months since he had seen Dominic. Ever since his transfer to Porton Down, the UK's Defence Science and Technology centre in Salisbury, Dominic had come back to London less and less frequently. Whatever work he was engaged in down there had changed him, making him more distant somehow and, Christopher acknowledged to himself, more cruel. It had been so much easier when they had first met at University - a golden time when they had discovered their opposite, but so complementary natures. For the first time in his life, Christopher had been able to release that hidden part of his self, a part so hidden he hadn't actually known it existed until Dominic released it.

It hadn't happened straight away of course. At first they had simply fumbled with each on that first night, both of them very drunk, which at least allowed them to pretend the next day that nothing had actually happened. If it had been a normal gay relationship, he would have been fine with it, as would everyone else. But his relationship with Dominic, whilst of course sexual, was also much more than that. Christopher discovered that he liked to be abused and receive some measure of pain, and of course Dominic excelled in giving both. He could never quite shred his dread of being discovered and the inevitable ridicule that would follow.

He remembered that first time when Dominic had slapped him across the face and then pinned him on their tatty old sofa. He had come in his boxer shorts, without Dominic even touching him. Dominic had that kind of power over him, a power that both of them enjoyed in different ways. Their games had gradually become more and more elaborate as they explored the boundaries of their desires. He checked his wig one last time, ensuring the bangs just fell onto his cheeks in the dressing table mirror, as he heard Dominic opening the bathroom door.

*

"Oh I can't tell you that, sir, it's forbidden." Christopher, or Chrissie as he had now become, said, using the high-pitched girlie voice Dominic liked.
Dominic twisted his nipple harder, his knee pressing hard onto Chrissie's exposed cock, causing him to gasp.
"Nothing is forbidden to me, you little slut, or have you forgotten?" Dominic said twisting harder. "Now tell me!"
Christopher Jennings, the efficient and dedicated civil servant, tried to protest as once again his submissive alter ego told in gasping sentences the arrangements for Operation Unify, and what he thought Dominic was really interested in, Hawksworth's dominance of Gregory Mablethorpe. They had done this once before, and it was almost as if the telling of his most professional secrets somehow heightened his debasement, making his submission to Dominic more complete and more satisfying.
He continued to spill state secrets, knowing that if Dominic was pleased with him, he would allow him to suck his cock till they both came.

Afterwards as he lay in the crook of Dominic's arm, his earlier tears still damp on his cheeks, his worry at what they had discussed came back to

him.
"I shouldn't talk about work, Dommie, its wrong!"
Dominic stroked his hair, "I've told you before, Chrissie it's OK. Anyway, I have a higher security clearance than you do, remember, so stop worrying your little head about it!"
"But you won't talk about what you do! You won't even tell me if it's dangerous or not."
"But you aren't in charge, Chrissie, are you?"
Chrissie sighed, snuggling up, aware that their time was short, "No I'm not, Dommie. I'm sorry!"
"It's OK, little one," Dominic said looking at his watch.
"You have to go?"
"You know I do," he said, starting to get up.

Once Dominic went into the bathroom, Christopher stripped off his clothes and dressed quickly into his tee shirt and jeans. They had an unspoken rule that when Dommie went to shower that that was the end of their special time. It would be Dominic not Dommie who would return to the room fully dressed, where they would chat for five minutes about their old university days as if the previous three hours had never existed; and then Dominic would leave. Only then would Christopher shower and examine the damage to his painfully bruised buttocks. Yes, Dominic had become crueller, and at some stage he would have to rein him in. But not just yet he thought, folding his new outfit and carefully placing the skirt, the wig, blouse and his beautiful new shoes under the unused gym clothes in his sports bag.

*

Dominic Weston let the scalding needles of the shower cascade across his skin. He felt the old anger surge back up in him as he thought on what they had just done. Jennings disgusted him, the man's weakness and mewling gratitude as he would slap his buttocks or shoot his semen down the wretched man's throat; he was a disgusting little creature! Yet, Dominic also knew he needed him. Jennings was his release, the pressure valve that allowed him to subsume and bury his anger and sadistic desires in order that they remained controllable in his day-to-day life.

Without Jennings he feared the urge he sometimes had to do the unthinkable would overcome him, and that would take him down the path to non-consensual harm, and then what? This...thing with Jennings had for the first time allowed him to be in control, real control of another human being. For a long time he had denied his feelings, seeing them as something to be ashamed of. But then hadn't he spent most of his life denying to himself who he really was, even re-inventing himself on occasion? He had left the grey smoky Yorkshire town that he'd grown up in and got on the bus to Cambridge University - the first ever to do so from his school. His teachers and parents were so proud of him. Yet even before the bus had pulled out of the station he had already decided he would never go back there. He left his family, his teachers and friends behind with no twinges of regret. He shed them all like a skin, and along with them he shed the last traces of the coarse Northern dialect of his peers and family. By the time he was lodged in his rooms his accent, at least most of the time, sounded more like he was raised in sunny Cambridge rather than the rainy North.

Ironically, his new best friend at Cambridge, Michael Deveron, someone who had real aristocratic credentials, was heading in the exact opposite direction. Though Deveron's family owned half of the Scottish countryside and a sizeable chunk of Cornwall, Michael was a leftie going on marches and dressing in a way that belied his wealth. They had gelled in part as they were roomed together, but more because they were both outsiders to the smart crowd, albeit for different reasons. When Michael had taken Dominic for a weekend at one of his father's country houses, he felt like he had come home. Even though Michael had spent much of the weekend berating his father over the 'stolen wealth' of the British aristocracy, it hadn't managed to lessen Dominic's feeling that he was meant for such a life. They had been close, he and Michael. Even though they were opposites, they shared something between them that neither if asked would be able to describe. Maybe it was just that they were both at ease in each other's company.

It was Michael who, after numerous hints and nudges, had reluctantly introduced Weston to the 'Harrington Boys', which at that time included the current Prime Minister, Gregory Mablethorpe. The Harrington Boys were named after the private club that ,courtesy of their fathers, they attended for frequent bouts of drunken dinners and meetings of the Young Tories Cambridge Association. They were everything that Dominic aspired to be, and to his great joy they had accepted him at least into the outer circle of their ranks.

He had known of course, even then, that they did so because of his friendship with Deveron, whose father was a powerful Tory peer, but it didn't lessen his happiness.

It was after that that his friendship with Michael Deveron began to break down, as he began to attend functions and even joined the Conservative Party. He wasn't particularly interested in politics, but the way that

Mablethorpe and his 'pals' lived their lives was a magnet to him. In the end Deveron had moved out of their shared rooms to live with some whacky fringe environmental group he was involved in. They never fell out, and there weren't any cross words or anger from either of them. The friendship just dissolved through an increasing lack of commonality.

One night at the Harrington, when they were all particularly drunk, Jeremy Fortescue had picked up on his accent which, despite his best efforts, would slip back sometimes, especially when he'd been drinking, and allowed the odd word or phrase to twang out of him. Fortescue of course had spotted it immediately, and he was one of those people who could be really funny - but only when he was being so at someone else's expense. He had pushed and prodded Dominic over his background and what his family did, throwing in lots of Northern jokes about coal merchants, cloth caps and whippets. Dominic had had to laugh it off of course and play along with them all. He had seen what happened when they had all turned on Simpkins that day. His ostracism had been sudden and complete, and turned out to be devastating in its consequences, as the boy had hung himself in his rooms only six months later.

Mablethorpe, who had been one of the main instigators of the banishment of Simpkins because the boy had had the audacity to call him a spoilt brat one night, was the one who gave the eulogy at his funeral. So Dominic took Fortescue's jibes as best he could, and laughed right along with them as they talked about cobbled streets and characters out of Dickens. Then Mablethorpe had suddenly declared that henceforth they should all call Dominic 'Turveydrop', a fellow who Dickens had described as a 'very model of deportment'. The name had stuck to the point where even some of the Masters called him by it, assuming he didn't mind, though at least they didn't use the more vulgar version which Fortescue preferred of 'turd drop'.

If that had been the worst of it he would have probably been able to let it go. Even though he detested the name, he would have been able to dismiss it as just the foolish antics of spoilt rich boys. It was the other thing that Mablethorpe did, though, that even all these years later when he thought on it (which he did often), still made him want to crush the life out of Mablethorpe with his bare hands. He had taken his career path extremely seriously as a young man. It was why he ended up choosing science in the end, not just because he was good at it, which he was, but because unlike Medicine and the Law it was a profession that didn't judge you by how well -connected your family was.

Then he had stumbled across the ancient order of Freemasonry when he had been receiving extra tuition from Mr Glendell, a retired Science teacher. Mr Glendell had an impressive and substantial library on a vast array of science and history subjects. Dominic had asked if he could borrow some on occasion, and Glendell had been happy to let him, providing he made sure he returned them in pristine condition, which he always did. There were a section of books that Glendell kept in a locked glass case that he wasn't allowed to read, but had fascinating titles, and which he later discovered were all related to the ancient brotherhood of freemasonry of which Glendell was a fraternal brother. Glendell, who had taken a great liking to Weston who he found to be an attentive and respectful pupil, began to teach him some of the ancient mysteries. It quickly became clear to Dominic that, though Freemasonry was truly an ancient order and was consequently full of arcane rituals and mumbo jumbo, it was also a tremendously powerful organisation that looked after its own. He devoured the Masonic works that Glendell allowed him to read, and spent as much time quizzing the old man on Freemasonry as he did on their science lessons.

Professor Glendell had written to him later whilst he was still at Cambridge to advise him that, now he had reached the age of twenty-one, he himself would be happy to sponsor Dominic's induction into his local Lodge. He was disappointed when Weston wrote back and thanked him, but said he had decided he would wait until the conclusion of his studies. The truth was he knew through his studies that, whilst theoretically all Freemasons and their lodges were equal, some were more equal than others. His study of freemasonry also allowed him to recognise, when the drunken Harrington Boys were passing supposedly secret signs to each other, that at least half of them including Mablethorpe and Fortescue were Freemasons.

He had approached Mablethorpe in strictest confidence one afternoon in Mablethorpe's rooms. As usual when he wasn't playing to the gallery, he was friendly and considerate and listened attentively as Dominic told him about Glendell, without naming him of course. He told Mablethorpe about his own studies, and his now earnest desire to become a Freemason, and said he would be eternally grateful if Mablethorpe would consider introducing him to his lodge. Mablethorpe had looked at him wide-eyed for a moment and then laughed 'Why, of course I will, Turveydrop old chap, of course I will!'

*

Four weeks later on a freezing November night, he was standing completely naked with a hemp noose around his neck, the end of the rope draping over his left shoulder, a dagger and pentagram drawn on his chest with charcoal. In another five minutes, at precisely midnight, the ceremony would begin, along with his new life. His hands were bound behind him with more hemp rope, as were his ankles, allowing him to move only in small shuffling steps. The six of them were standing on the ancient paving outside the massive doors of King's College Chapel in the University grounds.

Mablethorpe had explained to him previously that the order he was being invited to join was of ancient and royal assent, and therefore that all who became Brothers in it were initiated inside the King's Chapel itself. Mablethorpe and the four others with him, including Fortescue, were all wearing full-length dark cloaks with large hoods that they had left hanging down their backs. The five of them looked more sombre than he had ever known them. He shivered, not only from the cold midnight air, but as he listened to the words which Mablethorpe was reading in a quiet voice from an ancient-looking scroll.

Essentially the words repeated what he had already been told - that he should do whatever was asked of him this night and, without question or doubt, place his trust, indeed his very life in their hands. He'd agreed readily, knowing already that the ceremony was quite arcane in its ritualism and form. Mablethorpe had also told him the night before, that he must understand that he was joining a very privileged and ancient order within the hierarchy of freemasonry, and that therefore the rituals would be of an even more ancient form than that, of which he might have read. He had also given him a passage that he said he must learn by rote for the coming evening, and that he must speak the words loudly and clearly when the bell rang three times. He also told him confidentially that the other Brothers waiting inside would try and shout him down before he could complete his task, but he should not let them do so.

Mablethorpe nodded at him, a small smile on his face as he placed a red velvet sack over his head, blocking out all light but still allowing him to breathe. He heard the large door to the chapel creak open and, at a gentle push in his back, he began as previously instructed to shuffle forward. He could make out the ancient black and white flooring below his feet, which he thought had started to turn blue on the cold marble floor. He heard a gasp or some kind of exclamation, and then he heard the bell ring three times very close to his ear and he began to shout as loud as he could the words that were burned into his memory.

'Whosoever heareth me

Clear my path of Sin."
He heard the shouting begin and was grateful that his friend Gregory Mablethorpe had warned him of it.

"I will not be cowed by demons such as thee
For I seek light and-"

Suddenly the hood had been yanked roughly from his head and he had blinked confusedly at the fifty or so men and women who were staring at him, shocked at being wrenched out of the quietness of their weekly midnight mass. He had wailed in blind panic, unable to stop himself from screeching as if he'd been on fire. He tried to hobble out of the chapel, his cold feet betraying him as he crashed heavily to the floor. He could hear the laughter outside, fading as the others ran away.

*

At first he thought that he would be thrown out of college and was seriously considering following Simpkins by putting an end to it all. But the Dean for some reason had seemed to take pity on him, and informed Dominic that he had managed to pacify the clergy. He made it clear to Dominic though that it wouldn't help his future career in academia, should he choose to tell anyone else the names of those who Dominic had willingly told him were behind the stunt.
He was given three weeks off to recover from his 'aberration', and Mablethorpe had come to see him the first morning he got back. He had explained that it was all just a laugh and no harm done blah, blah, blah! Dominic had smiled and shook hands with him, assuring him that of course he wasn't going to bear any grudges.
'Good man!' Mablethorpe had said slapping him on the back, 'You're a good bloke Turveydrop, a bloody good bloke!'

Twelve months later he had been allocated as mentor to Christopher Jennings, a raw and quiet freshman who was clearly intimidated by the majority of his fellow students. He had, unusually for Dominic, felt sorry for young Christopher and taken him under his wing and shown him the ropes. He often wondered if even then he had recognised Jennings' potential for his desires. But he didn't think so; he was, he still believed today, simply giving a lift up to someone who needed it, in the same way Michael Deveron had done for him. He was completing his Masters degree while Jennings still couldn't find his way around the quadrangles, and maybe he just saw someone who reminded him of his younger naive self.

It was a wonderful irony then that one of the very few altruistic things he had done in life-ended up with the vulnerable undergraduate he had helped working directly for the man who had mocked and belittled him. At first he had simply been fascinated at the link itself and that Jennings had so many unflattering anecdotes about Mablethorpe's' private behaviour. When he began to get Jennings to divulge the private details of cabinet business, he did it simply to exert control, to prove to both himself and Jennings that, however high-powered Jennings' role was, it was Dominic who remained superior. He didn't know when that had changed, when he had first thought about being able to actually exact revenge on Mablethorpe and the rest of the Harrington bastards and not just fantasize about it, but nowadays he seemed to think of little else. It was almost as if Christopher's closeness to Mablethorpe had reignited the burning shame of all those years ago so it felt like it had only happened yesterday. And soon he would get his chance. He wasn't sure how~~,~~ or when, but it was close. He could feel it. Fate had cast this chance his way and when it showed him the direction or path to his revenge, he would walk it without hesitation. They would rue the day they had mocked him, all of them.

He soaped his body again, trying to scrub off the scent of Jennings cheap perfumed body. It wouldn't just be Mablethorpe he would settle with, he reminded himself. There was also the idiot Director of Porton Down and the equally idiotic military scientists who looked down their noses at him. Three times now they had passed him over for promotion, even though he was the most qualified and committed scientist in the base. Worse still, the last time he had applied for Departmental Head status, that bitch HR Director Susan Houghton had suggested he undertook life coaching classes! Apparently, many of his colleagues found him 'difficult to bond with, and he needed to develop his leadership skills'.

He knew differently of course. It was the damned fucking Freemasons, that group of corrupt fucking bastards that he had once wanted to join. It was they who were holding him back with a whisper here, and an innuendo there. His mother had always told him; drummed into him on a daily basis, that he was special, that the whole world would one day look at him and admire his achievements, and she was right. He would keep Jennings close and, at some point Jennings~~,~~ without even realising it, would give him the key to exact revenge on Mablethorpe and the others. He wasn't stupid or reckless of course, he would wait for the right moment, the right opportunity, but when it came he would grasp it with both hands.

Chapter Five

Sunny Taylor was beginning to feel it. True the club was only half full, and most people were paying him and Johnny Sticks little attention. But that didn't matter, never really had mattered for Sunny as long as he was feeling it, sliding into that groove where the music just became a part of him. The audience, if not entirely irrelevant given the pittance of a fee they paid him, were nonetheless at most an added bonus.

He was playing an old Robert Johnson song and had spent hours rearranging it and perfecting the screeching slide and counterpoint bass. The bottlenecks wail on the guitar strings contrasted with his stomping boot on the oak box he always placed on the floor in front of him. Johnny Sticks was feeling it too, Sunny could tell. Sticks' snare brush was skittering between the spaces in Sunny's vocal, his bass drum picking up the rhythm of Sunny's boot but slightly and deliberately off-time, creating a kind of false echo. The audience were starting to focus now, he could see them as he squinted through his old school Ray Charles shades, and from under the peak of his snazzy purple fedora. The conversations were tailing off, heads were starting to roll side to side. He could see through the haze of the club's dim blue smoke filled lighting, Frankie Johns, the club's owner, who was leaning on the post in his usual spot at the rear, raising his glass at Sunny.

Sunny began to amend the lyrics on the fly, something he could do when he was feeling it.

"Why don't you go down and tell that man Frankie Johnson
Yeah why don't you go and tell the man Frankie Johnson?
He got water in his beer and it's in his whisky too
But the prices are still so high for me and you."

The crowd whooped and laughed including Frankie, who threw his head back laughing as Sunny wound it up and finished his second set of the night.

"Bourbon on the rocks, my friend," Frankie said as Sunny came over to the bar.

Sunny smiled, taking the heavy tumbler, it was an old and comfortable joke. They both knew he hadn't touched a real drink since, well... he couldn't remember when exactly, but he only counted each day so it didn't really matter how long.

"Shit, Frankie, this tastes more like ginger ale than whisky man," Sunny said, playing out his end of the gag.

He liked Frankie Johnson for many reasons, but one of the main ones was his ability to make Sunny laugh about himself. When he had first come to Riverside just over a year ago, laughter wasn't something he thought he'd ever share again.

A female voice interrupted their script, "Hey there, hero. Nice set!"

Sunny smiled at Jo.

"Why thank you, ma'am, 'twas my pleasure."
Josephine Johnson, or Jo as everyone called her, was one of the other reasons he liked Frankie so much. Frankie's daughter was everything he thought a woman should be - smart, sassy and funny and with curves that caused men to stare open-mouthed when she occasionally got up to strut her stuff.
Unfortunately, he knew she wouldn't touch a reformed alcoholic with a barge pole and Sunny couldn't blame her, even if he was currently clinging valiantly to the wagon.

The three of them sat down at one of the back tables and fell into a companionable silence as Sadie, tonight's guest artiste, began to sing an old Ella song. Sunny had played a couple of sessions with her out of town and knew she was the real deal. He swirled the glass in front of him, watching the ice cubes melding with the straw coloured liquid and, for a moment, his imagination could actually smell malt whisky rather than ginger ale, causing the hand that held the glass to tremble slightly. He remembered his companions and looked up quickly, but they were too engrossed with Sadie to have noticed anything. Good, he thought, relieved. There hadn't been a day since he quit that he hadn't wanted a drink, not one. Still, there was no gain in advertising that need, especially to Jo.
He suddenly felt something prickling on the back of his neck and looked over his shoulder. At the far end of the bar, a man sat nursing a beer was staring at him. It's the copper - what do they call him? - 'the hammer', he remembered. What the hell does he want?
The man held five fingers up and pointed at his watch, signalling he wanted five minutes of his time.
Sunny felt tempted to ignore him, he had little liking for the police, and usually the feeling was mutual. He sighed taking out his small tobacco pouch, placing it on the table. If he had to talk to the man, at least he would do it without a large spliff on his person. He stood up quietly and looked at Frankie and Jo; they were both engrossed with Sadie's voice, so he slid off toward the old cop taking his ginger beer with him.

"Didn't think you dug the blues, Sarge," Sunny said sitting down. "Is there a problem?"
"There are always problems Sunny, or Charles if you prefer?" Mallet said sipping from a beer bottle.
"Sunny's fine. You want to cut to it Sergeant? You aint' exactly doin' my street cred much good you know?"
Mallet looked around, "No I guess I'm not. What time do you get off?"
Sunny felt a tremor of the old panic run through him but his voice was calm when he spoke.

"I'm done now."
Mallet nodded and Sunny thought, but you already knew that of course.
"Then walk with me Sunny...please."
Sunny looked back at Frankie and Jo but they were still enraptured with Sadie's haunting voice. He threw his stage hat and shades onto the bar and followed Mallet outside.

He had to rapidly draw the collar of his jacket up around his neck, as he ran across the cracked and potholed car park outside the club. It was raining, not too hard but with that typical Manchester drizzle that seemed to find its way into every seam of clothing and footwear. Mallet was already standing in the doorway of the burnt-out storeroom on the far side of the car park - a cigarette lighting his face momentarily in the shadowy doorway.
Sunny took the offered cigarette, lit it with his Zippo and waited for Mallet to speak.
Mallet was looking at him, waiting for him to say something, then he half smiled as if accepting that Sunny wouldn't be naive enough to fill in the empty silence, though it always surprised him how many did.

"I need to get a message to some people." he said.
Sunny drew on his cigarette, keeping silent.
"Look Sunny, I'm not going to spend a lot of time on bullshit here, there isn't time. I'm also going to ask that you don't divulge where you got this information from, I'm going to trust you in other words."
Sunny dropped the cigarette, ground it out with his shoe, and remained silent as Mallet carried on.
"There are a group of people, some of which are friends of yours, some of which are also subversives or subversive sympathisers......"
Sunny tensed and turned to go as Mallet grabbed him by the shoulder,
"Wait Sunny, this is important, or it is if you want to keep people safe, people like Jo and Frankie."
Sunny pushed Mallet's hand off his shoulder; his voice a hard whisper,
"I don't know anything about subs, Mallet, nothing, do you hear me, and neither does Jo. You are way off with this crap." He turned to go.
"In ten days time the whole of Riverside will be evacuated and its people relocated, forcibly so if necessary."

Sunny stopped, his back to Mallet. The rain already soaking through his jacket added to the chill he already felt. He turned slowly, stepping back into the doorway.
"What is this, sergeant? It's some kind of weird setup, right? What do you call it - a sting? You tell me your secret plan and I'll tell you mine, right? Well, here's the thing - I don't have one! I don't know any subversives and

never have. I am a musician; I play the guitar and sing a bit, full stop. Anything else you think you know about me is just bullshit. Oh, but I forgot, you don't have time for bullshit, right?"
Mallet lit another cigarette, not bothering to offer Sunny one this time.
"OK, here's the thing, Sunny. I know who you are, what you are now, and what you once were. So don't give me the old simple 'busker man' routine OK? Oh you don't believe me?" he said at Sunny's indifferent shrug. "Charles Windsor Taylor, finance whizz and high flyer, right? What do you want me to talk about - when you worked for the World Bank? Or maybe what came after when you spent a little vacation time in the West Tennessee State penitentiary?"

Mallet could see the shock on Sunny's face but the man's voice was steady when he spoke.
"If you know so much, then you also know that these days I am what I said. I am a guitar player, that's all. I don't know any subs, subversives, or if I do then I don't know they are. So you may as well turn off the tape and go and find another set of balls to squeeze, OK?"
Mallet looked at him for a long moment then offered Sunny another cigarette, who took it with no embarrassment.
"Sunny, if I thought that any of the subversives in Riverside were violent anarchists, then I would just pick them up and have them banged away. No-one would object, in fact I'd probably get a commendation. I already know who the lefties are in Riverside, at least the old hands. But I know that people like Jo aren't violent radicals - believe me, I understand that. And it's why I need you to speak with them, to warn them so they don't get caught up in something dangerous."
"Then talk to them yourself," Sunny said, "you don't need me."
"If I try to talk to Jo, or your friend Doc, for example... you think they'll believe me, John Mallet... the Hammer? No, my friend, they'll either run a mile or they'll put my name across every media outlet in the country, in the vain hope of stopping what's going to happen."
"I seem to be missing something here," Sunny said, "You're telling me they are going to move us all out of Riverside...OK I can see how that could happen. There have been rumours for long enough and we all saw the TV this morning. Still, I don't understand what that is to you. You're a copper, that's what you are, and it's written in your genes, Sergeant, we both know it. So tell me why on earth you would want to stop it?"

The magnitude of what Mallet was doing suddenly swept over him again. This is crazy, he told himself for the umpteenth time. Yet he couldn't simply stand aside and do nothing -that would mean turning his back on everything he believed in. This morning had been bad. Allen Carlisle, one

of the district Superintendents, had turned up unannounced and sent Smith and Lewins off to get coffee..... as he pulled a chair close to Mallets desk and told him that his name had come up as a possible subversive sympathiser.
Mallet had laughed out loud, all the time thinking what a shitty little prick Pat Dixon had turned out to be. Carlisle was a good man who had come up under Mallet's tutelage. He was taking a big risk himself by ignoring his instructions and telling Mallet directly what had been said in London, including the ultimate irony of Commissioner Hawksworth defending him. Carlisle told Mallet that he knew it was all bullshit, but he needed to be careful who he said what to, and that he should keep his head down over the next few weeks. Mallet had assured Carlisle that it was indeed all bullshit, but thanked him anyway. But if what he was doing now came out and it all blew up, they would all remember what Dixon had said, and then he really would be finished.
His gut told him Sunny was someone he could trust...but if he was wrong, if Sunny did tell the others who had tipped him off, then he would be hung out to dry, his career wrecked and maybe even face some jail time of his own.
He looked up at Sunny who was waiting patiently for an answer.
Mallet looked at the young man who could, if his instincts were wrong, lose him his pension, his reputation, everything he had worked for, and sighed. When he spoke it was with a weariness that did more to convince Sunny that Mallet was telling the truth than any amount of words.

"You can't stop it, Sunny. The powers that be have decided it's going to happen, so anything you or they try and do won't make any difference. You need to make them understand that-"
"Then why-"
Mallet held his hand up, cutting Sunny off, "Why? - because, if any of your friends put up anything more than token resistance, it will get very ugly. Because, if your friends, as I believe they might try to, do try and stop it, they will be crushed. There will be no TV cameras, no media coverage of any kind. Riverside will be totally isolated. It will be you few against an overwhelming force."

Mallet took out another cigarette, looked at it in disgust and put it back in the packet shaking his head.
"Sunny, this is going to happen and, though you might not believe it, I don't like it any more than you do. I have spent my life protecting this community, and now I can't. It's over, Sunny. All I ask is that you help out by convincing people not to resist. If they do, they will be hurt...or worse."

*

A few hours later Sunny sipped his coffee and looked across at Jo and Doc. Katy was wiping down the counter but the café's main lights were out and the door was locked, the 'open' sign turned to 'closed'. Jo looked concerned, worried not just about what he had told them, which included everything but his source, but she was, he realised worried about him, a realisation that caused a momentary flutter in the pit of his stomach. Doc though just looked pissed, and Sunny had to admit pretty formidable. He was still the same bespectacled skinny academic with a floppy mop of unruly dark hair but, as Sunny had laid out the facts, he had seemed to become more solid, his voice sharper and focussed, his eyes boring into Sunny as he spoke.
"I ask you again, Sunny, who gave this to you?"
Sunny shook his head, he had thought long and hard before speaking to Doc. Why shouldn't he give Mallet up? The man wasn't one of them, and this could still all be a set-up. Except Sunny didn't think it was. For some reason, though why he wasn't sure, he trusted old Sergeant Hammer, and sometimes he decided that just had to be enough.
Doc was still staring at him.
"OK, so this source, is I assume a friend?"
Sunny had the fingers of his hands steepled together in front of his mouth, remaining silent, but he could feel that he was beginning to get a little pissed off himself.

"OK so if you won't tell me, tell us," Doc said waving his hand, "then tell me why we shouldn't think that you are just trying to set us up?"
"Oh for Chrissakes Doc!" Katy said banging her hand flat on the counter behind them.
"Katy, please, stay out of this-"
"No Doc I won't! I've known Sunny for as long as you have. You have spent hours chewing the fat with him at that very table, and now he's setting you up?"
Doc held his hands up in surrender, smiling for the first time since they had sat down over an hour ago.
"As ever, my queen, your beauty is surpassed only by your wisdom, however....." he ducked suddenly as she threw the wet dishcloth at his head.
The laughter dissipated the tension in the room like smoke in a breeze, and then Jo spoke.
"If Sunny's 'friend'..." she held up her hand forestalling Sunny's protest, "If this... person is correct then we have to warn people and at least give them the chance to get away, to inform the media-"
"None of that will work, Jo. It's too late," Doc said.
"Riverside lost all access to the country's media, including to the internet and the mobile networks at six o'clock this evening. Check your phone if

you don't believe me!" he said seeing her expression.

Jo grabbed her mobile from her bag and stared at the screen. No signal. Katy had the cafe phone to her ear. She looked across the counter at them and shook her head, replacing the receiver.
Sunny felt freaked out,
"Jesus Doc, this can't be happening, Christ its illegal... We have to get..." he trailed off as he saw Doc shaking his head.
He had decided earlier that Mallet was being straight with him, but now he realised he had simply thought the old sergeant though sincere was simply batty, and had gotten himself wrapped up in some imaginary conspiracy.

He had expected Doc and Jo to laugh at him when he delivered Mallet's message; instead Doc had asked Katy to close the cafe early and had spent the last hour grilling him over every detail, and now the phones were out?
Doc leaned across the table and placed his hand over Sunny's.
"This is real Sunny, and it's happening right now. It's something we have been expecting of course, though I admit not quite so soon-"
"Then Jo is right, we have to get out of here and alert people?"
Doc leaned back and lit one of his stick-thin cigars, the ones Katy said smelt like horse shit. When he spoke his voice was low but decisive.
"Your friend is right, Sunny, we can't get out now; it's too late for that. Listen to me both of you. We have one chance of stopping this evacuation and only one, and that is if we can expose what they are doing to the wider world."

Jo was still staring at her phone as she spoke, "But you already said the net and all the phones are down?"
Doc smiled at her, "Sunny's friend was right, Jo, the authorities have shut down everything. But he's also wrong. Yes, the internet and phone network is down. But...we do have a few alternatives available!"
He couldn't quite keep the satisfaction out of his voice as he continued.
"Right here in Riverside, we have the means to communicate directly to the world, independently of the state-controlled networks, and that my friends, means we also have the means to stop the government in its tracks."

Sunny interrupted, "Doc, it doesn't make any difference! Firstly, they will find your phone mast or whatever it is and shut it down; second, the fact that they have decided to do this means it has been in the planning stage for a long time. They will know what you are planning and will know how to deal with it."
"You're wrong Sunny - not that they will expect us to resist, not even that we might have a sat phone or something similar - however, we have been

waiting for this next development for months, and believe me we are prepared. It's why I came here, to set it up," he paused and smiled at Katy, "it isn't the reason I decided to stay, though. That was something else."
Katy tossed her head, though the flush on her neck belied the nonchalant look she gave him.
"Who's 'we' Doc? Sunny asked. "You said 'we'!"
"You already know the answer to that my friend. All you have to decide now is whether you will join us in resisting them, or be led like a sheep to new-town slavery?"

Sunny tilted his head back and blew out a sigh of frustration. He didn't want any of this. He had been part of resisting powerful people before and the experience had not been pleasant. He didn't think he could face being banged up again, which is what was going to happen if he made the wrong choice.
He looked at Doc."Tell me exactly how you'll resist, Doc?"
"I will when you say whether you are with us or not."
Sunny shook his head, "Sorry Doc but that isn't good enough. If resistance is about alerting the world to what is happening whilst we, I assume, barricade ourselves in, then that's a scenario I can accept. But, what about other types of resistance - violence, guns bombs?"

Doc smiled, shaking his head, "Sunny, I give you my word that there is no intention of, and that there will be no form of armed resistance. Even if I supported such a response, which I don't, it wouldn't work, not when we are faced with a powerful state apparatus and the resources available to it. Our resistance will be to show the world what is happening; that should be enough, we think, to bring the approbation of the international community and a real threat of action by the International Criminal Court. All we have to do is hold out long enough for the world to act on our behalf, and we can save not only ourselves but also help the thousands who have already been sent to the New Towns."

Sunny tried to fault Doc's logic, but couldn't. The UK since pulling out of Europe had become virtually a pariah within western democracies. It had welded its future to a partnership with the Democratic Republic of China, a decision that had without doubt shored up the country's failing economy, but it had been at the cost of an increasingly polarised and fractured society. The New Towns were only the latest and most blatant example of that. Sunny wasn't one of those who doubted that the stories and video clips which had been smuggled out about what was going on in the New Towns were true. The New Towns were labour camps, pure and simple.

He turned to Jo, "Do you trust him?" he said, nodding towards Doc without looking at him.
He could see that she understood that her answer would decide him one way or another. She didn't smile at him but looked him directly in the eyes as she placed her hand over his and said simply, "Yes!"

*

The three of them talked for another hour as Doc laid out the detailed plan for Sunny and Jo, and the roles he needed them to undertake. Doc was pleased that Sunny had come in with them; he genuinely liked the man, even if his almost paranoid aversion to taking responsibility could be extremely frustrating at times. Doc knew he needed people like Sunny and Jo if he was to have any hope of holding the community together in the coming days. He had told Sunny the truth. They had the means to show the world, and in real time, what was happening. He had also been telling the truth when he told Sunny that it would be enough to stop Mablethorpe and his thugs in their tracks. What he hadn't said of course, was that it would only work for a short period - a few days, maybe even as long as a week - but then they would need something more, and that would depend entirely on the world's response to their plight.

Chapter Six

John Mallet stood to one side of the cenotaph square. The usual detritus of carrier bags and general litter was swirling around with the biting wind that had sprung up overnight. He thought the rain which looked like it had been coming an hour ago would now hold off for a few more hours, but the sky was still full of dark scudding clouds, reflecting his mood as he surveyed the scene in front of him. PC Lewins was trying not to laugh as she had finally noticed her colleague Smith's personalised lamp post, which even now he was slouching against. Mallet had informed them both this morning what was about to happen, and that they were instructed to only observe. Lewins had surprised him again as she had seemed as shocked as he had been at the forced evacuation plan. Smith on the other hand had winked at her when he thought Mallet wasn't watching, mouthing 'sooner the better.'

He could see that Sunny had informed the others of their discussion, as a significant majority of the residents, maybe as many as a thousand, had collected on the far side of the square. They had also spent the last few hours erecting a makeshift barrier of old wooden pallets and dustbins, and had even managed to drag an old burnt-out van across the main street. He knew that Sunny hadn't told them his source. If he had, then by now he would have picked it up in the expressions of people like Jo. He looked over at Sunny who was standing slightly to the left of his friend Doc. It was Doc who was clearly co-ordinating the different parts of the crowd, and Mallet could see several runners handing out home-made placards, as they all finally started to gather behind the barricades before the coming attack. Sunny held Mallet's gaze for a moment, then shrugged imperceptibly as if to say I told them, but they are going to resist anyway. Mallet nodded in acknowledgement. He didn't like the fact that they were going to resist, and he also didn't like how relieved he was that Sunny had kept his confidence. Still, he had done as much as he could, and at least now they all knew the odds were heavily against them. Hopefully that would be enough to ensure it would all be over without too much violence from either side. He had done what he could, he told himself again. Now he had to do what he had told Lewins and Smith to do, which was to stand aside and observe. He hadn't been able to shake off the feeling of self disgust though, at least not until he had written out his resignation letter in the early hours of this morning. True, he would lose about five grand a year from his early retirement, but he had felt a sense of release when he had sealed the envelope, ready to put in to the Superintendent's hand after this morning's events had been concluded.

*

The Chief Constable of Greater Manchester, Malcolm Denning, banged his hand flat on the table in the mobile HQ which was set back a hundred yards from the Riverside gates. The victim of his wrath, Superintendent Shawcross, was staring fixedly above the bank of monitors that showed the gathering crowds in Cenotaph Square. The crowd was beginning to change from a milling group of misfits into an organised mob. Placards were being passed around and a large white bed sheet had been attached to the front of the barricade emblazoned with the words 'No to Prison Camps' in bright red letters. The paint had run down from the letters looking almost like they had been written in blood, an effect that Shawcross felt was not accidental.

"I told you that this was to be a low key operation, and now look at it hundreds of the scum boxing themselves in! Now I ask you again, Superintendent, who the hell tipped them off?"

Shawcross was an old hand at superiors blowing off. The worst thing you could do in such circumstances was to try and answer a superior when they were in rant mode. He continued to stare stoically six inches above the monitors. Dennings shook his head, scratching the back of his neck, as he

spoke. "Well, no matter now, but I expect to be told by the end of play today where this leak originated, am I clear?"
"Very clear, sir," Shawcross replied promptly. The man's a bloody idiot, he thought. There were something close to eighty security personnel on rotating shifts at Riverside. Half of them were probably having it off with the people they were supposed to be securing and, if he was any judge of such matters, the other half were probably in receipt of backhanders. He looked across at Dixon, the SSC security chief who was on the opposite side of Dennings. The arrogant shit was smirking at his discomfort. "I'm sure it's not any of our people, sir!" he said, sounding petty even to his own ears.
Dennings leaned back in his chair, putting his hands behind his head. "Oh, on that, Superintendent, I think we can agree." This time it was Shawcross's turn to smirk.
"In any case," Dennings went on, "as it turns out the leak will probably make the whole operation that much easier, as the idiots have mostly gathered their selves in one place, which means they'll be much easier to round up." He turned to Dixon. "Mr Dixon," he said, deliberately avoiding any honorific. "We will commence Operation Unify in fifteen minutes on my mark."
The three of them synchronised watches.
Dixon started to leave then stopped as Dennings spoke again.
"One more thing Mr Dixon, please remember that you and your people are to create a twenty metre boundary on the inner gateways, and that is all that you are required to do. After that I will require your people to stand clear and not get in the way of the professionals. My team under Superintendent Shawcross here will advise you if we require anything else from you. Clear?"
Dixon nodded silently and left the cabin, the sound of the slammed door reverberating behind him.
"Bloody rent-a-cops," Dennings said.
"Absolutely sir!" Shawcross replied, already heading out of the door so his grin wouldn't be noticed.

*

Doc was shouting into the child's walkie-talkie. The things looked stupid and amateurish but, as he had explained to the co-ordinating committee, they would continue to work despite all the sophisticated jamming technologies of the police. "What do you mean it isn't working?" he said, putting a hand over his other ear to try and block out the sound of the surveillance helicopter that hovered above the gate.
"Right, Danny. I do understand, but let's be clear that if it isn't on in the next ten minutes then I wouldn't bother!"
"Problem?" Sunny asked.
Doc shook his head, "It's just Danny being a drama queen. He'll get it

going, trust me!"
Sunny nodded, "We might have another problem!" he said nodding towards the gate.
Doc winced as he saw a small group of boys who were being led by the ginger kid Schofield. They were walking across the square toward the SSC guards who had begun to create a perimeter between the gate and the square.
"For Chrissakes! How many times did we go through this, Sunny. We have to keep everyone together, or the whole plan will just collapse."
Sunny folded his arms across his chest. He was committed now and felt the sense of calm that always came on him just before a fight. It didn't stop him wondering though if Doc's plans, which he'd set out at last night's hastily arranged meeting in the sports hall, were going to work out quite as planned."

*

Mallet was only twenty feet from Schofield and the others as he watched them approaching the guards. He touched Lewins on the arm as the woman began to intercept them. "We are observers remember?"
She shook her head in disgust but stepped back.
Schofield was standing in front of one of the guards who, despite the man wearing full riot gear, Mallet knew without doubt was the same man Schofield had wound up the previous day. Schofield's voice carried across to them.
"Hey fuckwit, remember me?"
The guard didn't answer but pumped a baton round into the shotgun he held across his chest.
"Ooh look, the plastic pig has got his new toy gun out, is he going to shoot the nasty boys?"
The small group around Schofield all laughed, one of them high-fiving Schofield.
Mallet saw Dixon heading down the line ready to intervene, and his own hand went to his nightstick, gripping it for a moment then letting it go with a sigh. He looked ruefully at Lewins. At least she hadn't had to remind him that they were here only to observe.
Schofield had turned his back on the guard, bending over and pulling his jeans low to show his bare behind. "Kiss my arse you fucking pri-"
The crack of the baton round as it hit the back of Schofield's head plunged the whole of the square into a shocked silence, as Schofield's body slowly spun backward with the force of the entry of the projectile. Blood was flying outward from the back of his head in a red spiral as his body jerked spastically before he slumped to the floor, unmoving.
Mallet made some kind of guttural growl deep in his throat, pushing off Lewins' attempt to restrain him. He reached the guard before anyone could

snap out of the frozen stillness that had fallen across them all. He jammed his night stick hard under the bottom edge of the man's stab proof jacket, eliciting a large woofing sound from the guard as he doubled over. Mallet kicked the firearm away and went to cuff him. One of the other guards went to stop him and Mallet stiff-armed him in the chest. A second guard smacked the stock of his gun across the side of Mallet's head which exploded in red heat. As he fell, the first guard started kicking him in the ribs, whilst the one he had stiff-armed stamped at his face, which he just managed to turn aside. The heavy boot missed his skull but still caught his ear which, he felt burst open.

Pc Gillian Lewins snapped her mouth shut which she realised was hanging open with shock, and turned to Davies, "Come on, we have to help him."

Davies stared at her, then deliberately leaned back against his lamppost, smiling at her. "Observers only, remember?"

She turned away from him, charging at the guard who was trying to stamp on the old Sergeant's' head, managing to knock him to one side before someone grabbed her from behind. She heard Dixon the SSC chief growling in her ear,

"Stand down constable," he breathed into her ear, clamping her arms tighter behind her back.

Across the square, Sunny could see the police starting to move through the gates, banging their sticks on their riot shields. He could see the SSC thugs kicking Mallet as the man tried to cover his head with his hands. He felt the old rage blow up inside his head, "Baassstaarrrds!" he roared, charging across the square toward the two fallen men. There was a great roar behind him as he ran forward, as a couple of hundred people began charging after him, their own shouts of outrage joining with his own. Bizarrely, he could still hear Doc above the melee screaming into the Toys R Us radio, "Now, Danny; it has to be now."

As he raced across the square, Sunny saw the fear in the SSC personnel as a couple of hundred people ran screaming toward them. Their chief was screaming at them to form a line, but they were panicking and began to charge back through the gate, straight into the armed ranks of the police who had already started to come through the gateway. The resulting melee jammed up the entrance in a mass of confused and yelling bodies.

Sunny got to Mallet and began to drag him backward; someone else shouted at him, "Leave him, he's one of them, the bastard!"

Then someone else, Reeko, Sunny thought his name was, the same kid who had high- fived Schofield, grabbed Mallet's other arm. He looked at Sunny, tears in his eyes.

"He tried to save him!" he said.

Sunny looked across at Schofield. The kid was dead, the side of his head

split open like a watermelon that had been dropped on the road.
He nodded at the kid, "He tried to do more than that. Come on."
They pulled Mallet's unconscious body across their shoulders and began to run back toward the barricade. Sunny's own eyes were streaming now as the tear-gas began to flood the part of the square nearest to the gate.

*

Chief Constable Malcolm Dennings was furious. His men had only just now managed to clear the gateway of the SSC security people, he had a fatality, and now Dixon was screaming at him.
"I told you that fuckup Mallet was dangerous. I told you, and what did you do about it eh? Fuck all... I told you!"
Dennings pushed Dixon hard in the chest and turned to his left.
"Superintendent Shawcross, take this man into custody."
"Yes Sir!" Shawcross said, taking Dixon's arm.
Dixon pushed him off, "You can't arrest me! For what, you fucking idiot?"
Dennings looked at the Superintendent without speaking. The man nodded and grabbed Dixon, this time spinning him round to zip lock his wrists behind his back.
As he was led away, Dixon started laughing, "You Muppet's, you don't even know who's in charge any more!"
Dennings turned his attention back to the square. The crowd had split into two distinct groups now, the sheep and the wolves, as he named them in his head. The sheep who had been happy to wave a few placards and shout abuse had bottled it when they had seen the level of violence that had taken place. They had moved away from the barricade and to the side of the square, dropping their placards on the floor as they moved to what they hoped was a place of security. Most of them had their eyes cast to the floor, others holding their hands over their heads in surrender. He reckoned that left a hardcore of wolves, maybe four or five hundred strong, who were clustered behind the barriers. His men were now arranged into two square blocks of five hundred each, as they walked slowly toward the barriers. Behind them were two armoured vehicles armed with tear-gas and water cannon. His men had live baton rounds, tear gas and tazers at their disposal, and Dennings knew that, after what had just happened, they would be using them all. He looked across at the corpse of the kid; the pool of blood around his head had now spread into a large crimson pool that was dripping down the kerb stone, and slowing as it coagulated into the storm drain.
He began to order someone to cover the body when his Sergeant interrupted him, 'Sir, it's Chief Commissioner Hawksworth for you!" he held up the secure phone.
"Shit!" Dennings thought. He can't know already - it isn't possible?
He took the phone and spoke "Dennings here Sir, I-"
"Listen to me very carefully Dennings and don't speak."

Dennings bit down a retort but did as he was told.
“I want you to cover that body and remove it. I want you to stand down your men, and withdraw behind the perimeter-“
“Sir I don’t think-“
“I said don’t speak man! Right now, this very instant, I am sat in the operations room and I am watching everything that is happening live. How is that possible, you are doubtless asking yourself? It is possible, Dennings, because they have a FUCKING TRANSMITTER! They are broadcasting three live streams across the Free Press Network, which in turn is distributing those live feeds to every international broadcaster including our own. Now, I want you to-”
Dennings felt like someone had punched him in the stomach. The whole debacle that was now in front of him - the shooting, the evacuation, Mallet, the chaos between his own men and Dixon's - he could see it in his mind, broadcast across the world’s media. He tried to clear his head, tried to focus, but he couldn’t. He was finished, he knew it, he would be a laughing stock. Worse still, he knew he would be the scapegoat they would now need. Hawksworth would make sure of it. He suddenly clutched his throat as he began to hyperventilate, convinced he was having a heart attack as he sat down heavily on the ground He didn’t even try to resist when Superintendent Shawcross took the phone off him.
“Sir, this is Superintendent John Shawcross-“
“What? Where the hell is-”
“I’m afraid the Chief is feeling a little unwell, sir. Sir, if you would care to instruct me as to your orders?”

Chapter Seven

Of the seven of them who were meeting in the cafe, six of them were sitting around two pushed together tables - Doc, Sunny, Katy, Jo, Danny and Reeko. Mallet was propped up in the corner, conscious now, but still in a lot of pain. Ten hours had passed since Schofield had died. The whole front of Riverside was now lit up with halogen floodlights and the flashing blue of the dozens of police vehicles that were parked outside. At Doc's urging, they had conducted a quick head count after the fracas and estimated that three hundred and fifty of the estates residents had made it back to safety behind the barricades, which had now been extended to cover all the streets running downhill to the wharf. In the immediate aftermath of the chaos of the square, everyone had gathered as previously planned in the disused sports hall, which was the only building large enough that they could all barricade themselves in. The night before, everyone had gathered for Doc to tell them what they had learned was to happen in the morning. He had also told them about the food supplies and generating equipment that had been smuggled in over the last few months, meaning that they would be OK for food as his 'people' had two containers stuffed with provisions, and a further container had generators and various other bits of equipment that Doc said they would need if they were going to hold out.

Sunny had been surprised at how easily the people in the hall accepted that Doc was running things, though he had witnessed a similar thing once before in Africa. It seemed to be, when people were cornered and direction-less, someone would always stand up and take charge, and people would follow them... at least for a while. That wasn't always the soundest decision of course - which he had also witnessed first-hand. His judgement, for what it was worth though, was that Doc at least seemed to know what he was doing. He certainly had a strategic plan - if of course he got to carry it out. Despite his physical appearance, Doc had a real presence and, Sunny recognised, no little stagecraft. His voice carried to the back of the room easily. He spoke to them all with an assured calmness and authority, as he delivered a brief but detailed analysis of what was about to happen. He had climbed up on the table at the end of the hall, holding his hands up till the babble of noise fell into an expectant hush. He went through in detail, without naming his source, the details of the government's plan to forcibly evacuate them. His job was made easier and had greater credibility as most people had seen or heard the Mablethorpe interview. He also ran a series of video clips that he said had been smuggled out of the New Towns, which left no-one in any doubt that what they were going to be sent to were effectively bonded labour camps. He had then signalled to Danny, who seemed to be Doc's techno wizard, to change the large projection screen he had set up. The screen projected a series of camera shots which covered most angles of Cenotaph Square, including one that was clearly outside the estate and was high enough to look through the security gates onto the front of the square. He told them that whatever happened in the morning would be instantly broadcast around the world.

After Schofield had been killed and they had all barricaded themselves in the hall, the panic and fear, and a lot of anger bubbled in the room. Doc, rather than try and shout people down, got Danny to light up the projection screens again. People started to fall silent as they looked at the screen, which was split into four squares - three international feeds as well as the BBC news channel, which was now the only one not covering the Riverside events. The ticker-tape running across the bottom of the Free Press News channel said that the Hague was discussing sending an international delegation to observe 'these most concerning events in the United Kingdom' .

The Doc had pointed at the screens.
"They can't stop these broadcasts. We are controlling them, and for as long as they are running they daren't move against us. The world is watching us tonight, my friends. Think about that - the whole world watching the lowly Riverside estate. If we hold out long enough we have a chance, but only if we stick together and only if we show absolute commitment to each other. If we do that we can win, we can get back our lives and we can tear down this fence that's caged us in like we are animals in a zoo."
Once or twice someone would interrupt or shout some inanity. Doc didn't argue with them or try to argue. He would wait till they'd finished and then simply pick up where he had left off. He told them that they needed to be co-ordinated and that he had a preliminary steering group in mind, pointing at Sunny and the others including Reeko, who Sunny had persuaded him reluctantly to bring on board as the 'Yoof' representative.
It was at that point that someone at the back shouted.
"Who the fuck put you and your fucking subversive mates in charge?", quite a few people murmured showing they were in agreement.
Someone else shouted, "Shut up, you prick!"
Most of the gathering though waited to see what he would say, waiting for his denial that he wasn't a subversive, wasn't a terrorist.
Doc looked around the room slowly, waiting till there was complete silence before speaking.
"No-one, I repeat no one is in charge here and everyone has choices. Anyone who wants to can simply walk across the square out there and leave. Though, I would suggest they if they do so, they keep their hands above their heads to avoid being shot."
A few people laughed.
"As for our friend at the back there, who I didn't quite spot....", he said looking across the sea of heads, holding his hand above his eyes as if scanning a far horizon. "Nope, still can't see you!", he said, which brought a few more laughs.
"There are people here of differing faiths and of no faiths, people who are right wing and people, yes like me, who are of the left. Of the Left didn't used to be seen as subversive by the way, it never really was unless you accept the warped views and propaganda of people like Mablethorpe and his cronies. So when did someone having left-leaning convictions become the same as being subversive or being a terrorist? When did that change exactly?"
He smiled. "Well, maybe that's a debate for another time! The truth is it doesn't really make any difference right now does it? The only thing that matters right now is that everyone in this room has something in common. It doesn't matter right now what your political beliefs or your religion are.

Your age doesn't matter, nor your ethnicity, or even your cultural backgrounds. All of us have one thing in common, and that is that tonight, and for the coming days, we are all people of Riverside. We, all of us in this room, are the people that our government has given up on. We are the people who the government have declared to be so unworthy that we no longer have the right to choose how and where we wish to live. We are the people that they have decided they can treat like animals, like livestock that they can cage in, like beasts of burden to fetch and carry at their command."

The room was silent, other than the sound of shuffling feet as people looked down at the floor or anywhere but at each other.
Doc had paused, taking a swig of water from a plastic bottle. The room had started to become stifling with so many bodies trapped inside, and with the doors and windows nailed up tight. He took a deep breath as he continued. "So out there the government sees us simply as a commodity to be utilised as they see fit. But we are also the people who just this afternoon stood up for each other in the face of overwhelming force. We are the people who today stuck two fingers up at Mablethorpe and his corrupt stooges in Parliament. We are the ones who declared that enough is enough!' He paused, and for the first time raised his voice so that it reverberated around the damp and graffiti-stained walls.
"Today, right now, the world is watching." He pointed at the screen which was carrying live footage from the meeting across the globe. "The whole world is watching and waiting to see what comes next!
"My friends, I say that we, the people of Riverside who are gathered here now, reject this modern day slave trade; that we will resist the forces that seek to steal our very lives from us; and that we will hold out for as long as it takes for the world to come to our aid! So what do you say? Do we stand together and speak with one voice, or not?'

Sunny clenched his fists, and saw from Jo's face that she was as tense as he was. Doc had rolled the dice, and it was shit or bust time. The accompanying silence to Sunny had felt like a deafening shout of denial, of rejection. Then one person, an old guy at the front, stepped toward where the Doc still stood, his head now bowed, waiting. Sunny had seen the old guy a few times. He was the one who would come and clean the graffiti off the cenotaph and bag up the rubbish that gathered on its steps, and one of the few old soldiers who would wear his medals on Remembrance Day. The old warrior was standing and staring up at Doc for what seemed an eternity before finally he started to clap, the sound echoing around the room. A woman a few rows back joined him, then a few more, and then a hundred, and then the whole room was suddenly clapping and stamping.

Some of the younger people started chanting "Riverside, Riverside" and soon everyone was joining in including Sunny and Jo, who were looking at each other, both grinning and both both teary-eyed.

*

The euphoria of the meeting had lessened somewhat by the time they had got back to the cafe. Reeko had broken into the local pharmacy and gotten some painkillers for Mallet, though he did ask Katy to give them to him, just in case the cop asked where they had come from. Mallet had told them earlier that, in the morning, he would leave and deal with the consequences of what had happened. None of them were surprised. Sunny had decided to tell them that it was Mallet who had tipped him off about the evacuation. In large part he did so because a few people wanted to tie the old sergeant up, despite the fact that he was bleeding profusely from his head wound and was clearly no threat to anybody. In the end it was Reeko who had once again stood up for his old nemesis. He had pulled out a twelve inch knife and stood between Mallet and the crowd.

'You wanna tie him up, OK, but first you gotta tie me up!' After that the small group who had proposed the idea decided that Mallet wasn't really a threat worth bothering with. That was when Sunny finally persuaded the Doc that Reeko should become part of the steering group, as Doc had now christened them.

Jo tried again, "Listen, we have the ability to broadcast live, you already said."

The Doc blew smoke above his head, "I've already said, Jo, that......"

"I know, I know 'it isn't the right time' but, Doc, I saw you before, the way you spoke, the way you pulled everyone together. What's the difference between broadcasting the meeting and you doing a straight piece to camera? The way you ran that meeting, the power of what you said, it moved people, Doc, and you could do the same across the networks. Make another broadcast and people would rally to us."

"No they wouldn't Jo. What we have to do is follow the plan, and that means we wait for our people to start the international campaigns. Our support has to come from out there-"

"But if you go on air you can-"

He held his hand up, "Sunny, please explain to Jo why it wouldn't work."

Jo gave a bright smile that looked dangerous, "Oh yes, Sunny, do please explain it to me!"

Sunny gave the Doc a dirty look before turning to Jo. "They aren't scared, Jo, out there, I mean," he said nodding at the screen on the muted television set. "The reason why Doc's big 'fight them on the beaches' speech worked is because the people on this side of the barriers are frightened. Sure everyone's up and on a high right now, but that's just the adrenaline, the after-buzz from what happened in the square. Inside

themselves our people are shitting bricks. Basically Doc has told them to close their eyes and wish for the best, so for a little while at least they don't have to think about reality. And the other part of it is that this can't be seen as about Doc or any one individual, otherwise you can guarantee they will pick us apart one by one.
The Doc stubbed his cheroot out in the ashtray. "Well, remind me to come to you again, Sunny, when I want a ringing endorsement of the strategy."
Katy laughed, slapping his back with the flat of her hand and knocking the air out of him with a whoosh. "Serves you right for being a patronising and pompous ass my love!" she said, winking at Jo.
Sunny burst out laughing, then whooshed himself as Katy give him an only slightly softer whack across the back of his head.
"Ow! What was that for?"
"For laughing at my man!" Katy said folding her arms.
Reeko and Danny stared fixedly at the table as she glared in their direction.

"Turn it up," Mallet said, his voice still shaky, "The television, turn it up."
Reeko grabbed the remote and turned up the volume just as Gregory Mablethorpe was finishing speaking.
The Prime Minster was seated in the centre of the table flanked by Chief Commissioner Richard Hawksworth and General Sir John Moncrieff, Head of the British Joint Services Command.
They could all see what had startled Mallet on the screens, as behind the three men was a series of electronic photographs containing around twenty to thirty people.
Hawksworth the Commissioner was speaking now, picking up after the PM. "Ladies and Gentlemen, firstly I would like to endorse and support what has already been said by the Prime Minister, about the tragic loss of a young man's life that we have all witnessed on our television screens today. Our deepest sympathies of course go out to his loved ones." Hawksworth looked for a long moment into the camera before continuing. "You will have course already heard the wild accusations and claims by some of our international neighbours. Quite frankly those claims would be laughable if they were not so badly misplaced. The young man who was shot today I can now inform you was actually an undercover police officer who-"
"No fucking way!" Reeko shouted, jumping up out of his chair,
Sunny grabbed his arm, "Reeko, wait please. We have to hear this-"
"But Sunny, it isn't fucking true, I'm telling you-"
Doc put his own hand on Reeko's, "Sunny is right, Reeko. We have to hear what they are saying."
Reeko slumped back down in his chair as Hawksworth brought up a photograph of a young man who, despite one eye closed and his face being covered in bruises, was clearly the guard who had killed Schofield.

"Indeed, we have now established beyond doubt that Groves , an SSC security operative, was in fact a subversive infiltrator, who we now believe was recognised by Officer Schofield, and as a consequence was shot dead by Groves at zero nine twenty three this morning."
Suddenly the screen filled with Doc's face, then panned back to Hawksworth.
"We have established that this man is one of the key ringleaders of the terrorist acts we have seen carried out today. He has been on our Code One watch list for three years and is wanted in connection with a series of bombings and atrocities carried out over several years, including last May's bombing of Kensington Palace."
Katy put her hand on top of Doc's, and looked across at Mallet, "He was here all last May, John, you know that as well as I do!"
Mallet nodded his acknowledgement and looked back at the TV.
"This man's terrorist code name is 'The Doc'. His real name is Michael Bartholomew Deveron. He is the son and heir of Lord Deveron of Eastleigh who, as many of you will know, is one of the most distinguished members of the House of Lords and a privy councillor." A murmur ran around the press briefing room accompanied by a myriad of camera flashes. Hawksworth waited till the room stilled before continuing. "I would like to emphasise that Lord Deveron has behaved impeccably in these matters and has voluntarily chosen to stand down from all official duties until his son is apprehended. The noble Lord has also made it very clear to us that we will have his fullest cooperation to, in his own words 'help capture this shameful traitor to his family and country.'" Hawksworth nodded to his aide and the picture changed to one of Sunny, though instead of being in his normal tee shirt and jeans, the picture showed a Sunny with neatly cropped hair and wearing a three piece grey business suit. The photograph had been clipped from a larger one, as you could still see parts of the other people at what looked like some kind of conference.
"This man is one of Deveron's key lieutenants and goes by the name of Sunny Taylor, real name Charles Windsor Mountbatten Taylor-"
Reeko started to snigger then stopped just as suddenly, as Hawksworth went on.
"Taylor is a convicted felon who has served a prison sentence in the United States and has also been identified as one of the key conspirators of an attempted coup in East Africa. He is also wanted in connection with the embezzlement of millions of dollars from the World Bank's famine relief fund, for which he once worked. We have managed to identify, with the cooperation of our international partners, that those funds have financed terrorist atrocities around the globe as well as here in the UK."
Sunny was sat with his hands pressed over his mouth. He could feel everyone looking at him, waiting for him to say something, but he couldn't.

Hawksworth was relentless, with picture after picture being brought up on the large screen, many of which had clearly been taken from the surveillance cameras this morning, as they were blurred and hazed with tear-gas. Everyone in the cafe had been named as a subversive and terrorist, even Katy. Everyone except Mallet.
Hawksworth blanked out the screen and took off his glasses to polish them. He sipped a glass of water and dabbed his forehead which, despite the desk fan blowing onto his face, he could still feel the sweat starting to bead across his brow. He replaced his glasses and looked once again directly into the camera.
"As I have already said, a number of misinformed individuals and foreign powers have reported that this morning's operation was some kind of evacuation attempt." He paused, shaking his head at the ridiculous idea.
"I'm afraid that people have fallen for what I am sorry to say is a typical and wholly expected subversive strategy of misinformation and lies. This morning's operation was planned to prevent the tragedy that you have all seen. There are hundreds of good citizens in the Riverside estate who are trapped behind the subversive barricades. They have been duped by the people I have previously identified. We have been monitoring the estate for some considerable time, and our planned operation this morning, if unhindered, would have allowed the safe removal of these terrorists and secured the safety of the estate for its legitimate residents. This afternoon I offered my resignation to the Prime Minister as the senior responsible person for the operation, but that offer was declined. The Prime Minister reminded me that duty is not something that can be cast off in the face of adversity." He looked across at the Prime Minister and nodded respectfully.
The camera panned across to Mablethorpe's stony expression which, as he realised he was on camera, changed to a statesman-like nod.
"Part of the reason that I offered my resignation today was my shame and deep regret that the police force, of which I have been proud to serve for forty years, has been betrayed by one of its own."
John Mallet's face appeared on the TV screen, and everyone in the cafe heard the sergeant grunt as if he'd been punched in the stomach.
"The man on the screen behind me is Sergeant John Mallet; a man who was entrusted with the details of operation 'Save Riverside' and who, up to this morning, I believed was a man who exemplified the highest traditions of service."

*

The seven of them watched the rest of the briefing, where smudged photocopies of John Mallet's bank accounts were brought up on screen, showing multiple deposits made in his name and totalling hundreds of thousands of pounds. Pictures and lurid details of Mallet's father, 'Red Danny' the trade union baron, who had long ago been retrospectively

designated a subversive, were also shown.
Jo got up and switched the TV off, looking at each of them in turn until they finally met her gaze, before she turned towards Doc.
"I think you need to revise the strategy Michael!"
He looked at each of them. Everyone in the room had been designated as a category one subversive which, if proven, was a capital offence. These people along with himself were now the walking dead. They were also the people who had trusted him to lead them. He looked at Sunny, who nodded at him, then at Mallet who still looked grey and ashen, though whether from his injuries or the broadcast Doc wasn't sure. Finally he nodded to himself. He had expected that they would be vilified in the media but the degree and speed of it had still come as a shock. He turned to Danny, "Danny, set up the studio and be ready to run in forty minutes. Sunny, please go to the meeting hall. We are going to have to speak to everyone before I go on air-"
"You will be lynched, my friend!" Mallet said, sitting up so he could swallow a couple more painkillers. "Everyone in that hall will have just watched the same thing we did. They have just seen the Prime Minister and the country's most senior police officer condemning us, all of us, and you know that most, if not all, will believe it!"
They all fell into silence, not looking at each other.
Reeko stood up, "This is just bullshit! There is no way this will carry, are you kidding me? Rusty fucking Schofield as an undercover cop; ha, give me a fucking break! Anyone who knew him, which believe me is a lot of people, know that he didn't know his arse from his elbow. Rusty is...was my mate, God love him. But I tell you he was as thick as fucking pig shit. And anyway, his mother is back there for fuck's sake! Do you think she would be living in this fucking shit-hole of a place if he was an undercover cop? And Jesus fucking Christ, the fucking Prime Minister, you think he has any kind of credibility down here? Those people up in London are nothing to us, nothing. I mean really, you're talking about the same fucking twat who put a fence around us, caged us in like fucking animals and now he speaks to us and we all say 'Oh, OK then old chap, fair play. Of course we believe you, old boy!' "
The Doc smiled at Reeko's imitation of Mablethorpe, which he thought was pretty accurate.
Reeko walked over to Mallet and stared down at him, then he gestured his thumb back toward Sunny and Doc, "These two need to explain themselves; they aren't real Riversider's. Sorry guys!" he said turning briefly toward them both. "But I reckon they can do that. Sunny is a good guy, I would bet my life on it, and even Lord Deveron the Doc here, despite being a poncey toff, has some respect from people. But listen to me, old man, your top cop has just made two huge fucking errors. The first of

which is Rusty, but even worse than that is him putting you up there as some kind of bent cop. John Mallet, the Hammer! Look, everyone knows you are miserable old fucker, but bent............!"
Mallet grimaced but stayed quiet as Reeko looked down at him and carried on.
"For fuck's sake don't you know anything about this place? Don't you think we know who the bent coppers are? Like your chum Oinky Davis! Believe me we can smell 'em quicker than you would believe, old man. They stink in a very special way, bent pigs, and believe me there are enough of them. But you, everyone knows you smell of pure pork, one hundred percent straight, and there is no-one who knows you, whether they are your friend or whether they hate your fucking guts, which a lot of us do by the way, there is no way we will believe any of this bollocks about you."
John Mallet had received many commendations over the years, yet bizarrely he thought what Reeko had just said was possibly the nicest thing anyone had ever said about him. None of that showed on his face of course, which remained deadpan. He levered himself up with a grimace, and spoke to Sunny.
"Come on Mr Taylor, lets you and I, along with this foul-mouthed little scrote go and get lynched together!"

Chapter Eight

Carl Stevens liked his job. True, Porton Down was in the middle of nowhere and he only got one weekend off in three, but he pulled twice the money he could earn as a security guard anywhere else, and by and large the people were OK, if sometimes a little wacky. Talking of which, he thought, as he turned his tablet off hiding it under the desk console, here comes the number one Wacko, Dominic Weston. Carl didn't like Weston. There was something about him - he was arrogant for one thing - most of the staff were of course, especially when dealing with a no mark like him. But, it was more than that with Weston he was a cold fish. He was also a royal pain in the arse, he really was, and especially tonight when Man United were in the Champions League final and the kick off was in five minutes. If it was one of the other professors or scientists, it would take little more than two minutes to process them through. Of course all the other boffin's were happy to use the lab-provided pens and stationary, everyone except Weston that was. Still, Carl managed to put on his most efficient smile as the man came though the last transparent airlock.
"Hello, Professor Weston. Working late again?"
"Hello, Carl. Needs must I'm afraid! I know it's a pain for you night guys?"
"No problem at all Professor. That's why we're here," Carl said, his face

falling as he saw that Weston had four new pens in his hand, and knowing he would have to scan each one, record each one, and then do the same thing all over again on Weston's exit.
Weston caught the look and grimaced in sympathy, "I'm sorry, Carl, and I know it seems odd to you, but if I don't have the right pens I can't work, and it drives me nuts!"
"They're that special, eh?" Carl asked, being polite but not remotely interested Weston had actually used his name which was a first, he normally just mumbled. Carl glanced quickly at the desk clock and groaned inwardly as he realised he shouldn't have asked anything. There were just five minutes to kick off, and he could see Weston was now going to give him a lecture, on pens!
Weston, put three of the pens in his shirt breast pocket and held the other in front of Carl as he spoke. "Oh, these are more than special, Carl. These are the foremost academic pens in the world. They were designed by a German mathematician Max Koffler, titanium casing, with a double ink cartridge, waterproof, and, uniquely, fireproof. Interestingly, a lot of people think they were designed for space, but actually Koffler, as well as being a mathematician, was an accomplished marine biologist..."
Carl zoned out. He would be lucky if he saw the last ten minutes of the first half at this rate and the boring bastard would probably decide to leave during the second half. He looked down at his cheap Biro with its chewed top, thinking 'a pen is a pen', you fuckwit." He was startled out of his inner gloom as he realised what Weston had just said.
"Sorry, sir?"
Weston smiled, "I said, here I am boring you over my Koffler and you're probably thinking a pen is a pen, right?"
Carl felt his face heat up, "Sorry sir I-"
Weston laughed, something else he didn't usually do, "It's OK, Carl, I know you're a good man, even one of our best from what I hear from George Graham."
Carl definitely felt hot in the face now. George Graham was Acia Securities top boss. Shit, I've only met him twice, he thought, maybe that means I'm finally in line for a promotion... He looked quickly up at Weston, making sure the guy wasn't taking the mickey out of him.
Weston smiled, "Look, Carl, I shouldn't have told you that. It's just, as you know, the senior staff meets regularly to discuss how everything is going here in the labs, and... well, your name came up and George agreed with my assessment, that's all. I'd appreciate it if you didn't say anything."
Carl grinned, "Don't worry, sir. My lips are sealed and, sir, I appreciate your support!"
"You're welcome," Weston said as he removed his watch, looking at the time as he placed it in the storage box Carl had placed ready on the desk.

He put the pen back with the others in his breast pocket before speaking.
"I thought you would have been watching the game tonight, Carl? It's OK. I know you night-shift guys like a little live streaming now and then," he added.
Carl nodded; maybe this guy wasn't so bad after all, he thought.
"And now you have me and my stupid pens to scan!"
"That's OK, professor-" Carl started to say, stopping mid-sentence as he saw Weston take the four pens out of his pocket and put them in the side pocket of his lab coat.
"You know, sometimes I'd forget my own head if it wasn't screwed on, at least that's what my Mother always said. Anyway, I best get on if you can buzz me through?"
Carl looked at Weston, and then down at the desk clock. Three minutes past the hour. The rules of entry were really strict, nothing went into D section unless it was scanned and notarised, no deviations. But, this was Professor Weston, a good guy, and one of the top brass, and Carl knew the guy was just trying to help out a fellow colleague. Anyway, whilst he didn't know exactly what went on inside D section - well in truth he didn't have a clue, weapons research he guessed - one thing was certain, you couldn't sneak a nuke out in a piss-ant little pen.
He smiled up at the professor, "I guess I'm a bit that way myself, Prof," he said as he buzzed the door open.
"Enjoy the game, Carl." Weston said smiling as he walked into the airlock which sealed the access to D section, the UK's most secure biological weapons and research department.

*

Weston had stripped three of the Koffler pens down to their constituent parts and laid them out on the desk. The unaltered pen, the one that still had ink in, he returned to his breast pocket. As it turned out he hadn't needed to write anything, but as a precaution he had left it intact, just in case. Anyway, the three other re-engineered Koffler's would suffice. It had taken him several aborted attempts with the model lathe he had purchased to turn the new titanium ink cartridges into the exact shape of the originals. The trickiest part had been making the tops threaded and hermetically sealed with non corrosive 'O' rings. As he looked down now at the six slim cylinders, he felt a wobble of uncertainty. If they leaked or fractured...... He shook his head, clearing his mind. He had done the best job he could, and if anything the cylinders were stronger than the canisters that the lab used. The difference being of course that the 6/707 canisters were in a vacuum-sealed environment. Anyone exposed to 6/707 in that room would be fatally compromised, but the room itself would be contained along with anyone unfortunate enough to be inside at the time. He looked at the wall clock. He had fifty six minutes to fill the Koffler cylinders, decontaminate the work cell and leave the room. By then the second half of the dreaded football match would be in full sway and the idiot guard Stevens would hopefully still be drooling over his beloved football team. It was ironic, Weston thought, that he had indeed been going to speak to George Graham about Stevens - though that would have been to ask for his dismissal, as the man was both lazy and inept. The fact that he brought an illegal tablet into work to watch football as well, as the porn channels that Weston knew he also watched, said it all really. He had held off at the time for the simple reason that, when he was first formalising his plan to take some of the 6/707, he felt an idiot guard could be a useful asset or even a scapegoat if it became necessary. Three nights ago he had planted one of the 6/707's labels under the pile of junk in the man's holdall whilst he was on one of his numerous 'toilet breaks' again, just in case things went wrong and he needed a fall guy. He placed his hands into the reinforced silicone gauntlets, allowing him access through the glass cabinet, congratulating himself once again on the simple brilliance of his plan.

It was fate, or rather destiny, that had led him to this. There were just too many coincidences for it to be anything else, everything had fallen into place at the same time -even the fact that he never normally watched television news broadcasts in the morning as he preferred the radio. Yet this morning he had switched the television on and why? Because fate and destiny had decided he should! He had heard the voice first, and recognised it even though it was deeper and less polished than when he had last heard it all those years ago. It was Michael Deveron's voice coming out of the TV set as Free Press News kept running the same group of clips. First was the graphic footage of the boy being shot in the square, followed by the police and SSC people in seeming confusion. Then they had shown Michael speaking to a motley group in some run- down estates meeting hall. After that they would cut to Mablethorpe denouncing the people of the estate, which was called Riverside, as subversive terrorists. Free Press News had a panel of experts arguing both sides of the debate. Peter Rankin, the well- known exiled radical, was arguing that unless the international community stepped in to support the resistance, the authorities would crush them easily. At one point he had looked into the camera and called directly for people with a sense of justice to come to the aid of Riverside and support their cause. Dominic felt like Rankin was speaking directly to him, even though he knew rationally that was crazy. The UK government were calling Michael 'The Doc', a dangerous subversive and terrorist. Dominic could easily believe the first charge Michael Deveron was already into left-wing politics back in their Cambridge days. But the other stuff about him being a violent terrorist he knew without any doubt was pure fabrication. Michael was a pacifist by conviction, he had always been so, and there wasn't any way he knew that that would have altered. Michael had been a radical campaigner, a radical leftie, and for a long time after Cambridge Dominic would occasionally come across some anti-capitalist treatise from Michael on the web. 'Manifesto for Change' he remembered had caused quite a stir at the time, and there was lots of other stuff that he couldn't really remember now, as in truth he had found it all rather boring and irrelevant. This was of course years before the anti-capitalist brigades were given the new label of subversives and driven underground. Back then it was still the case that many people openly claimed to be left of centre in their politics. The change had been gradual at first, at least until the 'Net Wars'; but after that one government after another chose to move toward the U.S. model, where politics were confined to what CEOs, financiers and city economists thought. After all, the argument went, these were the people who created the wealth and understood how the systems worked, they managed the wealth of everyone. So it made sense that their views would become the driver for societal change and betterment. In this new paradigm, there was no place for politics. Economics were irrelevant and simply interfered with an innate science. Alternative views became increasingly sidelined to the internet, which in itself led to many developed nations continually creating legislation to try and control the World Wide Web. After the crash in 2018, and the massive riots that followed across Europe, very few people in public life (and especially in the UK) claimed to be anti-capitalist any more. To do so would in effect be declaring that you were against a civilised society and only sought to undermine basic law and order. After the UK ceded from the EU, those who still promulgated leftist views were officially classified by authorities and state-friendly media groups as unpatriotic. Dominic had watched from a distance as Michael had been ostracised by mainstream academia, and vilified in political journals, before eventually he had simply dropped out of sight. He had regretted at the time and over the years that he hadn't done something, or at the very least made contact with him, but the truth was he had been too afraid at the time.

He had snapped back into the broadcast as Gregory Mablethorpe was declaring directly into the camera that 'he would stand firm in the face of subversive terrorism and would not be cowed by threats wherever they came from'. As Dominic watched Mablethorpe, who was now looking directly at him through the TV screen, he could swear he heard him say 'and that means you Turveydrop!'

*

He waited for the airlock to go through its three-stage cycle. The feeling of calm satisfaction that he had felt on successfully finishing suddenly flooded out of him as he took a sharp intake of breath. There was someone outside the airlock talking to Stevens, the guard. What the hell is she doing here, he thought, dismayed as he realised it was Houghton, the bitch of an HR Director. It didn't make sense. She was strictly nine to five, so why was she here now? He felt a rising panic beginning to take hold of him and had to force himself to control his breathing, his mind frantically trying to think what could have gone wrong. The Koffler pens in his side pocket felt like they weighed fifty pounds each and seemed to be screaming aloud 'Containment Breach'! At least by the time he had exited the airlock though his voice was steady and even when he spoke.

"Susan! You're working late. No problems I hope?" he didn't smile at her as that would immediately arouse her suspicions.

The woman looked up from her conversation with Stevens; he could see she wasn't in good humour.

"Oh, good evening, Professor Weston. I'm afraid we do have a problem, but nothing that concerns the scientific department." Houghton looked back down at Stevens, shaking her head as the man looked down at the desk his face blood red.

Weston's feeling of fear and panic vanished at the same speed as it had arrived, leaving only the adrenalin that was still causing his heart to run faster than it should. Of course she isn't here for me, he thought. If they knew about the 6/707 it wouldn't be Ms Susan bloody Houghton, it would be twenty armed personnel, and the lab would be on lock-down with alarms blaring out all over the place. The tablet! He suddenly realised, she was here for Stevens - that's why the man looked so dismal. His first instinct was to think, it serves him right, and just leave, but he also knew he couldn't take the chance that the man wouldn't tell her about the pens. And he might do that because, if he gave her some good dirt on what was really common knowledge about her least favourite Professor, he might get himself off with just a warning. Or maybe Stevens would simply want to do as much damage to others as he could before he lost his job, Dominic thought - because that's exactly what he would do himself.

He placed his hand on Houghton's arm to attract her attention; she flinched back as if he had pinched her, which gave him not a little satisfaction as he mistook her loathing for his touch for one of fear.

"I'm sorry, Susan. As the head of D section, anything that happens here concerns me!"

He could almost see her visibly biting back a retort as she recognised he was right. She gave him that idiot simpering smile she used in formal meetings. Her voice when she spoke was the one her breed of human resources always used with him, the voice of contrived and insincere sincerity.

"Of course, Professor, you're quite right. My apologies. I am afraid that Mr Stevens here has seriously breached the organisation's appropriate behaviour code."

"Really, in what way?" he asked, looking sternly at Stevens, who continued to stare fixedly at the top of the security desk.
"Well, it may shock you, Professor, but it was reported to me, confidentially of course, that Mr Stevens has been bringing unauthorised equipment into a Category Four control area. As you know, Professor Weston, that means I am obligated to suspend Mr Stevens with immediate effect, and I have already advised him that it is likely he will be dismissed - though, obviously," she added quickly, "only after a fair and impartial hearing of the facts of the matter of course!"
Weston felt his heart suddenly skip a beat as the pens in his pocket threatened to start yelling of their presence again, but he managed to keep his expression neutral.
"Actually, I'm surprised you didn't see or hear it on your way in, Professor?"' she said, pointing at the tablet which had been shoved hurriedly halfway under the desk.
He looked down at the tablet, then back at her complacent face and smiled.
"I'm sorry, Susan, but I'm afraid it's you that are mistaken."
"Oh?"
"That's right. Carl, that is Mr Stevens here asked me yesterday if it would be OK to watch football this evening and I gave him permission. It's a big game, you know!"
Stevens looked up at him like a grateful Labrador looks at his master, and Dominic had to force himself to resist the urge to ruffle the top of the man's head and say 'good boy'. If Stevens looked like a docile Labrador, though, Houghton looked more Rotweiller-ish, he thought, as her normal cutesy mouth had now transformed into a sneering curl.
"You!" she said. "You gave him permission? I'm sorry, Professor, but you don't have the authority to override a directive in that way."
"Oh, don't I?" he said, shrugging in what he hoped was a nonchalant way. He placed his hand on Stevens shoulder as he continued, "Still, I gave Carl here permission, so I don't believe he has done anything wrong, do you?"
He could see her calculating, as she went through various scenarios in her head before finally replying.
"No, in this instance, I can see that he hasn't." She turned to Stevens, her HR voice back on. "However in future, Mr Stevens, you will clear any such requests with my department, and they will not be granted. Are we very clear?"
Stevens, nodded still looking stunned, as he mumbled "Yes, Miss Houghton."
"Ms Houghton."
"Ms Houghton." Stevens agreed quickly.
"Of course, Professor, you realise that I will have to formally report this very serious breach of protocol to the Director?"

"Of course you must Susan; indeed I would expect nothing less of you." He smiled again and winked, just because he knew how much it would irritate her.
"I'm not sure you appreciate the seriousness of what you may be facing, Professor, I have to advise you that-" She stopped suddenly and stepped back as he lifted the palm of his hand out in front of her.
"No, Ms Houghton," he said, his voice hard now, his face unsmiling. "No, you really don't. Now why don't you run back to your little office and file your little report whilst I consider the seriousness of the situation for myself."
She went bright red, began to speak, then appeared to think better of it, turned and walked briskly away. The sound of her heels clicking like an old clock that had been wound to fast echoed down the corridor behind her, as she rounded the corner out of sight.
Weston watched her go as Stevens touched his arm, "Jesus, Prof, I don't know what to say!"
"Forget it."
"But that snooty bitch, she's right, isn't she? The shit is going to hit the fan when the top brass find out what's happened tonight?"
Weston looked down at him, then at the tablet, his fingers caressing the pens in his pocket, which now contained the most contagious and deadly biological agent since anthrax.
"Oh, the shit will hit the fan, Carl" he said "Of that I can guarantee you!"
He began to laugh then, and he laughed even harder when he looked at Stevens face, which was moving from a confused smile to one of slight concern.

Chapter Nine

"Hello, Christopher Jennings"
"Christopher it's me."
"Dominic?"
"Yes, I need to see you urgently."
"I can't, Dominic I'm really sorry but I'm not in London, I'm in-"
"I do watch the news, Christopher, I know where you are. Now where are you staying?"
"I'm in the Midland Hotel, but I can't meet you here, there are too many people. What's wrong, Dominic, you sound-"
"Meet me in one hour, I'll tell you all about it then. Get a taxi to Piccadilly

Square, Central Manchester, and then change taxis-and go to the Metropole Hotel in North Manchester. I will meet you in the reception bar."

"I don't know if I can get away, it's hectic here, you must have seen how everything has gone pear-shaped-"

"Listen to me, Christopher, you need to meet me in one hour or the Riverside thing will look like very small fry. Now make sure you do what I said about changing taxis."

"But I can't just drop ev-?"

"Christopher, listen to me. Certain people, nasty people, have found out about us and, if you want to keep a lid on it, you need to do exactly what I say. One hour!"

"Hello? Dominic?"

*

Just over an hour later, Christopher sat in the Metropole hotel room, his hands unconsciously covering his mouth as he watched the video on Dominic's laptop. When he had arrived at the hotel, Dominic had met him in the reception area and told him to follow him to the room he had booked them into. He hadn't spoken again, other than to tell Jennings to sit down and watch the video. It showed everything, every explicit detail. It also had his face in full view and, despite the wig and the rouge, he was very easily identifiable. At one point Dominic seemed to look straight into the lens, though he knew that was just a coincidence from the positioning of the hidden camera. He watched as Dominic was loudly slapping his exposed buttocks and telling him what a dirty little slut he was whilst, in a stupid squeaky voice, he asked to be slapped harder as he had been such a naughty girl. What had been a highly erotic experience then, now just looked a hideous farce, making him want to crawl in a hole and die.

When it had finished, Dominic removed the data stick from the laptop and held it up in front of his face, Jennings' tear-stained eyes following the stick as if mesmerised.

"Listen to me carefully, Chrissie. This is the only copy, the only one, do you understand me?"

Jennings blinked, and shook his head.

"The people who had this made had two options, they could cash in with one of the tabloid sites or they could sell it to us. Fortunately they have chosen the latter."

"But how... I mean why? Why would they do that? This would have been dynamite in the press?"

Dominic smiled at him, "Not really. Oh, if it had been Mablethorpe or one of his Ministers on here, then yes. But, and I don't mean this unkindly Chrissie, you are not the Prime Minister, just a civil servant, albeit a high-ranking one. It would be a seven day wonder, but it wouldn't have touched

Mablethorpe, they would have made sure of it."
"But still it's worth a fortune, Dommie. the tabloids would pay tens of thousands for it !"
"Sadly, my friend, much more than that; and it is certainly the case that I won't be buying that second home I dreamed of..."
"But it's me that works for the PM; I'm the one that has everything to lose by exposure...Oh God, I'm sorry, I didn't mean that the way it came out. I just meant, why didn't they come to me?"
Weston smiled down at him, "It's OK, Chrissie. I know what you meant and you're right. But these people are clever, they don't just research their targets, they also discover any little weaknesses in those targets."
Weston could see that Jennings still didn't get it. He tried again.
"Chrissie, they know how I feel about you. In fact one of them actually said they knew you were like my little brother. Could you sell your kid brother out? Anyway, they wouldn't have come to you. If you had gone and told all to Mablethorpe, he would have set MI6 on them, maybe even before they had chance to sell it on. This way they have made a tidy sum and, other than this data stick, no evidence of crime or blackmail exists. They are home and free in other words."
"How much, Dominic, how much did you have to pay them? I want to pay my share. It isn't right. And why didn't you tell me? I could have supported you - we could have dealt with them together.'
Weston smiled and put his hand briefly on Jennings' cheek, "Ah my dear Chrissie, why would I make us both suffer that. But there is something I want you to do. Here, hold out your hand. Now, I want you to take the stick and, when you get back to London, I want you to burn it so we are both safe."
"Can't you do it?" Jennings asked, staring at the three inch stick of black plastic. Such a small thing to destroy two people's lives, he thought.
Weston placed it in his hand and closed Jennings' fingers over it.
"I want you to do it, Chrissie. I know you remember, I know what you're like. This way you know without doubt that it's gone forever, and you won't have to worry about it ever again!"

*

Later, the two of them sat companionably, at the back of an old fashioned run-down pub that Dominic had guided them to through a warren of littered, badly-lit back streets. The place was empty, apart from a surly barman and a couple of old winos, who alternated between swearing at each other and bursting into half-remembered songs.
Jennings sipped on his pint of dark stout and wiped the froth off his mouth with the back of his hand. "How do we know they haven't copied it?" he asked for the umpteenth time as he stared into space.
Weston sighed, "I've told you, Christopher. There is no gain for them in

doing that. These people are professionals; they take the money and leave. If they tried to hit us again they would risk all sorts of consequences. They hit hard and fast so you have little time to think, then they go and you never see them again. Professional blackmailers never hit the same mark twice; only amateurs do that, which is why they get caught."

"And the money, you won't change your mind?"

Weston shook his head and sipped his beer. "It's done and, anyway, at the moment it's the least of my worries."

"Why what else-""

"Oh, it's not to do with this!" Weston assured him quickly. "But it does seem to be my week for helping friends who are facing disaster."

"You mean Deveron don't you?"

Weston looked at him genuinely surprised.

"You're not the only person who reads people well, Dominic," Jennings smiled.

"When you rang earlier, I know it's awful, especially now I know what you've been going through for both of us, but I thought it was over him. I know how close you both were. I was worried you were going to try and help him, or do something crazy."

Weston stared down into his half-empty beer glass and spoke into it, not looking up at Jennings, his voice flat and emotionless.

"I am going to help him, Christopher. I'm not someone who leaves his friends in the lurch, ever. And don't try telling me that you believe all this subversive terrorist nonsense either. Deveron is, and always will be a pacifist - you know that."

Jennings shrugged, "People can change."

Weston shook his head, "Not him! Anyway, I'm going to go into Riverside and I'm going to bring him out. I know it's all locked down, and I don't know how yet, but I am going to go in to Riverside. I'm going to get him away from all those crazies in there and take him to the authorities, and make sure that they realise he is innocent."

Jennings placed his hand on Weston's arm, then quickly withdrew it as he realised where they were. "Dominic, you really can't go into Riverside. That whole area is under Marshall law. You'd be arrested or worse - you could be killed!"

Weston nodded, and smiled at his friend, "You may be right, Christopher, but if you're my kid brother, then once, a long time ago, Michael Deveron was like a father to me. If it weren't for him I wouldn't have made it through that first year at University. I have to try and help him, Christopher. I owe him and I know I can get him to listen, and if he does... It's funny, though, how life works out, because ironically, if he does agree to come out with me, I'll actually be helping that bastard boss of yours, Mablethorpe, to solve a major crisis!"

"But, Dominic, I'm telling you there isn't any way for you get to him-"
Weston held up his hand, "Enough. I wasn't even going to tell you about this. It's too dangerous for you, and I won't have you damaged for my antics if it does go wrong. Anyway," he said, standing up and downing his glass, "I'm for another - what about you?"
Jennings nodded, staring at his best friend's back as he walked to the bar.

*

Weston was surprised at what a different, confident person Jennings suddenly became when he was dealing with the various minor civil servants, and the junior police officers that stopped them as they drove through the outer cordons of the estate. He had just the right amount of arrogance that made people jump to it. A look at his watch here, or a rolled eye to the sky there, as someone would ask to see their authorisation. It did make it easier of course that they were in a ministerial Range Rover, and Jennings security clearance automatically made everyone stand to attention, so invariably they were waved through the various checkpoints. It had been unbelievably easy to allow Jennings to come up with the solution. He could get Weston into Riverside. He could drive him down there right now and no-one would question it. Weston had refused his offer outright at first; he became angry as Jennings insisted it was the only safe way to get into the estate. Jennings had argued it was his right as his friend to help him. Weston had allowed Jennings to move him gradually to where he was no longer angry, only desperately worried that Jennings could get himself into serious trouble for helping him. Jennings had become excited the more he thought it through though, as he assured Weston that he was an expert in the way officialdom worked. No-one will even bother to record me going down there. I work for the PM you see. They will all assume that it's hush-hush and that you're some kind of spook, he'd told him. In fact, if you succeed, I might even claim credit!

They exited the car at the main gate and were met by the Chief of SSC Security. The man was respectful of Jennings, but didn't seem to accept that he should just allow in a 'covert operative' without clearance from his own HQ. As Weston stood with his hands in his pockets slightly to one side, watching the two arguing, he felt like he had 'imposter' stamped across his forehead. It isn't going to work, he thought, his mind beginning to churn on the best way out when someone spoke behind him.
"Mr Jennings, sir, what seems to be the problem?"
All three of them turned toward the man, Jennings clearly recognising him.
"Ah! Superintendent Shawcross."
"Actually, it's Acting Chief Superintendent now, sir."
"Yes, yes, of course. Congratulations, by the way, you did a splendid job in what were very difficult circumstances."

"Thank you, sir, I appreciate it. I wasn't aware you were coming down this evening?"
"No, well, I'm sorry for that, but I'm sure you can appreciate that things are moving rather fast?"
"Of course, sir."
"Well, as I was just trying to explain to the gentleman here from SSC, we have an opportunity for," he paused, nodding at Weston, "Mr...Smith here to enter Riverside, and we need that to be done quietly and without any record of his visit, which is why it has been delegated to me of course, rather than ministerial level. I believe they call it plausible deniability, so I am sure you can-"
"I have already told him we need written authorisation before anyone goes in," the SSC man interrupted.
Shawcross smiled at Jennings and nodded, "I understand completely, sir," he said, before turning to Pat Dixon. "Chief Dixon, this is an official UK government matter, so there's no need for you to concern yourself."
Dixon stared for a long moment at Shawcross, as if debating whether to take it further. Then he shrugged. "It's your call, Mike," he said, turning to face Jennings and Weston. "Good evening, Mr Jennings, Mr...Smith," he said, before he walked slowly back toward the office cabins.

Christopher stood watching as Dominic Weston walked across the floodlit square toward the barricade of pallets and piled-up junk. He could see a couple of dark shapes to one side of the barricade, Weston's reception committee he assumed. Now it was done, he realised just how much he had been swept away by the pace of events, and he acknowledged the huge buzz he had gotten from taking charge on behalf of both of them. He squeezed the data stick tightly in his fist, as the potential consequences of his actions began to replace the adrenalin in his system.
"A brave man, sir!" Shawcross said.
"Yes, yes he is, Chief Superintendent." He turned to look at Shawcross. "I'm afraid I do have to emphasise how critical the security aspect of Mr Smith's work is-"
"Don't worry, sir, I totally understand the need for discretion. " He followed Jennings glance toward the SSC cabins and smiled, "And don't worry about Pat, sir - Chief Dixon I mean - he's been around a long time and knows where his bread is buttered."
"I hope so, Chief, I really do," Jennings said sincerely.

Chapter Ten

The committee of seven, which consisted of Doc, Danny, Katy, Mallet, Reeko, Sunny and Jo were now supplemented by two additions - Carl Timms, who Katy put forward, had been a GP for thirty years before being struck off for his addiction to Novocaine. Katy pointed out that substance addiction wasn't such a big deal in Riverside, and nobody could argue that Carl wasn't still a good doctor, something that they were going to need. The ninth member of the committee had been brought forward by Reeko, who said they needed someone who looked like they could break heads should it come down to it - and, much to everyone's surprise, Mallet had agreed to support Reeko's suggestion after he had spoken to Reeko and his friend 'Bear' privately.
Eight of the committee were seated on the long bench toward the back of the dilapidated stage, looking out at the sea of faces arranged around the sports hall. People were seated on various busted-up chairs, packing cases and old ripped sofas that Bear and Reeko and those they had co-opted had dragged over to the hall. A lot of people sitting in the hall were still wearing visible signs from two nights ago - cuts, and black eyes. A few had their arms in slings, and one man had his arm in plaster expertly provided by Riverside's newly-restored GP, Dr Timms. To the right of the committee also on the dais, sat Dominic Weston, his neat shirt and tweed jacket making him stand out to everybody, even if he wasn't seated so obviously alone.
Doc tapped the microphone that rested on the lectern, that Reeko had 'liberated' from the Salvation Army hall, and called for quiet over the sound of a hundred different arguments and heated discussions. He could see how wound-up people were, even before they heard what he had to say. Danny had the cameras, running but only to record what was said. They had all agreed that tonight's meeting was definitely not going to be streamed live. Doc looked back at Sunny, wondering again if he hadn't been wrong to insist that they do it this way. Sunny nodded at him encouragingly, letting him know that, despite their differences, he would support him now it was happening.

Last night had been a roller-coaster meeting as, item by item, they had attempted to repudiate the government's accusations about them. Reeko had been remarkably accurate in his assessment. There were very few in the room who believed that Mallet was on the take and, when Reeko himself had dealt with the Schofield-as-undercover- cop story, people had actually laughed at its ridiculousness. Then it had been Sunny's turn to explain that, whilst he had worked for the World Bank in Africa, he hadn't, as claimed, embezzled anything, though his explanation was a strangely stumbling affair. Fortunately Danny had, at Doc's request, managed to source from one of his hacker friends a number of supportive articles and clips from the time. These, supported Sunny's story that he had been the whistle-blower who had exposed the embezzlement, which had been done to fund the military coup, rather than the perpetrator of any fraud. Doc had simply told them in a calm and steady voice that, rather than being a violent anarchist, he was a lifelong pacifist and peace campaigner. Danny had again accessed a number of clips of Doc speaking at fringe meetings over the last twenty years, which he put up on the screen. Doc had been shocked, not only that Danny had done so without being asked, but that he had been unaware that footage of many of those meetings even existed. Danny told him later that the tapes were actually hacked covert security footage, and had only winked when Katy had asked him how he had managed to access them. The meeting had been much briefer than they had expected, and quickly moved off the Government's accusations and on to what happened next. They had gone over again the strategy, which was to harness international support, and the whole room had been rapt as they had watched the numerous international news channels which, with the exception of the US and China, were largely condemnatory of the forced evacuation plan. The UK media had declared the 'Riverside situation' as the most dangerous terrorist threat the country had faced in twenty years. Most international news media had carried the live streams from the sports hall meetings, but the BBC and Sky News had shown none of them. Doc said that they would all be under what he called a 'D' notice, which effectively meant the Government had a veto on anything it didn't like.

The committee had decided that tonight's meeting would not be broadcast live and it would depend entirely on what they decided tonight whether it ever would be.

Michael Deveron, the Doc, looked down at the microphone and tapped it again but a little harder, making a dull thud echo round the room before speaking. "OK, people, if we can just quieten down here..." A few people at the front stopped talking and looked up at him, but the majority were oblivious and if anything seemed to be getting rowdier. Reeko shook his head, stood up and walked over to the lectern, " 'Scuse me, Doc," he said leaning down to the microphone. The volume of his voice as he spoke caused a high feedback that screeched through the speakers. "SHUT THE FUCK UP!"

The room fell silent, some people putting their fingers in their ears at the level of his voice and the whine of feedback.

Reeko turned back toward Deveron, stony-faced, "I think the Ladies and Gentleman are ready now, Doc!" Everyone laughed and, as they did, Doc could feel the tension popping like a balloon. He nodded at Reeko, who winked and sauntered back to his seat, casting a grim look as he went toward Dominic Weston.

Doc looked around the room at the several hundred faces staring expectantly, many apprehensively, at him and removed his glasses, then quickly decided to put them back on again as the room went blurred. He took one deep breath, pushed his hand through his hair and began.

"Forty eight hours ago we, everyone in this room, did something remarkable. We stood up not just for ourselves; we stood up for each other. We drew a line in the sand that told Them.," he gestured over his shoulder toward the gates, "those people who think they can buy and sell us as if we are servants or farm animals that can be harnessed to the plough. We told them enough was enough." He paused and looked around. "We did that, and the whole world watched us do it! Think about that for a moment. Think about how a group of people who amount to nothing, scum, lazy idle wasters who are nothing but a drain on society, people who our illustrious Prime Minister calls 'the enemy within' and 'the undeserving poor' could do that."

There were a few grumbles and shouts of 'bastard Mablethorpe' and 'they are the scum, not us'. Doc held his hand up and waited till there was complete silence before continuing. "We have managed to stop them in their tracks. We have also shown the whole world that we are good people, people who have pride and courage, people who stand up for themselves and more importantly for each other. We did that! You have all seen the broadcasts so you know by now, those who hadn't guessed it already that I'm not originally from the Riverside Estate." He said Riverside Estate in a perfect mimic of Mablethorpe's' clipped aristocratic accent and a got a good laugh and a few wolf whistles. "Last night we spoke at length about this terrorist nonsense that the Government have put out, so I know we've dealt with it already. But I'd like to add my own thanks on behalf of all of the committee for the support you have shown us." He leaned his hands flat on the rostrum, and had a sudden memory of back when he was still a respected Professor, rather than public enemy number one, as Richard Hawksworth had described him today. He looked back up at the sea of faces, and knew that his students had never been quite so eager to hear what he had to say next.

"About four hours ago, a man," he turned to look at Weston, who continued to stare at the back of the room as if meditating, "a man I knew twenty years ago, and a person I still consider a friend arrived in Riverside and offered his...assistance." Everyone looked at Weston, then swung back to look at Doc as he continued. "That we need assistance is not in doubt,

we know now, assuming our information is correct, that we have at the most three days before the Government will be able to knock out our broadcasts, and after that they will undoubtedly come for us."
The room erupted into a torrent of shouts and cries, people standing up and waving fists.
Doc didn't try to speak, but stood calmly staring ahead, waiting till eventually the room went quiet.
"I believed two days ago, and I still believe today, that the International community will not allow the Mablethorpe regime to forcibly relocate us. It was, and it remains my view, that we should continue to peacefully resist, and continue to broadcast our pleas, in order that the whole world remains aware that we are just ordinary people and not scum - well, not all of us!" he said, though this time only a few people laughed.
"Whatever decisions are taken here tonight, we will only be successful in my view if we remain united and hold to our position of passive resistance. However, the committee was offered two alternatives earlier tonight and, quite frankly; we are divided on the best way forward. What we are not divided on, though, is that we have all agreed that any decision made on behalf of this community should be made by this community, and not by the people who you have asked simply to organise things." This got a few nods and "well said," and one shouted, "fucking yay, Brother."
"Earlier, a couple of us held a video conference with the authorities where they offered us a way out if we want it." The room began to buzz excitedly as people sensed that they might have had a breakthrough, though they fell back into stunned silence as he continued. "They have agreed to give us twenty four hours to peacefully leave Riverside 'without reprisals'. In other words, we go back to where we started from, and they have attempted to assure us that none of you will be punished or singled out for what has happened so far. That means, if they are genuine, that none of you will be arrested or charged with insurrection. I was also told that, should we to choose reject this offer, then in the words of the Metropolitan Chief Police Commissioner, Richard Hawksworth, 'All bets are off, and the situation within Riverside -will be brought to a swift conclusion.' So my friends, that is the first choice before us. If we accept Hawksworth's offer, you will not be prosecuted-"
"We still get dragged off to Chinatown though!" someone at the back shouted.
Deveron nodded, "Yes, I'm afraid so! We do though have another alternative, courtesy of Dominic here." He gestured again at Weston, who this time smiled and nodded at people.
Dominic is a scientist who works, or should I say worked, for the Ministry of Defence at its weapons' testing base at Porton Down. Porton Down is, though it is illegal under international law, also the home of the UK's

biological weapons research & development facility. Dominic has 'liberated' a small quantity of one of those chemical agents and has brought it here."
The panic that Sunny had predicted didn't arise, but the whole room seemed to sit up straighter, and he could see people almost physically leaning away from Weston as they looked at him in a new light.
"I will ask Dominic to answer any questions that you have about the agent at the end of the discussion but, first, let me emphasise that the 'agent' is totally harmless unless activated. And that activation cannot happen by accident; in other words it is safe and contained. What you are going to be asked to vote on this evening is whether we use the threat of this weapon to protect ourselves."

Doc set out the same description he had given Reeko and Bear of how that would work, he had been surprised that neither of them had even heard of the Soviet Union though, given how political history had been gradually rewritten for decades in the UK, he didn't know why he was. Reeko had been impressed in perhaps not quite the way he had intended, and had asked him to repeat the same discussion tonight. He pushed his glasses back up his nose and began.

"Seventy years ago the USA and the Soviet Union, Russia as it's now called, were locked in an arms race, where both had the power to destroy each other and, in reality, most of the world by the pressing of a few buttons. The arms race pulled in huge amounts of resources and billions of dollars to both sides. Yet after all that time, energy and money, what they ended up with was a stalemate. Why? Two reasons. The first reason was that no matter how many nukes each side had, no matter how powerful or sophisticated they were, the other side could always replicate the threat. The second reason was that no matter which of them launched first, the other side would always have just enough time before they were destroyed to fire back." Doc paused to take a sip of water before continuing. "At that time, believe it or not, this nuclear arms race was aptly named MAD! MAD stands for Mutually Assured Destruction! Each side had the power to destroy each other but, if they chose to do so, then the very act would lead to their own destruction. In short, it was a stand-off. Many still believe that it was one of those old cold war Soviet nukes that was set off in Israel - which, in response of course, nuked Lebanon and Palestine which in turn, as you all know ,resulted in the destruction of most of the Middle East. The truth is that, given the level of desolation over there, no one will ever really know who launched first. So why tell you all this now, tonight? Because, friends, right here in Riverside, we now have a similar power."

It took a good five minutes this time for people to quieten down enough

for Doc to carry on.
“The weapon that Professor Weston has brought into Riverside isn’t nuclear, of course; it is biological. This chemical weapon, which is called 6/707, is a weapon that was designed to kill people, not destroy property. Military strategists will tell you of course that such a weapon is much more cost effective, as the assets remain largely viable and undamaged. The 6/707 apparently has a lifespan of approximately three to seven years once it’s released into the atmosphere, after which the area and any assets are completely retrievable. This weapon that Dominic Weston has brought here, if it is triggered, could cause upwards of a million deaths if released into the UK atmosphere - maybe even more, depending on how efficiently they can set up viable quarantine zones. It is transmitted through aspiration, that is by humans and some animals, specifically mammals, inhaling and exhaling.” This last Doc had been reading from the notes he had taken earlier, when he had questioned Weston on specific details. He removed his glasses and rubbed the bridge of his nose between his thumb and forefinger, then looked around the room.
“So that is what we have now at our disposal, and that is what we can threaten the authorities with - mutually assured destruction! If the government won’t back off, we can launch the weapon. If they leave us alone and allow us to live here, then we don’t. It really is quite a straightforward thing when you look at it in that way. In a moment I’m going to hand over to another member of the committee, who is going to argue for us to use this 'weapon' as a threat. But before I do so, I want to say that there is no going back if you choose this route. It is a choice that, once made, is irreversible. We will be locked into Riverside, and we will never be allowed to leave without surrendering the weapon and, if we did so...what then?”
He looked slowly around the room at the now sombre faces.
“And finally I want to say this. I am against this, my friends.”
He took a long swig of water, then slowly placed the bottle back down, staring at it for a moment before continuing.
"Dominic, Professor Weston, has come here to Riverside with only the very best of intentions. He believes in our struggle not because he is from here, not because he knows anyone here other than me. He is here simply as a response to our broadcasted calls for help; he believes he is offering us a way out of the trap we are in. He is a good man who wants to support our stand against tyranny. I believe this to be true with every fibre of my being. Yet I am still against it. In the same way I was against the use of nuclear weapons; in the same way I have always been against those elements of resistance that the government calls subversives, those who chose to move from civil disobedience to armed struggle I am against it. We have a choice to make tonight, and my choice is based on the simple principle that you

don't beat evil by becoming more evil still. You don't save a few hundred by sacrificing millions more. If we choose this position, there can of course be no going back on it, and I hope that I have been clear on that if nothing else. Now I will ask Jo, who you all know, to give a counter view, after which we will throw it open for discussion, and then we will make a decision...all of us!"

Michael Deveron sat down to silence, apart from a few coughs and shuffling chairs. He had been shocked that it had been Jo of all people who had supported Weston 's proposal so vehemently. He had thought maybe Sunny, had even expected Reeko would be up for it, but no, it had been Jo and that had shocked him. As she began to speak though, he felt calm about the decision whatever it was. At least they had all been of one mind that it wasn't their decision alone. As Reeko had said in his inimitable style, 'If we do that, then we're no better than the fuckers who put us here.' He smiled to himself. Reeko was a good kid and, the more he watched him organising and running their little rebellion, the more he felt sure that Sunny had been right to recruit him. He turned his attention back to Jo, knowing already that if it went against him he had no choice, not any more. Most of his life had been spent running away from things he despised rather than standing up to them, so whatever the people decided tonight he would stay and see it out.

It was obvious to everyone right away that Jo didn't have Doc's years of practice at public speaking and giving lectures. Her voice started off too quietly, a clear tremor in her voice, causing someone to shout up from the back.
"Speak up girlie or get off the stage!" A few people sniggered; Jo stumbled to a stop, staring down at the lectern. Sunny put a restraining hand on Reeko's arm as he started to get up to deal with the big-mouth. He looked at Sunny, who shook his head; Reeko sat back down, though Sunny could see his hands had curled into tight fists, the knuckles of his hands going white with the force of the grip he made.
Jo saw that her hands were trembling and remembered what the Doc had said, and she placed them flat so people had one less sign of her nervousness to see as she started again.
"I'm sorry; I'm not used to this-"
"Not as sorry as we are girlie, believe me!" the same man shouted.
Jo went red and snapped, "Is that you, Ryan Bailey, because it sounds like your great stupid gob? I tell you what, why don't you walk up here and take the microphone and show me how it's done?" She paused for a moment, then carried on. "No? I thought not. Now, as my good friend Reeko likes to say, shut the fuck up and let me say what I'm here to say."

The room erupted into laughter and hollers. Jo cast a quick glance at Sunny, who tipped her a wink and nodded encouragement.
"As I said, I'm not used to this." she said again, but this time her voice was stronger and sounded much more confident.
"I was born here in Riverside and, back when I was a kid, this place wasn't a dump. Of course, back then, most of the people that lived in Riverside had jobs. We weren't seen as scum and parasites by the rest of the country... When did that happen by the way? When did we become like this, people left with nothing but handouts? Did we make a choice not to work, or did they move our jobs out to Asia and Africa or anywhere else where they could make more money for themselves?"
"That's right!" a woman Jo didn't spot from somewhere in the middle of the room shouted.
"I have known many of the people in this room for most of my life, and for good or bad," she paused, and looked in Ryan Bailey's direction, "for good or bad, this is my society...my home. I know it isn't much, but it's where I come from and its part of who I am. Those people outside, that great arse Mablethorpe, Hawksworth and their like, they have absolutely nothing in common with me and you. They live in a different world, a world where profit matters more than people. Now they want to move us to the so-called new towns, or slave camps as they should really be called. Professor Weston has offered us a chance to resist, a real chance to make a stand for ourselves. Don't get me wrong. If it was about using this thing, this 6/707, I would be with Doc -in fact," she looked back over her shoulder, "I know we all would. But, it isn't about that. We don't have to really use it to use its power. The very fact that we have it in our possession is enough for us to defend ourselves. Even Doc will tell you that Mablethorpe can't even tell the world that we have it! Why? because his government shouldn't have made it in the first place. It is illegal for any state to develop these weapons. Mablethorpe himself would end up in the international criminal courts if it came out that his government was making biological weapons. Professor Weston himself has made it clear that he has absolutely no intention of harming anybody. One of the reasons he felt confident enough to come here was because he knows Doc, and knows what his views are on such weapons. But they don't know! Out there they don't know that; and even if they did they can't take the chance that they might be wrong, and that it we might actually be desperate and crazy enough to use it. Now I respect Doc," she continued, "In fact I'd go farther than that; apart from my father, he's the most honest and trustworthy person I know. That we have managed to get this far is largely down to him and, what he hasn't told you even now, is the price that he will pay for that if we fail. What he didn't tell you is that, although you will all walk out of here, not to freedom of course, we all know that, but still you'll live, at least until you work yourself to death

for the Chinese. But not Doc, he won't be going with you, neither will Sunny or Sergeant John Mallet. If we give in, they are to be tried for treason! Treason, the penalty for which if found guilty, and we all know they will be don't we, is death by hanging. That's the part of the deal that Hawksworth said wasn't negotiable; it's also the one thing that I promised Doc and the others I wouldn't tell you about." She turned again and looked at Deveron, who looked up from staring at his feet. "Sorry, Doc. I lied!" She looked around the room at all the faces, many of which she had known for years, yet unable to read any responses from them, and finished what she had to say.

"I believe we should fight. I believe we should fight for these three men who we all know are not terrorists. I believe we should fight for the young man they murdered in cold blood two nights ago. Most of all, though, I believe we should fight for ourselves, for our right to choose where we live, for our right to choose who we want to speak with or associate with. I think we should fight for ourselves and for each other. I say what the hell have we got to lose? Thank you for listening!" She walked back toward the bench, the only sound in the hall the clip of her boot heels on the wooden stage. The room suddenly erupted into a huge clatter of knocked over chairs and crates as people got to their feet cheering and clapping. Jo, still with her back to the room, looked at Sunny who had sided with Doc, but who now gave her a theatrical bow. She looked at Doc, who gave her a thin smile that seemed to mirror her own thoughts. They were committed now, all of them.

Chapter Eleven

Chief Commissioner Richard Hawksworth grimaced at having to turn sideways on in order to fit through the ridiculously small door of Operation Unify's mobile HQ. He had spent the morning being chewed out by Mablethorpe over the chaos of the last few days. The worst thing was that he had to take it on the chin, as Mablethorpe was right - there had been a massive intelligence screw-up. No one could have reasonably expected that Deveron would have been able to smuggle in such an array of sophisticated broadcast equipment, and at the end of the day he, Hawksworth, was responsible. Mablethorpe had spent the last two days fielding calls from the UN Secretary General, who was demanding that he be allowed to send international observers onto the estate. The Prime Minister had quite rightly

refused, of course, but Hawksworth knew he had a very small window in which to shut these bastards down.
"Good morning, sir," Acting Chief Superintendent Shawcross said, as he got smartly to his feet.
Hawksworth looked at him, "Nothing bloody good about it, Shawcross. Is everyone here?"
"Yes, sir," Shawcross said ,opening the door to the cramped meeting room where the six members of the Riverside tactical team were already standing briskly to attention, probably having been tipped off on his arrival, he didn't doubt.
Hawksworth slumped into the vacant chair, which creaked under his weight, and nodded at Shawcross to begin.
"Sir, we can now confirm that the antenna and transmitter are located on an old dredging vessel that is moored on the estate side of the Ship Canal. Though it isn't directly accessible from the bank side, we believe it would be a relatively straightforward seizure by air. Commander?"

Special Forces Commander David Willets clicked on his laptop, which projected a satellite view of the dredger and surrounding areas. He pointed with a laser pen to various points as he spoke.
"Operation 'Capture' would commence at 21:00 hours this evening, and would consist of two Apache helicopters; the first, Taylor One, will take up a strafing position twenty five metres above the vessel, whilst Taylor Two will be used as the rappelling vessel to land eight Special Force ops on her decks. At the same time, two aqua units will close on the vessel from the stern and bow-"
"How long will it take to shut the damn thing down, Commander?" Hawksworth asked, in no mood for fancy presentations.
"That depends on the resistance level, sir. If they are armed, then clearly it will take longer, as we have to neutralise any terrorist resistance before we can take out the equipment. In an unarmed scenario, we estimate six minutes; if they are armed, probably ten to twelve, given that we have been given a go on deadly force."
"You understand I'm sure, Commander, that whatever happens over there has to be done with the minimum fanfare; we can't rule out that these people have more than one transmitter, and we can ill afford another international TV special!"
"Yes, sir, I understand that. For completeness, sir, you should know there is an alternative scenario which would be codenamed 'Hell-fire'. Hell-fire would consist of a helicopter strike utilising a single Tomcat missile fired from a thousand feet. Timing would not in the Hell-fire scenario be a factor, as they would be dead before they even heard the rotor blades."
Hawksworth banged the flat of his hand on the table. "For Chrissakes man,

have you actually been watching the news at all? This whole situation has to be done as quickly and as quietly as possible. Am I clear?"
Commander Willets looked at the sweating obese desk jockey who was now bawling him out in front of one of his junior staff, and considered whether or not the laser pen he twirled in his fingers would, if jammed hard enough up one of the man's piggy nostrils, reach to his brain. Probably, he thought, as he replied without any inflection, "Of course, sir, that is perfectly clear."
Hawksworth nodded, mollified. These military types like it when you give it to them straight, he thought.
"Jennings, you've been advised by now that we have agreed to meet these subversives directly, I take it?"
"Yes, Commissioner. We have erected a small screened gazebo in the centre of the cenotaph square. The meeting will take place at two this afternoon. There will be six attendees from each side. It has been agreed that the meeting will be in camera, and that no weapons will be allowed."
Hawksworth nodded. He was against the meeting, and had told Mablethorpe so in no uncertain terms that he shouldn't have agreed to their request. Mablethorpe, however, was desperate to be able to show that he had tried to facilitate a peaceful solution, even though he had already signed the orders for the assault on the dredger. 'This is politics' he had told Hawksworth, 'something I think I know rather more than you about, Chief Commissioner'. Given the balls-up of the initial evacuation, Hawksworth had had to agree to the meeting, but he would make sure it was brief and to the point.

Hawksworth gave the order to Commander Willets that operation 'Capture' was a go, and waited for Willets to turn off the projection screen off before speaking.
"Alright, gentlemen, what most of you won't be aware of is that we have a deep cover operative inside the estate."
Jennings looked at Shawcross, who raised his eyebrows at him for a brief moment. Shawcross thinks it's Dominic, Jennings realised, the sense of relief nearly overwhelming him as he quickly looked back at Hawksworth, who went on.
"This operative has strict orders to remain silent and observe only. The operative's testimony will be vital we believe. in securing a treason conviction when this is all over. In the event, however, that the operative feels they have been exposed, or that their life is under threat, they will reveal themselves by the codename Avenger One..."
Hawksworth snapped a glance at Commander Willets, who had put a hand over his mouth in an attempt to stifle a snigger.
"If Avenger One declares him or herself as being in danger, then their extraction is a priority and they must be secured regardless of the costs.

Commander, you have something to add?"
"It would help my team considerably if we had an ID on...Avenger One, sir, in the event-"
"Out of the question, Commander Willets. The security of Operation Unify has been compromised once already, and it would appear that these subversives have sympathisers in the most surprising of places."
Commander Willets decided that, yes, the pen would definitely reach the man's brains - he would make sure of it.

*

Hawksworth, Jennings, Shawcross, Commander Willets, Pat Dixon and Hawksworth's secretary and note-taker, Alice Drayton, were seated with their back to the perimeter fence and security cabins. From their vantage point, they had a view over the square, which allowed them to see the barricades which had been placed across Renshaw Street, which itself ran down to the main wharves. Nobody spoke as they all watched and waited for Deveron and his henchmen to arrive. Jennings looked at his watch; there were five minutes before the subversives were due. It had been eighteen hours since he had watched Dominic walk into Riverside, and he had heard nothing from him since. He had texted him a dozen times, and even tried ringing, till he had cursed his own stupidity as he remembered that the government blackout was blocking all cell phone signals, in and out of the estate.

He had hoped the meeting would by now have become redundant as, if Dominic could have gotten Michael Deveron out by now, the whole thing would have been over. He stared across the square, hoping that Dominic would at least be one of the six that were coming to the meeting. At least that would mean that he had probably succeeded in persuading Deveron to surrender, and more importantly, that Dominic himself was OK.

As he finally saw them walking across the square, his heart sank. Dominic wasn't with them. He quickly identified the six of them from the briefing they had all received earlier that morning. Deveron was in the centre, flanked on the left by Charles Windsor aka Sunny, and the woman with the man's name - Jo, he remembered. On Deveron's other side was the woman from the cafe, who they had now identified as Kate Marsh, and who as far as they knew had no subversive links. To his surprise, he realised the man limping at her side was the rogue police officer, John Mallet, and, even from fifty yards away, Christopher could see how badly beaten up he was. Just behind Mallet, his head swinging from side to side as if looking for an ambush, was a young black kid who as yet they hadn't identified, which meant he had no known links and a clean criminal record. He could see the kid was talking to the old Sergeant.

"Hey, old man," Reeko said catching up with Mallet, "this is kind of cool, like one of them gangster flicks, you know?"
Mallet shook his head, and grimaced to hide the fact that he was trying not to smile.
"Remember what we agreed, everyone," Sunny said in a low voice, "Doc does all of the talking; no-one else says anything." He looked meaningfully at Reeko, who mimed a zipper across his mouth. Nobody laughed.

They sat down in the same order they had walked in across the square - Deveron in the centre facing Hawksworth, who hadn't bothered to look up from his notes as they arrived and seated themselves. Doc had told them to expect them to start playing 'meeting games', and told them not to react, but to sit patiently.
"Good afternoon," Doc said.
Hawksworth carried on reading his notes, still not acknowledging their arrival. Doc had also told them that this might happen - but that it was unlikely as it was such a tired stratagem - but, if it did, they should just stay silent and wait. Doc frowned to stop himself from smiling as Reeko leaned into the middle of the table, and grabbed two fistfuls of the boiled sweets that had been placed in the bowl, and began to stuff them into his jacket pockets. As he went for a second handful Hawksworth's pudgy hand snapped out like a cobra and pulled the bowl away from him. He didn't look at Reeko, his eyes boring instead into Michael Deveron's, willing him to look away. Doc didn't blink as he removed one of his stinky cigars from the tin and began to light it.
Hawksworth pointed at Doc as he spoke, "Don't light that, Mr Deveron, or I'll add smoking without a permit to the list of charges you are already facing. That's good for a mandatory six month sentence, by the way, as I'm sure Sergeant Mallet here will be able to tell you!"
Doc looked down at his miniature cigar and smiled.
"According to what you've told the media, Chief Commissioner Hawksworth, I and my colleagues are already facing a death sentence, so threatening to lock me up for six months first hardly seems much of a deterrent." He lit the cigar and blew the smoke up in the air.
"OK, then, enough of this bullshit!" Hawksworth said, his face reddening. "Here are some simple facts for you, Deveron, and I want you to listen very carefully, I want all of you to listen to me very carefully." He paused to look at each of them in turn before turning back to Doc.
"You have one opportunity to come out of this situation alive. This government doesn't negotiate with terrorists, ever. You and your motley crew have caused enough embarrassment to the country, and this situation will be brought to a quick end. All you have to decide and right now is how

it ends, and you need to understand very clearly what the consequences of making the wrong choice means for you. Now, I am sure that the riff-raff," he looked at Reeko, "and the degenerates back there are all feeling happy with their fifteen minutes of fame. But you, Deveron, you know better. You know as well as I that very shortly we will be able to block your transmissions, and that will leave you totally isolated."

Doc stayed silent, calmly waiting for whatever offer Hawksworth was going to make.

Hawksworth unscrewed a bottle of mineral water and poured himself a glass The Doc smiled at the fact that water and glasses had only been provided for Hawksworth's side of the table.

Hawksworth's face tightened at Doc's smile.

"As I have already said to you, your behaviour has embarrassed the country and damaged our international reputation with this subversive propaganda you've have been promulgating. Now I'm going to give you the opportunity to address the damage you have done in the following way." Hawksworth began reading from a prepared script. "At ten o'clock tomorrow morning, you will give a final online press conference where you express regret for your actions. You personally will tell the press that you have now realised that you were wholly misguided in your actions, and that you were in fact influenced by foreign powers. You now accept and understand that those foreign powers were trying to undermine the legitimate elected government of the United Kingdom. Finally, you will say that you have met with the people of the estate and told them of your errors in judgement, and personally apologised for misleading them. You will then say that the residents of Riverside have since met together without you, and decided unanimously that they now wish to take up the opportunity of a fresh start in the new towns. Immediately after that statement is broadcast, we will issue a statement that the British Government has agreed to help them in every way we can."

Doc could see Reeko waiting to explode, and he wasn't the only one. He just hoped they would keep their discipline a little longer. It was important that they got their message over in a very clear way. He looked at Reeko and then the rest of them in turn before turning back to speak to Hawksworth.

"What you are suggesting, Chief Commissioner, doesn't sound very different than three days ago?"

"No, you're wrong, Mr Deveron. Three days ago you and your lieutenants here weren't facing the death penalty!"

Doc inclined his head, "That's true, Chief Commissioner! So then, am I to understand it that, if we agree to your...suggestion, that we, that is all of us, will leave for the new towns with your, how did you put it...every

assistance?"
For the first time since the start of the meeting Hawksworth smiled as he shook his head, "Oh no, Deveron. You gave up the opportunity for a new beginning when you undertook this subversive operation of yours. However, and against my better judgement, the Prime minister has decided to show leniency. You and your colleagues here will, if you do what I am strongly advising you to do, be given whole life sentences."
"Whole life?" Katy quietly asked Sunny.
"No parole," he replied without taking his eyes off Hawksworth.
"Mr Windsor is right, Ms Marsh. No parole!" he said, smiling at her.
To his surprise, Doc saw Katy hold her temper as she smiled back and put on her best plumby voice, "Ooh sounds super!"
Hawksworth's smile disappeared, "Right. I believe we are done here. Think it over Deveron, but if you're not in front of the cameras by ten am tomorrow, and quite frankly I really hope you refuse the offer, then matters will take their course." He started to close his folder.
"Wait!" the Doc said, his voice low and flat.
Hawksworth looked at him, "Ah! I thought you'd see sense; your type are always the same when it comes to the crunch-"
He stopped speaking abruptly as Deveron started to reach into his inside pocket.
Commander Willets drew his weapon in an instant, and pointed it at the Doc's head before Doc could even start to remove his hand from his jacket.
"Remove your hand from your jacket, Professor. Move your hand very slowly, and make sure it's empty or I will shoot you dead," Willets said, then blinked as he heard a familiar click across the table. He turned toward the kid, Reeko, already knowing what he would see.
Reeko held the chrome plated handgun steadily in both hands, "No, fuckwit, you won't!"

Doc wasn't shocked that the other side had come armed despite the agreement, but they had all, including Reeko agreed to do it his way, and he felt let down, even though right now the kid was the only thing that stood between him and a bullet in his head. He removed his hand slowly and placed both hands flat on the table, his voice steady as he spoke.
"Commander I have in my pocket a pen. I am going to open my jacket and remove that pen and place it on the table between the Commissioner and myself. If you choose to shoot me whilst I am doing so, there is nothing that I can do about it." Though my young friend Reeko seems to have a different view on how to handle these matters, he thought.
He could see Willets debating the situation, and hoped that his judgement of the man as being a calm professional was right, as he drew his jacket open so that Willets could see the pocket. With his other hand, he drew the

pen from the pocket between his thumb and forefinger, holding it up so Willets could see it clearly. The Commander gave a small nod, and Doc placed it gently on the table in front of Hawksworth. Willets eased the hammer back on his service revolver, but didn't lower it from pointing at his head. The Doc let out a breath he didn't know he had been holding.
He turned toward Reeko, satisfied with what he saw, as the kid looked as calm as the Commander. Finally, he turned back to face Hawksworth whose face was blood red, though with fear or anger the Doc couldn't tell - probably both he decided, not that it mattered. He was committed now, they all were.
"You and your government have treated us like animals, Hawksworth, and the responsibility for this," he said nodding toward the pen, "is I am afraid a direct consequence of your oppression and mistreatment of your own citizens."
"What the hell are you talking about, Deveron. You've had your warning. Now unless you have something sensible to say-"
"I would like you to contact the UK's biological weapons facility, based at Porton Down I believe, and ask them to check their stores of 6/707."
Hawksworth looked at him incredulously; then he looked at the pen and laughed, the sound like a harsh bark, which made Katy jump.
"Deveron, this is pathetic even from you! "
"Nevertheless, I suggest you make that call."
Hawksworth shook his head, "Indeed I will not. I-"
"Sir, I think maybe we should check on this before acting pre-emptively." Jennings suddenly spoke up, his voice shaking.
"Be quiet, Jennings. I will not be dictated to by this filth-"
"I'm sorry, sir,' Jennings said, swallowing to try and get some moisture in his suddenly dry mouth, "but, as the PM's direct representative, I must insist."

Everybody around the table looked at Jennings, and then at Hawksworth, waiting for the explosion. To Deveron's surprise, the Chief Commissioner simply smiled, "Well Mr Jennings, as you believe this matter would be so important to the Prime Minister, and indeed you are as you say his official spokesperson, I have to believe you know his wishes on this matter. Commander, you make the call. Oh and, Commander... "
"Sir?" Willets said, pausing as he started to get up from the table.
"Once you have established that this is all nonsense, I'd like you to escort Mr Jennings here off site, where I will seek to have him charged for interfering with a police officer during the carrying out of his duties."
Willets face was a mask as he nodded curtly, before walking back to the main cabins.
Deveron looked at Jennings, then took out another cigar and lit it, his mind

racing. It was a strange intervention from the man who was clearly not comfortable at challenging the overbearing Hawksworth. Yet he had seen the brief look of shock on the man's face as he had mentioned the 6/707. It's probably just a coincidence and my own paranoia, he decided in the end. He was pleased that his hand appeared steady as he had lit the cigar, and even more pleased that no-one could see his left leg under the table which was trembling involuntarily.

*

The wait for Willets' return seemed interminable to Sunny but, as he watched the Commander walking back toward them, his watch told him it had been no more than ten minutes. He could see Doc's knee twitching under the table, though no one else could, and he was impressed that his old debating partner was holding it all together so well as his own head felt like it would explode any moment. Reeko pulling the gun out had nearly sent him over the edge as he had expected that any moment they would all be shot by the snipers they had seen on the rooftops beyond the gates. He was glad that the fabric of the gazebo stopped anyone from having a direct line of sight on them, and looked at Doc again with renewed respect, as he realised Doc had arranged a covered area for precisely that reason. He looked up as Willets signalled Hawksworth to join him, whilst still some distance from the meeting area. The Commissioner heaved his bulk out of the chair and stomped over to the Commander. Sunny couldn't hear what was said, but they could all hear Hawksworth's voice go from angry grunts to a tone of disbelief. Hawksworth kept looking from Willets to them, and then back to Willets again. Finally, the two men walked over to them, and Hawksworth's whole demeanour was now one that threatened violence as he stayed standing, his hands flat on the table leaning toward Doc.

"This is a very dangerous game you're playing here, Deveron. Now I suggest you stop all this nonsense and tell me very quickly-"

"Within this pen is a sealed vial of the biological weapon 6/707," Doc said, his voice matter of fact. "Doubtless the Commander here has already ascertained that such an agent exists, and that it is indeed manufactured at the Porton Down facility. I understand that you will need to make further enquiries as to whether," he placed his fingers on the pen and ran them down the length of it, and as he did so they all clearly saw Hawksworth flinch, " we are actually in possession of it and then we can talk further. On that basis, Chief Commissioner I propose that we adjourn this meeting till tomorrow morning, by which time-"

"Shut up, Deveron; just shut your stupid fucking mouth. You and your cronies are going nowhere and, if you attempt to move away from this area without my permission, the six of you will be shot dead. I don't believe for one minute this little fairy tale of yours, by the way, but it is clear that you people believe you have gained information on an issue of national strategic importance. If you think you can use it to bluff your way to freedom, you can't! You will remain here until I have resolved matters."

Sunny watched his friend Michael Deveron, or 'The Doc' as they were now calling him across the web. For the first time he was looking thrown by Hawksworth's very real threat. He was trying to decide whether to speak, even though he'd said he wouldn't, when the decision was taken from him by of all people John Mallet, who Sunny now realised had been watching Doc as closely as he had.

"I'm afraid we won't be doing that, Chief Commissioner. We are going to go back behind the barricade and, as Doc has said we will return tomo-"

"My god man, I really can't believe that you can go along with this...this... betrayal!" Hawksworth said."Have you forgotten that you swore a solemn oath to this country? "

"No I haven't forgotten. But, just twelve hours ago, Chief Commissioner you declared to the world that me and my... my friends here are all subversive terrorists. You know that is a lie. It is you that is prepared to forcibly remove people who have committed no crimes, been tried before no court of law, and imprison them in one of your shiny new towns. No, I'm afraid it's you, sir who has betrayed your oath, and it is you who have soiled the uniform- and for what? Power- Money? "

Hawksworth looked at his old nemesis with utter contempt. "How long have you been a Sergeant now Mallet, thirty five years isn't it? Have you ever actually asked yourself why? Why you have been passed over time and again, whilst those around you gained the promotions you always wanted? I'll tell you, though my guess is that somewhere in that thick skull of yours you already know the answer. You're a bleeding heart liberal Mallet, you always have been one, I suppose it's in your genes. You seriously still believe that rehabilitation or more community workers is the key to fixing crime? What scum like these Riverside people need Mallet is an iron fist; they need a government that governs for the vast majority of our decent upstanding citizens, a government that won't hesitate to stamp out those who won't conform. I didn't declare you to be a terrorist Mallet, you did it yourself by allying with this trash. And now you and your comrades here show what people you really are by this latest hollow threat-"

"Enough!" Sunny said, suddenly banging his hand flat on the table. "We're not interested in your bullshit Hawksworth. We are going back into Riverside right now." He looked at Commander Willets as he continued, "If you choose to stop us Commander, then of course you can. But you need to understand that you have left us with no choice any more and if we are killed then the agent will be released. God knows we... none of us want that, but we will do it!" Sunny turned to Deveron, "Doc?"

Doc smiled at Mallet and then Sunny, "Thank you, gentlemen. Now, Chief

Commissioner, you have a decision to make, because we are going back across the square. If you are right and we are just bluffing, and if this is just a pen then you can shoot us in the back and that will be the end of it." He stood up from the table, Sunny and the rest of them immediately standing up with him. "Till tomorrow morning, gentlemen."

As the six of them left the cover of the gazebo and started across the square, they all heard Hawksworth tell the Commander to have his snipers take them out.
Katy took hold of Deveron's hand, 'Have I ever told you how much I love you, Professor Deveron?'

Chapter Twelve

Six hours after the Riverside meeting, Christopher Jennings sat in his hotel room staring at his reflection in the dressing room mirror. Surprisingly, he didn't look as bad as he felt inside. He looked down at the cursor blinking on his laptop at the end of the salutation, 'Dear Prime Minister', waiting for the next line to be written. He had written the resignation letter three times so far and deleted it three times. He had known instantly when Deveron said the name of 'Porton Down' that he was finished. He knew it was only a matter of time before it was discovered that he had been the one who helped Dominic get into Riverside. If it wasn't the private security man, Dixon, then it would be the other one, the policeman Shawcross who would report him to Hawksworth. His eyes flicked again toward the family sized bottle of aspirin he had left open at the side of his laptop. He had purchased the pills from the same supermarket as the craft knife lying next to the pills, on his way back to the hotel. He didn't want to do it, the thing with the knife and the pills, but, he couldn't face going to prison. Even the thought of going into one of those places gave him a feeling of dread and panic. There was no other way out; he had been betrayed and played like the most gullible of lovesick teenagers. He could admit it now finally that he had loved Weston, and had done for a long time. He had known that Weston's feelings for him weren't the same, but he had believed that they shared something special that was more than just the sex. Above all else, he would have bet his life, had bet his life, he corrected himself that they were at least friends. Now he understood that everything they had done, everything they had shared was a lie, it had all meant nothing to Weston. How could he have not seen the hatred that Dominic had for Mablethorpe? He had seen how he would light up whenever he told him about one of the

PM's many faux pas.

The rap on the hotel door made him jump and spill some of the wine he had been drinking steadily for the last half hour onto his lap top. He clumsily wiped the sleeve of his shirt across the laptop keys as he tried to stop the liquid from getting inside. The rap on the door came again, sharper, more insistent, then a man's voice which sounded angry and impatient.
"Jennings, its Shawcross. Open the door I know you're in there!"
All the dread and panic that he had felt in waiting for this moment to come simply drained out of him as he realised it was all over, leaving just an empty numbness. "I'm in shock" he said aloud as he abandoned the wine spill and opened the door.
Chief Superintendent John Shawcross was alone as he brushed roughly past him. He walked over to the small bathroom, making sure that Jennings was alone as well, and then sat down his eyes taking in the spilt wine, the pills and the unfinished letter still flashing on the laptop.
"Close the door, Christopher."
Jennings did as he was told.
"Sit down."
Jennings sat on the edge of the bed, his hands flat on his thighs, waiting for Shawcross to formally caution him.
Shawcross picked up the pills, and then the craft knife, then threw them back on the desk. He leaned back balancing on two chair legs, as he faced Jennings.
"Tell me what Weston's plan is Christopher."
"I don't know."
"Hypothesise."
"I tell you I don't know! He...look, shouldn't you be arresting me or cautioning me or something?"
"What's his plan, Christopher?"
"I've told you I don't know, I thought... Look he knows the Professor-"
"Deveron?"
Jennings nodded, "They went to Cambridge together. He, that is Dominic, he said he could get him to come out, to surrender."
"And you believed him?"
"Why wouldn't I?"
"What was your relationship with Dominic Weston?"
"I'm sorry, Chief Superintendent, but I am not going to make any further statement until I have some legal-"
One moment Shawcross was leaning back in his chair, the next he had closed the space between them, the heel of his hand crashing into the side of Jennings' head. Shawcross grabbed the back of his hair, wrenching him

off the bed. Jennings started to protest, then felt himself flung over onto his stomach, his face forced into the soft mattress as Shawcross used his knee to force him flat so he couldn't breathe. He tried to push himself upright on his hands, then collapsed as Shawcross jabbed him so hard in his side he felt certain he must have ruptured a kidney. He was suffocating and helpless. He could feel his consciousness falling away when he was slammed down on to the floor, where he managed to sit up, retching and staring wide eyed at Shawcross, who was now sat back in the chair, his voice was calm and measured as he repeated the question.

"What was your relationship with Dominic Weston?"

Jennings looked down at his hands and clasped them together to try and stop them shaking. He didn't know which was worse-the violence that Shawcross had just demonstrated, or the calm way that he was now restating the question as though nothing had happened. He could kill me, Jennings realised. Right now, he could kill me, and there would be nothing I could do about it. Then he realised something else-that no one would care. He was the arch betrayer, a senior aide to the Prime Minister, and someone who had actively assisted a terrorist who, if Deveron was right, had access to the most terrifying of weapons. If Shawcross killed him here right now, he would probably be awarded a medal. Shawcross was staring at him, as if he was allowing him the time for the position he was in to fully hit home. Ten minutes ago he had been contemplating his own death, a romanticised picture of crimson streams running into the bath water as his life left him. Now he had a different picture- the stark terror of suffocation, the burning lungs that begged for oxygen. He didn't want to die, not at all, he suddenly realised and definitely not like that.

"We were lovers." he said, looking directly at Shawcross now, knowing that if he once lied to this man who had seemed so civilised whenever they had met before, this man would know it- and Jennings thought that he wouldn't blink at ending his life.

Shawcross continued to stare at him, waiting for him to go on.

Jennings began to stumble through the details of his relationship with Dominic. Even now though, he didn't tell Shawcross about the data stick and the video, the same data stick that he realised was still sitting on top of the bureau right next to the Chief Superintendent's arm. The thought of someone like Shawcross or of anyone watching him as he did those things- well he couldn't tell him, could never let anyone see it, even to save his life. It was strangely comforting to recognise that his fear at least had some boundaries.

"So what now Christopher? You pop the pills, slit your wrists, and let the rest of us take the consequences?"

"I don't understand?"

"Really? Well it's pretty simple, or don't you think that anyone will ask how you got Weston in, or doesn't that matter-"
"But you didn't know what I was doing. I would have... I was going to put that in my letter explain-"
"And you think that would just make it all OK? Don't be so fucking dim, Christopher. Now, it may surprise you to know this but, I actually don't give a flying fuck about whether you decide to end your miserable little life; and most of what you've just told me I already knew about three hours ago. You see, you're not too good at keeping secrets Christopher. First there is the diary you keep in your apartment- and this might surprise you Christopher, but it wasn't too difficult to figure out who 'Chrissie' and 'Dommie 'were, even for someone as slow-witted as me. Then there's the credit card that you always use to book your cheap hotel rooms, the same one incidentally that you buy your 'special' little outfits with." He smiled without any warmth and shook his head, "You know it never ceases to amaze me how you intellectual Cambridge Wallies are quite often as thick as a wooden plank when it comes to common sense-"
"Then why bother asking me if you already knew?" Jennings said, correctly deciding that now would not be a good time to complain about the illegal breach of his privacy.
"It's an old- fashioned thing, Christopher, you see you can look at all the data, sift through all the evidence, but in the end it comes down to gut instinct, that's what you have to go with. You have to look people in the eye to know whether they are all they seem to be. You see, this conversation so far has been a little test, and so far you've done well, as, if you had lied to me about any of this, well... Let's just say you wouldn't have needed the pills. But, anyway, you didn't lie to me, Christopher, at least that's what my gut tells me. So far you've told the truth, and that was a very smart thing to do, it's saved your life for now at least. You see, when you let your 'little 'Dommie' into Riverside, you didn't just fuck up your own future. You also fucked up mine, and you fucked up Pat Dixon's. It doesn't matter that we didn't know, you see, because we fucked up, me more than Dixon of course. But that doesn't matter. If it came out that we allowed Weston into Riverside we are finished, dismissed at best, more likely imprisoned for treason. You know how it works, Christopher, when the shit hits the fan- the more scapegoats you can find, the less shit sticks on to yourself; and both your boss and mine, whatever happens, will make sure that none of it sticks on them."
Jennings wiped the moisture from the corner of his eye, trying desperately not to cry at the enormous weight that had suddenly fallen upon him. He looked up at Shawcross, about to apologise again, but he knew now that wasn't why he was here. He took a deep shuddering breath before speaking.
"What do you want me to do, sign a statement or what? I'll do it whatever it

is."
Shawcross leaned back on the chair again and nodded, "I know you will, Christopher, do you know why I know?"
"Your gut told you." Jennings replied dully.
"That's right it did! OK, so here is what we are going to do. In about, oh," he looked at his watch, "fifty minutes, we are going on a drive to the airport and then we are taking a little trip to your chum Dommie's laboratory. When we get there, I will inform the Chief Commissioner that it turns out, by an amazing coincidence, that you and this lunatic Weston are acquainted with each other from your Cambridge days. Don't worry, though, that won't be a problem as most of you top boys pissed in the same pot, didn't you? The same schools, the same Universities, the same back thumping ladder to success. In fact, I guess that if you asked you'd find half of Whitehall went to school with him!"
"Mablethorpe!" Jennings said.
"What about him?"
"The Prime Minister and Dom- Weston, that is- they went to Cambridge together at the same time. They knew each other!"
Shawcross leaned across and patted Jennings' knee, then hunched back into the chair, his fingers steepled under his chin. "That's good, Chrissie. You don't mind me calling you that, do you? No, of course you don't. Anyway, that is what you can do Chrissie, you can give me every single thing that you know about your chum, and I mean everything, however small it is, however trivial it seems; however much it embarrasses you, I want it all."
"And then what?"
"Why then we bring Mr Weston down, Chrissie, you and I together. We will be the ones who bring that nutty bastard down See we can be heroes!"
"You're forgetting something Chief Inspector; there were three of us there when Dominic went into Riverside..."
"Pat Dixon, you mean? Don't worry about Dixon, Chrissie; he's all boxed off with this. You see, Pat has a big fat pay cheque coming in every month, a company Mercedes and a nice big company house. He also has a large, and I do mean large, gambling habit that has left him with a lot of debt. Not a run of the mill debt, by the way, where they repossess your car and your house if you don't pay it. No Pat owes money to one of the most vicious cartels in the country, and if he doesn't want to end up minced in a pork processing factory, he needs to keep his job. He might even be useful for us if we decide we have to send someone in to that shithole Riverside to get at Weston!"
"Hurt him you mean?"
"That still bothers you Chrissie? After what he did to you and knowing what it would mean for you when he did it?"
Jennings stared at the fists he had been clenching unconsciously in his lap,

his eyes flicked again toward the data stick. He knew now with absolute certainty that Dominic had made the film himself, maybe not for this purpose, maybe it had just been for his own gratification. But he knew now that the blackmail story was a lie, it was as bogus as Dominic's supposed affection and friendship for him. He owed nothing now to Dominic Weston, nothing at all. He looked across at Shawcross, his voice a little steadier as he spoke. "No Chief Superintendent, I don't believe it does."

Chapter Thirteen

Carl Stevens, the Safeworld Security guard who had allowed Dominic Weston to leave Porton Down with a deadly bacterial agent, was colder than he had ever been in his life. His knees trembled, his arms trembled, his teeth chattered. He sat naked on a cold hard metal chair; his bare chest was going blue, apart from the red skin where they had roughly shaved his chest to attach the monitoring electrodes. His legs were spread wide, his ankles secured to the table legs with zip lock ties. There was a short chain that ran out through the centre of the grey metal table, which connected to an upright stainless steel T-bar. Attached to the end of the bar were metal wrist cuffs that kept his hands suspended three inches above the surface of the table, causing excruciating pain in his wrists and forearms. As bad as it was though, it was still better than before. Before, they had tied him flat on his back to a wooden bench, with his head lower than his body so it tilted backward. They had poured water over his mouth and nose in a continuous stream that almost, but not quite, caused him to drown. Five times they had lifted him back up and strapped him in the chair, and five times they had tied him back on the bench and poured that cold stinking chlorine water over and into him. No matter how long he had tried to hold his breath, eventually he would have to try and breathe, and each time they did it to him, it felt longer and worse than the time before. It was called water boarding, that much he had known already. He had watched all those CNN clips of first the Ay-rabs, then after the nuke quieted down the Ay-rabs, they had used it on the Greeks and the Spanish. All those foreign terrorists had been given the old water boarding treatment! He had laughed at the bleeding hearts that had said it was inhumane, that it was torture, and that people should be treated as innocent until a court had proved otherwise. Whenever he heard one of the whiners complaining about what was being done, he would shout the same thing at the TV screen. 'They deserve what

they get, or they're fucking terrorists, a bunch of subversive bastards. That's why they're there in the first place you dumb bastards!'And his favourite rant, 'Why waste money on a trial? Fuck em!' Julie, who was his sometime partner, at first used to try and argue with him, 'What if they're innocent, Carl, what if they really didn't do anything?' He hated it when she started putting out all that leftie liberal crap. Most times she would end up crying, as he would stop shouting at the TV and start shouting at her. He never hit her though, he had never hit a woman in his life but, boy, Julie would bring him close sometimes. Eventually, she quit arguing with him; well no, eventually she just quit on him altogether and didn't come around any more. But now here he was, freezing his fucking balls off, the water still dripping down his nose, strapped to a chair in a locked room, and oh how he wished Julie was here now, ready to take his part and to tell them that he was innocent. He knew they were watching him through the large mirror opposite, knew that they would have seen him piss down his own legs earlier. They would have watched him cry gently at first, and later the big racking baby sobs. Whatever he had said in answer to their questions, they had just tied him down again right after and poured the water into his mouth and nose all over again. He had told them everything, even about the porn he had watched. He told them about the stationary he had been nicking for months, but, they just nodded saying nothing as they belted him back down on the bench.
He stared at himself in the mirrored glass opposite, hardly recognising himself.

"Report," Hawksworth said still looking through the one-way glass at the now darkened room.
The psych tech adjusted the glasses on his nose and looked down at his clipboard, unfazed by the man's abrupt manner. He looked first at Porton Down's CEO, Sir George Caithness-Millar who nodded permission before answering the fat police chief.
"We can say with a 94% probability that what he has told us is the truth, or at least the truth as he perceives it. We can also say with an eighty nine per cent probability that he has told us all he knows of the incident, and any relevant factors."
"Why only eighty nine per cent? Why so low?" Hawksworth asked.
The psych tech shook his head smiling, "Oh, that isn't a low score, Chief Commissioner, not for a single day's evaluation. You have to remember that the subject will evince high levels of stress and disorientation. If you would allow us two weeks of continual treatment, we can firm his scores up quite a bit."
"Just give me your best guess, son."
The psych tech smiled again, "We don't deal in guessing sir. We deal in

known certainties, and sometimes in probability matrices, but one thing we never do is guess."
Hawksworth's mouth drew into a tight thin line, but he only nodded at the man. "OK, thank you for your input."
George Caithness-Millar waited for the psych tech to leave the observation room, and the door to hermetically seal itself, before speaking.
"He does seem to be merely an innocent dupe..."
"Hardly innocent!"
"No, but in terms of the gravity of his misdemeanour's, it's hardly a-"
"The gravity of his misdemeanour's, Sir George, is what has led us to the brink of disaster. We can't afford to have him talk to anyone, whether it is in a prison cell or a work camp."
"Still, if he understands that-"
"Oh, he'd understand it alright, he'd be scared shitless for about a month, and then suddenly he'll stop being scared shitless and only be frightened. Then he'll start to get angry and indignant at how he's been treated. Then the next time we see him, he'll probably have his face blanked out in some foreign TV studio, spilling his guts out about whatever he thinks he knows. No, I'm afraid the decision is made, I want your people to continue questioning him until we are certain we have all he knows, and then he will be executed under the Emergency Powers Act. Now about the other one, the woman what's her name? Ms Huffton?"
"Houghton, her name is Susan Houghton," Sir George replied, his cheeks beginning to redden.
"The same situation applies, I'm afraid. We can't afford her disclosing the details of this...incident to anyone."
"Listen to me, Chief Commissioner. I don't like the fact that you are going to execute a security guard, I don't like it one bit. But Susan Houghton is the one who uncovered this mess in the first place, and she's a senior manager for God's sake! She's also one of my personal senior team members, and I will not allow-"
Hawksworth clamped his hand on top of Sir George's, and pressed hard, causing the man to wince and fall silent.
"I'm not sure you fully understand the gravity of what we are dealing with here, Sir George. This is a matter of the gravest national security, and the PM has directly authorised me under the Emergency Powers Act to contain the situation. You understand what that means, I'm sure. All I have to determine is what level of sanction constitutes secure containment. At the moment I have a view that disposing of the guard and Ms...Houghton will be sufficient to secure the information stream. Now tell me, Sir George, if I am underestimating the situation?"
Sir George, who had been a decorated soldier in his earlier career put his hand over Hawksworth's own and applied direct pressure to the nerves,

causing Hawksworth to hiss.
"Listen to me you pompous little man, Susan Houghton is not only a Director of this establishment, she also sits on three multi-national boards, three quasi-government committees, and is generally well known throughout the human resources industry, understand? She isn't some piss-pot little guard you can dispose of silently. She will be missed. Now, I suggest that you release her immediately-"
Hawksworth wrenched his hand out of the man's grip, his cheeks bright red, "She is a direct security risk man, she can't be allowed to just wander around the place!"

*

Susan Houghton had worked at the Porton Down facility for five years and, as the Human Resources Director, she had a level five clearance – which meant she should have known already about the group of 'interview rooms', one of which she had now been kept in for almost five hours, but she hadn't. Unlike the unlucky Carl Stevens, she hadn't been stripped or handcuffed to the table. She also hadn't had water poured over her face so that she would say anything, admit to anything to make it stop. The CEO himself had taken her down to Underground Level 3- a place she hadn't even known existed until the Military Policeman escorting them had unlocked the lift switch panel, and inserted an electronic key which allowed the lift to descend beyond its advertised stations. Sir George had told her not to be overly concerned, and then quickly left with what, even at the time, she had thought had been undue haste. It had all been quite civilized. She had gone through the events of two nights ago regarding Professor Weston and the security guard Stevens. She knew that she had done everything correctly, and in line with both HR and the facility's protocols. She had also followed correct procedure in properly recording Stevens and Weston's transgressions. She knew she had done everything by the book, as she had been part of the team that had written it. She was also the person responsible for overseeing that everyone in the facility both understood and followed procedures correctly. It was clear to her now that something had gone badly wrong in the lab, and that Weston himself was involved. Whatever had gone wrong, though, wasn't her responsibility, so she had no need to be overly concerned; but she was. The people who had interviewed her were polite and not in any way aggressive, but they were all military personnel, and of all of senior rank, and there was a cold remoteness to the way they repeatedly asked her the same things over and over. It was the first time she had been on the receiving end of such an interview, where everything you said was written down and reinterpreted when repeated back to you in a follow up question. For the first time, she thought about the many times she had put people through this process where she had been the inquisitor. She could even see them using some of the techniques she herself had used on numerous occasions. The little eyebrow lift, or widening of the eyes in incredulity at some comment she made. Or the sudden written note that they would take down as she was speaking, as if she had slipped up with something she had just said. The strange thing was that, even though she understood the psychology behind it, it still worked, causing her to stumble and second guess herself precisely as it was designed to do. She had been fine for the first hour, even the next two hours as they would question her over and over again. 'Was Weston carrying anything? Did he seem stressed? Had he ever given her cause for concern in his behaviours?' On and on, over and over again the same questions each time worded slightly differently. Then they would break off and leave her alone for twenty minutes or so. They had left her coffee, bottled water and a tray of biscuits- even bringing her a sandwich at one point, though she couldn't have eaten anything, the way her stomach was churning. Then, for the first time, she'd heard the muffled crying and then shouting from somewhere down the corridor. She thought it was the guard Stevens, something about the man's whining voice managing to sound familiar, despite the fact that she was unable to make out what he was actually saying. That's when she began to be frightened by what was happening. She wasn't stupid. She knew they were deliberately allowing the sounds of the man's interrogation to leech out to her. And she didn't doubt that that's exactly what it was- an interrogation...or worse. Whatever Weston had done had been so serious that they were prepared to go to any lengths to find out the truth. About twenty minutes ago she had spilled her coffee in her lap when she had heard screaming; and then the man's final shout of his innocence followed by one last scream, made all the more chilling by the complete silence that followed. Since then, the only sound had been the subliminal hum of the air conditioning.

Her imagination was running through the various possible scenarios of why he had suddenly gone quiet, none of which were pleasant. They had left her alone for forty minutes now, and she had tried to bring the calm ruthlessness to bear on her own situation that she had always used in both her career and her personal life. Just by doing so, she felt calmer as she ran through the various schemes that Weston and the guard could have been involved in. She felt calmer as she went through the possibilities, including potentially espionage, but she could also still feel the dread and panic bubbling below the surface, waiting to spill over. She knew already that Weston had absconded; the questions they had asked her had told her that much. She started as the door suddenly opened and two men walked into the room.

"Ms Houghton," the policeman said, "my name is Chief Superintendent

Shawcross; this gentleman is Mr Jennings from the PM's office."
She nodded at them both, folding her hands across her lap to cover up the coffee stain on her light grey pant suit.
"I realise that this must be a stressful experience for you Ms-"
She interrupted him, "What has he done, Professor Weston I mean?"
The policeman smiled, "If I told you that I'd have to shoot you."
She smiled stiffly at him, knowing he was joking but, given where she was not entirely certain. She decided that, if she was going to survive this...whatever this was, she had to be assertive, had to make herself of value somehow. She had realised over the last five hours that whatever Weston had done was so serious that they were going to close everything down tight. They would want to stop any possibility of leaks in whatever way they deemed necessary. Stevens' screams and pleas of what she assumed were his protested innocence told her that, as did the fact she was being questioned in a secret basement that, even as a Senior Director she had been unaware of.
The police officer was looking at her still, smiling, the other man, the one from the PM's office looked as nervous as she did. That along with the fact that these were the first non-military personnel she had seen since being brought down here, made her decision for her.
"I think," she said, "that Professor Weston has done something- no, I mean taken something from the facility and, whatever it is, has gotten everyone scared out of their wits." She looked up at him, waiting for confirmation. He just stared at her, the half smile still in place.
"Given the nature of his research, which I only have a vague idea of," she added quickly, "it must be something that is extremely dangerous, and something that is probably illegal- sorry, I mean highly classified?"
Again, she got nothing, not even a flicker of response, the other one though- Jennings was it?- had begun to doodle on his notepad sharp jagged lines that she knew from her years in the job, observing people under stress, meant she was right. "I can help you get him!" she said, almost blurting it out, and cursing inwardly at her clumsiness, but also knowing instinctively that this was her one opportunity to avoid... what?
The man tilted his head at her, still half- smiling, "What makes you think we don't already have him?"
"Because if you did, I wouldn't have been sat here for the last five hours answering the same damn questions over and over again. Because if you had him, then you wouldn't have arranged for me to overhear that idiot security guard Stevens being... You don't have him!" she finished finally, knowing now she was right. "But I could help you get him!"
The police man leaned back in his chair as he spoke, "And how would that work exactly, Ms Houghton?"
"Because, more than anyone I know what a sick twisted bastard he is!" she

said causing the man Jennings to suddenly look up at her for the first time, before quickly looking back down at his notepad.
"Go on," Shawcross said.
"I have been watching and waiting for Professor Weston to screw up for a long time, I knew the man had something wrong inside him. Not anything like this, of course. if I had thought that, I would have said something."
"Of course you would, I can see that."
She began to warm to what she was saying, began to smell a half- open door to freedom. "In a way, Chief Inspector," she said her voice unconsciously moving from one of a frightened woman to the professional manager, "our jobs are not dissimilar. I mean, I'm not comparing what I do to the role of the police, of course. What I mean is that we both have to study people, have a sense of their truthfulness ... of their worth, if you like. Weston was already here when I took up my position but, shortly after I arrived, I conducted interviews and evaluations with all of the Senior Team members, so my insight-"
"It's more than that though, Susan," Shawcross said quietly, "I mean, it's more personal between you and him," Shawcross said.
She felt herself begin to flush- how dare he! She caught herself, and took a long slow breath. This was her one opportunity to come out of this situation unscathed, and she had also instinctively recognised something of Shawcross in herself. This was a man who studied people, watched them, and he would smell any bullshit she gave him from a mile away. She composed herself so her voice was steady when she spoke.
"We, that is Professor Weston and I, went out together for a short time, back when I first arrived at the facility; it didn't come to anything. "
Shawcross stayed silent, waiting for her to tell the rest of it.
She looked down at the table where her red varnished fingernail was unconsciously tapping as if she was trying to send Morse code. Even now, she was deciding how much of it she could leave out.
Shawcross pushed the cuff of his jacket back to look at his wristwatch, and for a moment the feeling of dread rushed back into the pit of her stomach, as she realised he might just close down the interview and leave her here.
"He...he had only been here for a couple of months before I was appointed, so he said he knew how I felt being the new kid. He was very charming- he can be that way when he wants to be. He's very good at making you feel like you're very special to him, but he uses people too, at least he used me and I doubt very much if I was the first."
She looked back up at Shawcross, who had that half- smile back on his face; he nodded at her to continue. The other one, Jennings had put his pen down and was now sat staring at his hands, which were clenched into fists on top of his notepad.
"At first I didn't see that his behaviour was deliberate, I just thought he

was... Well, anyway, afterwards it was easy to see why. It was the evaluations, you see; that was part of the reason I was appointed, to run a series of psychometric tests. Psychometric testing shows what a person's real motivations are, it shows their fears and their hopes, and it tells us whether they will make a positive or negative contribution to the organisation. I am an expert in the field of human resources, Chief Inspector. The tests I use are designed to weed out the chaff, the malcontents; they identify very accurately those individuals who won't contribute the maximum to the organisation that employs them."

"You didn't test him!" Shawcross said.

She felt her eyes widen in surprise for a moment, then shook her head.

"He told me that he had a morbid fear of testing and that it went back to something that had been done to him as a child, some kind of abuse he had suffered, sexual I think, but he would never say. 'In time I'll be able to tell you,' he told me, 'when we can be more certain of each other...'"

"So you faked his results?"

"No! Well, not faked exactly, you see I felt I knew him better than most people. In a way I was continually testing him, I mean I was testing him whenever we were together. Look, Chief Inspector, does this have to come out? I mean my career would be in-"

Shawcross cut her off, the smile gone as he spoke. "You have a decision to make. Susan. Either tell me all of it right now or don't. But, before you decide you should understand that your decision will determine more than your career!"

Susan Houghton nodded, "Yes I see that, I..." she sighed before continuing. "You have to understand something about Weston; he could be, can be so charming so...nice when he chooses to be. I know we can all be like that of course, but it isn't that with him. He's like an actor, a very good actor, except he plays the part that you want him to play, he says the things that you want to hear." She saw Jennings in her peripheral vision give an almost imperceptible nod. "I didn't see the other side of him, the ugly side till much later. Well no that isn't true," she corrected herself, "I saw it almost as soon as the psychometric tests were concluded."

"After you'd given him a clean bill of health, you mean?"

"Yes, and the thing is, that it seems so stupid and obvious after the event, but I suppose that's always the way when someone uses you, when they aren't what you thought they were. It's only afterwards that you wonder how you could be so-"

"Tell me about afterwards, how did he change?"

She took a deep breath before going on. This was the most difficult part to talk about. She was essentially a very private person, not that she was a prude or anything. Sex had never been an issue for her, it was no more than if she went to the gym, just another form of enjoyable exercise. She looked at Shawcross, who seemed to be debating with himself whether she had any further value and decided if she was going to come out without a stain on her career, she couldn't hold anything back.

"He became very different. At first the intimacy was, well it was good, very good, but then he began to do different things...cruel things." She looked at Shawcross hoping that he would spare her this but knowing he wouldn't. It made it worse that there were two of them in the room. If it was just Shawcross she thought she'd be OK with it. She considered asking if the other one, Jennings, could leave them alone, and almost laughed at the absurdity. "He liked me to talk about the job...when we did it... had sex, I mean, he seemed to get off on me talking about the other faculty members. He liked me to tell him about, about their weaknesses, their failings. It was just a game I thought, I didn't see it as a problem..." she said, stumbling to a halt as Shawcross gave a small shake of his head a shake that said 'don't lie, Susan.' "

"OK, that isn't true. I did see it as a problem. But I thought it was just a weird sexual thing, you know. People have all sorts of weird fantasies. But then he started to become physically abusive."

"He beat you, you mean?"

"No, not that, he...he would pinch me in... well, in painful places, and he slapped me a couple of times and called me names.... bad names. He'd done it a little bit before, and I could tell. it got him off... but, later, well it frightened me as to just how far he would go. That was when I broke off our relationship."

"And how did he take that?"

"Very badly, He made it very clear to me that if I said anything he would expose me over the tests."

Shawcross stared at her for what seemed a long time before nodding. "OK, so now explain to me how you think you can help us, Ms Houghton."

She felt a tear forming at the back of her eyes as she realised he wasn't going to probe her further on the sex front, and squeezed her eyes shut for a brief moment before continuing. Her voice when she spoke sounded more confident and assured, as she was once again back on known territory.

"Well, as I said, I couldn't really do anything because of the tests, I would have lost my job! Still, I decided that it would be only a matter of time before he did something that would allow me to-"

"Bury him!"

"He was dangerous, I knew that; he was, is in my opinion pathological. I have observed him discreetly ever since I realised that, and I have compiled quite a considerable dossier on his background and his previous employment relationships."

Shawcross shrugged, clearly unimpressed.

"Chief Inspector, I don't think you understand what I am saying. I have got inside this man's head, I know how he thinks, and I can predict how he will act in most given situations. If he hadn't done whatever it is he has done, well, I believe I would have been able to have him dismissed from the lab. It was just a matter of time, you see, a culmination of small things that he did. The way he spoke to some of the other board members, and how he treated the junior staff."
"You still haven't sold me, Susan," Shawcross said leaning back and stretching his hands behind the back of his head.
"I've told you, I know this man, I can predict how he will act in certain situations, more than that I believe I can make him react. Look, I know you have all sorts of experts who can analyse him and come up with the same conclusions-"
"Then why do I need you?"
She looked directly at him now, her self-assurance back to where it should be, knowing that she was as good as anyone at what she did.
"Because, Chief Inspector, you don't have time for that, do you? Whatever he's done has sent everyone here into a panic, which means you don't have the time to analyse and study his profile. But I've already done that you see? And I have something else that all your analysts don't have."
"Go on," Shawcross said.
"I want to bring the arrogant cruel bastard down! For me it's personal, Chief Inspector. He used me, he betrayed my trust and he made me compromise the thing that matters most to me, my career. Get me out of here, Chief Inspector, and I'll do whatever it takes to help you."
Shawcross stared at her for a long moment, then turned his head toward Jennings, who looked up briefly and shrugged. Shawcross turned back toward her, the half smile back as he spoke.
"OK, Susan, but I'm afraid that getting you out of here isn't quite as simple as it sounds. There are some very senior people who think we'd all be a lot safer if you were to remain at the facility."

She made a conscious effort to keep her hands flat on the table so he couldn't see them shaking.
"However, I believe that you may actually be of some use to us, and my colleague Mr Jennings I'm sure agrees with me, that you have the necessary... motivation to be of some use. Also, you are fortunate that your boss, Sir George, has also been quite insistent that you should be free to leave the facility this evening, which my boss has surprisingly agreed to. However, I will require that you attend here tomorrow morning at 07:00 hrs. and that, when you arrive, you have with you every last scrap of information that you have on Dominic Weston so that we can begin to go though it together."

*

An hour later she was sitting in the snug of the Wagon and Horses, which nestled on the edge of the A138, linking the laboratory at Porton Down and her own village of Embury. She was staring into her second glass of an acidic and tepid house red. The bar was empty, apart from an old boy in the corner drinking cider and mumbling to himself, and the sweaty landlord who had barely managed to turn away from the TV on the wall as he had served her. The place was a dump, and not somewhere she would ever frequent. Ironically, the only time she had been in before was with Weston, one afternoon, when they had both skipped off early and wanted somewhere they wouldn't be spotted by any colleagues. They had sat in the far corner where the old boy was now, and Weston had persuaded her to unzip his trousers under the table and stroke his hard cock, while an old pensioner couple sat a few tables away eating fish and chips. She blushed now as she remembered how exciting it had been at the time. The risk that they might have been discovered had made her horny enough that she had let him take her over the bonnet of the car, just down the road in a small country lane, in broad daylight. She took another swallow of the wine, aware that she was becoming a little buzzed and, though only a mile from home, she would still have to watch it driving back. She looked up, startled at the sound of sirens, the shakes she had been unable to control when she had finally gotten out of the lab and made it to her car threatened to return. She sighed with relief as she saw that the sirens were actually coming from the TV which the bar man had turned up, as they were reporting the latest events at Riverside. The woman she liked, the Arab one who sounded English, was standing outside the cordoned off area, police lights flashing blue lightning behind her as she spoke into the camera.

"Well, Seamus, we haven't been able to get any confirmation of this story, either from the Government's spokesperson or from the Chief Commissioner himself, Richard Hawksworth. You certainly do get the sense down here, though, that there is something holding back the security services from entering the estate, especially given that we now know from our sources that, other than sticks and knives, the residents are actually unarmed. Seamus."

"You say that, Nasri," Seamus said, "but the blogs are full of rumours that the people in the estate might have gained access to some kind of weapon, and it's that that's stopping the police and security services from going in. Are you hearing any of that from where you are?"

"Well as you know Seamus, the blogs are never short of wild and wonderful theories when it comes to what's going on down here. But as far as the authorities here are concerned, they refuse to move away from their original statement that they are 'simply allowing matters to play out peacefully'. Of course, the other theory that seems to be gaining more traction, at least with some of the mainstream bloggers, is that the leader of the so called Riverside Revolutionaries, Professor Michael Deveron, who as you know went to University with half the current Cabinet including the British Prime minister Gregory Mablethorpe, has some kind of embarrassing information. What that information is again can only be speculated upon, but it would have to be pretty significant if it has been enough to stop the authorities in their tracks. Seamus."

"So what you're saying, Nasri, is that you pay's yer money and you take's yer choice?" Seamus said, winking at the camera in that way he had, that Susan Houghton had always found mildly irritating.

"That's right Seamus, though as you can see from earlier this evening, the Prime Minister didn't look particularly concerned as he arrived here for a security update."

Susan Houghton didn't hear anything else as she watched the clip of Mablethorpe and his team crossing the small walkway from their blacked out Range Rovers to the enclosed security compound. She didn't notice that the glass she was holding had slopped red wine over her hand and down the cuff of her newest business suit, which was already ruined with a coffee stain. Instead she stared at the screen, her mouth unconsciously hanging open, her eyes fixed on the two men who walked behind the Prime Minister and the fat policeman, the same two men who she had been interviewed by only an hour or so ago. Chief Superintendent Shawcross looked briefly across at the gaggle of international cameras, and for a brief moment she felt as if he was looking directly at her.

She had, like most people interested in current events, watched the Riverside fiasco as it had rumbled along. If anyone raised it at work lunches, she would of course feign ignorance to avoid getting involved in any kind of discussion. Riverside had polarised the UK, and had brought the whole issue of the Zoning, New Towns and China's increasing presence in the country to the fore; and the one thing Susan never did was take any position that could impact her career, at least not without being ninety nine percent certain of who was going to come out on top. When she had seen Shawcross and the other one, Jennings with the PM, she had known instantly and without any doubt that Dominic was involved in some way with what was happening. She kept hearing Seamus O'Donnell saying, 'blogs today are full of rumours that the people in the estate have some kind of weapon'. And she knew, didn't she? She knew with more than ninety nine per cent certainty that this wasn't just the usual conspiracy story, this time it was true. The link was obvious really, she had seen it in his CV when she had been doing his last set of psych tests, not that it had meant anything then that one of his historical listed referees post university was one Professor Michael Deveron. And that was the real problem, wasn't it, because although Riverside hadn't happened at the time, she should have picked up that Deveron was a proscribed individual and had been for more than three years? The background checks she should have run when he had done the test screening would have flagged that up, Weston would have been interviewed and almost certainly 'let go'. Simply being associated with a suspected subversive and known leftist would debar him from working at the facility. Except, she hadn't run fresh background checks, had she; she had nearly done it, or at least was going to have it done by one of her staff, but what was the point if she was only going to pass him through anyway, especially given how tight the departmental budget was lately. But tomorrow or the next day, or the day after that, when Shawcross and his team started to go through everything, which they were bound to do...then they would see it straight away, and then what? All at once she was back in the austere room down in Level Three, she could hear in her head the security guard, Carl Stevens as he had screamed from somewhere down the corridor. Suddenly she had to run to the toilet past a startled looking barman, so she could throw up into the water stained sink.

*

Ten minutes later, she sat in her car still in the pub car park. She was going methodically through her personal calming ritual, which consisted of repairing her make-up. First a careful use of her lip pencil, and then filling in her lips which she always worried weren't full enough, with a deep red lipstick. The red lipstick contrasted well with her bronzed skin tone, which she ensured was always just right with her expensive monthly spray tan. As she moved onto her eyes, the mascara brush began to tremble in her shaking hand, causing her to smudge liner onto her upper cheek.

"Shit...shit...shit," she looked into the mirror and burst into great racking sobs, throwing the mascara brush onto the passenger seat of the car, leaving a black splatter of mascara on the tan leather seats, which made her feel even worse. She was staring into the abyss, she realised, and at this moment, for the first time since she was a young girl, her career path was not even a consideration. She wasn't lying when she'd told Shawcross that she had compiled a lot of information on Weston; she had, it was all securely encrypted on her personal laptop at home. And that was her problem, Shawcross didn't need her, he could just take what she had and then what value did she have? She started to feel angry at Shawcross and at Weston, but mostly angry at herself; she was better than this. Strategising, or 'plotting' as her mother would always sarcastically call it, it was what she was good at. Working out people's agendas, their desires, their fears, that was what had gotten her to where she was now, the youngest HR director in the history of the service. And now here she was behaving for the second time like some simpering idiot. The first time was with Weston she hadn't even seen it coming, the way the man just conned her. And wasn't Shawcross now doing the same thing? She thought about his half smile as she'd told him what she had- stupid, stupid, stupid. She wiped the smudge of her cheek with the heel of her palm, and forced a smile in the car mirror. She had to take back control, and she could only do that by doing what she had always done best- to 'seize the moment', she even had it printed on a plaque on her dressing table at home, so she would see it every day before she went to work. Ever since Weston had appeared in her life, rather than taking the advantage she had been simply reacting. She had allowed events to control her, and that was going to stop right now. It was time to stop being a victim; it was time as good old Teddy Roosevelt would say to 'seize the moment'.

Five minutes later, still sat in the car she was turning the full force of her will onto the limp sounding Carlton, who declared himself to be the 'servicing person' for the female reporter Nasri Jaheel.
"And I am telling you, Carlton, that Nasri will most definitely want to speak to me directly; this is a big story, the biggest!"
"Yes, I understand that Ms Houghton-"
"Susan, please."
"Susan. Yes of course, but even if what you say is true Susan and I'm sure it is, it is the strict policy of the station that we don't give out direct contact numbers. Now, as I have said, if you apprise me of the nature of your story, I'll pass that on to Nasri directly and-"
"Listen!" she said loudly, almost shouting before she caught herself. She couldn't afford to alienate him even if he was a pompous little prick. "I'm sorry, Carlton, I apologise. I don't mean to be rude, I really don't, but I have a very small window in which to operate, and I need to speak to Ms Jaheel urgently."
Carlton repeated himself again sounding as if he was reading from a script which he probably was, she thought.
She would have to take a chance. "OK, Carlton, you win; but I need you to assure me that what I tell you is recorded accurately and passed on immediately?"
"Of course," he said sounding bored.
"OK, it's about Riverside, the estate that is. I have information about the weapon they have inside..."

*

As she drove down the road she blew out a huge sigh of relief. For the first time since this dreadful day had started, she actually felt in control. She could hear immediately the change in young Carlton's voice as she had told him she had evidence of a weapon, and who had taken it in to the estate.

The boredom in his voice vanished instantly, as he had tried to get more details from her; and she only just stopped herself from laughing aloud as she told him that it was her policy only to deal with the organ grinder, and not the monkey. In the end she had given him her personal mobile and home telephone numbers, and made it clear if she didn't receive a call directly from Nasri Jaheel within the next three hours, she would take the story to another broadcaster. With that, she had ended the call. The sound of his pleas for more details as she cut him off actually caused her to laugh aloud.

She looked into the rear view mirror and pulled in just opposite the small group of shops that bordered the village. She would treat herself to a budget bottle of fizz for after her shower, and wait for the call she had no doubt at all now would be coming soon. As she stepped out of the car she was still deciding the best way to play it. Certainly she would need a secure place to stay until the story broke. She thought Paris would be politically secure, given its hostility to the UK these days. It was also where Jaheel's organisation, Free Press News, had its headquarters and crucially, of course, it would be outside of the reach of Chief Inspector Shawcross and Co. She had been chewing over what her demands should be; clearly any monies would have to compensate for her loss of her career, as well as recognising the international importance of the story. But that was OK she was not just good at negotiating and closing a deal, she was one of, if not the best, in her field. She would also insist on only doing live interviews, so she could control the pace of what she said. In fact, she thought, I should demand we do an hour special. Then who knew? She was photogenic, intelligent and articulate; maybe a whole new career awaited her. She smiled as she checked both ways for traffic before crossing and decided that what the hell, she might even buy a very expensive bottle of fizz, instead of the usual cheap crap. The road as usual was pretty empty at this time of day, a black van, probably delivering, as it was parked twenty feet away with its hazards flashing, was the only vehicle other than her own in sight.

A moment later, she tried to puzzle out how she had come to be lying across the grass verge, and why her legs seemed to be pointing at a bizarre and impossible angle to the rest of her body. She still hadn't worked it out as the black van, a Mercedes she realised now reversed suddenly back over her instantly crushing her spinal cord before speeding off down the road.

Chapter Fourteen

Gregory Mablethorpe stared at the cognac as he swirled it around his glass, the amber liquid refracted the flickering reds and yellows from the grand fireplace. He had never been particularly fond of Chequers, the country residence of British prime ministers since 1921. Despite the many years of substantive refurbishment, it always seemed a damp and draughty place. The Hawtrey Room where he now sat opposite the Chinese Ambassador, His Excellency Hunshai Tan, was one of the few rooms he did like. Its oak-panelled walls and low lighting gave it an air of understated power, whilst still retaining a feeling of cosy intimacy. He also always felt a connection to Great Britain's proud history when he sat in this room, where heads of state and presidents had sat drinking brandy on these same comfy sofas, whilst they decided the fates of countless millions. However, in his peripheral vision, he could see that his friend the Ambassador felt no such comfort, as he sat perched on the very edge of the opposite sofa his hands flat on his thighs, his back upright. Mablethorpe took a small sip of the vintage brandy, savouring its taste before reluctantly placing the glass back down on the small side table. He sighed drawing his fingers through his long mop of silver grey hair and tried again.

"You have to understand, Hunshai, that there are certain proprieties that I have to observe and, as I say it is in neither of our interests for this thing to end badly. But you should know that I remain very confident that if-"

"Two weeks ago, Gregory, you were also as I recall very confident. You were confident that the population of these three estates would all have been relocated to our New Age facilities by now. Instead of which, I have been informed that we have a subversive terrorist grouping in Manchester that threatens to destroy all of our endeavours!"

"Hunshai, my dear friend-"

"I use the term 'informed', Gregory" Hunshai, said ignoring Mablethorpe's protestations "because I was not told about this by yourself- someone whom I have valued as friend and a Brother. It was not you, Gregory, who told me that these terrorists have access to a highly illegal weapon which, under international law, should not of course even exist. Yet these subversives have somehow managed to take it from this Porton Down,

from ... how you say it, from under all your noses!"
Mablethorpe was still immensely irritated at yet another leak to the Chinese, despite his instructions that security had to be beefed up. He tilted his head to one side, a small smile on his face as he spoke. "Your sources of information once again are impressive, Hunshai. I'd be quite interested to learn, as your friend and brother, just who it was that informed you so quickly?"
Hunshai gave a thin smile and steepled his fingers under his chin, changing tack. "We both know Gregory that deception in the defence of one's nation is an entirely honourable thing; indeed, is it not expected for those of us who must carry the heavy burdens of leadership?"
Mablethorpe nodded, staring at the fire.

"I do of course, Gregory, remain fully confident that you will bring this matter of Riverside to a conclusion. This conclusion must not only be swift, but must also ensure that no information pertaining to this weapon enters the public domain. If, my dear friend and Brother, those things are not achieved, then I am sure you will understand that the interests of the People's Republic of China will in all circumstances take precedence."
Mablethorpe could feel a cold slither of tension beginning to slide into his stomach; he kept his voice relaxed as he spoke. "The interests of your government and mine, Ambassador remain, I believe, inseparable in this matter."
"This...incident at Riverside, Gregory, it has become a how do you say it, a 'cause celebre' on the international stage. As of this moment, this small and isolated resistance is, we believe, manageable, at least for a finite period. However, if information about this weapon becomes public, we in the People's Republic of China will have no choice but to disavow both you and your government."
Mablethorpe leaned toward Hunshai Tan, unable as ever to see the man's eyes through the slight tint of the heavy black rimmed spectacles that he wore. "Are you telling me that China does not have its own biological weapons Ambassador?" Mablethorpe smiled, "No, my friend, you need us every bit as much as we need-"
"We have been approached by the Greek government which, like your own country as you know, ceded from the European Union-"
"Greece!" Mablethorpe almost shouted, "Greece, my God Hunshai you cannot seriously be suggesting that you could... What about the billions of yen that you have already invested here?"
Hunshai shrugged, "We Chinese are very different than you British. For us a short term investment might be fifty years, a mere blink of the eye, whereas for you British five years would be an eternity. That is one reason why we lead the world, Gregory, we don't invest for short term capital gain,

we invest for the continuing security and prosperity of our great nation."
"But Greece Hunshai, it's an agrarian country full of olive pickers and goat herders. Here we have an industrial heritage, a skilled and progressive workforce."
Hunshai smiled not unkindly and waved his hand around the room. "Gregory Mablethorpe my good friend please look around you! This room where we now sit is a symbol of what you once were. Your Great Britain was it's true and for however fleetingly once a great empire. But now you are left only with the vain adornments and mementos of power. Your country has survived in the world since its empire fell by its clever attachment to more powerful allies. You are not unlike those pilot fish that clean the teeth and mouths of sharks and by doing so manage to hide from those who would eat them. For a long time you swam with the great white shark of the United States until they abandoned you for the greener pastures of the Pacific world. Then you found us, the 'inscrutable Orientals'." Hunshai could see that Mablethorpe was offended he shook his head and smiled thinly. "I tell you this Gregory Mablethorpe not to injure or insult you or your nation's honour, but only so there is truth between us. You must bring this Riverside nonsense to a suitable resolution and you must do it quickly my friend as the hawks in my government are not patient men. For now I have persuaded them that the United Kingdom is still our route to the domination and absorption of the greater European economies. I have personally assured them that through you Gregory Great Britain remains a loyal vassal state. But their patience is not without limits and both you and I will I fear not survive if that patience wears out."
Mablethorpe drew himself straighter in his chair, "The United Kingdom is no vassal state Sir I-"
"Did I not say this was a time for truth Gregory Mablethorpe," Hunshai said his voice in quiet contrast to Mablethorpe's.

Mablethorpe stood up abruptly and refilled his glass. His family had been members of the British parliament since the 17th century. He was the third prime minister to come out of the Mablethorpe and Wessex lineage; leadership was stamped through his very genes. Yet sometimes he felt so inadequate and unsuited to the task. Yes, he could deliver a rousing speech in front of hundreds or thousands; he could negotiate with Kings and Presidents, and come away with great diplomatic victories. But inside in his deepest self, he had a dominant fear that it would be him, after all these centuries, that would fail his distinguished ancestors. He could never tell anyone about the imaginary conversations that he sometimes had with his long dead ancestors, conversations where they often berated him for being weak and a coward. Hunshai was right, of course. Britain was no longer a world power, not even if he was truly honest a significant player on the world stage any more. Yet tonight Hunshai had revealed in stark terms the real nature of their relationship. He should throw the arrogant slitty eyed devil out on his arse. He could do it with the press of a button. The room would be swamped in less than thirty seconds by his personal bodyguards. But what then? Where would he go? His hand shook as he picked up the brandy glass. Perhaps the ghosts of his ancestors were right, and he was a coward. Yet, was it cowardice to acknowledge the truth? Was it weak to understand that to survive and prosper, Britain needed strong allies? His courting of the Chinese... No, he acknowledged to himself now in this time of truth, their courting of him, had started before he was even elected as leader of the opposition. They had offered their private support financial and more, and he hadn't hesitated, he hadn't blinked at what he knew were going to be golden chains. They had offered, and delivered him, the leadership of the fractured Conservative party, and then they had delivered him the country. There were stories of course, but then there were always stories, stories about his opponents being blackmailed and compromised, stories about payments to potential supporters. There were even some tragic accidents that happened to potential opponents or to their close family members. But stories and conspiracy theories weren't facts; so he could decry them in public and could deny them to himself in private. Except now Hunshai had pulled away that veneer of respectability, 'a vassal state' he had said. He wasn't even trying to insult him, he realised Hunshai was simply stating the truth as he saw it. To be a vassal could mean two different things, Mablethorpe knew. India and half of Africa had been vassal states in the glory days of the British Empire, yet India today was a world player exceeding far and above what its old colonial masters had achieved. Suddenly Mablethorpe knew that this was his real destiny. He would accept this current relationship of vassal status as necessary to his personal survival. He could he decided, become a most loyal and trusted vassal. But Hunshai was wrong about China. They were in the end just another empire. They too would begin to fracture and crumble. Many said that it had already started, as the capitalist ring-fences the Chinese had allowed and encouraged in their great cities were slowly expanding, and creeping into the wider country. The Chinese ruthlessly suppressed any attempts at reform of the government's total authority, but they would not be able to do so for very much longer if Mablethorpe's own analysts were to be believed. Capitalism could not by its very nature allow any master other than itself. The Chinese would, like all those before them, soon come to realise they had uncaged the beast that would eventually devour them. That would be the moment that he would lead Great Britain to a golden age that had not been seen since the reign of Queen Victoria. He could hear the clamour of blusterous outrage at the risks he was taking emanating from the ghosts of his ancestors, but for once was able to silence them with ease.

He turned toward Ambassador Hunshai Tan and smiled his most winning smile, the one which had so endeared him to the media, the one that said here was a man who could be trusted.
"My dear Hunshai, I feel it is time that I took you completely into my confidence in all matters pertaining to Riverside and elsewhere!"
Hunshai bowed his head in thanks, which also had the advantage of hiding his own smile.

*

Richard Hawksworth's own meeting with the Chinese Ambassador was somewhat less genteel, as Hunshai told him what he had agreed with Mablethorpe earlier in the evening. The motorway service station had only half a dozen customers- the usual array of truckers and night workers who were the only people that used such places at two in the morning. Hunshai's ever present bodyguard, Zhi, was seated discreetly on the opposite side of the restaurant, ready to leap into deadly action should circumstance require it.

Hunshai had just told him that that little piss-ant, Jennings, had gotten agreement from Mablethorpe that he and Shawcross were to be given full intelligence access to the Riverside operation. This was completely outrageous and in his view risked undermining his command. He had also learned that Shawcross and Jennings had, without his knowledge gotten Mablethorpe to agree they could add the woman Houghton to their little cabal, and that really was wholly unacceptable, something which he had just told Hunshai in the bluntest manner. The Ambassador had merely looked at him not speaking, his mouth slightly uplifted in that infuriating way he had.

"Are you bloody listening, Mr Hunshy?" Hawksworth said, leaning slightly toward him.
Hunshai Tan, Ambassador to the Peoples Republic of China, whose ancestors had wielded power for even as long as the Yuan dynasty, and had managed to hold it for all those centuries even through the great purges of Mao, looked at the fat sweating Chief of Police and recited the names of all the rocks in his garden. This was Hunshai's way of never succumbing to anger, an emotion he understood made noise, but was devoid of skill. He took off his heavy black rimmed spectacles, and removed a white linen handkerchief from his breast pocket, his eyes not leaving Hawksworth's as he breathed on one of the spotless lenses and began to polish it. He had seen Zhi, his number one guard, readying to move at Hawksworth's aggressive and disrespectful body language, and had taken his glasses off which signalled to Zhi that he should wait. Hawksworth seemed to sense

that he had committed some kind of error as he began to explain.
"You have to understand Mr Hunshy, that I need total control if I am-"
"Hunshai, Mr Hawksworth. Hunshai two distinct syllables- or Mr Ambassador if that is easier for you?"
Hawksworth grimaced, "I apologise, no slight intended." Hunshai stared at him silently. "Really, I didn't mean anything by it; no big deal, alright?" Hawksworth spread his hands wide and smiled.
"Ah, but I am afraid it is indeed a 'big deal', Mr Hawksworth, for a person's name is not that person's own property. A person's name is something that he or she only carries for and on behalf of his or her ancestors, and even then only for the fleeting period of their mortal existence. A person's name must then be protected and cared for, to be passed on unsullied to that person's progeny. I am, of course, used to dealing with you westerners who mispronounce the names of our cities and the names of our ancestors. Most times I let such insults run through me like smoke through the air. Zhi, however;" he inclined his head towards where his number one guard sat like a coiled spring, one hand inside of his suit jacket. It amused him, though he did not show it as he watched Hawksworth look across the short distance into Zhi's stony stare, then turn back to look at him whilst at the same time seeming to take on the shape of a deflated tyre at whatever he had just seen in the bodyguard's eyes. "Zhi, whose name means- how would you say it?- yes, 'wilful intention'. If you mispronounced Zhi which should of course be pronounced 'Gee', he would be deeply insulted."
"I have said I am sorry, Mr Hunshai," Hawksworth said as correctly as he could. Realising that he was in a dangerous situation, he awkwardly bowed his head first toward Hunshai and then as he began to turn back, to bow toward towards Zhi, Hunshai interrupted him.
"No need for that, Mr Hawksworth. I think we have had enough lessons in Chinese etiquette for now." He replaced his glasses, knowing as he did so Zhi would relax into mere alertness.
"It is my opinion that we should give Messrs Shawcross and Jennings some latitude, which does not mean to say that we will relinquish control."
Hawksworth confined himself to a respectful nod.
"It transpires that Professor Weston's karma has touched upon this man Christopher Jennings in surprising ways-"
"But I don't see why Mablethorpe would agree to-"
"We have a saying in my country, Mr Hawksworth, 'that he who seeks to understand has only ears!"
Hawksworth flushed slightly, and nodded for Hunshai to continue.
"It seems also that, as well as Mr Jennings, the Prime Minister himself has some personal knowledge of Professor Weston. In fact, it is only your man Chief Superintendent Shawcross who doesn't appear to have a personal connection. It is my view that this Shawcross merely wishes to curry favour

with your good self by achieving the capture of Professor Weston. It may well be, therefore, that Jennings controlled as he is by Shawcross, along of course with your inside source," he smiled at Hawksworth's surprised expression, "will be useful in not only neutralising Weston, but may well assist in bringing the whole edifice of Riverside to its knees. Of course, if that does not come to pass, then I assure you it will become public knowledge that it was the Prime Minister himself who authorised this pairing, and directly against your express wishes, yes?"
"I see Mr Hunshai, and I agree of course. But, it is still difficult for me that Shawcross will be given such leeway, as my subordinate, you understand?"
"We have looked at your new Chief Inspector, and his only motive appears to be ambition. He has no connection otherwise, and I'm sure you will agree that those who are ambitious are always useful assets to men such as ourselves?"
Hawksworth smiled warmly now at Hunshai's description of his standing, "What would you have me do Mr Hunshai," he said, carefully pronouncing the name correctly.
"Why, just what you are doing Chief Commissioner. Our plans though somewhat delayed, remain sound. When the time is right, we will inform you and you may then act with your renowned ruthless efficiency by carrying out our mutual aims."
"Mablethorpe won't know what hits him, Ambassador; I can assure you there will be no mistakes."
"Good. His removal will be the first real test of your leadership of New Britannia."
Hunshai started to get up, then stopped as Hawksworth started to speak. "What about the woman, Houghton?"
For the first time Hunshai smiled, "Ah yes! I had forgotten about that. Do not concern yourself with Ms Houghton. Her part in this little story is concluded!"

*

Later in the car Hunshai could feel Zhi watching him in the rear view mirror of their Range Rover. The car like the support Audi behind them was armoured and unmarked.
"What ails you, little brother?" he asked using the familiar, as always when he was alone with his most loyal and trusted friend.
"I don't know how you put up with that fat pig; his manners are appalling, even for a gweilo!"
Hunshai laughed out loud as only Zhi could make him, "Not every foreigner is a devil little brother- though in this case you may be right!"
"Then why trust him, why offer him so much?"
"Whatever is given can be taken back, Zhi, eh? Yes, for a brief moment we give this devil, this gweilo great power, but it is only a temporary gift, and I

will make sure it is you little brother who restores it back to us when the time is right. Now be quiet so I can sleep for a while."
Zhi turned off the car's rear reading lights, and dropped his speed down to a steady fifty six miles an hour, contented now in knowing that at some stage the fat gweilo who'd insulted his family's lineage would be properly accounted for.

Chapter Fifteen

Jo sat on the balcony of her second floor apartment which overlooked the canal side wharves whose great cranes stood rusting from their years of idleness. When she had borrowed the deposit from her father to buy the place, it had been on the basis that it was a sound investment. Only five years ago, Riverside had been seen as potentially the next buzzing thing. The plan was to link to the wealthy new waterside developments which were just five miles further up the ship canal. They themselves already adjoined 'billionaire's row' which was another five miles further downstream. The price had been good, given the projected growth in property values. If everything had gone as planned, it would have been the springboard to buying what she really wanted which was a place just like the one she grew up in. Though only a kid, she had loved the tiny little cottage which was surrounded by fields, even though it was only a few miles from where she now sat. Her parents' divorce was hard enough on her but when she and her father moved out of the house she loved to a modern apartment, it had felt like her childhood ended overnight. She went back once a few years ago, but all the fields and the row of little cottages had been replaced by a large retail park. She already knew Riverside before they moved here as it was where she went to school and hung out, as the majority of her friends had lived there. So she took the plunge and bought the flat about three months before everything went pear-shaped, and all the rioting started which immediately scared off the money people. For a long time she had almost given up hope of ever climbing out of the negative equity that the plummeting property prices had plunged her into and, when they declared the estate a Zone 1 area she gave up completely. She wasn't alone, of course. At the same time she was sinking her hard earned money into buying the place- dozens of others, the artisans, musicians artists and writers, or collectively 'the bohemians, ('boho's as the locals still called them)- had bought into the same bullshit. For Jo, the boho's setting up shop in Riverside had been the thing that finally convinced her that it would be a good investment to buy the apartment. Their presence should have led to Riverside developing into a thriving artistic community full of café bars and bistros.

She looked up as a police helicopter thundered across the canal, and could see clearly the gantry mounted camera spying on them all. For the first week, it had freaked her out every time it thundered overhead, rattling windows and whipping up little whirlpools of dust and litter. Nowadays she would either wave at them or give them the finger, depending on her mood. Sometimes, like now when she had her mind on other things, she didn't do either.

She smoothed her hand across the large hide bound diary on the table in front of her. Sunny had given it to her three days ago, saying,
'You keep saying we're making history and someone should write it down? I think that someone should be you; I also think you'd enjoy it!' he'd said placing it on the table in the bistro in front of her, after one of the late night committee meetings.
She had laughed and shook her head, 'No way Jose'. I am way too busy'
And it was true she was busy, in fact she thought she'd never been as busy as she was now. Organising resource distribution alone was nearly a full time and certainly a tiring job. She was also on a dozen sub committees that had sprung up, covering everything from kid's schooling to ideas of self sustainability. Still, although she wouldn't tell him so, Sunny had been right; the more she'd thought about it, the more she felt she would actually enjoy writing down what was happening. It wouldn't be a historical record though, as Sunny had suggested, simply a diary of her thoughts and her impressions of what was happening to them all. She'd decided it might be cathartic, and hopefully would bring some sense of order to the chaos of what was going on all round her. She also hoped it might give her the necessary distance from events in a way that could stop them overwhelming her.
She stroked the suede cover, liking the way it was soft almost silky, but at the same time tough and durable, just like me she thought, and laughed aloud. It was big was more than A4, A3 maybe? She didn't know, but anyway it was big and very expensive maybe even handmade. Not just the cover but even the paper inside had a richness she had never seen. One thing for sure though, Sunny had not paid for it. It would be yet one more item that had been 'liberated' as they all now described what, if she was honest, was basically theft. She still couldn't figure out who would have had such an expensive luxury item here on the estate though. The first pristine page stared at her as she opened the cover, daring her as it had been since Sunny gave it to her, to begin. She wasn't a writer and had been crap at composition in school; and her University work was, according to the

description of one particularly delightful female Professor, 'solid but unimaginative'. Still, if she was going to do it, she was going to do it. Nobody will ever read it anyway, she told herself. She looked across the hundred metres or so to the canal's opposite bank, at the armoured police vehicles which toured constantly up and down and began to write.

Friday 8th June.
It has been exactly six weeks and four days since 'D Day', as we call it around here. It has been tragic and scary, funny and frightening, sad and frantic and, well, every other adjective I can think of. That's how it's been! It's also been, as bizarre as this sounds given everything that's happened, uplifting and rewarding! Anyway, what's happened? I don't think I'll use this diary to write everything down about the cops and the government, most of that stuff is on the net anyway so, if you want to know that stuff, help yourself. Since they realised we really did have the virus, the 6/707 to give it its proper title, the authorities have backed right off. We are still locked inside the estate as tight as a drum, but as part of the 'truce', they have agreed to keep the essential utilities on; so electric, heat and water is all OK. Similarly, we managed to get them to agree certain provisions, mostly perishable foodstuffs etc. They also offered to set up a patient's clinic twice a week where people with specific issues, like the half dozen or so diabetics we have, can get their insulin. We insisted our own struck-off GP, Carl Timms, be in attendance and, though their medicos hate it, they agreed- though they do insist on keeping him in a separate but adjacent room. It's quite funny really. (I know this cos' my Dad's one of the aforementioned diabetics,) but the first thing our people do when they have seen the Government quacks is go into the next room and check the advice and medicines are all OK with Carl, before they actually take them!

What else? Well, the first few meetings with the authorities were terrible of course, especially that first one where everyone was pulling guns on each other. I swear I was convinced we were going to be shot in the back when we walked back across the square. It still wakes me up in the night if I'm honest. Obviously, though, we weren't shot in the back as I wouldn't be here writing about it! I was really proud of us all at that first meeting, even Reeko. The Doc was really pissed at him for bringing the gun but I'm glad he did so, otherwise, well who knows what would have happened? Reeko's been a star; he's funny and sharp as a knife and it doesn't matter whether he's talking to one of the Governments senior hacks we meet once, sometimes twice a week now, or if he's dealing with one of the bombed out drunks (of which there are a fair few) at one of our town meetings, he's constant and 'straight as a die' as my dear Dad is wont to say. He's also usually the one who cuts through all our wrangling and terminal debates with an, 'OK. Enough of the gob wobbling, are we doing it or not?' type of remark. I know the Doc really likes him, we all do I think; most surprising though is how well Reeko and the Sarge get on. They'd never admit it of course as they fire barbs at each other all the time, but there is definitely real respect there, and it's interesting how they both without realising it look at each other to see if they're of a similar mind on any action, before they commit themselves! The rest of the committee- well, there's Professor Michael Deveron who we all still call Doc! Where to begin? Suffice to say he is one cool dude (Reeko speak), he's the one who holds us all together, the one who's shown all of us that if we work together, help each other, then we have a chance of making something special. And the amazing thing is everyone (well, not everyone, but most of us) get it. The people here are really diverse and I suppose, stuck up cow that I am!, I knew and expected the Boho's to switch on quite easily to a communal type society. It's what bohemian type groups do, after all. But the non Boho's- the Mums the unemployed Dockers, the kids who used to spend most of their time stoned behind Frankie's- have really bought into it. It's almost because, for the first time, someone has given them real ownership of their lives, allowed them to make decisions, and made them responsible for the consequences of what they decide... Well there's just a buzz about the place, people are helping each other, Boho's helping Riversiders and vice-versa. Someone printed up some t shirts and badges 'We're all Riversiders now!' and everyone seems to wear them, especially at our big meetings.

That's where Doc impresses me so much; he laid out to our ad hoc committee that first week that, if we encouraged the community and implemented certain things, then the community would respond and he was right. He also doesn't shove his politics down people's throats and if he hears a good idea from someone, whether he likes them or not, whether it's what he would have chosen to do or not, he usually supports it.
Who's left? Oh yes, Sergeant John Mallet, or' Sarge' as most of us call him, or 'Rusty Hammer' as Reeko calls him when there are just the five of us together. It's been hard for the Sarge. We all see the looks of contempt and disdain from the goons at the gate and, even at the meetings with the Government people when (which he rarely does) the Sarge makes a comment, one of them usually makes some snide crack at him. Even our own people are funny around him- surprisingly the Boho's more so than the Riversiders. (Oops, forgot we're all Riversiders now!) Still, one of our first mass votes was to agree we had to have some kind of law and order, and he and Reeko were elected, though Reeko refused to accept the role officially at first, only agreeing to tag along with 'Rusty Hammer to make sure he doesn't revert back to type!' I worry about the Sarge, though. The goons and cops treat him like he's betrayed everything he was supposed to stand for, and I think part of him believes that he has, even though the opposite is true. Katy summed it up for all of the committee the other night when she told him she had never been as proud of someone in her life as the day he stood with us. She had given him a big sloppy kiss on the cheek and we had all laughed at how he had blushed as red as a beetroot. But he was pleased, I could tell. Katy is probably the person I'm closest to. Reeko once said her'tits were so big because she had such a big heart,' Fortunately for him, she took it as it was meant!

She winds me up a lot about Sunny, of course, and I know she's right. We should get it together if not now, when? But, that whole alcoholic baggage freaks me out. Mum was an alcoholic of course, and I know that's at the root of my fears. Anyway, we'll see! He's a good man and funny, although I can see why they called him Sunny as a joke, given how dour he always seems, or at least if you don't get to look behind his shop window!

Anyway, that's our happy band, except of course for our newest recruit.
It was inevitable I suppose, given he was the one who brought the weapon, that he would have to go on to the committee; and Danny was all too eager to step down and let Professor Dominic Weston take his place. Well, anyway, the Doc likes him, Sunny too which really surprised me! Me and Reeko though, we don't like him, not one bit. We talked about it not long ago and agreed. We don't trust his smiling bonhomie, the whole hale fellow well met routine. There's just something about him or, as Reeko put it, 'he's a fucking weirdo!' and I guess I agree, though if you asked me to spell out why I think so, I couldn't.

15th June
Things are going surprisingly well!
We now have a school for the little kids (all twenty of them) and a bunch of people have started repairing the old bust up playground.
We've also started work on the old allotment site and even planted a few crops. At first people said it was a crazy thing to do, plant vegetables and stuff, as if we are going to be here forever, but we are doing it anyway.
In fact about half the things we are doing don't make sense, unless you're someone who believes we are going to be allowed to stay here! I know that a large part of it is just PR for the outside world- Doc explained that at the outset. We have to show the outside world that we are ordinary industrious people just trying to survive against the odds. Planting the crops, the school, cleaning up the square and whatnot are all part of the campaign to show we are good people, not some terrorist cell. Yet, everywhere we clear up or every piece of land we plant, you can see how people get off on those things. You can see people are actually proud of making a difference. We have lost quite a few more people of course. The government requested that they be allowed to make weekly representations to everyone in order, as they said 'to ensure people weren't being held against their will'. And a few have listened and chosen to leave for the new towns. I don't blame them. Underneath everything good we are doing everyone is still frightened.

Both sides agreed after the first meeting that we wouldn't give any more public statements as part of the stand-off situation, but they still manage to slip the odd propaganda piece out. Pictures of happy and relieved people leaving for a new life with their fat relocation cheques in hand etc. We do the same of course with pictures of the new school and the cleaned up allotments mysteriously appearing on the news nets. Neither side mentions the real deal of course- the weapon- and to be honest I'm not even sure who's most scared of news of it getting out, us or them!

21st June
We had a bad issue crop up last night. Caitlin, Sally Smith's sixteen year old daughter, was drugged up and assaulted by three pigs in Renshaw Street Park. They denied it of

course but the Sarge says there isn't any doubt that they did it. Physically, she isn't too bad, a few cuts and scrapes but, inside, in her head she's broken, for how long I don't know. The fact of the rape is bad enough, but the reaction of some of the 'free citizenry' was frightening in its ferocity. A large group wanted to hang them from the trees they had raped her under and probably would have done if the Sarge hadn't pre-empted them. He has them locked up in the back of what was the old Nat West bank, and under constant guard. It hasn't been a bank for years of course, in fact it's a loan shark's office (or it was up until D Day) when they had been one of the first groups to flee! Anyway, the old bank vault is still there and the Sarge and Reeko just chained up the doors with the three scumbags inside. One thing is clear- we aren't geared up for this sort of thing, it's too soon and it's too heavy. There is a town meeting tonight and we have to decide what to do. I'm really afraid that this could split the community wide open; Christ it's already split the committee!

It's funny (not ha ha funny). the Sarge told us that law and order were going to be a problem right from the outset and that we should consider what systems we were going to operate to. I confess I was with the majority and wearing my full rose coloured membership glasses at the time. But I guess you just don't think in this day and age that there are people still like that, especially not here and now, when we have all this other shit to deal with. Well the Sarge was right and now tonight will probably shape for good or bad what sort of people we are going to be.

The other big concern is that we're pretty certain the government has a source inside the estate itself. They know too much about what we are doing, and I don't mean just general stuff like the kid's school and the planting of crops. They could get that from the helicopters and surveillance cameras. Well to be honest it's all over the net a lot of what we are doing. The real concern is that they know stuff that we have only spoken about on the committee, not that they have said so directly, but a couple of times they have boxed us off or pre-empted us when we were due to raise something. So it's pretty obvious really. A few days ago we had arranged for a camera crew from a German news channel to be smuggled in via one of the delivery trucks. Only us six knew about it, but the police were waiting for them in the exact location of the pick-up point. I talked to Sunny about it last night. I said it had to be Weston but he said that couldn't be right because, a couple of other times it has happened, and he wasn't then part of the six. Sunny thinks it's just careless talk, one of us confiding in someone else and he might be right, but I'm not convinced. In two days time we are having our first 'Grand Ball'; it was the Sarge's idea, he said we needed to pull people together socially and not just for meetings. That was before Caitlin of course... but we discussed it last night and decided if we cancelled the ball, it would probably do more harm than good, though I suppose that depends on how tonight goes!

*

The meeting hall was rammed to the rafters, the atmosphere tense and unlike anything they had witnessed before. The agreed plan that they should have an orderly debate and proper consideration of the facts and evidence was looking increasingly shaky. The Doc had, at the opening of the meeting, begun to list the agenda items when someone stood up at the back, wanting to know where the 'accused' were?

'Bring them out!' someone shouted at Doc's attempt to explain the order of business. The shout was quickly picked up, at first only by a few people but, within a few moments, most of the room were banging their feet and chanting, 'Bring em out, bring em out now!' Mallet watched Doc's shoulders slump as he stood at the lectern trying to call for order. Mallet had tried earlier to tell him where this was going to end up, but Doc had insisted that they had to try a reasoned approach, as that was the only way they could have a calm debate. Doc turned now and looked at him. Mallet kept his face neutral as he nodded and stood up, taking no pleasure in being proved right. As he walked past Doc to the lectern, he had no clue what he would say. Part of him, a large part, was with the crowd wanting to string the vicious little trio up from the nearest lamp post. But the other part of him, the part which had kept him all through his career from taking the easy path, was greater. It was the same with the bribes that, when they started, were just 'favours' and 'no harm done'. It would start out with the small things- maybe a free coffee, then perhaps a whole meal, what about a holiday or a car, until eventually the bastards ending up owning you. That part of him knew that, if they were truly to amount to anything, to become more than a minor self-preservation group, then they had to have a better way, however tempting it might be to give in to mob justice.

He placed his hands flat on the lectern and looked slowly from one side of the room to the other. The chants were deafening, the anger had taken hold, and the mob mind set was written clearly on people's faces, many of whom he had known for decades. He tried to imagine what the three scumbags felt as they waited; the crowd didn't know that they were being kept behind the stage with Reeko's deputy 'Bear' guarding them. He hoped that they felt at least as scared and frightened as the young girl they had held down and raped. Some of the people were beginning to wind down as he stood immobile watching them, not attempting to speak. Slowly more and more people were falling quiet, as if recognising the futility of making demands of him. He removed his notebook from the breast pocket of his shirt and laid it open on the lectern, and slowly took out his reading glasses and perched them on the end of his nose. There were only half a dozen at the back now chanting 'bring em out, bring em out'. People started to shush them, telling them to sit down and listen. Only when the whole room had quieted did Mallet attempt to speak, his voice carrying clearly to the back of the room, the microphone he had forgotten to switch back on unnecessary.

“The three suspects, Carlson, Jones and Clarke, have this morning confessed to the drugging and forcible rape of Caitlin Smith. They did so without coercion and in front of three independent witnesses.”

The room erupted into a buzz of conversation. At the back someone shouted, “Then why are we waiting? let’s hang the fuckers!” which was greeted by a great cheer around large parts of the hall. The chants started up again, ‘bring em out, bring em out’.

Mallet closed the pad and pocketed his reading glasses, deciding that what he had written earlier about appropriate sentencing and legal precedence would do nothing in this situation. That was something else he had told Doc earlier when he’d asked him to prepare notes. What should he say to them now, these people who wanted justice, who were entitled to justice if they were really going to be any kind of a real community? He waited for them to quieten down again, which didn’t take nearly as long this time, before he began speaking.

“There is anger in this room,” he began, “There is anger that a young girl, one of our own has been hurt this way. That anger is in all of us,” he gestured with his hand toward the dais and back toward the crowd. “All of us.” He saw people nodding, waiting for him to go on. “As well as anger though, there is power here tonight, an ultimate power that very few of us have ever held in our hands before. This ultimate power to give life or to take life is in all of our hands. Remember when Doc told us all those weeks ago that we, all of us here, could decide our futures from now on. That sounded great didn’t it? -when we were talking about a future, for however long or short it might be, where we mattered, a future where we got to decide for ourselves who and what we could be, what we wanted to be? And you know every single decision that we have taken since that day has made us stronger. It’s shown even an old cynic like me, that if you allow people to choose for themselves, if you give people the power to shape their lives, they will do it better than any government could ever do; it makes us free right?”

A few shouts of ‘right’, lots of nods of agreement as people waited to hear the rest.

“Two nights ago, a few of us had the right to choose for ourselves what we did about the three men whose futures we will all decide here tonight,” he paused and unclipped his revolver from its belt, held it up for everyone to see and pointed it at the side of his temple. A murmur ran through the hall. ‘I could have chosen to hold this gun to each of their heads and pulled the trigger!” He pulled it now, the dry loud click of an empty chamber made everybody jump. He held the gun back up in front of them, “I wanted to do that, I wanted to see their brains and blood and fragments of bone spatter everywhere. And I had the power, right? This gun gave me that power, and you elected me, you gave me the power to protect you, so what stopped

me?" He put the gun back in its holster, "It's strange but what actually stopped me was the same anger that you all feel tonight, it called to me in such a way that I hungered to pull this trigger. And it wasn't for young Caitlin that I wanted to do it, and it certainly wasn't for any of you. No, I wanted to do it for me. It would have made me feel good, righteous even-"
"Then you should have done!" someone shouted from the back of the room, someone else shouted, "Do it now," and again "Do it now" as they tried to get another chant going. Matt Johnson stood up and shouted towards the hecklers, "For Chrissakes why don't you shut up and listen to the man?" There was a smattering of applause.
"That's OK, Matt, I understand that people want their say on this." He smiled briefly at Johnson, showing his appreciation for the support. "There is a lot for you to decide tonight. Sure there is the biggie, the main question of kill them or don't kill them, or maybe you prefer the term execution? Well, anyway, I guess we can decide what we call it afterwards. By the way you people at the back, there are some seats down at the front here if you want to save yourselves from having to shout? No? Didn't think so!" He stopped and took a sip of the water that Doc had left on the rostrum, then coughed and spluttered it back out in a big spray that reached the front seats, as he realised it was nine parts gin. There was a burst of laughter from the room as most people guessed what had happened. Reeko came over with a bottle of water, laughing uproariously. Mallet tried to give him a mean stare, but his eyes and throat were still stinging too much so he settled for a drink of the water- and then stared over at Doc who shrugged sheepishly, looking down at his feet, which brought another gale of laughter from the room.

Mallet looked around the room at the people, some still laughing, most smiling, and told himself again that these were good people, or most of them at least. They deserved the truth. "I know that passions are high and that you are looking to do the right thing, we all are-"
"Then stop the waffle and bring them out here!"
This time Mallet saw who it was- Gobby George as Jo called him. More concerning, he remembered that he had seen Gobby George along with a few others on several occasions in Dominic Weston's company over the last few days. The Professor is getting quite a little entourage he suddenly realised, annoyed with himself for not picking up on it earlier.
"George says I am waffling. I know some of you agree with him; I suspect some of you also think that this committee is going to try and argue you out of what you want to do? Well, we're not! If you decide to kill these men, there is no one up here who will try and stop you, including me. Oh, we've talked about it believe me, though the truth is we don't even agree on this amongst ourselves. Some of us want to see them killed, some of us don't.

All of us want them punished, all of us want them to pay a price, and I guess that's at least one thing everybody in this room does agree on."
A rumble of affirmation greeted this last.
"We can decide how and what that price is when it goes to the vote, but that won't come from people shouting anyone else down, or from a show of hands. Everyone will walk down to the front here and sign their name for or against-"
"That's not how it's done!" Gobby George shouted, not hiding now he'd been named, "How someone votes should be secret!"
Mallet shook his head, "That's the old way. That's the way it was done before, where you vote for something without consequence. If this is to be done, it will be done openly and everyone will be party to the decision, and everyone will be responsible." He paused and took a breath, and did something he had watched Doc do often over the last few weeks. Raising his voice, he called the question and gave them the answer. "Is that agreed? Say aye!"
A roar of 'Aye!' filled the room and he nodded, thinking wow that was easy, as he watched George and his small band of merry men sit back down, all with their arms uniformly folded across their chests in silent protest.
"OK, thank you. There are a few other things we have to decide before we can take the vote as well, and they are matters of simple logistics." He started to count them off on the fingers of his right hand in a calm and matter of fact tone. "First, if we decide on the death penalty how do we do it, kill them I mean? I think there are only two realistic options; First, a firing squad. We have a few revolvers and I think that as long as the shooters, say four of you, are close enough, let's say two metres, then that should be OK- though we will have to find some way of restraining their heads against the wall as otherwise the kill won't be clean, and I don't think any of us want that! The second option has already been mentioned, hanging. Though I think if we do that, it can't be on a tree limb or a lamp post, as it could take them half an hour or more to die. No, we would have to build some kind of scaffold, and it would need a trap door- we can get the specs off the net- but we definitely need a scaffold and trapdoor as that would make sure their spinal cord is jerked and crushed onto the knot of the rope, as it's the knot that actually breaks the neck of course." As he said this, he broke an imaginary neck in the curled fists of his two hands, and made a cracking sound with his mouth that echoed in the silent hall. "Thirdly," He paused as an audible groan ran through the room before carrying on, "Thirdly, we need to decide what to do with the corpses after we cut them down-"
A man in the second row suddenly stood up and ran from the room, holding his hand over his mouth. People could hear clearly as he vomited in the corridor outside. Mallet never missed a beat.

"Now, this is important, obviously we don't have a crematorium here in Riverside, and I guess it wouldn't look so good to the outside cameras if we're seen burning bodies in the square, right. So we need to think about a suitable burial site! Finally, we will need to elect a number of people for either the firing squad or to operate the hanging scaffold, as well as a burial team. Now, any questions?" He looked around the room slowly taking in their faces. A lot of people avoided eye contact with him as they looked down at their feet or off to the side. 'Not so easy now you might be the one who's doing it,' he thought but didn't say.

A woman in the third row back stood up, "The chair recognises Susan Doyle," Mallet said.
"Sergeant, you said we have to choose whether to...execute them or not, and I understand that. But what do we do with them if we don't do it, execute them I mean? Sorry, it's a stupid question I know..."she said colouring bright red then sitting down.
"No, Susan, it isn't stupid; in fact it's one of the things the committee has asked itself, and to be honest has been unable to come up with an answer. We don't have a prison, or anything remotely suitable for one. We also don't have guards who can work twenty four hours a day and, if we locked them up, there are a whole raft of other problems- food, and clothing, not to mention for how long?"

There were a few hands starting to go up now that the first person to speak hadn't been ridiculed. Most questions required a simple yes or no. There were a lot of anti-capital punishment speeches mostly from the Boho's which he received without making any comment. When anyone said something that he thought was just stupid or dangerous or even just particularly unhelpful, he heard himself saying, 'Hmm interesting!' Just like my dear old dad would do he thought, and swore he could almost feel the greasy fingers of political management trying to get a grasp on him. Gobby George stood up, and he recognised him before others who had had their hands up longer.
"We can talk all night about this and that, and about prisons which we don't have. But that's all just stalling or gob wobbling; you said they are guilty, you said that they've confessed. So I say we cut this short and do them, and, if you want someone to pull the trigger, then I volunteer." He sat down with a few whoops from his comrades.
Mallet smiled, "Thanks for that George. You are a man of conviction, everyone here knows that!"
George nodded, oblivious of the snigger that ran around the room.
"We have then one volunteer, and we will need a few more. However before anyone else rushes forward, I want to sound a note of caution. If we

vote to kill these three, then that will of course be a Riverside decision, and in that sense it will make it lawful within our community. Of course as yet we have very few laws and no trial system, but if we here tonight decide that's what we will do, then that is that. Outside of Riverside of course, it won't be seen that way. Outside, it will be classed as murder by the individuals carrying out the act, an unlawful killing in terms of UK law. Those of you who don't directly take part in the killing of the three men, and that will mean all of us, will still be classed as being accessories to murder-"
The room erupted back into pandemonium, as people stood up and started shouting at Mallet and at each other. This was the other prediction he had made last night when they had talked it through and what would happen. This rape would tear them apart, whatever they decided. The Riverside Revolution, as the Free Press were calling it, would be effectively over, fallen at its first real hurdle of self governance. He felt an overwhelming sadness start to fill him up as he realised that, without noticing exactly when, he had started to believe that they might actually make something good here. After tonight though it would be over, because they would do it, of course they would. He knew that, with passions running so high, and in their moral outrage and righteous indignation, they would take the three of them out and shoot them; they would not want to wait and build a scaffold.

He also knew that when that happened though, he hadn't told the others he would be done. Some of them, probably most people in the room in truth, would be surprised when they saw him later voting against the execution. But he would vote against it, he had always opposed capital punishment and voted against it when the UK reintroduced it five years ago. He looked across at Jo, about to tell her to bring the voting ledger forward so they could begin the inevitable. Her eyes were wide as she looked at him. He thought at first that she was feeling the same as him as she had been one of the three who had argued on his side, but she was nodding at something else, directing him to look to his left at the corner of the dais. He turned back and saw Sally Smith, Caitlin's mother, standing with her hand raised wanting to speak. His heart sank even further but, if anyone had the right to demand the men's execution, then it was surely her. He started to call for order, but other people had noticed her at the same time and the room was rapidly growing quiet. When he invited her to speak there was complete silence.

"The chair recognises Sally Smith and, Sally, why don't you come up here so everyone can hear what you have to say?" He walked across and took her trembling hand, helping her up. She smiled at him then walked to the lectern, whilst he stayed at the side waiting for her to speak and for her to

pronounce sentence.
She stared out at them all seeing only blank faces and didn't know how to begin, but then she saw someone she knew, her neighbour and friend Alice Tompkins, who smiled at her; and then she saw Jane and Allan from the next street down and she remembered who they were- just people like her, friends, and neighbours. She took a breath and started to speak, her voice quiet but steady, not shaky as she feared it was going to be. She guessed that was because she was speaking for Caitlin now.

"Caitlin wanted to come here tonight. She wanted to speak to you herself, but Doc Timms says she needs to stay in bed at least for a few more days to... heal. She knows what's happening here tonight though. John, that is Sergeant Mallet, came to see us, to tell us...he's been very kind, everyone has." She looked over at Mallet who nodded at her, his arms folded across his chest to hide his embarrassment.
"Anyway, I've heard what's been said by everybody, I was sat out the back, and I hoped I wouldn't have to speak but I think it's important that you should hear what Caitlin wants, if that's OK?"
The whole room nodded almost in unison. That was OK they were telling her, and that made her feel just a little better.
"Those of you who are parents, well I guess even those who aren't will know how I feel about... about what's happened to my little girl..." her voice caught on the last word and she almost couldn't go on; but she gripped the lectern firmly, steadying herself, unconscious of the tears that glistened on her eyelashes readying to spill, "They hurt her, those bastards, they hurt my little Caitlin, they took her and they held her down and raped her, and... they laughed while they were doing it! That's what she told me, 'they laughed while they hurt me, Mum'. "
She shook her head and wiped her eyes with the back of her hand. "I want you to understand how I feel about these... these three...these vermin. They're not men, they don't deserve to be called men; they are vermin and I would put them down like vermin. I would put them down and I'd smile while I did it!" She closed her eyes and bowed her head, the shuddering sigh she let out audible around the hushed room. She looked up at them, a small smile on her tear-stained face. "But that's what happens, isn't it? With people like them I mean, they drag us all down to their level, and then what are we? You know these last weeks, for me and Caitlin they have been the greatest we have ever had. We mattered, if that makes sense, we were making a difference. I mean, Christ, I've been teaching in the school, me a teacher, who'd have thought that was possible? And Caitlin, she's been working with Doc Timms in the clinic and she likes it, is good at it. We talked about it last night, about all of it, and that's why I'm here to speak for her because she asked me to. She doesn't want you to kill these men." A

surprised murmur ran around the room. "She doesn't want you to do it in her name and, God help me, neither do I. They would win you see? That's what she told me last night, and she's right. All those people outside who just think we are subversives, terrorists, those people who think we are scum, that we can't make anything good of ourselves... if we do this, then we will be doing exactly what they expect of us, do you see that? We would be doing exactly what they expect us to do."

A lot of people were nodding, others just looking blank, as she went on, "Caitlin wants them gone. She wants them out of our lives, she wants them out of Riverside, she doesn't ever want to see them again, and neither do I."

Mallet was watching the crowd as they listened; he could see people were puzzling out what that would mean. Did the three of them just get to walk out scot free? But Sally hadn't finished.
"I know some of you won't like that idea, the idea that these men will just walk out of here. But, and this is me speaking, by myself you understand, not for Caitlin, I want more than that and if you want to avenge my daughter then this is," she paused remembering how Doc said it, "then this is what I propose."

*

In the end it was the women who took charge of it. Sunny and Doc sat on a graffiti sprayed bench about twenty feet away, observing. It seemed that everyone left in the estate was lined up at various points across three sides of the square. The police helicopter had been buzzing overhead all morning filming the whole thing.
"You ever seen anything like this before?" Doc asked as he sat cross legged smoking, as if they were watching street theatre from a metropolitan café.
Sunny stretched and rubbed his neck, "Not exactly like this but, when I was in Africa, I once saw three men given a necklace." He could see Doc didn't understand. "It's where they put a tyre around a man's head, fill it with diesel and set it alight."
"That would be worse then!"
Sunny nodded, closing his eyes for a moment, "Oh yeah, much worse."
The three rapists had been tied to the same lamppost by their wrists and ankles so they faced outwards. Sunny and Doc watched as half a dozen women including Sally and, to the surprise of both of them, Jo, were methodically cutting away the three men's clothing with pinking shears. One of the men, Clarke, had begun cursing and spitting at Jo. She went right up to his face, her words loud enough to reach Doc and Sunny on the bench.
"Do that again, in fact speak again, and I'll cut off more than your pants."
Clarke started to retort, but must have seen something in her face as he fell

quiet, his head falling down onto his now naked chest.
"This quaint custom, it's from Ireland before they reunified, right?" Sunny asked.
"No, they were tarring and feathering people centuries before that; in fact the Irish adopted it from the British soldiers who used to tar and feather the Irish rebels back in the 1700s."
Sunny looked at him, "I don't know how you remember all this stuff, Doc. You're like a walking encyclopaedia!"
Doc shrugged, not looking at him, "How come you remember all the lyrics and chords to hundreds of songs? It's just what we do! By the way, it's not actually tar in the modern sense of the word," he went on, as they watched the women start to roughly chop the hair off the three men, who were by now looking completely cowed, one of them starting to sob softly. "It's actually pine tar from the trees. Sally Caitlin's mother looked it up and then located some from the old municipal garden stores."
"Tar is just tar, right?"
"No, not really- if they used tar like the bitumen used for roads, they would be burned so badly we may as well have just hung them in the first place; but it's still not going to be pleasant!"
"They were facing much worse."
"Yes, they were. You surprised me the other night, Sunny. I wouldn't ever have had you down as pro capital punishment?" Doc said turning to look at him.
Sunny continued to stare fixedly at the three men as Sally, standing on a pair of step ladders, began to pour the hot tar over the three men's heads. All three of them were starting to moan now and were doing a macabre jittering dance, at least as much as their bindings allowed them to.
"I guess that's where we're different, Doc. You have the belief that everyone is basically good or, if they're not that they can be turned around or reformed in some way."
"And that's wrong?"
"I think it is, yeah! I know there are people who have bad breaks, poor upbringings, difficult circumstances or whatever. And I know that many of them can be helped to see a better way- we've even seen the evidence of that whilst we've been here. And I suppose I even fall in that category myself, but what you don't get, Doc, and with respect people like you never do-"
"People like me!"
"Yes, people like you who grew up in a safe world, a world of law and order and social rules, where people don't see casual violence as the norm... Well, just let's say I think there are good people and bad people, and most of us fall somewhere in between. We try to do the right thing even if we don't manage it a lot of the time. But these three," he said, gesturing dismissively

at the men just as the feathers were being poured out of the pillow cases and sticking to the rapidly setting tar. Their eyes were white staring circles as they had instinctively squeezed them shut as the tar was being poured. "These three are just bad, and people like them...well, I just think they are getting off lightly!"
They turned to watch the end of the process, both aware that there was suddenly a distance between them which neither liked, but which neither was willing to try and bridge.

Sally was fastening three white placards around the necks of the men, the words 'Child Rapist' in dripping red painted letters. She stood back for a moment, her hands on her hips as though admiring her work, then turned and nodded at Mallet who had been standing to one side. He was in his dress uniform, the line of medals a splash of colour against his black uniform. He walked across the small space and stood in front of the three men, who had been untied from the lamppost, but were still had their hands tied behind their backs. The three of them were shivering and moaning uncontrollably. Mallet's voice rang out across the square as he began to read from the front page of a sheaf of documents contained in a clear plastic A4 folder.
"John Carlson, Hugh Jones, and Noel Clarke, you have been found guilty of the brutal assault and rape of Caitlin Smith by a jury of your peers. The sentence carried out here today is in accordance with the express wishes of the citizens of the Riverside Estate. The sentence is that you be tarred and feathered, and that you then be driven out from this community. The full list of charges, the physical evidence, and the recordings and papers of your signed confessions, as well as the trial documents, are contained in this folder and will be posted online." He handed the document case to Jo, who hung it around Noel Clarke's neck so it dangled halfway down his back.
Mallet looked across the square at the gates and silvered windows, knowing full well that outside they were watching and recording every action, every word. "Let those outside do with you what they will. You are hereby banished, now be gone."

For a moment the three men stood jittering as if rooted to the spot. Sally and two other women walked behind them holding thin three foot canes, and began to drive them across the square. The sound of the canes striking the men on their calves and tar covered behinds was quickly masked by their wails and screams. In the end the three of them began to half jog half run as they tried to outpace their tormentors, before finally passing over the yellow painted lines in front of the gates.
"What happens if they don't let them out?" Sunny said, holding his hand above his eyes against the watery sunlight which was reflecting from the

barred windows of the security cabins.
"They will.' Doc said and, almost as if they had heard him, the gates swung open and the men ran wailing into the arms of a half dozen SSC guards, who bundled them roughly out of sight.

Chapter Sixteen

Nasri Jaheel did her slow breathing exercise, the one she always used to try and stop the nerves, which appeared without fail whenever she was going to broadcast live from the Free Press main studio, or FPS as they all called it. It was weird because, when she was on the road, pieces to camera, whether live or not, didn't faze her, but she behaved like a cub reporter whenever she came in to this glass and chrome monolith. She watched Seamus O'Donnell as he chatted to the floor manager about some swanky Paris restaurant that they both frequented. Apart from a perfunctory nod when she'd arrived and sat down, he'd ignored her as usual. Wherever she went, people would talk to her about Seamus O'Donnell- 'good old Seamus' they always called him. The man had been with Free Press News for almost five years now, which was a lifetime in this business. When FPN had launched its multi-national news service, they had based themselves in Paris and quickly recruited some 'star names' from the international news circuit. O'Donnell had been at his peak when he had abandoned the News Corp stable and moved across to FPN, pocketing a rumoured five million just for signing up. The public loved his warm twinkling eyes and his soft Irish brogue, and of course his droll 'man in the street' comments on topics of the day. 'Good old Seamus, he's one of us that one', they always told her, and she would always give them her brightest smile as she agreed with whoever said it. And though she hated to admit it, he had brought a lot of viewers with him so was a big part of why FPN had become one of the top three TV news providers in the world. She looked at the studio clock- thirty seconds- and straightened her notes for the fifth time, rehearsing again her opening comments to O'Donnell's first question. The script had been agreed in advance by their production assistants, and would be about Mablethorpe's comments this morning on Riverside, which would lead them nicely into the bulk of her report.

The floor manager started his five second hand count, holding each digit in front of them as they went live to the more than 100 million world citizens

who tuned into FPN daily.
"Good evening folks, and welcome to Free Press News coming to you live from our Paris headquarters. Tonight we have a lot of big breaking stories to bring you, with some of our top correspondents but before any of that, we have 'our Nazzy' in the studio to discuss what people are now calling the 'Riverside revolution'." O'Donnell turned toward her smiling warmly, his eyes twinkling as he spoke, "So Nasri, what's going on over there in the UK? I see the Riverside revolutionaries have taken to some ancient forms of punishment today?"
She wanted to punch him not just for the intro, but for going off script. He had just thrown her whole report into chaos, and the autocue would now be totally fucking useless! She hesitated for probably half a second, which she knew would look an age to the viewers, before the adrenalin of the live cameras kicked her into motion.
"Well, Seamus they certainly have," she said smiling warmly back at him, then turned to face camera two, hearing in her earpiece as she did so the Producer screaming at her to stay on camera one, so they could keep Seamus in shot. She smiled into camera two and imagined, as she always did when she was live in the studio, that she was talking to her grandfather, who she knew would be sitting in the high-winged chair he had 'liberated' from Oxford University on his retirement. He was the first Pakistani-born Principal of Jesus College, Oxford, a fact he would remind her of often. If she reported to 'Gramps,' and only 'Gramps' she didn't have to think about the faceless millions whose homes she was now inside.

"At two pm UK time, three men were tarred and feathered and hung with placards declaring them to be rapists. The men who are now in the custody of the UK authorities, were forcefully evicted from the Riverside Estate by the remaining residents, who'd decided on this archaic form of punishment. The images which you are about to see, and which are exclusive to FPN, are graphic and contain scenes of nudity." She continued speaking as the images of the men being stripped and tarred and feathered came up on screen. "Despite the scenes you are witnessing, the Prime Ministers Press Spokesman Christopher Jennings said that, 'The prime minister is said to be 'relaxed' about the Riverside experiment and believes that, before too long, the people of Riverside will come to realise the Government remains on their side.' Contrast that, Seamus, with just a few weeks ago when Gregory Mablethorpe called the Riverside residents 'terrorist subversives'. So what's changed?"

The producer called play VT, and Gregory Mablethorpe appeared on the screen being barraged by the international press at his weekly press conference.

Nasri flinched as O'Donnell banged his pudgy hand on the table, "What the fuck are you playing at, girlie?"
She stared back at him, *I could ask you the same, you fat smarmy shit-bag*, she thought but shrugged, "I'm sorry, Seamus, I got confused with the order changing. I thought we had signed off the running order of the piece." She held her hands up in a 'what can I do gesture' knowing that, if he insisted on it, the studio would probably fire her. For a brief moment she considered whether that would be such a bad thing, but she also knew this was her one chance to move into the big leagues and, if she blew it here, she would only be on a downward slide. O'Donnell would make sure of it. She put on her most glum face, the one with the big hurt eyes, "I'm truly sorry, Seamus. You know how I struggle with the whole live studio gig!"
He looked at her as if deciding whether she was taking the piss out of him or was just an idiot. He shook his head deciding she assumed that she was simply what he always described her as to the Producer, 'A dumb fucking cunt!'
By the time the VT ended, his eyes were twinkling as well as ever.

*

"That went well, I thought!" Tony Ferrin FPN's Senior News Director said, as Nasri flopped down in one of the big squishy chairs he had ringed around his office.
She blew out a big sigh, "I know Tony, and I'm sorry but, as I said to Seamus I got conf-"
"Bullshit, Nas. You saw your arse with him, and you knew exactly what you were doing. He's been going ballistic on the phone, says he wants your head!"
She looked over his shoulder at Paris's grimy grey skies.
"Listen to me, Nas... are you listening?"
She looked at him and nodded, trying to stop the tears she could feel pricking at the back of her eyes.
Tony leaned toward her, "I hope you are, because we can't do this again. Jeez, Nasri, you're what- twenty eight?"
"Nine."
"OK, twenty nine. You're a great journalist, Nasri, one of the best I've seen. You have the nose, as we used to say in the old days and, if you can keep that sharp temper and even sharper tongue of yours in check, then you can have a great career. But understand me, Nasri; no matter what I think about it round here, Seamus O'Donnell is the main man, Numero Uno. I was at a board meeting yesterday where the accountants reckoned he brings in an additional 33% in our ratings, which is huge in advertising revenue terms."
"I know that, Tony, and I really am sorry. I'll apologise again to him tonight."

"I think it's probably better if you leave him alone for a few days, OK?"
She nodded, feeling the tears threatening again as she realised Tony wasn't going to sack her...this time!
"OK let's move on. Riverside, where are we? I gather this woman Houghton has disappeared?"
"Yeah it's weird, Carlton was convinced she was the real deal, but neither number she left exists, so..."
"Well, shit happens. Maybe she was genuine or more likely maybe she was just some nut. Anyway what else?
"I told you about the texts?"
Tony nodded, "Have you sourced their origin yet?"
"No, but what's more interesting than that is I've gone through it with a guy I know, and he tells me that it is a really deep encrypted send-"
"In English, Nas!"
"Sorry!' she said laughing, "I forget you still use chalk and slate! Anyway, basically every email or text you or I send has a number of identifying parameters, which means you can identify the sender's location and, if you have access to the right databases, nine times out of ten you can identify the user themselves even if they mask the IP- the address of your computer, that is. So, as you know there are lots of systems for disguising media origin. They range from the freeware stuff, all the way to blue chip company systems like we have here. But the two messages I have had so far are, at least as far as my friend can tell, pretty much untraceable. As I said deep encryption."
"So they could just as easily be coming from an intelligence agency as from Riverside?"
"They could, but my friend doesn't think so. He thinks they are from Fringe Net, because they self delete once opened, and because they only appear on my phone and not on any of my linked devices, which shouldn't be possible!"
"OK, but that isn't news is it? We have always assumed Deveron is hooked in with Fringe Net, given the way that the Riverside lot managed to access the world satellite feeds."
"Yeah, that's true, but get this. My techie friend also says that the level of encryption being used here is like at a core level. He says that the usual anarchist and subversive groups who use Fringe Net wouldn't be allowed within a mile of this level of coding!"

Tony stared into space. Nasri could see his cogs whirring at even a remote possibility that they would be able to crack into Fringe Net and the people behind it. Since its launch ten years ago, it had been impossible to identify how it had been financed or why. When governments across the world had moved almost as one against a free world wide web, they had done so with lightening speed, the leaders of dictatorships joining with the leaders of so called democratic states in common purpose to introduce through the UN the 'WCPO' or World Citizens Protection Order. Almost overnight, tens of thousands of sites worldwide were shut down, with who knew how many of their owners simply disappearing. Within a couple of months, Fringe Net had managed to hijack six satellites and, for now at least, the world of uncontrolled web access was back in business.

Nasri watched Tony shake his head, as he forced himself away from the potential of a Fringe Net breakthrough, to focus back on the immediate, "Alright, so the messages seem to confirm what we suspected- that they have something in Riverside that is stopping the Government from shutting them down?"
Nasri nodded.
"You think it really is a weapon?" he asked, sitting up straighter.
"Maybe, but all my background stuff tells me that that doesn't fit with what we know about Deveron, who's a lifelong peacenik. So I don't think the weapon idea fits with his profile. I think it's more likely that Deveron has some sort of personal hold over Mablethorpe. We know they were at Cambridge together, so maybe it's something from then, but either way it's stopped the authorities in their tracks, even to the point where they are provisioning the rebels inside."
"So why has he contacted you? Assuming of course that the texts are actually from Deveron, then something doesn't fit, especially if he already has Mablethorpe by the short and curlies- sorry!" he said quickly at her grimace. "But I'm right, Nas. There's something that we aren't seeing yet!"
Nasri nodded. She'd had the same thought herself but...
"It could even be MI6 or Hawksworth's bunch leading you into a fall. You know your reports have ruffled a lot of feathers over there!"
She grinned at him.
"I mean it, Nasri. Seamus isn't the only one calling for your head. The British have even threatened to refuse FPN access to future press conferences-"
"They wouldn't dare-"
Tony held his hand up, forestalling her freedom of the press speech, "No, they wouldn't, but that doesn't mean that they won't do everything in their power to discredit us on this issue; and the easiest way to do that it is set us, or rather you, up!"
"I know, I know, and I am being careful, but these communications however light on real detail feel legit, so..."
"I understand that, and I agree you have to follow up on it but Nasri, you need to be careful. We are offending some very powerful people here, including the Chinese. If your friend is right, and Fringe Net is part of

this...well, there are worse things than being discredited!" He looked at her to make sure she was taking him seriously.

*

Four hours later, she let herself into her Kensington flat, picking up on the way in a pile of mail, most of which would be used in the cat litter tray. The place was too expensive now she was no longer sharing with Jorgen. It also felt empty, which was weird given how little of his stuff he had ever kept there. It was almost as if he knew they wouldn't last together so had brought only his clothes, his computer and a couple of 'manly' gadgets. The two bureau desks they had bought at an auction one tipsy afternoon were still side by side in front of the grand Georgian windows. They looked lopsided nowadays, although in truth they always had done. Her own was as usual overflowing with various papers and books or, as Jorgen used to describe it, 'crap!' Jorgen was the neatest man she had ever known, and it was a constant source of irritation for him that she was such a slob domestically. Anyway, she thought, trying to shrug her sudden gloomy mood off it's done now. No more endless arguments about politics and social issues, no more heated debates about whether it was India or Pakistan who had sparked the Middle East war, a war which annihilated nearly a million Israelis and Palestinians. On the downside of course, she was back to her more usual state of celibacy as there was no more of the glorious sex he had introduced her to! Jorgen had awakened her sensuality in a way she had never thought possible, allowing her to kick off all her inhibitions and still feel utterly safe. He had that Scandinavian thing about him that which made the notions of shame and overt modesty she had been raised with simply fade away. Still, he was gone and, apart from the sex and the companionship, she knew it was a good thing. They were just too dissimilar and argued about too many things, and in the end their differences were greater than the things that kept them together. She did miss him though- or maybe it wasn't him she missed. Maybe what she mostly missed was simply the presence of another human being.

She felt the hairs on her arms prickle up as she finally noticed what had been in plain sight since she had first entered the room. The chaos of her desk was largely the same, the usual jumble of papers and folders, but something was different. She didn't know how she knew it, but she did- small things like the folder that she hadn't looked at for weeks which was now on top of something that was current, and the drawers were closed, something she never did. In part she didn't because it was one of Jorgen's bugbears, 'close the fucking drawers,' he'd always say in his most pompous Danish- which she always replied to in Urdu just to irritate him further, knowing he could never be quite sure what she was saying. Her stuff had definitely been moved. Someone had been in the flat and it wasn't Jorgen, though he still had his key. She knew he was in Mogadishu covering the African Security Council, had even seen his live report for CNN whilst she was flying back from Paris. She flinched her shoulders, hunching unconsciously as she heard the rustle of a plastic bag coming from the kitchen. Her fists clenched, the nails digging into her palms as she tried to calm her racing heartbeat from the adrenalin rushing into her bloodstream. She would have to pass the kitchen to leave the flat, and whoever was in there would see her as she tried to leave. She started to slowly back up toward the window directly opposite the dark kitchen doorway, her hand fumbling in her jacket for her mobile phone. She almost screamed as the bag rustled again louder this time, then gasped out loud as she heard a frustrated yowl. Her legs felt like jelly as she shook her head at her own stupidity, most but not all of her fright draining out of her, as she forced herself to walk towards the kitchen, standing slightly back as she leaned forward and switched on the kitchen light.

"Captain, you bad cat. Get off that!" she said, her voice sounding squeaky and too high to her own ears.

The cat looked at her with disdain, and went back to trying to shred the bag containing the cheese crisps he had such a liking for. He yowled again, this time directly at her, and strolled across the worktop to receive his homage. She stroked her hand down his back, running her hand from his head and down his spine, and then from the base of his tail to the top. His purring sounded like a distant riverboat in the quiet apartment. She fed him quickly, and even opened the bag of crisps, scattering a few on the work surface for him. As she did so, she could hear in her head Jorgen's snort of disgust at how she allowed the cat to walk wherever it chose. Towards the end of their relationship, she had even encouraged the cat to do it just to irritate him. Captain rubbed himself around her legs as she made a cup of coffee then, deciding there were no more treats, he left without looking back through the small kitchen window she always left open for him. She went through the other two rooms, switching all the lights on to satisfy herself that whoever had been in the place was really gone, then sat down at her desk and tried to figure out if anything had actually been taken.

Ten minutes later, she was feeling much calmer as she sat with a half eaten micro-waved pizza in one hand, and a glass of cheap red in the other. Jorgen had always told her she had no palate, and it was true. She was as happy with a three litre box of plonk as some arty farty bottle that cost a week's wages. 'Pakistani families aren't big on wine', she had told him once, 'unlike the pickled Danes'. She'd argued with herself over whether she should draw the curtains, or whether she was simply being paranoid, but in the end she had got up and closed them 'just in case' she told herself. She'd also put the security chain on the front door. Tomorrow, before she headed off to Manchester, she would get someone in to change the locks. She felt a sudden chill run through her as she realised that, if they really were watching her, whoever 'they' were, changing the locks would be as good as hoisting a flag telling them she knew they had been inside the flat. She had known from that first anonymous text that she was on the verge of a big story. It might even be the biggest story of her career, but now she also knew the stakes were far higher than she had realised. Tony was right. The people she was now investigating were not only powerful, but almost certainly dangerous. Tony was a good boss and she trusted him, yet she still hadn't told him about the last message. Why not tell him, she thought again, looking at her watch. Because you won't let me go inside, Tony, and that is where the real story is! She could almost hear his lecture on acceptable and unacceptable risk. She understood why, of course they all did. He had lost a reporter Freddie, in Syria, Not long after FPN had got started. Freddie was beheaded by a Syrian fundamentalist group who said they would execute any 'Zionist media dogs whose presence polluted the purity of the Islamic State'. That Freddie Jong was a Muslim himself didn't of course feature in their judgement of him. Tony intellectually knew he wasn't at fault, but he had never forgiven himself and, if he could avoid his reporters being put at risk, he did so with a fervour. On the reverse side, that meant that quite often his reporters didn't tell him if they were getting into potentially hairy situations.

*

The next morning she phoned Dave from the car and asked him to take the broadcasting unit back down to Riverside. She could tell he wasn't happy. They'd already spent weeks down there, and still couldn't get within a half mile of the actual estate.

"Look, kiddo. If you want us there, we'll be there but...well, unless you have something that you aren't telling us, is there any point? I mean, we have a static feed set up already, so if anything happens..." he trailed off, and she could hear his kids screaming in the background as Alice was trying to get them ready for school.

She had worked with Dave her cameraman ever since she had joined FPN. He and Ian were almost like family now, the big brothers she had always wished for as an only child. She didn't like keeping them out of the loop on this but, if her fears were right, she wouldn't risk discussing the invite from Deveron to go into Riverside on the phone. She had even debated whether it might be better if she went in alone, as she didn't want to put either of them at risk. She shook her head, smiling to herself. Now I'm beginning to think like Tony, she thought.

She made her voice sound light, "You know me, Dave; always looking for glory! Anyway, you know that Al Jazeera nearly got a camera crew inside. Just imagine if we pulled it off and could actually get in and do a live piece with Deveron?'

"It's not gonna happen, kiddo. The place is locked down like a drum! "

"I know, I know, but give me some wiggle room, ok? My gut tells me something will come up."

Dave sighed, then shouted, "I'm on the phone here!" making her wince and pull the phone from her ear. The kids fell quiet for all of thirty seconds then started up again louder than ever.

"What time do you want us, Nas?"

"Tomorrow afternoon will do. I'm going to go and see Gramps on the way down. Oh and can you ask Ian to sort out the accommodation?"

"Err, I think not, or we'll end up in another flea pit. I'll do it myself and text you when I know where; and give my regards to the Professor when you see him."

Chapter Seventeen

Frankie Johnson stood looking out of the window of his cramped office overlooking the community centre building. It was strange that the familiar thrum of bass and drums weren't coming up from the floor below, but from the normally empty hall opposite. He was glad that in the end they had all agreed the party should go ahead, despite what had happened to Caitlin. It would be the first whole estate celebration since they had been barricaded in. It would also be the first time they could all come together without speeches or life changing decisions having to be made. Frankie had donated the use of the club's sound equipment for the night, and Danny had wired some projection screens in the hall which flashed lights and images across the ceilings and walls, and did a good job of hiding the damp and flaking paintwork. People were milling around the doors outside the hall where a buffet had been laid out on covered trestle tables. He watched Jo and Sunny talking together, his daughter suddenly throwing back her head and laughing the way she did when she was really happy.

Frankie liked Sunny, though liking him didn't mean he was necessarily overjoyed at his daughter's obvious infatuation with him. She knew of his past, the drugs, prison in the States for possession etc., Sunny had volunteered that to her himself without any prompting from Frankie. He also did so long before the craziness of this so called 'revolution' had been even thought about. But Jo hadn't seen him the way Frankie had, hadn't seen him smashed out of his skull- the food stained clothing, the dirty bitten nails, the hands that shook whenever he had one of his all too rare sober moments. And when he was sober, the man could barely make a C chord, so only ever played live when he was either high or drunk, and usually both. Like any father, the thought of his daughter, his little girl, turning into a woman and giving herself to a man freaked him out. Fathers and daughters were a weird and complicated thing, he knew that. Maybe, though, he was even more paranoid than most. Jo's mother Maggie was, he accepted now, an alcoholic even when he'd first met her. He hadn't seen it then of course; she just seemed a happy bubbling personality. But then, as she progressed to other various chemical addictions along with the attendant lying and stealing that always accompanies addicts, she became someone he no longer knew. She finally ran off to Tangiers with a pianist he used to manage, and took a sizeable chunk of their joint savings with her. It had been a relief though when she went- even though Jo was just three years old at the time- trying to juggle being a single parent with a full time career. In the end he had done ok with Jo and, by the time she was twelve years old, it was difficult to know who looked after whom. She was a good person, he knew that, and he was so proud of her, more than she would ever realise. But she was a rebel, always had been really. She got that part of her from her mother of course. Even as a twelve year old tomboy, she would out dare any of the boys in the gang she had hooked up with, and the few that would try anything on with her never made the same mistake twice. So he liked Sunny. The man had a good soul and Frankie admired that he seemed to have finally conquered his demons but... he let out a long sigh as he watched the two of them entering the hall. The truth was Jo would do what Jo wanted to do, she always had, and he couldn't see her changing now. All he could do as her father was protect her in the best way he could, even if she would end up hating him for doing it.

He sat down at his desk, his fingers running lightly over the parchment documents he had laid out in front of him earlier. It was strange to think that all these links to the past would end with him, unless of course Jo had a son; but, no, even as unlikely as that was, she would have no truck with the lodge. He had tried on many occasions to explain to her what a noble thing Freemasonry was, but she had been brainwashed by her leftie friends who believed all the rubbish conspiracy theories. It was ironic, he thought, how the one thing they could never agree on, Freemasonry, was the very thing, probably the only thing now that could save them both from this god awful mess. It was also, of course, why he had been tasked with Sunny in the first place, not that either Sunny or Jo knew that. He looked at his watch- half past six. He would go over to the party at seven, but first he would need to make his weekly call.

*

Danny smiled at the bank of his computer screens, as one by one they began to run their trace patterns. There was no mistaking it as an anomaly this time, the radio spike was definitely there and it was coming from inside the estate. He had three trackers set up in what everyone called his Mission Control. In reality it was the top floor of the old bakery. Some of the battered dough mixing machines were still gathering dust in the corners of the room and, when it rained you could still smell the yeast that had impregnated itself in the building. He had chosen it for a couple of reasons, not least of which were the stainless steel benches that dominated the room and were perfect for the equipment he had installed. The place also housed a huge walk-in fridge that he had lined with lead sheets, and then covered the lead with stainless steel sheets, making it an eavesdrop-free space should they need it. Downstairs was an ad hoc studio that he had set up to allow them to make reasonably professional broadcasts. It hadn't been used much lately as, although they still had the ability to live-stream to the web, they had reluctantly agreed not to do so as part of the 'truce' reached with the Government. If the shit did hit the fan, Danny reckoned they would be able to manage a live stream for maybe thirty minutes or so, before the authorities could shut off the signal.

Dominic had pointed out to him one afternoon though that, if they suddenly decided to drop a bomb on the bakery roof, worrying about how long it would take jam the signal might be somewhat superfluous. He liked Dominic Weston, despite what some of the others felt. The guy, probably because of his scientific background, was one of the few people who seemed to appreciate how important Danny's tech work was to their survival. He'd also been a big help to Danny in rewiring some of the more jerry-built wiring loops he had set up in those frantic first few days. He was unconsciously tapping his pen on the counter, as he watched the tracking software trying to triangulate the signal. The call had lasted for six minutes so far, yet the caller's location position according to the tracking devices, was in up to any one of thirty buildings within a two mile radius. Whoever was contacting the outside had state of the art technology- 'spook tech' most likely, he thought. The call suddenly flipped out, leaving a flat line on the screens, the words 'Tracking Failed' flashing on each monitor in red letters. He closed it down and leaned back into the battered leather swing chair, his hands clasped behind his head. Oh, these people are good, he told himself; but I'm better and all I need to do is think a bit more creatively. He began to write an encrypted message to send to Chen, laying out the data he had cracked so far. Chen would complain but he would do what he could- he owed Danny and besides Chen would be desperate to solve the riddle first. One thing you could always count on with the hacking fraternity was that everyone had a giant ego, especially when it came to who could hack the most 'hack-proof' systems first. He sent the message which would show up on the government monitoring software, if at all, as an email about the price of wheat in Pennsylvania. A deeper search of its code would show that the message originated from a grain trader in Washington DC who was emailing a feed company director in Memphis Tennessee. It would also self delete two minutes after it had been shunted to an encrypted trapdoor receiving folder. "Yeah, I'm better," he said aloud, and laughed. He decided to wait till the morning before telling Doc there had been another call to the outside. Why spoil the man's evening and, more importantly, he thought why get on the wrong side of Katy when you didn't need to?

*

Sunny was glad he'd decided not to play tonight. Everyone was enjoying themselves to the sounds of the bubblegum pop that he personally detested, and he just knew that the dreaded karaoke would be starting up soon.

"You're tapping your foot!" Doc said.

Sunny looked at Doc, who was sitting opposite him and looking more relaxed than Sunny had seen him for a long time. Katy had even got him to put on a new stylish black shirt, one of those with the latest trendy Cee Collars.

"What did you say?"

"Your foot. You were tapping it to the hep sounds of the Battle Bopsters!"

"Don't talk through your arse, Doc. I hate this shit and you know it-"

"Jo?" the Doc said, looking at her.

"Yep, there was definite foot- tapping going on!" she said straight faced.

Sunny shook his head and grimaced at them, whilst unconsciously flattening his feet to the floor.

Katy burst out laughing, and turned to Doc, "You dancin' Doc?"

"God, no!" he said, looking genuinely horrified.

"No, my dear Professor Deveron. The correct response is, 'if you're askin' then I'm dancin'!"

"No, I mean, I would...and, well, maybe I might do later, but Sunny needs to talk to me about something first." He looked across at Sunny, raising his eyes at him.

Sunny grinned, his normally serious expression instantly transformed as he did so, "No, you go ahead, Doc. I'm too busy right now groovin' to these Battle Bopsters!" he did a little Battle Bopster's wiggle with his shoulders as he said it, and then belly-laughed at the look Doc gave him. Doc could still hear Sunny laughing as Katy, not to gently, hoicked him out of the chair and onto the dance floor.

"That was cruel," Jo said, smiling.

"Oh yeah baby!" Sunny said, still laughing. Then his smile faded suddenly, his eyes narrowing slightly as he looked across the room beyond the dance floor.

She followed his gaze, knowing as she did so who she would see- Weston. She had spotted him earlier sitting surrounded by his small entourage, like a king holding court. Her father had always told her that you could tell a lot about someone by the company they kept and, if that was true, then the ragbag of dissenters and malcontents who were waiting on every word or comment made by Professor Dominic Weston told her all she needed to know. Not that she had needed telling, she had disliked the man from day one, didn't trust him. Simple as that! She had tried to give him the benefit of the doubt, of course. He was a friend of the Doc's, and she even tried to like him for the fact, that without him, none of them would still be here but... It wasn't anything specific, Weston was always charming and self deprecating in the meetings they had, but there was something hidden. It was almost like he was playing a part. It was also the way he looked at people when he thought no-one was watching him. As she watched him, she felt sure he was playing a part right now. Julie Coppull was leaning into his side, her gormless face turned up towards him in adoration as he was holding forth to 'his boys'.

She turned back to Sunny, ready to go over yet again why she didn't trust the man. Sunny was watching her, that mischievous half smile of his playing around his eyes and mouth.

"What?" she said, smiling despite herself.

He shook his head, still smiling.

"You wanna dance, big fellah?" she said in her best southern drawl, forcing thoughts of Weston and weapons and everything else back into the shadows. Tonight they all deserved a break.

He grinned at her, "Why Miss Josephine ma'am, I thought you'd never ask."

Weston watched them both walk onto the dance floor, the placid smile he wore as a permanent mask since his arrival fixed firmly in place. He watched the woman Jo dancing with the nigger Sunny, the way she was leaning on him like some cheap slut. His smile broadened suddenly to cover the simmering anger that was never far from him now, and had begun almost from the moment he had set foot in this god awful estate. Part of his discontent, he had finally admitted to himself today, was that he had misjudged the Riverside situation quite badly. Worse still, and unforgivably so, he had based his decisions solely on the distorted media and press coverage he had watched. The truth was Riverside was no hotbed of subversive terrorism, as the press had described it; there were no anarchist cells here bent on destruction and mayhem. He had sacrificed everything, all those years of patiently waiting for an opportunity, and at the last hurdle he had lost his discipline. He had behaved impetuously and irrationally, carried away with the romantic notion of hijacking a revolutionary movement. In his mind, Riverside would become a movement that would shake the world, toppling Mablethorpe and his cretinous cronies from their privileged perches. Instead, he had found himself surrounded by a bunch of hippy trippy do gooders who wanted nothing more than to live in some communal version of Walton's world. They weren't even prepared to go public with the 6/707, preferring to sit and plant tomatoes in this stalemated shit-hole. It was unbelievable, really. He had given Deveron the means to change the world, and the man just sat here waiting for some do-gooders to save them all. He had taken a great risk to come here, the greatest risk he possibly could have taken, yet nobody outside even knew his name or what he had done. Still, all that was about to change, and this time the whole world would know about it.

Chapter Eighteen

What should have been a four hour drive to her grandfather's house ended up taking nearly six, as the motorways jammed up with early bank holiday traffic. Caravans and supermarket lorries were vying in the usual competition for who could block as many lanes as possible at the slowest speed. At one point, the motorway was so jammed she nearly abandoned the journey altogether and turned off to Manchester, which the motorway passed, as she headed for Gramps' house nestling on the border of the Yorkshire Pennines. In the end she stuck it out, feeling in need of his company and advice. Foulridge, where Gramps lived was, as many Yorkshire villages are, dourly named. As Nasri turned off the A road and down into its narrow streets, she had the familiar sensation that she was driving back into an earlier and simpler time. It was raining of course, as it always seemed to be when she came back these days- a fine drizzle which made the grey stone houses look even more dark and sombre than usual. Yet, despite its sombre exterior, Foulridge itself was a friendly village, surrounded by magnificent countryside. Whenever she made the effort to come down here, she always promised herself she would do it more often. As a child, she had loved the long school holidays which were always spent with Gramps as her father would go back to Pakistan for business. She went to Pakistan with him once and felt like an alien. The whole male dominated culture, and the expectations that her father's family had of her that she should marry well and become a home-maker, just didn't fit with how she had been raised. She couldn't remember her mother, other than the odd fuzzy feeling of warmth she felt when she looked at old photographs. Those photos always made her feel like she was looking at a more stylised and sophisticated version of herself. She had asked her grandfather, more than once as she got older, why Daddy was the way he was with her- so cool and distant, even though she wanted for nothing and she knew he loved her. Gramps had told her she was being silly, but she knew she wasn't, and in the end she'd decided it was simply that she reminded her father too much of her dead mother.

She pulled the car onto the small drive, squeezing in next to Professor Alhim Jaheel's trusty and battered Volvo estate, which was hardly moved from its current spot in front of the old lock-keepers cottage he had bought some thirty years ago. The car was covered in berry-stained bird droppings and wet decaying leaves, as if it was part of the landscape. She could see him now in the bay window, sitting at his desk as he squinted over his reading glasses at her car. She suddenly realised that he wouldn't know who it was as, the last time she had driven down, she'd still had the old Beetle, not the swanky silver Mercedes that she'd been given when she got the job with FPN.

He was already standing in the open doorway by the time she got out of the car, his stoop slightly worse than she remembered and his hair, though still thick was now a shock of white against his dark skin. He could still pass for a man in his mid sixties though she thought- rather than the decade older he actually was.
"Nasri, is that you girl?"
"It's me Gramps. Sorry, I should have rung first. "
"Nonsense, child!" he said, grinning at her as he stood with arms open wide, the way he always did when he hadn't seen her for a while.
As his still strong and vital arms wrapped around her, she closed her eyes, breathing in the familiar smell of his old-fashioned aftershave, mixed with the aromatic Turkish pipe tobacco he loved to smoke, despite the ban. Gramps held her away from himself, looking her up and down, then gave his verdict, "Too thin little Nazzy. What? Have you been eating all this trendy rabbit food, or this sushi nonsense I keep reading about?"
She laughed and took his arm as they walked into the house.

The kitchen was as spotless as ever, draped with copper bottom pans that reflected the glowing fire like burnished gold. She sat at the big knotted pine table whilst he made them both some jasmine tea.

"I can only stay tonight, I'm afraid. I have to be down at Riverside in Manchester tomorrow. We are-"
"How about some English crumpets, Nazzy? They should still be fresh enough!"
"OK, that would be nice. I was saying that-"
"And I have that local butter, 'Grimshaw's', the one you like, "he said, cutting her off again.
She looked at him, the dark shadow of dementia suddenly rearing like a spectre in the back of her mind; he was only seventy five, but still...
"I remember how you would always demand Grimshaw's," he said looking at her. He put his finger across his lips as he spoke, "only Grimshaw's for my little Nasri, right?" He shook his head as she again started to speak, and put his finger back on his lips.
"Crumpets sound lovely, Gramps," she said slowly as he stared intently at her.
He smiled, "Perfect! In fact I think we'll take them down to Alitheia and toast them on there; and don't look like that, as it happens I lit her stove over an hour ago. We'll be as warm as toasted crumpets ourselves!"
She groaned inside, and smiled at him as he started to pack the crumpets and butter into a small basket.
*

At least it's stopped raining, she thought as she followed him outside, stepping gingerly down the steep, leaf covered and winding path that led to Alitheia. He had bought the old barge, or narrow boat as he would constantly correct her, twenty years ago. She had been an old wreck when he got her, and he had spent every spare weekend and all his holidays restoring her. She was sixty feet long, painted in a rich blue with gold piping. To Nasri, Alitheia- which was the Greek word for truth always seemed more like one of those old Pullman train carriages than a boat. She hated Alitheia... well, no, that wasn't strictly true, as the boat itself was ok. In fact Alitheia was quite nice really. Nasri's problem was she was terrified of the water, any water, and that was really the truth! She had never learned to swim and, although Gramps had told her the canal wasn't deep enough to worry about, that if she fell in she could just stand up and climb out, she had a morbid and, she accepted irrational fear of falling in to the green inky canal and being dragged down to-.
"Here you go!" Gramps said, holding out the orange life jacket for her whilst he hopped onto the back of the boat like an excited teenager. If she hated the canal, she hated the bloody life jacket even more; it was her badge of shame and shouted scaredy cat to everyone who saw her in it. Still she pulled it on and clipped the belt tight against her waist before taking Gramps hand, closing her eyes as she stepped over the all of twelve inches

gap between the bank and the solid steel deck. Her hands clamped on to the stainless steel rail tightly as she sat down on the open rear deck. Within five minutes, Gramps had Alitheia chugging down the Leeds and Liverpool canal at a steady four miles an hour, the smoke from the wooden stove puffing contentedly against the steel grey of the sky. Gramps whooped with delight as the red traffic light changed to green just as they rounded the last tight bend that would lead them into the mile long Foulridge tunnel. She smiled at him, thankful that they at least wouldn't have to wait the half hour for the lights to change. The tunnel was just wide enough for one boat, so entry was regulated by traffic lights. Gramps sounded Alitheia's horn, signalling in case any tardy boats were coming through, and switched on the front spotlight. As they entered the gloomy dark tunnel, he threw her a wide brimmed wax hat which she jammed over her head. The tunnel's blackened brickwork always dripped like a sieve, and the water was always freezing irrespective of the time of year. The tunnel closed around them like a dark shroud as they began to round the slight curve which meant there was no natural light for most of its length. He slowed the boat to half speed- a magnificent two miles an hour and sat down next to her, his hand resting lightly on the tiller. She pulled her collar around her neck, as she could hear the cold drips start to patter onto the boat's roof and her hat.

She could just make out his face from the reflections of green light coming from the instrument panel, and she took a deep breath before she spoke.
"Gramps, how have you been feeling?"
"Me? You know me, I'm as fit as a butcher's dog!"
She smiled in the dark; he loved picking up English colloquialisms and throwing them into academic conversations, fully aware of how incongruous they sounded with his still strong Pakistani accent.
"Oh, I see!" he chuckled. You're worried I'm going a little doolally?"
"No, I-"
He laughed his big hearty laugh, the one that always made her giggle as a child, "It's ok Nazzy. The dreaded devil of dementia hasn't visited me yet... though if and when it does, of course I'll probably be the last to know. Now to business. How deep are you into this Riverside fiasco?"
She felt a sense of relief flood through her. That was the real Gramps the renowned scholar was finally being himself again.
"Well, strangely enough, that's why I came to see you. I need your advice. There's been some very strange things happening-"
"Tell me granddaughter."

*

She ran through everything she could remember as they chugged through the darkness of the tunnel, the dark and cold fitting in nicely, she thought, with how paranoid she must sound. When she had finished, she saw him nod as he corrected the steering of the boat slightly, the tunnel bending to the right as it followed the contour of the hillside fifty feet above.

"Around two weeks ago, I had a visit from the telephone company," he said. "They told me they were upgrading local junction boxes and that they needed to check my data stream speeds. Very efficient chaps they were too, spent a whole hour checking all the connection points and said there would be no charge. Splendid eh?"

She shrugged in the dark, a little bemused.

"Then last week I had another visit from an old pal in the service, brought him out here as a matter of fact," he laughed, " I think he actually hated this tunnel more than you do if that's possible!"

Her hands gripped tighter onto the railings as she waited for him to continue. She realised now that he had taken them onto the boat to avoid any electronic surveillance. The tunnel suddenly felt colder than ever.

"Anyway, this old chum of mine- well he's quite young really probably not a day over sixty- he tells me that they are watching me because of your public sympathy toward the Riverside terrorists."

She started to protest, but he held his hand up, forestalling her as he went on, "Whatever is happening down there on this Riverside estate, Nasri, has them frightened out of their wits; and believe me, these people are very dangerous, most especially so when they are frightened."

She suddenly felt her ire rising, "We should expose this. Look Gramps, it's bad enough them watching me but, if you're right and they are bugging your house-"

"Oh, they are definitely doing that," he said, chuckling. "I'm not so out of touch I can't track their simplistic methods."

"But this is wrong, Gramps. Christ you are one of them-"

"Don't blaspheme, Nasri, not on our deity or on anyone else's."

"Sorry, "she responded automatically, "but it's true, isn't it! You risked your life, your career-"

"All that may be true my darling girl, but a greater truth is this that, no matter how many years you serve an adopted country and no matter how well, you are, and always will be to many, the 'other'. To those people, you will always be 'Johnny Foreigner' and, worse, a Muslim, both of which, but especially the latter, mean that you will never be above suspicion."

She rested her chin on her fists, knowing it was true that, despite all the years he had worked as a distinguished Professor, despite all the years he had helped the British and the Americans following the annexing of Pakistan by China, he was still 'not one of us'. She even felt it herself sometimes that, despite being born in the UK, to some people she would never be seen as truly British.

She jumped involuntarily as Gramps sounded the horn, catching her by

surprise that they had reached the end of the tunnel already. He steered Alitheia expertly to the nearside bank, and stepped off smartly to tie her off onto the large steel rings set in the bank-side, before jumping back on the stern smiling at her.
"Now I think it's time for you to toast those crumpets, while I take you through a few things that should help to keep the dogs off your scent for a while."
She nodded glumly and followed him down into the fire warmed galley.

*

Seventy two hours later, Nasri would gladly have given up a year's salary to be back on board Alitheia. Instead of the bright cosy cabin and comforting warmth of the wood stove, she was squashed along with Ian and Dave and all their gear in the dank and rusting hold of an old canal dredger. The only light was from a grating above their heads, which let flickering and intermittent light in as they lumbered along the black waters of the Manchester Ship Canal. At least they were now starting to pass under the shadows of the old mill buildings which adjoined the Riverside docks, which meant they couldn't be far off. Earlier they had entered the maintenance yard jammed under a dirty tarpaulin cover, in their contact Gazza's pick-up truck. That had been at ten to six this morning, which was the time of the yard's shift change. None of them had been happy that they had to spend all day hidden at the yard, but Gazza had been insistent that the shift changeover was the only time he could get them in. He'd explained that today was turnover day, when he would switch from days and double back to the night shift, which meant he would have access to the truck. The yard, which belonged to the Manchester Ship Canal company, was a series of tin huts stuffed with dredging gear and various bits of broken and abandoned machinery, much of which looked as old as the canal itself.

The day had been interminable, the three of them sitting around inside an old disused shed at the back of the yard, listening to the rain hammer down incessantly on its leaking tin roof. Gazza said they had to wait inside until the shift supervisors had gone for the day, and then he'd return and take them onboard the 'Gaelic Rose', whose delights they were now enjoying. The Gaelic Rose had spent her whole life dredging sludge and oil deposits from the main channel of the ship canal, ensuring there was sufficient draft for the large grain ships and oil tankers which made their way through the Mersey estuary from the Irish Sea. The Rose was one of the few unescorted craft currently allowed to go anywhere near the locked down estate. Nasri doubted that, even a month ago, they would have been able to try getting into Riverside via the dredger but, although the estate was still locked down as tight as a drum, inevitably the intensity of the initial security operation had lessened. The security forces had now become more confident and familiar with the operation and the coming and going of craft such as the Gaelic Rose. Gazza had assured them that, although they would be stopped and possibly boarded, any search would be cursory, or 'nuffink much' as he had described it. When she had tried to quiz Gazza about who his contacts were inside the estate, he had brushed her off to the point of rudeness. In the end she had shrugged helplessly at Ian and Dave and given up. Later, Dave had managed to get him talking a bit as they smoked a cigarette, and had managed to get out of him that he was originally from Riverside and still had some family inside. He told Dave that his brother George, who he had been supplying with smokes and 'stuff', had asked him to bring them in. Dave's view was that it was cash rather than brotherly love that had gotten him to take the risk of bringing in a camera crew. Dave said Gazza's view was his brother George was a 'fucking loony for not getting out of there while he still can'. He also said that the Gaelic Rose's Captain, or 'Skip' as he referred to him, knew that he did some business on the dock, and was happy to turn a blind eye so long as Gazza left him a present of cash or goodies in the wheelhouse. Skip didn't know they were aboard though, and would 'shit himself' if he found out. Hence why they had been hustled onto the boat and down into the dark hold, with Gazza giving hurried instructions to Dave, who he had clearly decided was the group's real leader, that they should stay quiet, They had been huddled in the dark hold ever since and hadn't seen Skip, but they had heard him grunting at Gazza to variously 'shift his arse' or 'light the bank, you lazy fuckwit' and other such nautical terminology. This was interspersed with Skip's coughing up of copious amounts of phlegm which, to Nasri's great dismay, were frequently directed down the grate to splatter near her feet. Gazza had said that during daylight the boat had a crew of five, but quite often there would just be the two of them at night, when all they had to do was shunt the boat down to the next morning's dredging spot.

The three of them tensed as they heard three sharp raps on the steel deck just above their heads. This was Gazza's prearranged signal, and meant that they were being approached by one of the security boats which now patrolled the canal constantly since the Riverside revolution. Almost simultaneously with his signal, they could hear the whine of a powerful outboard, which was accompanied by a slight rocking of the dredger as the skipper pulled the Gaelic Rose into a grumbling and shuddering reverse thrust before he killed the engine. Dave and Ian leaned forward, and began to pull the oil stained tarpaulin above the three of them as Gazza had instructed them do if they were boarded. The security boat's large spotlight cast streams of flashing light across the rusty grate above their heads. Nasri couldn't help but squeeze Dave's hand tight, as she felt a nauseous panic as the claustrophobic plastic was drawn over her head, plunging the three of

them into pitch black darkness. She could smell, almost taste, the stale oil and dankness, and could hear the swell of the rank deep water as the wake from the security boat slapped against the Gaelic Rose's hull. She was trying to breathe to stop the rising panic she could feel overtaking her, when Dave leaned close to her ear whispering softly,
"Stuck up bitch!"
She tried to make sense of what he was saying through the rising panic of being unable to breathe, "What? I-"
"He said that's why he wouldn't talk to you- Gazza that is. He said you were one 'stuck up fucking bitch'!" Dave whispered into her ear, even as she heard the heavy thud of boots as someone boarded the boat.
She felt her irritation push out the fear, just of course as Dave had intended, and dug her nails hard into his hand, feeling just slightly more in control as she felt him wince in pain.

*

Michael Winstone, or 'Bear' as he was known to everyone except his mother, had watched the old dredger as it was stopped and boarded by the cop boat. He had strolled down to the dockside earlier, just as the sky gave out the last of its grey daylight, a few people shouting out at him 'Hey, Bear' or 'Whatcha doin', Bear?' He knew people smiled when they saw him doing his patrol thing, and he didn't mind. Most of them were ok and were good people who appreciated what he did. Some of them, though, what he thought of as 'the nasties' would go a little further than a gentle ribbing. The nasties wanted to mock him not just for his size but for how seriously he took the job he had been given. The truth was though that for the first time ever, he didn't give a shit what they thought, so long as they didn't mock him to his face and, of course nasties rarely did that. He had stood a foot taller than most of the kids his age by the time he was eleven years old, and it was then someone had called him Yogi Bear, which later got shortened to just 'Bear.'

He knew his size was intimidating to people (six feet four inches last time his mother had checked him, which was three years ago on his sixteenth birthday. He had tried to be less menacing, often unconsciously stooping in the way that some tall people do. He knew his sheer bulk and powerful build tended to make people who didn't know him so well a little cautious when they were around him. But some people would still mock him behind his back even now, in just the same way they had when he was a kid, treating him like some great dimwit. 'Corporal Bear' was the new jibe. 'Where's Sergeant Reeko? Oh, he's out patrolling with 'Corporal Bear'. Yeah he had heard them, but it really didn't matter because he was finally doing something that actually made him feel good about himself. He had never had a job, ever, and he didn't get paid for what he was doing now but it was a job, a real job where what he was doing mattered. Reeko had always been the clever one of course. At school, he had been the one who would get them both into trouble, and most times he would also be the one able to talk them out both out of it. That was only fair of course, as most of their troubles came about when one of Reeko's crazy schemes went pear-shaped, which to Bear seemed always to be the way of it. Bear didn't pretend to understand everything that the others said, Doc and Sunny and the rest of them. The Doc was the worst of them though. He used ten words when two would do, and usually words that Bear wasn't even sure were English. But for the first time he actually felt like part of something, what Doc called a 'system of cooperative society'. Reeko had explained to him later on that it just meant that people shared their shit and looked after each other. Anyway, whatever they wanted to call it, it felt good to Bear. They still had problems and Bear didn't think that they would be able to last out much longer. The cops and the Government wouldn't let it carry on like this. Him and Reeko had talked about it only yesterday, but there was nothing they could do about it. And while it lasted it was good; he liked that people were more caring, were looking out for one another. He had seen with his own eyes how people seemed to laugh more and were generally less angry about the place. Sure they still had some problems, arguments would break out, and there was still the odd fight. But even then it wasn't like before, where people fought with knives and stuff; mostly now it would be just a fist fight. There were other problems though, which was why he was out here tonight.

He watched as the cops boarded the dredger and thought it looked like the Sarge was right, and this was where the Dust was being brought in. They had all (well, not all) agreed that drugs were everybody's personal business, so long as they didn't send anybody loco or cause any problems, but Dust was something else. People who got into Dust could just go ape shit for no reason, and were a danger to everyone in the community. Mallet had first found some on one of the rapists, and then a week later, he had busted two spaced-out Boho's who were having a pissing contest (literally off the roof of the old library building). It was at that point that the Sarge had told him and Reeko that he thought someone was bringing the stuff in. Dust was a powerful drug, but it had a major flaw apart from potentially causing severe psychosis, that was. It only had a shelf-life of a couple of weeks at most, and that meant it had to have been brought in from the outside, as the facilities needed for making the stuff were way outside anything the estate could offer. So it was definitely being brought in, but why? Bear had asked the Sarge that very question, as the three of them were discussing it after the last council meeting.

"There's no money in it, Sarge, and everyone knows that dust is way expensive," Bear had said. "Nobody had much money to start with round here, and they've got even less now, so it doesn't make any sense for the dealers to supply it to us."
Mallet had looked at them both and nodded, "You're right, Bear, so what's the advantage, what's the play?" Mallet had asked him in that quiet voice, the one he used whenever he wanted Bear to work something through for himself.
Bear had stared hard at Mallet. Then he looked at Reeko who he guessed would already know the answer but was waiting for him to get it, to 'work it through' as Mallet would say. Before everything went crazy, before all the shit had happened, Bear didn't like working things through; it was one of the reasons he had hated school so much, if he did get asked something in class, the rest of them would usually take the piss. He would always take too long to work something out or worse, would get the answer arse upwards. Before he got his new job he would have just shut down, or become 'non-engaged' as his old school reports used to describe him. But that was before Reeko had asked him to be his deputy, and before Sergeant Hammer had agreed to it, and before the council had agreed with that, and appointed him as an official Deputy. Now when he was asked something, he wouldn't just walk away; he would try and figure it out however foolish he felt doing it. Someone's bringing in Dust he told himself now, unconsciously counting ideas off on each one of his fingers. If it was the dealers, they would want cash, but nobody has any. They could trade though, he thought suddenly, and looked up brightly at Reeko who sat waiting patiently, his chin resting on his cupped hand. Bear stopped himself from speaking whilst he thought about it some more- 'work it through' he thought again, 'work it through'. They had nothing to trade, least not anything that a dealer would want anyway, so it couldn't be... Now he looked up at Reeko and the Sergeant, who both nodded encouragement as if they could actually hear what he was thinking!
"Well," he began, ticking off on his fingers as he spoke, something he had watched Sunny do when he was making points in meetings, "first point, Dust is expensive, but nobody has much money in Riverside, so that's out." He counted off another finger, "Second, they could trade something for it, but what? Any of the good shit we have, like the cameras and stuff, would be missed straight away, so that's out." He saw Reeko nodding out of the corner of his eye.
"OK, so why? Maybe...maybe it's not the dealers bringing it in, maybe it's someone else. Maybe it's the Government sending it in to try and screw us up; I mean, if we end up with loads of 'dust heads'..." he tailed off suddenly, feeling foolish, and stared down at his boots.

"Reeko?" Sergeant Mallet asked.
"Works for me, old man." Reeko said
Bear was still staring at his boots, waiting.
"And for me!" Mallet said brusquely, nodding at Bear, who was now looking up at him grinning.

*

After that they agreed to keep the Dust investigation amongst the three of them and not involve the committee; nobody actually said outright that it was because of Weston, they didn't need to. None of them trusted or liked him, so that was that. Bear was allocated to watch the dockside, which is where they suspected the Dust was coming in, and Reeko and Mallet would keep an eye on the side streets leading down to the docks to see who, if anybody, was hanging around. Mallet had said he wanted the complete supply chain, so the job was to 'watch and not go off half cocked '. So Bear did just that, and watched as the patrol boat disengaged from the dredger and then roared off, plunging the quay back into darkness. The dredger's running lights glinted dimly on the surface of the water as it started to chug slowly to the quayside. Bear waited a moment for his eyes to adjust after the brilliance of the spotlight, then moved quietly, keeping carefully under the pitch black lee of the old granary sheds. He kept himself tight to the wall as he moved forward on the dock, listening to the old dredger as its tyre fenders scraped slowly against the concrete bank. Mallet had said he was only to observe, see what they did and how they did it and only if it was possible, to spot who it was that picked up any of the dropped packages. The dredger and the dock itself were still in near darkness despite the running lights, and Bear knew he had to get a little closer if he was to see anything useful. He half crouched and moved across the apron. He could see the outline of one of the crew who shouted up to the wheelhouse.

"Slow it down, Skip. I need a quick whizz!"
There was no reply that Bear could hear, but the boat's engine slowed another half notch. Bear watched as the crewman's silhouette moved to the centre of the boat then moved back to the edge. He could see other people moving behind the man as they began stepping off the side of the boat onto the quay. Bear felt the hairs on the back of his head stand up; it's the cops, he thought. They're coming for us! He started to turn back so he could run and warn Reeko and the Sarge, when the whole quayside suddenly lit up like a football stadium.

A metallic voice shattered the quiet, "This is the police. Stay exactly where you are, raise your hands. This is your only warning."
Bear watched bemused as the four people on the quay were frozen in the glare of the police boat searchlight. The first of them, smaller than the

others, looked back toward the light then back to the quay, then shouted to the others, “ Go, we can make it!” Then she- it was definitely a woman’s voice Bear heard- crouched and began to run for the rotted granary doors, which were hung crookedly on their rusted hinges. Two of the remaining people began to run after her struggling with the bulky holdalls they were carrying. There was a clash of gunfire which clanged against the old dredger and spit up cement from the quayside wall. Bear didn’t stop to think or work anything through as he sprinted forward, shouting as he ran, “This way! Quick now, this way!”

The woman turned and looked right at him, his frame already massive casting a huge shadow against the wall. I know her! I know her face, he thought, startled as the gunfire started again from different directions. The woman had almost reached him and the safety of the granary overhang; one of the men behind her let out a scream and fell hard onto the ground; the woman screamed out, “Ian!”
Reeko grabbed her arm and pulled her under the overhang whilst she tried to fight free. He shoved her back harder than he meant to. “I’ll do it.” he said, and ran crouching toward the man who was sprawled on the floodlit apron, yelping like a dog. Bear was almost there as he saw the last man, the one who had stayed near the boat begin to run toward the doors. He watched as the man suddenly twisted in the air like he was dancing. The blood, which looked black in the bright white of the spotlight, spewed from his gaping mouth, his body going from a pirouette to a crazy jitterbug as the bullets ripped and shredded his shirt, his chest erupting with multiple black liquid spurts. Bear grabbed the man who was whimpering on the floor- *shot in the leg* he realised, as he hoicked him over his shoulder and began to run back to the woman and the man whose outlines he could just make out. Another three paces and he would be ok. He gasped as he felt a sudden dizzying weirdness, and was surprised as he felt, and then saw a great ray of spit flying out of his open mouth. He thought something had slammed into the side of his skull, something that was causing his body to spin around back toward the lights of the boat; then he felt his knees buckling and he was falling, his consciousness fading into oblivion.

*

The outside of the makeshift infirmary was in chaos as groups of people blocked up the doorways, trying to look in to see what was happening. The shots had sounded across the estate, and people had come running out of their houses, clearly expecting to see hordes of police and security people charging across the square. Sunny stood outside the doors, his hands held above his head as he shouted for calm; he could see panic in many of the people who were shouting at him, demanding to know what was going on. He closed his eyes for a moment, and tried again to shout for order.

Reeko looked at Mallet. They could both hear the crowd becoming noisier, angrier.
"You want me to go and help him?" Reeko asked, nodding toward the doors.
Mallet shook his head and placed his hand on Reeko's shoulder, "Sunny can handle it; you and I need to see to our boy."
Reeko nodded, sniffing air through his nose to keep back the tears and grief.
They had arrived from different streets at the dockside in almost the same instant, both watching helplessly as the blood spewed from the side of Bear's head, the momentum of the shot sending him spinning, sprawling into the shadow of the dark overhang. Reeko could hear himself keep saying 'Fuck, fuck, fuck', knowing how stupid he sounded but unable to stop it, 'fuck, fuck, fuck'. He'd dropped down to kneel at Bear's side, big old Bear who had never looked as small as he did now, lying crumpled against the dirty wall. Mallet had been all cold fury turning on the woman and the man, who both looked in total shock. The other one, the one that Bear had saved, was shivering uncontrollably holding his thigh with both hands, the blood seeping rapidly through his fingers.
"You two get this man between you and follow us! Reeko! Reeko! Shut up, and help me get Bear to Doc Timms."
Reeko looked up at him "It's too late, Sarge He's gone-"
"No he's not, Reeko, but listen to me now, he will be if we don't get him help, so come on and help me get him up!"
They had slung an arm over each shoulder dragging him up the side street, neither of them looking back to see if the other three were following. Bear was making no sound his head drooping forward onto his chest, Reeko knew he was dead, he knew it.
As they had burst through the doors, Doctor Carl Timms had looked for a moment like he would collapse into hysteria, his eyes wide, his mouth hanging open as he lifted Bear's chin up and looked at the large flap of skin and hair which hung over one of Bear's eyes. He shook his head at Mallet, "I can't...I..."
Mallet adjusted Bear's weight onto his shoulder and held Carl's shoulder with his free hand, his voice still breathless from the effort of dragging Bear up the street and across the back of the square.
"Just try, Doc, that's all I ask. Just try!"
Carl Timms stared at Mallet, and then at Reeko, whose eyes were wide with shock; he took a deep shuddering breath and nodded toward the back room, "Put him back there and someone go and get Caitlin and Jenna." Mallet and Reeko bore Bear through the doors, then turned to look at the man who had been shot in the leg. The man nodded at them, sweat pouring down his brow, "I can wait. See to him first Doctor; he saved me out

there!"
Carl took another look at the man's leg and jabbed a finger at his two companions, "you two keep pressure on the wound. We don't have spare blood here. And give him this." He handed them a syringe and a vial containing enough morphine to dull the pain till he could get back from seeing to Bear.
The woman held the syringe and morphine up in front of her, "Doctor, I'm not qualified to do this. I don't know how?"
He smiled grimly as he spoke, "That's ok, my dear. I'm not qualified either. Just stick it in his backside and it'll be fine!"
As he turned back toward the treatment room, he felt a sudden calmness and clarity that he hadn't known since he was a medical student descend on him. 'I could murder a drink right now' he thought to himself as he pushed open the doors- to see that Bear's blood had already soaked into more than half the paper covering the first aid table.

*

Mallet looked up as Doc Timms came through the doors. The man's eyes were glittering as if he was coming down from an amphetamine rush. Whilst Mallet felt like he had aged ten years in the last hour, Carl Timms looked ten years younger.
Reeko leapt up from the chair he had been slumped in, "Is he...?"
Timms rubbed the sweat from his forehead with the back of his hand, and smiled, "He's ok Reeko; well as best as I can tell he is." He slumped down in a chair opposite and lit up a cigarette, inhaling deeply, "As far as I can tell he's been lucky. Most of the wound is superficial to the scalp; though the bullet has grooved his skull, it doesn't appear to have fractured it, but he's severely concussed. We have to get him out of here, John," he said, looking at Mallet," He needs a scan to make sure there's no haematoma in the brain, or the other half dozen things I can't check!"
Mallet nodded, "OK, I'll-"
"No!" Reeko said, putting his hand on Mallet's arm. "We aren't sending him out there, old man."
Mallet turned to look at him, "Did you hear what he said, Reeko? Bear needs help, help that we can't give him in here-"
"And you think they'll give it to him? Those bastards out there are the ones who shot him. You really think they'll send him to hospital and not to a prison cell, or worse?"
"Reeko, listen to me-"
"No, you listen to me! I know Bear and, if he could speak right now, he'd tell you he'd rather take his chances with us."
Mallet started to speak, then shook his head and looked across at Carl Timms.
"Jesus, John. I don't know!" Timms said, "He could wake up in a day and

be fine, or he could die in ten minutes with an undiscovered embolism..." he threw his hands up in a helpless shrug.

Chapter Nineteen

Nasri still felt in a state of shock from everything that had happened. Intellectually she had known what they were doing was dangerous, but that didn't lessen the impact on her now it had really happened. It looked like Ian was going to be ok. The Doctor had stitched up his leg and told her and Dave that another half inch to the left and he would have bled to death, as the bullet had just missed a main artery. They had left him sedated in a cot in the so called medical centre, and the Doctor had told her that he would see about getting him out tomorrow, if that was what he wanted. At least he's being spared this inquisition, she thought, shifting uncomfortably on the hard plastic chair which had been placed in the middle of a large dilapidated hall. They had taken her out of the bank vault where they had been put last night, leaving Dave there. She'd told him she'd be ok as he had protested at them taking her; besides, there wasn't anything he could do to stop them.

Opposite to her, sitting behind some peeling trestle tables, were the now infamous faces of the Riverside organising committee. Their camera bags and personal stuff had been brought into the hall, and the contents spread out across the floor space between the committee and her. No one had spoken for the twenty minutes that the man with the glasses, who looked every inch the IT geek, had spent examining every item, especially anything electrical. He had scanned each item with a hand-held device and then put their phones, PDAs, and even the cameras and sound equipment into what looked like metal mesh bags. Finally, the man stood up, putting his hands on his back stretching, and handed the smaller bag with her personal stuff to the man in uniform, who she knew was the renegade cop John Mallet.
"Anything?" Mallet asked him.
The geek shook his head.
Mallet turned and said something inaudible to Professor Deveron, who was sat in the middle of the long trestle table, flanked on both sides. Nasri forced herself not to smile, as she thought how bizarrely it reminded her of Leonardo's last supper. Her eyes flicked again to the man, Reeko, who was staring with ill masked contempt at her. She couldn't blame him. His best friend had been shot in the head because of them, and he was still critical. When he had almost frog-marched her down from the quay, she had tried to tell him, who they were; but he had almost spit out the words at her, "I

know who you are; now shut your fucking mouth until you're told you can speak!"

So she had sat and watched as their belongings were spread out on the floor, watched them gone through in fine detail including to her great discomfort her underwear, which felt like a violation of her privacy. When they had been first put in the vault, they had made them strip out of their clothes and given them bright orange overalls to wear. They at least had allowed her to undress privately; well, with only Deveron's partner Katy in the room with her. She had been able to keep Gramps present around her neck which surprised her, but she guessed that to the woman it was only what it appeared to be, a piece of costume jewellery. Even though it was just in the presence of the woman, it had still felt intimidating and, she admitted to herself frightening to have to strip naked. It brought home to her in stark relief the realisation that these people could, if they felt threatened enough do anything they wanted to them.

The Sergeant was holding her FPN ID badge, turning it over and over in his hand as he watched her. She held his gaze without flinching, she had nothing to hide and she thought he knew that. Finally, she spoke into the interminable silence, "Look Sergeant Mallet, isn't it?" She waited for him to nod in acknowledgement, but he continued to stare at her impassively, the badge slowly revolving in his fingers. She tried again, "Firstly, I want to say how deeply sorry we are that your friend was shot, and we will hold the UK government to account-"
"Why are you here?" Mallet said, cutting her off, "And on whose behalf, and who arranged passage on the boat?"
Nasri was a little nonplussed by the questions. She knew they were angry and didn't blame them for that, their friend had been shot and she understood that they needed to vent their anger but-.
"Shall I repeat the question's Ms Jaheel?"
She took a calming breath, "You know why we are here, Sergeant- to report the news!"
"Report it, or make it?"
"That's ridiculous! Do you seriously think we arranged to be shot at? Look, I understand the degree of paranoia that you all feel but we aren't the enemy here, and if you want people outside to hear what you have to say-"
"Who arranged the boat trip?"
"Really, Sergeant, this is totally unnecessary-"
"Reeko, put her back in the vault!" Mallet said, turning away from her.
She saw the young man, the one who had cried when he thought his friend had been killed, start to rise; she could see that he was barely able to control the anger he felt towards her. Whatever else she was unsure of, she knew

she didn't want this armed, unpredictable youth taking her anywhere.
"Wait! I'm telling you the truth. We are here to report on the story, we don't work for the Government and, if you know anything about the Free Press News you know that. For goodness sake, we are trying to help you."
"Help us!" Mallet said, a grim smile on his face, "You're here to help us! This morning we were in a state of truce, or at the very least a stand-off, but your little stunt down on the dockside last night has blown any hope we have of ending this thing peacefully. So tell me, Ms Jaheel, in what way is that helping?"
Nasri felt a tingle of a thread, the way she did sometimes, her desire for the story blowing away her caution, "A better question, Sergeant, is why they have been prepared to allow a 'stand-off'. What exactly have you got over Mablethorpe that has stopped him from shutting you down?"
The man, the crazy one, Reeko, stood up, "Enough of this bullshit old man-"
"Wait!" Nasri said, holding her hand out towards him, "This is crazy. It's you who asked us to come in here in the first place," she pointed at Deveron, "It was you, Professor, who sent the messages, and it was you who asked me to come here..." She stopped in mid-sentence, her own face mirroring the surprise she saw on Deveron's as they all turned to look at him. Deveron stared at her, then at Mallet, and shook his head almost imperceptibly in denial. The man Reeko was now pointing his gun directly at her, ready to march her off.
"But this is crazy. You sent me the messages, you told me to come here... you arranged the contact with the boat, all of it. Look, how did we know we'd be able to get in otherwise..." she suddenly stopped talking, realising she was wasting her time, they weren't going to believe her whatever she said.

Mallet held his hand up signalling for Reeko to wait. She could see how little he wanted to, but he stopped coming toward her, instead folding his arms across his chest but still holding the gun which he rested across his biceps. She looked back towards Deveron, then Mallet, whose voice though quieter somehow seemed more threatening.
"So these messages- how do you know they were from Professor Deveron?"
"He signed them," She said, pleased that her voice still sounded steady.
Mallet nodded, and held up the bag containing her phone and tablet, "And of course you can show them to us now, these messages?"
She closed her eyes for a second, "You know I can't!"
Mallet placed the bag gently down on the table in front of him, raising an eyebrow as he looked at her.
"Look, the messages deleted themselves almost as soon as I had read them,

but you know that. We tried to trace their origin but couldn't. So whoever does your encryption software must be pretty good, as the whole of FPN's IT people got nowhere." She noticed the young man, the geek with the glasses who was sat at the opposite end to Reeko, suddenly sitting up straighter, looking directly at her. She looked at Deveron directly, "The messages were from you...or at least they were signed from you, 'Prof D'. They said, if I came in, I would learn the truth, they told us when and where to meet, and the boat and everything!" She held her hands up and shrugged. Deveron was ignoring her and looking at the man to his left, the one she didn't know. He was sat with his hands interlocked in front of him, smiling at her.

Deveron looked as if he was going to speak and then thought better of it, turning back to Mallet and nodding that he should continue.
Mallet looked puzzled, but carried on, "And how did your IT people explain how these messages had magically managed to delete themselves?"
"They couldn't. In fact they said," she paused, knowing that what they had told her didn't exactly help her cause, "they said that the only people who could probably arrange that were government agencies."
Mallet started to speak, then stopped as the geek held up his hand as if in class.
"Danny?" Mallet said, nodding for him to speak.
The man ran his fingers roughly through his untidy brown hair as he spoke, "Well, that's not strictly true what she is saying. I mean, yes, there are a few states that have cracked Alpha Four tech, but not many, and definitely not the UK. There are a few of us 'civilians' who know how to do it, but only a few. The system is actually quite simple really. Well, not simple, but it's relatively straightforward, a matter of setting up binary gateways that have built into them a circular recoding, almost a reverse gear if you like. So, a text message goes out in what seems like a simple binary code that comprises the body of the text. But within each line of code is a simple command that returns the code string to its origin, shredding itself as it goes." Danny looked at Mallet hopefully, but could see that the sergeant thought he was talking gibberish. He remembered that this was the man who still used a desktop computer, and decided to change tack. "Look, all you have to know is that there are very few people who know how to set it up but, once it is setup, then anyone with a bit of tech savvy..." he stopped speaking and stared at the man that Nasri didn't know, the 'smiley man' as she had christened him. Danny cleared his throat and continued. "Then anyone with a bit of tech savvy, who watched carefully how it was done, would be able to use the system!" They could all see as he finished speaking how his face was flushed.
Mallet stared at him for a long time, then looked at Weston.

*

Hunshai Tan needed every ounce of his legendary self control to stop himself from exploding in a most unseemly manner, as the fat policeman Hawksworth sat perspiring in front of his spotless mahogany desk. He stared unblinking as the man continued to splutter out his explanation,
"So, Ambassador, as you can see we did everything possible in terms of interception, but these people got through. We have made a series of arrests relating to the transportation of-"
"You have made one arrest, Chief Commissioner, the tugboat captain who has told you precisely nothing, most probably because he knows nothing, mm? The actual accomplice though, the one who may have given your investigation some worthwhile information, what of him? Ah yes, I believe your men shot him dead, mm?" Hawksworth nodded miserably, causing at least two of his chins to bulge out over his crisp uniform shirt.
Hunshai continued, his voice flat and even, "Your incompetence has allowed the Free Press News Organisation to gain a physical presence in the estate. We must assume therefore that they will learn of the weapon that the man," he looked down briefly at his desk, "Weston, has taken inside. Should this become common knowledge, then of course my government will not only be required to disavow the United Kingdom and withdraw our support, we will also have no choice but to support any proposals put forward by the rest of the world to deal with it, mm?"
Hawksworth nodded again, remaining silent.
Useless piece of dog shit, Hunshai thought. How happily will I give you over to Zhi's wrath if you fail me. Indeed, I believe I will eventually give you to him even if you succeed in your task. This last thought made him feel a little happier and slightly calmer, allowing him to smile thinly at Hawksworth.

The fat creature in front of him looked unsure at Hunshai's smile, which perhaps meant he was finally beginning to learn something. Hunshai opened a drawer in the desk and removed a vanilla folder.
"The woman reporter, Ms Jaheel, perhaps she can yet be persuaded to understand the dangerous waters she has chosen to swim in, mm?" He slid the envelope across the desk toward Hawksworth who opened the front cover and, after a brief moment of scanning the documents inside, smiled up at the Ambassador confidently.

*

Michael Deveron twisted the butt of his small cigar into the half filled ashtray and looked up into the eyes of his friend. He still found it difficult to accept this seeming betrayal. John Mallet had said Dominic was the person who had been in contact with the FPN people, and he had waited for Dominic to protest and deny Mallet and Danny's accusation. Instead, Dominic had continued calmly to sip from the bottle of water he had been nursing, a smile his only response; if anything, he actually seemed pleased about the whole mess. Deveron had asked everyone to leave the two of them alone against a barrage of objections, the loudest of which came from Reeko. In the end he had stood face to face with Reeko, staring upward at the young man's furious gaze, until, to his great surprise, Reeko had backed down and stomped out of the hall, the rest of them trudging out after him. These were the people who had followed him on a path of hope, the people who, though he had known them for such a short time, he had grown to value beyond simple friendship. They were people now who, as they left, went with silent looks that seemed to say, it's over... the sky has fallen down. Katy had hugged him tightly and kissed him on the cheek, her eyes bright with unshod tears, before she too left. None of them had looked at Weston.

Now as he looked across at him, this man who he had thought he knew well, he was at a loss where to begin? Why had Dominic chosen to put them all in such mortal danger? His normal easy command of language seemed to have deserted him tonight; instead, he simply held his hands outward in a questioning gesture as he asked,
"Dominic, I don't understand?"
Weston had a kind and compassionate smile on his face, "I know you don't, Michael, but you don't have to worry about what's happening now. It's all going to be ok!"
Deveron shook his head.
"No, really, it is. You see what you've done here, Michael, is wonderful. I mean that, it really is. You have brought together a group of people; people who are the failures, the drop outs, and scroungers, including all these boho arty farty type wasters. These types of people, Michael, are the ones who always fall through the cracks, the people that society usually tramples underfoot. Yet somehow you have given them something wonderful, a belief in their own selves, and a belief that they are actually worth something. And they're so proud of this place...of you. They're proud of their little school and their vegetable plots, and their communal meetings, and especially the debates in the hall, where to their great surprise, they actually get to choose what will happen to them. But that isn't the most amazing thing Michael. The most amazing thing is that they truly believe that somehow it's all just going to carry on. They truly believe that the Mablethorpe's and the Hawksworth's and the rest of those bastards out there will just say 'Oh, good for them! Look they really aren't any trouble at all now, so we'll just leave them to it. Oh, and by the way why don't we just keep giving them food and power and medicine because... well, because,

after all they just want to be happy!'
"That isn't what we are-"
"Oh I know you don't think that, Michael. I know you don't believe that, except..."
"Except what?" Deveron asked. He felt numb inside as for the first time, (or maybe it was just the first time he had admitted it to himself) he could see the glint in Dominic's eyes, the way the man seemed not to be talking to him but talking only to himself.
"You have a genius about you, Michael- no don't look like that, you do- the way you can analyse things, the way you can bring ideas and people together, give them hope, belief... You could always do it even back then at Cambridge, and it's a rare gift, it really is. But I'm not sure you realise just how much these people have actually invested in you, Professor Michael Deveron, 'The Doc!'"
Deveron shook his head.
Weston laughed at his denial, "You see, that's you all over. You take power...no that's wrong, people give you power and then you give it right back to them. You always refuse to accept the responsibility that comes with that power, you see? You did the same thing at college. When you walked away from Mablethorpe and the rest of them, they were devastated; you were their leader and you didn't even realise it! They never forgave you for that, you know. That's why they treated me the way they did. For a long time I didn't realise that. I thought it was me, that there was something wrong with me; but there wasn't, they just couldn't forgive the fact that I was the closest to you. I realise now that they hurt me because they couldn't do it to you; they never forgave you for abandoning them, you know."
Deveron shook his head, "I don't know what you-"
"Gregory Mablethorpe and the rest of those bastards... they hated you for abandoning them. You made them bereft and very angry, but they couldn't touch you...hurt you; they wouldn't have dared because of your family, you see. So they took it out on me!"

Deveron stayed silent, watching Weston, who had suddenly stopped talking and was staring off to one side. He could almost see the man's lips moving as he was clearly reliving whatever Mablethorpe and the others had done to him. He forced himself not to interrupt; he would need to hear everything now if he was going to have any chance of dealing with this...whatever this was! He kept his expression neutral as Weston started speaking again, clearly unaware he had 'zoned out' for over a minute,
"They blamed me for it, you see! But I understand it all now, why they couldn't accept me as part of their group, why they were so cruel and hurtful. It wasn't ever about me you see. It was you they were trying to hurt: you they wanted to ridicule."

"Whatever they did, Dominic, it was a long time ago," Deveron said quietly, "It was a different world back then-"
"No!" Weston shouted, crashing his fist down onto the table. He shook his head, drawing a long shuddering breath with his eyes closed tightly; when he opened them again he looked calmly at Deveron, the smile he had worn earlier back now as though it had never been away.
"No, this is what I'm trying to tell you, Michael, this is the part you don't get...you never did! All this," he waved his arms around the room, "this whole place, it only exists because you took it and you took it with force. You exercised power, Michael. You understand that much surely?" He looked at Deveron and leaned forward impatiently. "Look, when I saw it was you on the television, I knew it straight away. It was almost like it was ordained or something. I mean, there you were Michael Deveron the kindest, goodliest man I have ever known. There you were bringing people together, defending people, and then he, Mablethorpe was trashing you, calling you a terrorist and a murderer. You! Sounds familiar, doesn't it? It's like history repeating itself. Except this time you see they won't succeed in humiliating us, this time they won't succeed because of this!' He held up the pen that contained the virus, and Deveron felt himself involuntarily wince, but still managed to force himself to smile as Weston grabbed his hand and placed the pen in between their two clasped palms. He could almost feel the poison leeching through the thin metal. He knew instinctively if he was to show fear now, he would have no chance of controlling Dominic's actions.
"You're a good man, Michael!"
"So are you, Dominic, but I don't see how any of this will achieve anything. You have to realise that the moment the woman Nasri files her story, the Government will have no choice but to move against us. And, instead of the support we will have been gradually building up, the public outcry against us will be huge, and then there will be nothing any of us can do to stop them!"
Weston smiled, shaking his head, "No you still don't see it, do you, you who are so good at analysing the nature of power, and yet you refuse to acknowledge the power we have? Look, what if I told you that this pen between our hands has been activated- No, don't let go Michael!" he said, suddenly gripping Deveron's hand tighter, "If you let go, then the capsule inside will be released and the agent will escape and we, all of us, will perish."

Deveron looked into Weston's intense gaze; the man had loosened his grip now enough that, if Deveron wanted to, he could pull free. You're bluffing he wanted to shout into this lunatic man's face whilst yanking his hand free. Instead he said quietly, "Well I assume you can deactivate it just as easily?"
Weston's eyes widened in surprise, then he burst out laughing, a genuine

laugh that Deveron remembered from their younger, more innocent days, "Of course I can, but you knew I hadn't activated it! But just then, for that brief second, Michael, I wanted you to experience what it would feel like to make that decision. Now, admit it. It made you feel more alive didn't it?"

"This won't stop them, Dominic, not now! Don't you see that? They'll evacuate a large enough area and then they will blast us into oblivion..." he stopped as Weston shook his head.

"No, they won't, Michael. You see, this agent between our hands is everything that I told you it was except...well, I'll be honest with you I did omit a few small details when I described its properties to everyone."

Deveron's eyes widened.

"It's ok," he smiled, "I've told you about your fear of taking control, about accepting responsibility. I mean, what would you have done if I had told you what this stuff is really capable of? You wouldn't have allowed me to stay whatever the others decided; we both know that, don't we." he paused waiting for Deveron to speak and, when he didn't, he nodded sympathetically. "I know it's hard to accept but truly, Michael, I was just trying to protect you. Anyway, it's all going to be ok now, because out there Mablethorpe and the rest of them, they know that this wouldn't be a small incident. If the 6/707 gets into the atmosphere, it can't be shut down! Oh, believe me, they've tried; that was why they brought me into the project in the first place, to see if I could re-sequence the thing, to make it switch off after a suitable time frame, one based on a couple of years rather than a couple of centuries. Otherwise, it has no practical application in the theatre."

Deveron shook his head, "I don't understand what you mean –"

"It's the future of modern warfare Michael. Everyone is trying to develop the same type of system-"

"But why would you...oh, I see!" Deveron said. "Kill the people not the assets. It's sick, Dominic!"

"Not really, well, not if you think about it logically, it makes perfect sense, at least from a military point of view."

He thought about it now, and knew that Dominic was right that to have something that annihilated a city, or even a whole country's population, but didn't destroy its infrastructure was, Deveron thought, the ultimate capitalist weapon. He tried to clear his mind and focus on the now, trying to keep his voice light, neutral.

"So what happens now, Dominic? You have this thing," he nodded down at the pen still clasped in Dominic's hand. He forced himself not to hold his breath as Dominic smiled at him and placed the pen back in his inside jacket pocket without even looking at it.

"What I mean, Dominic, is- and I'm assuming that for the moment you are right, by the way, and they don't simply drop some ginormous bomb on

our head- then what happens now?"
Weston leaned back in his chair and held his hands out in a shrug, "I don't get what you mean, Michael?"
"Well, have you not now become our Helios around which we must all perpetually orbit?"
"You're the classicist, Michael. You tell me?" his smile had faded now. "Maybe I'm the other one, his son, the one who burned the Earth. I can't remember his name Apollo?"
"Phaeton, "Deveron said quietly. "He stole his father's chariot and crashed it, burning heaven and earth in the process. Look, Dominic, I don't think you want to destroy us all; the man I knew, the man I know I mean wouldn't deliberately hurt anyone. But I do need to know what comes next, we all do."
Weston grinned at him, staying silent.
"You've said it yourself, Dominic, this is a weapon that can't be used unless..."
Weston nodded encouragingly.
"Unless you have discovered how to isolate it, and then it's worth millions, billions?"
"More than that Michael. And believe me we won't have any shortage of people who want to help us keep it safe and secure, the same people who will have the power to secure our futures!"

Chapter Twenty

For Professor Alim Jaheel, today was a day of firsts. For starters it was the first time in his seventy five years that he had ever been chauffeur driven. It was also the first time that, as a Muslim with Pakistani origins who sported a beard, that he hadn't been questioned at passport control. In fact, in yet another first, he had been driven directly to the steps of a small-sleek looking jet which was parked in a corner of the runway at Leeds International airport, where a customs officer saluted him and his companion as they boarded.

Only a few hours ago he had been planning on a leisurely morning sail up the canal and, depending on the weather, maybe mooring up at the Anchor for a pie and pint. Yet here he was now, sipping tea from a dainty cup, comfortably seated in the grand reception room of the United Grand Lodge of England. He had already known that this was the centre of the world as far as the history of freemasonry was concerned. He had been here once before, many years ago as an undergraduate as, like many newly sworn-in Freemasons, he had taken up the offer of a conducted tour of the Great Hall. At the time, he had only achieved the second rank of 'Fellow Craft', so the visit had been brief and restricted to the main halls. Nowadays of course, anybody could go online for an, albeit restricted video tour of the Grand Lodge. That would have been unthinkable in those early days, when membership of a lodge was shrouded in secrecy, especially for a young Pakistani Academic. When the British Ambassador to Pakistan had invited him, an earnest young graduate, to become an apprentice, he had almost refused the invitation. There were many in the one true faith who considered freemasonry as an insidious arm of Zionist empiricism. Fortunately for him, and to his great surprise, his own Imam Khalid (who it turned out was himself a brother, a fellow traveller as the brotherhood often called themselves) persuaded him that to be a Freemason was an entirely acceptable and righteous thing for a Muslim to do, though not something of course one would ever be let known in public.
He had often wondered how different his life would have become if he had not accepted the Ambassador's offer. Certainly he would never have achieved the academic standing he had done; nor would he have become a Principal of Jesus College, Oxford. He realised he was thinking about that first visit to the Grand Lodge now, as part of him felt almost like he did on that day, waiting for someone to ask who did he think he was, coming into such an august place. Ridiculous, of course, Alhim was no longer a lowly apprentice. He had reached the fifteenth level and become a 'Knight of the Sword and of the East'. He knew and accepted without rancour that he would be elevated no further. The Brotherhood was truly egalitarian, with no Brother who reached the third Rank of Master to be considered higher in import than any other-except, of course, that the financial obligations placed on the 'appendant' rankings meant only those with independent means could afford to go beyond that which he had attained. And today he would be meeting the highest of them all- the head of British and Commonwealth Freemasonry, the Grand Inspector General, or Grand Master of the United Lodge of England. His rank was of the thirty third-

degree and customarily, it was a role reserved for a member of the Royal Family.

He had met the Duke of Kent once before when his Royal Highness had toured the university, but this was different. He had brought with him his ceremonial robe, unsure as to whether he would be required to wear it. The Brother who had welcomed him and invited him to wait in the reception room had informed him, without being asked, that he needn't dress formally, but that it 'would be appropriate if he would don his badge of office'. He traced his hand across the face of the embossed box. He had other medals of course, but none meant as much to him as this one. Yet he suspected that his attendance here today was more about those former medals than his achievements in the brotherhood. It had been no surprise of course that the intelligence services would want to use him. His native tongue was Urdu, but he also spoke fluent Punjabi and had passable Arabic. Coming to England in those first years, it had been the Brotherhood of Free Masonry and the comradeship of the intelligence community which had helped him cope with the loss of all that he had thought of as home. As an academic, he had been able to legitimately attend conferences in all of the Middle East countries, and of course they had fast-tracked him for British citizenship as part of what he learned later was called 'bringing him in to the family'.

He had done things, things that even now his conscience wrestled with. He had done them for the right reasons, of course; even when his actions had led directly to the deaths of others, they had always been carried out to protect innocents. His rank of Knight of the Sword and of the East was both fitting and ironic, he thought. Ever since those early days, he had been a weapon of one type or another and, no matter how long and faithfully he served his adopted nation, he would be forever of the East. Sometimes, often in fact, he would simply act as a gatherer of information or as a talent scout for recruits in the Arab sphere. Sometimes, though, he had been required to do violence or worse against some individual. He had killed three times, and each death still haunted him even forty years later. The people he had killed, two men and a woman, were all guilty of terrorist acts- not the phoney terrorism that the UK government now branded anyone who had a counter view to their own with, but real terrorists, people who killed or ordered people to be killed indiscriminately. Nor had he ever had any difficulty distinguishing between freedom fighters and terrorists; for him the distinction was simple. Freedom fighters killed fellow combatants; terrorists killed civilians, full stop. Not that he promoted that view too often in the service of course. He never forgot that he was employed by the same organisation that had branded Gandhi a terrorist, the same people who for many years said that said Mandela was a terrorist, even that Curt

Kobella was a terrorist! He also never forgot- for how could he that he had never, would never, he corrected himself, be fully trusted despite all he had done. Still, he had been shocked and dismayed that whilst the nuclear fires were still burning throughout Israel and the West Bank, he had been 'rested' from active service. More than that, he had been 'interviewed' several times as to his sympathies in the conflagration. Nor had it been his service as a distinguished and loyal servant that had saved him from the fate suffered by many, if not most British Asians. Tens of thousands of men, women, and children had been rounded up and interned and not only for the six months immediately following the holocaust but, in many cases for years afterwards. No, he had been saved from such indignity, from such betrayal, because he was a respected member of the brotherhood of freemasonry, which lifted him in the eyes of those who mattered above the normal levels of Islamophobic paranoia and suspicion. He hadn't been interned, but he been 'rested' ever since, something that privately at least he could admit to being grateful for. The internments had changed him, changed his views on the principles and tenets that he had fought for, had killed for. They had taken away his trust, shaken his beliefs, and now they were calling him back. He knew without question that this was to do with Nasri; she had gone into Riverside and they were panicking but why?

He had followed the whole story of Riverside, of course he had, and he would have done so even if Nasri hadn't been covering it. He didn't believe that the stand-off was simply to avoid, as many commentators were saying, political scandal and embarrassment. More than most, he understood the power of the state to suppress information when it needed or wanted to, and that was still the case even today, despite the likes of Fringenet and to a lesser extent FPN, Al-Jazeera and the others. No, it was clear that the people of the Riverside Estate had access to weaponry of some type, probably nuclear he thought, shuddering inwardly at the memories of the last time the world had witnessed its use. Nasri was inside and she would get the story, he had no doubts on that, nor did he doubt that FPN would broadcast it. What he couldn't figure out yet was why that was such a problem politically for the Government? It was obvious that international sympathy would fall away from the rebels as soon as it became known they had obtained, and were threatening to use, a nuclear device. He was still missing some part of the puzzle. What though?

He let out a long sigh, and became aware that the young police superintendent a 'fellow traveller' was watching him, a not unkind smile on his face.

He held out the jewel case, and smiled back at the superintendent, speaking softly, "Would you like to look at it, my young Brother?"

The Superintendent took the case in his hands, "I have seen the sword once before, Brother, but only from a distance. It is a thing of beauty," he said opening the case.
"Can you interpret its meaning?"
The Superintendent stared at the star shaped badge for a long moment, clearly trying to remember the many hours of teachings and research he had been obliged to undertake. "The three golden triangles, they represent equality, liberty and fraternity... for all men and nations?"
"Go on," Jaheel said nodding.
"The two crossed swords stand for truth and justice, and the red velvet of the lined case signifies the kingly status of Masonry."
"Mm, ok. But the red velvet actually signifies that the gift of Masonry is more precious than the gift of kings, in other words, masonry bestows more than wealth and power." He smiled and pointed back down at the case in the superintendent's hands. "What about the triangles and that which lies within them?"
"The chains, you mean? No I can't remember. It's something to do with us being bound together though, that we are stronger when we are linked together... But to be honest I might be making that up!"
Jaheel laughed, "Still, it's a highly plausible suggestion. The chains are often neglected, yet for me they are at the crux of freemasonry. The chains are imprisoned inside the triangles, as we must try on our life journey to imprison the negativities they represent. They are the chains of the intellect and of tyranny and of superstition, and of course they are also the chains of privilege. And, though you are still new to the path, I am sure you will know that not all of our brethren quite manage to forgo all such evils!"
The Superintendent laughed, then looked around quickly to make sure he hadn't been overheard, which made them both laugh a little more.

He had liked the young policeman instinctively when he had introduced himself that morning at his front door, and handed him the prestigious invitation which would so dramatically change his plans for the day. The man had been a thoroughly pleasant travelling companion, and he seemed as impressed by their VIP treatment as Jaheel himself, which made the whole surreal experience somehow less stressful. Though he had known immediately that this had something to do with Nasri, the Superintendent clearly had no clue as to why he had been summoned or who he was, other than his name, and that the Chief Commissioner himself, Richard Hawksworth, had ordered him 'to escort the Professor to London immediately'. The Superintendent had introduced himself that morning, offering his hand in a way that told Jaheel that he was a fellow traveller and brother, He also allowed his hand to be enclosed, so that Jaheel's thumb could take a dominant position in the handshake, indicating that he was of a lower rank to that of himself. He had taken the plain vanilla envelope from the young man and ripped it open casually, in part to disguise that his hands were trembling slightly. They both recognised instantly whose Royal insignia headed the letter, the Superintendent unconsciously standing straighter whilst trying hard not to peer further at the contents, which were brief.

Dear Brother Jaheel,

Please accompany this young Brother to meet with us at our Grand Place.

Yours Fraternally

Nicholas

He looked up as the secretary who had greeted them earlier re-entered the room from one of the numerous unmarked highly lacquered doors that lined the hall. The Superintendent stood up quickly, standing to attention.

The man looked like he had a bad smell under his nose as he ignored the young Brother and spoke coolly to Jaheel, "Brother, the Grand Master will see you now."

He got up slowly and pushed his fists into his lower back to ease the ache he always seemed to get these days, when he sat in one place for too long.

Jaheel turned to the Superintendent who was already offering his badge of office, which he took back with a smile, pinning it quickly onto the lapel of his favourite tweed and well lived-in teaching jacket.

"A moment please, Brother," he said to the Secretary who was already walking back down the hall. The man paused, trying unsuccessfully to hide his irritation at any delay. Jaheel turned to the Superintendent, offering his hand, which he took with a smile, "Thank you for your help and for your company, Brother."

"It was my pleasure, sir."

He started to follow the secretary, who was now looking at his watch pointedly. Jaheel stopped again, "And do remember the chains, my boy, especially the last one." He said raising his eyes upward toward the now openly impatient Secretary.

"I will sir," the superintendent said, his serious expression only slightly betrayed by the hint of a smile.

As Jaheel followed the Secretary's retreating back through yet another angled corridor, he kicked himself again for baiting the man, who he was now certain was determined to present him in front of the Grand Master out of breath and sweating like a pig. He had known that the Grand Lodge was big, but not this big, surely? No, the man had clearly understood his little dig about the chain of privilege, and now he was quite rightly reminding Jaheel of the other chain, the one that represented vanity and intellect. Serves me right, he thought as the long striding devil turned yet another corner. When he stopped abruptly, Jaheel barely managed not to bump into him. They had stopped in front of another plain varnished oak door, with nothing to distinguish it from any of the countless identical doors they had passed on their way through the labyrinth of corridors. It suddenly struck him that maybe the long detour had been simply to disorient him, as he doubted he would be able to retrace his steps if he was ever asked to.

"You may enter freely, Brother." Jaheel realised with the formal words that the man was not a secretary but the Tyler of the Lodge and the keeper of the doors for the Grand Lodge. The man had a satisfied smile on his face, as he saw that Jaheel was breathing heavily after the brisk trot through the halls.

Jaheel simply nodded. He had behaved stupidly once today; he wouldn't do it twice he told himself self-consciously, straightening his posture before opening the door.

He had been expecting- well, he didn't exactly know what he'd been expecting, probably an opulent drawing room or a gentleman's club kind of thing, but the room he entered actually took his breath away. The whole of the far wall was stained glass divided into three large leaded sections. To the left, the horsed Knights of St John were riding down to what he guessed was Galilee. In the right panel, a group of robed Grand Masters stood around a large table with the Volume of the Sacred Law lying opened upon it. This was the volume that contained the sacred books of religion. For Jaheel, the volume of the sacred law meant the Holy Koran, for others it meant the Holy Bible. and for others the Torah. It was a key strength that masonry whilst insisting a man on entering the brotherhood must declare his belief in a supreme being, the religion itself was not proscribed. The largest panel in the centre was a dazzling rainbow of colour, separated into the 32 degrees of masonry. which stretched outward as though reflected by the sun itself. The centre contained the great eye encased within the golden triangle. He forced himself to look away from the magnificent window to take in the rest of his surroundings- the vaulted ceilings and domed apertures which were lavishly adorned with gilt the gold vivid against galazio blue panels. He was aware of the two men who were waiting patiently at the far end of the room, yet he continued as they would expect him to, to slowly take in the grandeur of the place, thereby giving proper recognition to the artistry of the building and its artefacts.

He walked slowly down the chequered black and white marbled floor, which was lined by serried ranks of the numerous bronze statuary which represented the majesty and craft of the brotherhood. When he finally

reached the low dais where they waited, he was unconsciously smiling. The Grand Sovereign General himself stood with his arms and hands shaped so that their meaning reinforced his greeting, "Brother Jaheel Knight of the Sword and of the East, you are most welcome in this place."
Jaheel began to make the signs of the three degrees, pleased that his hands were steady, as was his voice when he spoke, "Grand Master, I-"
"Now then, Brother," the Duke said abruptly, "let us dispense with these rituals, as sacred as they are, and talk as men must when a crisis confronts them!"
Jaheel nodded his assent, in part to hide his shock at the man's profanity in the face of their honoured and sacred rituals. He wondered for a moment whether he should now address the Grand Master with his civilian title of Your Royal Highness, then dismissed it. When they were in the lodge, however informally they spoke, they were after all simply brethren. The Duke indicated that he should follow him. Jaheel got up and waited until both the Grand Master and his right hand, the 'Keeper of the Royal Secrets', who he had met occasionally in his other role as Chief Commissioner of Police Richard Hawksworth. Despite the fact that the man was a brother he was someone Jaheel had little liking for. He went through the door and followed them out of the ritual hall into a small antechamber. The Grand Master indicated that he should sit, which he did, sinking into the old leather chair which felt as if it had been designed for his personal comfort. The Grand Master sat down opposite him whilst the Keeper of The Royal Secrets stood with his arms folded, leaning on the side of the white marble fireplace, the banked red coals flickering and making small forays above the grate as they sought feebly for new fuel and oxygen.

"You will have divined, I think why, we asked you here, Brother Jaheel?" The Duke said, his hands steepled in front of him, his legs crossed so his expensive handmade shoes reflected the flickering coals.
I wonder if he's ever shined his own shoes, Jaheel thought, whilst nodding gravely. "I assume it has something to do with the fact that my granddaughter Nasri has managed to get herself into the Riverside Estate?"
The Duke smiled, "Indeed so, Brother. We believe your granddaughter's presence amongst the terrorists places our nation in great peril and we, that is all of us, must do what we can to ensure this Riverside situation is brought to a swift end."

Jaheel nodded, "I see that, Grand Master, but my granddaughter, as I am sure you already know, is not with or for these terrorists as you describe them. She is simply a journalist, and as such she seeks to shine the light of truth on these matters."
"Yet are there not some truths, Brother, that benefit little from being

exposed to the light, else how do we justify our order?"
Jaheel smiled. This was apprentice level stuff which he wouldn't dignify with a response. The Duke nodded imperceptibly at Hawksworth, who stood up straight, his voice distinctly different from the soft, almost gentle tones of the Worshipful Master.
"Brother Jaheel, the people of Riverside have gained access to a weapon that places all which we hold dear in jeopardy. We, that is the Grand Master has summoned you here to ensure that your granddaughter does not magnify that danger."
Jaheel stroked the beading of the chair arm, addressing himself directly to the Duke,
"Brother, I am what you see before you, and that is simply an old academic. My granddaughter, like all those still blessed with youth, would take no notice-"
"Come, Brother!" Hawksworth said, causing Jaheel to look up at him, "we know what you seem to be, and we know what you are. How could we not?"
Jaheel inclined his head, "That was a long time ago-"
Hawksworth held up his hand, "Forgive my interrupting again, Brother Jaheel, but circumstances require that I speak to you more bluntly than is customary in this place."
Jaheel for the first time heard real sincerity in Hawksworth's words, "I can see that, Brother, and it is of little matter to me with what bluntness truth is expressed, so long as it is truth. It is true what I have said, I am but an old man whose influence and skills wane faster than even I like to admit."
The Grand Master unclasped his hands and leaned forward, "Brother, the weapon these people have access to is not nuclear as I feel sure you have assumed!"
"Then what is it?"
The Grand Master looked over at Hawksworth nodding for him to speak.
"It is a biological weapon capable of mass destruction if it's released into the atmosphere." He held his hand up, forestalling Jaheel's questions. "Brother we are talking in this place so there is no need to talk of confidences and keeping secrets. We are beyond that?"
Then why say it? Jaheel thought, irritated, but still managed to smile and nod his assent.
"The weapon, which is designated 6/707, was stolen from one of our facilities by one of our own scientists, who we now know has been in league with these terrorists for some time!"

Jaheel wanted to rail at the two of them. How had such incompetence become so embedded and entrenched in these people who ran his adopted country? That they had the weapon at all was bad enough, though

unsurprising as in Jaheel's opinion most states would still be working on such weaponry despite the international treaties. But what did it say about them that had they allowed a weapon as disgusting and deadly as this clearly was to be removed from a secure facility, right under their noses. That in itself was bad enough, but to then allow it to be taken through the heavily secured area that was the Riverside Estate really did beggar belief. He had unconsciously steepled his fingers together, almost mimicking someone in Christian prayer, which was simply his meditative stance when faced with a dilemma. It was true what he had told them, he was an old man now and full of aches and pains that he told no one about except his specialist. If he was right in what they were asking of him, he feared he really wouldn't be physically up to the task.
He also knew if he was to reject their request for him to involve himself that would clearly put his beloved Nasri at risk, something he couldn't countenance on any level. He looked up at the Grand Master, ignoring Hawksworth completely.

"What is it you would have me do, Grand Master?"
"We need you to speak to your granddaughter. We can arrange a satellite call for you to do so, and we need you, in whatever way you think appropriate, to get her to stop the report that she is currently preparing."
Jaheel shook his head, "You don't know her sir. She has a stubborn streak. Heaven knows where she gets it from!" he smiled to himself, "Nonetheless, Nasri will not walk away from a story like this, no matter what I say to her."
This time when Hawksworth spoke the Grand Master didn't stop him, "The brotherhood requires this from you, Brother Jaheel, and the sacred oaths you have taken require you to aide and assist your brethren when they are in need."
Jaheel continued to stare at the Grand Master, "Those oaths preclude doing anything that is injurious to one's own family and kin!"
The Grand Master smiled sympathetically, "That is true, Brother Jaheel, yet when events of such grave seriousness occur, we may all have to sacrifice ourselves on the altar for the greater good. Sometimes when it is for the greater good, we have to be prepared to carry out any acts required of us- you of all people know that!"
Jaheel looked away from the man's eyes; so they did know everything...even that! He realised now how desperate they really were, which meant they could still be manoeuvred, as all those who are desperate can be. This time he turned directly to face Hawksworth, "What if I decline this...request, Brother, what other options are available?"
"Only one."
Jaheel tilted his head to one side, easing the crick in his neck. Only one! Hawksworth, would have her neutralised, killed. He knew with absolute

certainty that they would do so in whatever way they could if he refused to help. He felt a sickening gurgle in the pit of his stomach, but his face remained impassive. He could get Nasri to stop her report, he realised suddenly. She would do it for him; especially if she thought doing so would save him from harm or danger, then she would do it. But she would hate him forever and would never forgive him- he knew that much about her. It was why he could never have told her the truth about her father the husband of his beautiful Aysha Nasri's mother. He took a long slow breath and blew it out. Hawksworth had moved to stand behind the Grand Master's chair. The two of them were watching him, waiting for his answer.
He nodded slowly, "Very well, I will do it. However," he said holding his hands up to stop them speaking, "there are a few pre-conditions and guarantees that I will need from you before doing so."
Hawksworth smiled at him; the Grand Master looked at his watch clearly already thinking about his next appointment.

Chapter Twenty One

They were in Woodcock's hardware shop, or 'Splintered Dick's' as Reeko told them it had been called locally. The place had been closed for maybe three years or so, and the only things not stripped out were the old wooden benches that used to be piled high with every screw and widget known to man. It was still basically a sound building, with unbroken windows; and the lead flashing even more surprisingly, was still attached to the roof. Woodcock's had been one of those old-fashioned places that existed before DIY superstores crushed them out of existence. It didn't matter how obscure, how large or small the screw, plug, wire, valve or tap was, Old Man Woodcock would be able to find one amongst the myriad of unlabelled cartons and boxes that lined the ceiling high shelves and wooden benches. If he didn't have quite the part you wanted, he would always heave a great sigh of regret. Then quickly lay his hands on something that would 'do just as good with a bit of a tweak', and most times he was right.

At first they had started using the shop as it overlooked the square, and was better than standing in the rain while they waited for a meeting with the Government. Then Reeko and Mallet had gotten hold of a primus stove and brought some mugs over for brewing tea and coffee from the bistro, and it had now become their unofficial pre-meeting room. It was less public than the bistro, which meant they didn't have to be as cautious when they were discussing stuff that wasn't necessarily for public consumption. The other advantage was that Danny had recently installed some filters in the place, which he assured them made the building eavesdropper proof, triggering an alarm if anyone tried to use any bugs, or even a parabolic microphone to hear what they were saying.

Without any conscious planning or discussion, Riverside had now split up its business arrangements. The normal everyday meetings that discussed everything from food growing to schooling to neighbour disputes, now took place in the large hall or, if they were just in committee, in the bistro. Security meetings, when they were all there including Weston, were now held in Danny's workshop. The problem was, whenever people saw the security committee as they were now known meeting, they would get edgy. Rumours would fly around the place as to what was happening, or about to. That had gotten worse since Bear and the sound man had been shot. People appreciated the work that Doc and the others did, and any meetings they convened always packed out the hall. But the truth was most people didn't want to have to think about Armageddon every hour of the day, and were glad to let them get on with it.

They were due to meet the Government shortly for a regular meeting except, since the journalist from the FPN had gotten inside the meetings had become tense and anything but regular. Hawksworth had initially demanded they send the reporter out with her equipment else he would launch an all out assault and had given them twelve hours to comply. It had been by no means unanimous to allow her to stay but, in the end, it was the knowledge that she was now probably in as much danger as they were that eventually swung the vote in her favour. They had also fallen out quite badly amongst themselves on whether to allow her to interview people, but the truth was it had actually helped. It didn't matter that ninety per cent of the interviews and footage she shot would never be used or seen, people clearly found the process cathartic. Even those like Reeko, who had been dead set against letting her and the cameraman Dave stay, had come round to the two of them. That was helped by the fact that Bear had come through ok, and both Nasri and Dave had taken more than their share of nursing him without being asked. Apart from a scar on his temple that would never fade, and which Reeko suspected Bear was secretly proud of, the big man seemed to be pretty much back to his old self. The fact that Bear had taken a real liking to Nasri and Dave also helped in bringing round Reeko to finally declare them as 'acceptable'.

The woman Nasri had been quite open about the stuff she was putting together, and didn't seem to have engaged in any of the typical cutesy media stunts. She was also quite willing to show them any footage they asked to look at. Still, her arrival had upped the stakes considerably, and threatened the uneasy truce that they had reached with the outside. When they had called Hawksworth's bluff and refused to hand her over, it had been made very clear to them that the only way they would survive, not just the committee but every man woman and child living in Riverside, was if news of the weapon didn't reach the outside world. This time none of them thought the Government was bluffing. That was emphasised when it was Mablethorpe's normally mild mannered aide, Jennings, who told them in his quiet and unassuming way that 'Should this information become, or even seriously threaten to become public, there will then be no need or incentive for the Government to show any measure of restraint.' Since then, as a committee, they hadn't really talked it through at length, but in truth they were all half expecting that the next meeting might just be the last before it, whatever it was, came to a head.

"What about asking Doc Timms if there is something we can give him that would put him down fast, like the stuff they use on dogs?" Reeko said, continuing the discussion they had been having.
"Come on, Reeko," Sunny said, pouring himself the last of the coffee, "we know that the thing is wired into his vitals somehow, so it doesn't matter how quick we do it. Killing him would still set the thing off!"
"We don't know that though do we?" Reeko said, looking across at the five of them. He was perched on his favourite spot on the old service counter, his feet propped up against a corner of one wall.
Jo stood up and stamped her feet. It was cold in here today and she had her hands thrust deep into her favourite too big flying jacket. "No, we don't, but the sick bastard has told us that the pen triggers a release if he stops breathing, if his heart stops, even if it's moved a metre away from him!"
"And you believe him?" Reeko asked.
Sunny had stood up whilst the two of them were arguing and started to vigorously rub Jo's arms to warm her up, and also to try and stop them all descending into the same circuitous discussion they had been having for days. "Danny says it's possible, Reeko, and we all agreed that we can't take the chance-"
"No, he didn't say that, Sunny. Danny said it was 'possible but not likely' that he had the tech to pull it off. Not likely, right?" Reeko said looking across at Danny who just shrugged.
Sunny shook his head at him. "It doesn't really matter, does it, because we agreed we couldn't take the risk that he was bluffing, or have you forgotten

that bit?"
"No, I haven't forgotten. But I tell you now that I am not gonna allow that fucker to lord it over us, make us bow and scrape around him and just... just use us till he decides to actually carry out whatever crazy shit he's got going on in his head. You've all seen him with his little gang, he's like some old feudal Baron or Lord, and it's getting worse you all know it!"

The room fell into silence. It was true. Weston had gone from the shy 'here to help' academic, to the smug and arrogant leader of a small but not insignificant group of Riverside misfits. He was rarely on his own now and, even when the security committee met, he always arranged to have a couple of people hanging around outside the cafe or wherever they met, keeping him in constant sight. He'd also told them that he wouldn't be attending any of the meetings with the Government, as he thought they might just be foolish enough to put a bullet in the back of his head. That was the same time he had told them all in front of a mass meeting that they needn't worry about him or their own security. He'd explained the fail-safe systems he had built in to the pen device to a hushed room. Someone had asked him what would happen if he just had an everyday normal accident, or a heart attack or something? Weston had grinned good naturedly as he replied 'then Lord help us all! It had been a chilling moment. A few people had laughed with him, but they were nervous laughs. Most people simply looked confused, unclear as to what exactly it would mean for them. The one good thing about his decision not to attend the government meetings was at least they now had a chance to talk openly about what, if anything, they could do about him, which was of course the main benefit of Woodcock's as a venue.

The day after Weston and Doc had had their private conversation, Doc had come to the six of them ashen-faced, speaking quietly as he told them that it was true. Dominic had invited the journalist Nasri Jaheel into the estate. He had told Doc that he felt the 'revolutionary aims' had been slipping into a cosy hippy trippy commune. The world needed to know, he had told Doc, that Mablethorpe and his coterie, had in direct violation of the 2019 International Treaty, developed and manufactured biological weapons of mass destruction. Weston believed, Doc told them, that the world would not forgive them for it, and in that much at least he was probably correct. When North Korea had used for the first time in modern history lethal mass biotics against their Southern neighbours, the world had been repulsed. Hundreds of thousands had died within weeks, and almost half a million within the first three months. Fifteen years later, one in three South and North Korean children were born with severe deformities, and the infant mortality rate was over sixty percent. The biotic agent used had been

carried in the faeces of livestock, and contaminated cereal crops and watercourses. It couldn't be switched off. The best minds in world science still hadn't managed to eradicate the agent, but in the last year had announced that they were trialling a counter enzyme that could digest the spores that the re-agent remade itself from.
Doc also told them on that day that he now believed Dominic Weston was a dangerous sociopath, and no one had contradicted him.

Katy finally broke the morose silence that had descended on them, "Well, whatever we decide to do is going to have to wait." She tapped her wristwatch.
"OK," Reeko said, "But we have to decide what we're gonna do; we can't leave it like this!"
"I agree," Sunny said standing up and stretching the ache out of his back. "but Katy's right Reeko. We don't have time right now to thrash it out. But whatever we do eventually decide, we have to all agree to it, and we also will need to be very clear what the consequences are." he looked across the room at Reeko who nodded seemingly satisfied at least for the time being.

*

Jo felt instinctively that something was off balance as she took her usual seat under the by now decidedly grubby looking gazebo. She looked around at the others, and could see they sensed it as well. The usual faces were sat opposite, although the woman who took notes had been replaced by an older Asian man, his kindly expression looking completely out of place alongside Hawksworth and the rest of them. Suddenly she had it, what was wrong. It was Hawksworth; he was smiling at them. We must really be in the shit, she thought, trying to keep her face blank.
"Good morning, ladies and gentlemen," Hawksworth said, still smiling in a way that Jo found more chilling than if he'd been in one of his usual rages
Doc nodded and opened the cover of his A4 notepad, his face impassive, seemingly oblivious to this new friendly version of the Chief Commissioner.
Hawksworth spoke as he indicated to his left, "This gentleman is Professor Alhim, and I have invited him here today to try and help us with our...current difficulties."
Jo looked across at the man who, nodded without looking directly at any of them.
"Professor Deveron," Hawksworth said, using Doc's honorific for the first time she could remember. "We understand that Professor Weston and your good self have, how can I put it, differing viewpoints shall we say as to the way forward for the good citizenry of Riverside."
Jo was Watching Doc as he kept his hands palm down on either side of his notepad, his face blank. He had this incredible ability to not show any emotion when under stress, especially in these formal situations where most

of the group, herself included, just wanted to reach across and punch the smug Chief Commissioner on the nose. Sunny had told Doc once that, if he ever turned his mind to it, he could make a fortune playing poker. None of them had expected or considered that Hawksworth would already know that Weston had gone rogue. She cursed herself and the rest of them for being so naive. They had known for weeks now there was an informant in the estate, even though they were no nearer to tracking down whoever it was. Danny was still saying it was only a matter of time before whoever it was stayed online just long enough for him to be able to pinpoint with 100% accuracy who the spy was. But until then, they could only guess, something she found herself doing far too often. Just please God that it isn't one of us, she thought again, not for the first time.

"What? No witty retort, Professor?" Hawksworth said, still smiling. "You disappoint me. Still, I will take it by your lack of response that you don't deny what we both know to be true, that you have lost control of both your friend Weston and, as a consequence, the 6/707." Hawksworth leaned back into his chair, waiting for Doc to respond. When he didn't, the smile slipped slightly from his face. "There is still time, Professor Deveron, to bring this whole sorry state of affairs to an end, without either your people or the wider population of this country being subjected to the horrors of this weapon. Even I do not believe that you wish to see that."

"Chief Constable Hawksworth," Doc said, his voice calm, his hands still flat on the table, "we would appreciate it very much if you were to come directly to the point."

"The point, Professor as you well know, is that we have for many weeks now been at something of a stalemate, or stand-off if you prefer. However, that position cannot be sustained if your friend Weston manages to get word out to the wider world that he possesses the 6/707. Now this TV reporter," he looked at his notes, "Ms Nasri Jaheel is as I understand it, making a documentary, including interviews with Professor Weston, and I am informed that Professor Weston has been more than forthcoming in his views?"

"Go on," Doc said.

"Ms Jaheel, as you are aware, is a prominent and highly-respected reporter for the Free Press News organisation, whose TV news bulletins are obsessing themselves and much of the Western hemisphere with the fact that she is being held incommunicado and under duress in the Riverside Estate." Hawksworth held his hand up, forestalling the protests that both Jo and Reeko were about to make. "Yes, of course we already know that she is not in fact under duress. We also now know that it was your friend Weston who arranged for her to be brought into the estate. Nonetheless, again as you are only too aware, the media, if it does not have a real story, is more than capable of making one up regardless of the facts. So, strange as it may seem, Professor, it would appear that for once we find ourselves on the same side in this matter. Do we not?"

"I'm listening," Doc said, his face impassive.

"I'm glad you are, Professor Deveron, because this situation is so very dangerous, for all of us. If this woman Jaheel has the ability, and is foolish enough... for laudable reasons of course," he added quickly, looking to his left, "If she does manage to get her report broadcast to the outside world, then we will be left with no alternative but to take the severest action possible." Hawksworth leaned forward. "You do believe me when I tell you that, Professor, I hope?" He smiled tightly at Doc's nodded assent. "Good. I told the Prime Minister that you would understand the significance of what is happening now."

Hawksworth leaned back in the chair, waiting for a response. For a moment there was complete silence around the table broken only by the faint and then getting louder thwump, thwump of a helicopter's blades as it passed to one side of the square, for the umpteenth time that morning. For a long time, Doc simply stared at his adversary before finally letting out long sigh and running his hand through his hair.

"So, Chief Commissioner, you've now succeeded in telling us what we already know, though I confess I am no clearer on what it is you are proposing. It would seem to me that the stalemate remains the same. There is of course little point in me trying to pretend that what you've said isn't true, so I won't. But, if you have a proposal you wish to make then please do so and I assure you we will be all ears."

Hawksworth nodded brusquely, as if satisfied with Doc's response. "As I said to you previously, this gentleman is Professor Alhim, his full name is Alhim Jaheel who, as well as being a distinguished academic, happens to be the grandfather of Nasri Jaheel. It is my hope and belief that, through the Professor's guidance and wisdom, he will be able to persuade Ms Jaheel how vital it is that she does not seek to publicise the presence of the weapon. What I propose therefore is to seek your cooperation in allowing the Professor to enter the estate to talk to his granddaughter."

Doc looked down at the table for a long moment before looking back at Hawksworth. "And I assume we are to take it simply on good faith that this man is who you say he is, and that he isn't simply an assassin?"

Hawksworth tilted his head to one side in what was clearly meant as a dismissive gesture at such an absurd suggestion, then he seemed to halt whatever sharp retort he was about to make and shook his head, smiling as he spoke, "Come now, Deveron. The time for games is over. We are all in deep, deep shit here- you and your people, me and mine- so I'm sure that you can appreciate that it would be to our mutual advantage to allow Professor Jaheel to speak directly to his granddaughter. For what it's worth

you have my personal word that he is who he says he is."
Deveron stared at Hawksworth for a long moment and then turned and looked at his people. Nobody said anything or gave any signal, although John Mallet gave a slight shrug that said your call. The strange thing was, Doc knew the old academic. He hadn't realised it when he first sat down, just thinking that the man looked vaguely familiar and assuming he was a member of Mablethorpe's Cabinet. It was when Hawksworth had said the man's full name though that he had remembered. He had seen Alhim Jaheel speak once at a debate he had taken part in, long before the Middle East holocaust. They were on opposite sides of the argument that day, and probably still are, Deveron thought. But, though he had disagreed with Jaheel's pro 'Western democracy fits all' solution, he had respected how the man had put his arguments, and Jaheel had clearly been uncomfortable at the time that he shared a platform with the 'all oppositionists are terrorists brigade'. That could be why they were using him, of course. They might well know that he would know him, remember him. Although he reminded himself that, back then, they wouldn't have been watching him to the degree they did later, when he was under constant surveillance. His gut instinct was that they should let the old man in, not because Doc believed he would be able to persuade Nasri to not broadcast her documentary though. Having spent however brief a time he had with Nasri Jaheel, Doc couldn't imagine her being moved off this big a story because her grandfather told her it was the right thing to do. And he knows that, Doc realised suddenly. The man he had seen debating in the Oxford Union that day, facing off a room full of angry idealistic students, was anything but naive, so he must have another reason for wanting to come in. What Doc had to decide was whether that reason was a good or bad thing for his people. He was snapped out of his ponderings by the old man's abrupt interruption.
"Before you give an answer to the Chief Commissioner, Professor Deveron, there is a further complication that I would like to try and resolve before you decide whether or not to let me in."
Hawksworth's neck started to suffuse red up into his cheeks as he spun in his chair, glowering at Jaheel. "Professor, I must ask you to-"
"Whilst I am quite willing to risk my personal safety," he said, ignoring Hawksworth," I will require additional assurances that I and my granddaughter will not be...how can I put it, abandoned and left to our fates, should some unexpected or unforeseen circumstance arise."
Doc kept his face impassive, resisting the urge to smile at the way the old boy had just hijacked Hawksworth's agenda. It definitely fit with his limited recollections of the man.
"I feel that, if I am to go inside and something goes wrong, Nasri and I would be of little consequence to either the authorities or your good selves,

and it is ever the case that pawns are the easiest pieces on the board to sacrifice. I propose, therefore, that I do not enter alone, but with a figure of authority, a person who would of course have to be of significant importance- that they had, well, shall we say a currency with both sides." He turned toward Shawcross and put his hand on his shoulder, "This young man, whom I confess to only meeting this morning, he is a high ranking police officer and would-."
"Unacceptable!" Doc said, not needing to look at the others to see if they agreed with him.
Hawksworth was still staring at Jaheel, seemingly unable to grasp for the moment what was happening.
"But you appreciate my dilemma?" Jaheel said.
"As I'm sure you appreciate ours, Professor Jaheel," Doc said.
"Right...yes, of course." Jaheel said looking down at his hands which he was unconsciously wringing.
"I could do it... that is, if it was acceptable to all parties?"
Everybody stared at Christopher Jennings as he went on. "I understand that you wouldn't allow the Inspector here to come in," he said not looking at Shawcross, though he should have been able to feel the man's eyes burning a hole into the side of his head. "I mean," he went on looking at Doc, "and without trying to sound grandiose about it, I am a senior civil servant and the Prime Minister's personal aide. Would that make me a bishop rather than a pawn?" he said seemingly to himself. "No probably not a bishop, but possibly a knight though. Certainly I would be worth more than a pawn!" He suddenly looked up, as he realised everyone was staring at him. "Oh; I'm sorry. I just thought..."
Hawksworth looked across at Deveron, and held his hands up in a well. 'what do you think gesture'.

Deveron looked across at Jennings. Throughout all the meetings they had with Hawksworth and the others he had, like the rest of the committee, come to know their opposite numbers strengths and weaknesses reasonably well. Jennings had been the archetypal civil servant, polite, efficient, and was quite often the one who would suggest a way out of their frequent impasses. Deveron didn't exactly like the man but crucially, he didn't dislike him, which was more than he could say for any of the others. Shawcross was wholly unacceptable of course- not simply because he was a police officer whom none of them liked, but there was also something about Shawcross that made him believe the man was ruthless possibly dangerous, and capable of anything. Jennings, in contrast, was not only mild-mannered but diminutive enough in his physical stature that Doc thought even he could 'take him'. He smiled to himself for a moment as he realised he was starting to use some of the local idioms, and made a quick mental note not to do it aloud, as he could already hear the gales of laughter that doing so would bring from Sunny, and especially Reeko. Once again he turned to the others, looking at each in turn. They either nodded or shrugged; once again it was up to him. He rested his elbows on the table, his hands flat together the fingers steepled in front of his mouth which the others knew meant he was about to throw the dice.

"Very well, Chief Commissioner, we will agree to Professor Jaheel and Mr Jennings coming into the estate, providing that it is done in the following manner."
Hawksworth leaned back in his chair, his usual belligerency clearly wanting to bubble through his Mr Affability mask.
"Don't look so suspicious, Chief Commissioner;" Doc went on. "I don't want much; in fact it is only this. The Professor and Mr Jennings must come now, immediately that is. We must all get up from the table together right now and walk across the square. Neither of them will bring phones, keys, any bags or documents, or personal belongings inside with them. You can send in replacement clothing later today as I am afraid they will have to give up what they are wearing now when we reach the other side of the barrier!"

Hawksworth stared into Deveron's eyes. he was being bounced he knew it and so did Deveron. First the old man Jaheel had sprung the idea on him- so much for the bond of Masonic Brotherhood, he thought. Jaheel was right, of course. Both he and his brat granddaughter would be sacrificed if necessary, and still would be. But Jennings! Once again the little twerp had usurped his authority. He would have had him locked up weeks ago if it had been up to him. The man was far too close to Shawcross, though for what reason he couldn't be certain. He had caught them on a number of occasions speaking together, and quite obviously changing the subject whenever he approached them. Jennings was clearly only here anyway to report back to Mablethorpe, and he had had to accept that, especially given the strain his personal and professional relationship with the PM had reached lately. He was almost certain now that Shawcross was colluding with Jennings by feeding detrimental information about him back to Mablethorpe via Jennings- and the reason was obvious, of course. Shawcross was an ambitious little shit. He should refuse Deveron's demands, he knew. At the very least, he should clear that it was ok to allow Jennings into the estate, as he wasn't actually under his direct line of command.... Yes, he should do that but he was damned if he would! Without realising it, Deveron had gifted him a huge advantage. With Jennings inside the estate, Mablethorpe would have no spy in Hawksworth's fiefdom. Shawcross he could deal with on his own very easily. He only had to wait a few weeks so it wasn't too obvious, and he could post the man anywhere he wanted to. I might even give the little shit a promotion, he thought. Northern Ireland needs a new Chief, and that would stop Shawcross from saying anything to anyone as he'd be too busy grasping up onto the greasy pole. Not for long though of course as, once this Riverside issue was finally done with, he would take great deal of satisfaction in dealing with Shawcross for good.

He rubbed his chin as if puzzling what to do, and shook his head. "Well, Deveron, it seems I am left with no alternatives here. Both the PM and I feel it is imperative that Professor Jaheel speak directly to his granddaughter..." He suddenly looked up as if the thought had just struck him, "You are of course prepared to give your personal assurance that they will be protected and safe whilst inside the estate?"
Deveron shrugged, "They will be as safe as the rest of us are. Other than that..."
"Very well then!" Hawksworth said, standing up as suddenly as his bulk would allow. "I cannot say that I am happy about this development. No not happy at all. But Mr Jennings here has volunteered himself for this...operation, as the recording of this meeting will clearly show. I have to accept therefore that both he and the Professor are fully aware and cognisant of the choices that they have made." With that he turned and nodded at Jaheel and Jennings and began walking back to the gates.
Shawcross leaned across to Jennings gripping his arm, "What the fuck are you playing-"
"Chief Inspector!" Hawksworth's voice thundered across the square.
Shawcross stared at Jennings as if he was going to beat him senseless, and then reluctantly let go of his arm, snatching his papers from the table in a scrunched pile and storming off toward his boss and the others, who had by now almost reached the security perimeter.

Deveron stared after them, trying to understand the interplay between Shawcross and Jennings. He had clearly seen the panic and fear that were in the man's eyes when Shawcross had grabbed his arm. In the end, he had to accept that he didn't have enough information to work out what was going on. Maybe later, he thought, as he lit a cigar and continued to watch Hawksworth and Co leave through the gates. Finally, he looked across at the two of them. Jennings had an 'Oh my God what have I done?' look on his face. The professor though, looked quite relaxed, as if everything was going splendidly.

*

Within half an hour, both men had been made to remove all items of clothing and were now donned in the orange Council boiler suits that now served as Riverside prisoner fashion ware. Mallet had said that he and Reeko would interview Jennings, whilst the Doc had a conversation with the old Professor. Doc said he would prefer to take Professor Jaheel to his and Katy's flat, and Mallet had okayed it. It was obvious to them all that any real threat would come from the younger man and, whilst that didn't mean that Mallet was dismissing Nasri's grandfather as harmless, it was Jennings' closeness to the Prime Minister which made Mallet highly suspicious of the man's motives.

Mallet had brought Jennings to one of the old warehouse offices, near to where Bear had been shot, which they had recently made into their unofficial police office. Mallet looked over at Jennings, who was seated in the middle of the stark room, his natural paleness exaggerated by the harsh fluorescent light above him and the orange boiler suit against his skin. That he was hiding something Mallet had no doubt, the question was- what? He continued to stare without speaking, as Jennings sat with his hands folded in his lap. Jennings attempt to look calm and confident was betrayed somewhat by the tremble in his right leg that was clearly visible to them all. Mallet had briefed Reeko on what he wanted from him and Bear during the interview. The two of them were now standing a couple of feet to either side of Jennings and as much again behind him, meaning Jennings could sense their presence but couldn't actually see them without turning his head. Mallet knew the man wanted desperately to look behind him to see what they were doing, but knew by doing so he would look weak, although he couldn't quite stop his eyes from darting side to side.
Mallet leaned back on the table behind him, his arms folded, his voice quiet, "So, Mr Jennings, Christopher, perhaps we can start by you explaining to us why you are here?"
Jennings shook his head and looked confused, "I don't understand, Sergeant. You know why I'm here. You were there when-"
Mallet shook his head, "Ah, Christopher. Therein lies the problem."
Again Jennings shook his head, genuinely confused now, his eyes darting to the left making sure the big one the one they called Bear hadn't come up closer to him, "Professor Jaheel said that he-"
"Please don't do that, Christopher! Don't start out by obfuscating. Don't lie to me or try and spin a yarn, not here, not now."
"I-"
"You see, things are different in here, Christopher. The law in Riverside, the safeguards to your well being, the legal rights that would normally apply to someone in your situation... well to put it simply, Christopher, they don't exist here unless we decide that they do. I mean, you understand that much surely? I've watched you for several months now you see, in our weekly get together. You're are an intelligent man, Christopher, a man who sees things

that others like the Chief Commissioner, for example...well, never mind, the thing is, Christopher, I know that what happened back there wasn't simple spontaneity on your part. Oh, Hawksworth didn't know. The old boy Jaheel blind sided him quite well I thought. But you, you knew exactly what was going to happen."
"I assure you, Sergeant-"Jennings began, then trailed off as Mallet shook his head as if he was disappointed with Christopher, and at what would happen now.

They all jumped, even Mallet as there was a loud banging on the locked door at the bottom of the stairs leading up the office. Mallet let out a tight breath of frustration, and nodded at Reeko to go and check out which idiot was down there. A moment later Reeko walked back into the room with a face like thunder, followed by Weston and his oppo Gobby George. Weston was smiling at Mallet like they were old friends.
"Professor Weston, I'm afraid this isn't a good time, we are conducting an interview-"Mallet began.
"Yes, yes, I realise that Sergeant, that's why I rushed over as soon as I was notified. Not by you or any of my other comrades on the committee, I might add! Still, that doesn't matter right now. And I have good news for you, Sergeant Mallet, this interview is over, it's unnecessary you see-"
"Professor, I must insist-"
Weston's smile stayed on his face, but looked like it was plastered on now," No Sergeant. It is I that must insist, I really must." As he spoke, he moved his hand deliberately to the apparatus that he always had strapped to his wrist, the one that he had told them would trigger the weapon.
Mallet raised his hand, forestalling Reeko who looked as if he was ready to throttle Weston regardless of the consequences.
"I'm afraid I don't understand, Professor Weston?"
"Of course you don't, Sergeant, "his smile grew wider, "but please allow me to explain. You see, it turns out that I know this man you are trying to interview, and I can vouch for him. He was, is, very dear to me. In fact I can honestly say that, if it wasn't for my dearest friend Christopher here, none of us would have got this far. Anyway, as I say, I can personally vouch for Mr Jennings as an ally and friend, and as such I'm sure you will want to release him immediately so I can give him the type of reception he deserves."
Mallet could see that Jennings had been as taken aback as he was himself by this turn of events. And Mallet noticed he had turned crimson when Weston had called him his dearest friend. Mallet closed his eyes briefly for a moment, trying to decide if this was the moment they had all feared. When one of them would have to call Weston's bluff and test the man's willingness for self destruction. He opened his eyes, and looked for a

moment at Jennings, unable to interpret the man's expression, though when he looked back into Dominic Weston's eyes, he could interpret quite easily that the guy was clearly certifiable. Oh, he looked calm enough and was smiling, but there was something, a glitter in his eyes, something that he had seen before... He suddenly remembered. It was the Lyebeck case, just before Lyebeck had stepped off the twenty storey rooftop, clutching his eight year old daughter too him. Weston had that same look in his eyes now that Lyebeck had had that day. Mallet had called the man's bluff then and took just one more small step toward him, not believing that he would kill himself and his little girl. He had been wrong. And now Weston had that same look in his eyes as Lyebeck had.
"OK!" Mallet said.
Weston looked momentarily confused, then Mallet thought he saw a flicker of disappointment. His smile widened, "OK?"
"If you can vouch for Mr Jennings, Professor, then that's good enough for me, though it would be useful for us, all of us that is, if I could debrief him on what is happening outside."
"Of course, Sergeant, but not right now. I think there has been enough excitement for one day. I think, Christopher, "he said turning toward Jennings "we should go and get you something to eat and a hot drink, eh?" he held out his hand, inviting Jennings to follow him.
Jennings nodded, his face still flushed and, as he was leaving he glanced briefly at Mallet as if about to say something.
"Come on, Chrissie let's get out of the Sergeant's way."
Mallet watched them go, grateful at least that Reeko had kept any objections till after the three of them were alone.

*

Doc had asked Katy to tell Nasri her grandfather was here, and to fetch her over to the flat. Sunny had joined them, and the five of them were now seated around Katy's polished dining table, the same one that Doc had once carelessly dropped cigar ash on. He had been made to smoke out on the balcony ever since, whatever the weather. Doc waited for the Professor and his granddaughter to finish their hugs and kisses; the relief that the two of them showed on seeing each other was clearly unfeigned. Katy had made tea and coffee and now all of them looked expectantly at Doc, who signalled that he would prefer the Professor to begin.
"I assume that by now you know who I am, so I won't go through my history?"
Doc nodded.
The Professor smiled at Doc, then patted Nasri's hand before continuing, "You may also be aware that over the years I have worked for the intelligence services?"
Again, Doc simply nodded. He had gotten Danny to pull up a lot of

information on the old boy and on Christopher Jennings in the two hours since they had come in to the estate.

"Very well, then. I am not going to go up and down the houses with you, Professor Deveron. I am as aware of you and your history as you probably are of mine. As I said, I worked for the intelligence services from time to time; technically I suppose I still do, as it isn't the sort of thing they let you retire from. I did so at the time for the same reason many of us did back then. We were tired of the fanatics and the fundamentalists besmirching the name of our faith. Even before the great devastation of the Middle East, the vast majority of Muslims were as they are today, peaceful law-abiding citizens of the world. Yet, as we watched our beliefs being hijacked by those ignorant medievalists who perverted for their own purposes the true tenets of Islam, we became determined not to allow such terrible distortions of our holy teachings. As a student of history, you know as well as I do, Professor, that the insidious disease of fundamentalism can erupt in any culture. Hitler's fascism, the Catholic Inquisition or the American evangelicals, whose crusades led to the failed neo-con experiment that bankrupted the world and ripped apart so many societies..." He stopped suddenly and smiled at Doc, "I think now I am going up and down the houses, is that how you say it?"

"It will do," Doc said.

"Very well then, but I want you to understand that in the eyes of many I have betrayed my own people. Whether that is true, I shall leave it to others to judge. But if asked I would walk the same path again, if faced with those same choices, because I believe that as- who was it said 'If good men do nothing? - "

"Edmund Burke," Doc said, "'all that is necessary for the triumph of evil is that good men do nothing'".

Professor Jaheel smiled again, "Burke, of course you are right. And so I did what I could. However, at some point... oh I don't know precisely when, I came to realise that the cure applied to these fundamentalists had become as bad as the original disease, and that the people I worked for had become as bad as those they sought to defeat. In some ways of course they were worse. At least when the fanatics looked into the martyrs camera and said, 'we will kill you and your families, on buses and planes, in school playgrounds, and crowded cafes', at least they were honest with us and suffered the consequences of their actions. The organisations I had become entwined with would not blink at the murder of innocents and quite happily blame it on the extremists, extremists who quite often they themselves had armed in their past dealings." He paused and rubbed his forehead with his fingers before continuing, "So I found myself in that place, that fulcrum of balance between two evils, trying to decide which one was worse. You of all people, Professor Deveron, must know how that feels?"

Deveron nodded, not trusting himself to speak. Though the circumstances were different, he had been, was still in that same dark place that Jaheel was describing. He had tried to defend what he believed to be right, and in doing so had allowed a madman to threaten mass destruction.
Jaheel looked at him a moment longer, then nodded to himself as if satisfied that Deveron understood.
"And so I come here, Professor Deveron, on behalf of the UK authorities to bring an end to this... this situation. The instructions I have been given are quite explicit- I am to neutralise the weapon. Or, to put it more bluntly- forgive me my dear," he said patting Nasri's hand, "I am to kill Dominic Weston in a way that will not allow him to release the 6/707."
Nasri snatched her hand back as if it had been burned, "Gramps, no!"
He took her hand back in his, stroking it gently with his thumb, before turning back to face Deveron who was leaning back in his chair, for once lost for words.
"Those are my orders, and I also bring an offer to you, Professor, one that comes from the highest authority. If you and your comrades enable and assist me in this mission, the authorities are prepared to let all of you," he chuckled, " make that all of us," he said twirling his hand in the air, "go free."
Doc leaned forward, his clasped hands steepled under his chin, "I assume that your mission allows for the fact that Weston has a device that allows him to trigger the weapon, and that it would be triggered automatically in the event of his death, and/or if he is in a state of unconsciousness?"
Jaheel nodded.
"And we just go free?"
"That's what they say."
"Ah, ok. What do you say?"
Jaheel let out another of his deep rumbling chuckles before replying. "They are frightened out there, Professor Deveron, not just of the weapon, though that frightens them a great deal. But that is not their greatest fear, as you will already have guessed I am sure?"
Doc nodded.
"Doc?" Katy asked.
"They are frightened of losing their power, Katy."
"I'm sorry, Doc I still don't get it! Given what this 6/707 can do, that it can wipe out so many people- but that's not what really frightens them?"

They were interrupted by a knock at the door. Katy got up, and then stepped back as Mallet and Reeko filed in.
Doc stood up, looking at Mallet, "John?"
Mallet quickly filled them in on what had happened with Weston and

Jennings.
"Where are they now?" Professor Jaheel asked him.
Mallet looked at Doc, who nodded.
Mallet shrugged, "Last we knew they were heading over to Frankie's place, I assume for a drink. Bear is keeping an eye on them and will let us know if that changes" he said, patting his kiddie's walkie-talkie.

The room was cramped now, with not enough chairs, leaving Sunny and Jo to sit on the floor as Doc asked Jaheel to go on with what he was saying.
"My dear," Jaheel said, looking once again at Katy, "Let me try and explain. You know or will have heard of the Free Net Wars?"
She nodded "Not much, though. It was a little before my time!"
He smiled, "Actually, without being ungallant, it wasn't that long ago. What are you twenty eight, thirty?"
"Now you're just messin' with me, Prof. OK I think I was around ten or eleven I guess."
"Well, you were still a child and I was still a slim and earnest and youngish Professor. It isn't a surprise that you don't know much about it given how well most governments, including ours, have airbrushed it out of history. At that time the UK, along with most nation states, was being rocked by a continuing series of protests- against the banks, the multinationals and against the political class, who had become increasingly disconnected from their electorates. Mass unemployment, collapsed social safety nets, stolen pensions, even lifetime savings were wiped out overnight across the western capitalist system. At the same time, the divide between the wealthy top ten percent and the rest was becoming wider and wider. Nothing new in that, of course, it was just history repeating itself, as it so often does. Except that this time there was a new factor in the equation. At first it was just the fringe groups, like Anonymous or Occupy Wall St, and the dozens of others who utilised the internet to organise significant propaganda campaigns and international protests. National governments could and did dismiss these groups as just the usual ragtag bag of anarchists and new age protesters who'd always been around; but then soon, others followed in their footsteps. It was the biggest thing to affect nation states since the dawn of the Industrial Revolution. For the first time, irrespective of their status, ordinary citizens across much of the planet could see and read and hear what was happening in real time. Not just in their own countries either but across borders, no matter how secure or repressive their own governments were. The secrets, the corruptions and lies of the most powerful people on the planet were being exposed for all too see. Information was suddenly being shared and disseminated on a global scale, resulting in targeted campaigns against corrupt and oppressive regimes, and greedy corrupt organisations.

If it had stayed at that level, then maybe Free Net would have survived, who knows? But there have been challenges before in history and it is accepted, indeed expected, as natural by proponents of a capitalist system, that the weak will fall by the wayside. But Free Net for the first time allowed people to start realistically challenging the ingrained economic orthodoxy of unfettered and unregulated capitalism. This then was a challenge to the whole monetarist ideology, the very heart of the beast itself, and was a fact which the neo-con free marketeers understood only too well. Freenet and its supporters were no longer challenging individual leaders, or even individual states. Now they were challenging the transnational corporations and financiers that had, over many decades, transcended the spatial limitations of geography and Statehood, people whose only accountability and obligation were to themselves."

"And that's when they shut it down," Katy said. "I remember it now, my Mum and Dad going on all those marches. They even took me in the early days. I remember it was like a carnival, whistles and drums, people singing. I remember sitting on Dad's shoulders... but then suddenly the whole subversive thing happened and, because they'd been on the marches, first Dad lost his job, then Mum, and then we lost the house, which is when we moved down here."

Jaheel was nodding, no longer smiling. "When they shut Free Net down, on the back of protecting us all from the subversives and the terrorists of course, they also broke the link that connected billions of individuals; and returned us all back under the constraints of national and geographical control, which in reality meant under the control of corporations.

Those who had the courage to stand up for freedom like your mother and father were ostracised or worse. And people like young Deveron here, who continued to speak out and continued to protest, were classified as unpatriotic or anarchists. Finally, of course, they were labelled as leftist subversives, those 'enemies within' that our beloved Prime Minister often likes to talk about." He paused, and sighed turning to look at Deveron briefly before turning back to face Katy. "People like me who should have known better, we closed our ears and stood aside, we let it happen in the belief that it was the lesser of two evils. I could give you our reasoning and justifications at the time, many if not most of which were sound. The holocaust in the Middle East and the Korean devastation, those things shook us; and they made us fearful of the cyber sphere and its unregulated and uncontrolled dissemination of information. Such freedoms were shown to be dangerous when used by those seeking to destroy us.

So people like me, who should really have known better, closed our eyes to the increasing controls and the oppression of legitimate free thought, as we believed it was a price we had to pay to keep us safe."

Sunny suddenly let out a big sigh from where he was seated on the floor "Excuse me, Professor. This is all very interesting but-"
"Hey, Sunny-"Katy began.
Jaheel held his hand up, stopping her, "No, it's alright young man, Sunny, isn't it? It's ok, Sunny is right, and we can talk about this later. Right now you will all have to decide if you will help me carry out my mission?"

"Tell me this, Professor," Doc said, "why now, why after all of these years do you suddenly seek to right the wrongs, why now?"
Jaheel stroked his beard as he spoke, "I could tell you that it is simply that my conscience will no longer let me sit by and watch it all happen again, Professor Deveron, and I wish that were true, but I am afraid to say that I have learnt to live with the decisions and choices I have made over the years. It's true that I have become increasingly concerned at what is happening in our country today, but that alone wouldn't have been enough to drag me from my very comfortable retirement. The well being and safety of my granddaughter of course is an entirely different matter, and it was made very clear to me that she like all of you, are in great danger should matters not be resolved satisfactorily."
"Kill Dominic Weston you mean Gramps. It's not like you not to say what you mean. I don't think I could be party to such a thing, no matter how crazy he is, or how much danger I am in!" Nasri said.
"Of course my dear I understand that, of course I do, but you will not be asked or expected to have any part of this."
"But-"
"The Professor is right, Nasri," Doc said, cutting her off, "your job is to report the truth of what you have found here and to get that out to the wider world, and that's your only job."
"And what if you don't like what I have to say?"
"Well, that goes back to our earlier discussion, doesn't it? If all this is to mean anything at all, then we need people to know the truth of it. And that means the whole thing- the New Towns, the forced relocations, why we resisted and, yes, how we allowed Dominic and the weapon to stay. And if we agree, then it must also come out what we chose to do about it. Afterwards, well as your grandfather said earlier, it will then be for others to judge."
"And that's the answer to my question, isn't it" Katy said, that's what they are truly afraid of. They are afraid of the truth because, like us, they don't know how people outside will react when they know all of it!"
"And when and if that happens," Sunny said, "What happens to us if the people out there think we were wrong, that we are the bad guys, and the

Government was right all along?"
"At that point," Reeko said, yawning, "Then I believe we is all fucked!"
"Eruditely put, young Mr Reeko!" Jaheel said smiling, "But perhaps not entirely accurate!"

*

Dominic had remained silent as Christopher followed him across to the club, other than when he'd instructed the two henchmen to wait at the bottom of the stairs and to not let anyone up. He had closed the door behind them and poured out a shot of whisky for the both of them, and now sat rolling the glass between the palms of his hands. Dominic was sitting in Frankie's high backed office chair in front of the grimy windows which, despite the dirt, still streamed sunlight onto his head and shoulders. Christopher had the feeling that the positioning wasn't accidental, and that Dominic knew it would make him look more formidable.
"It's good to see you, Christopher," he said finally, breaking the silence.
Jennings nodded.
"How that whole thing came about... well, it wasn't planned you know, it was just circumstances forcing events."
Jennings still didn't speak.
"If there had been more time, I would have... Well, anyway enough of that, what's done is done, right? What is more interesting to me right now, Christopher, is why you have come here? I assume that your boss is offering some kind of deal, am I right? Don't tell me, let me guess, he'll give me his word that I won't be harmed if-"
"He's given the order to have you assassinated...killed." Jennings said.
Weston physically flinched as if Christopher had struck him, his lip curling, his teeth bared as if he was about to leap across the desk.
"Not by me, Dominic," Jennings said quickly, "I mean that would be ridiculous!"
Weston gave a tight smile, relaxing slightly, and nodding his agreement that 'yes it would be'.
"They...that is the Prime Minister, Commissioner Hawksworth and some of the others, they believe that you can't be reasoned with. "
"They understand what I can do?" Weston said, holding up his hand and fingering the mechanism strapped to his forearm.
"They do."
"Then-"
"They think...they think that you will deploy the weapon regardless of what happens, and they would rather it was deployed here, where they think they can at least minimise the damage-"
"ARE THEY FUCKING STUPID?" Weston said, banging the heavy whisky glass on the desk. He stared down at the glass for several moments as if gathering himself. When he finally looked up, he had that winning

smile back on his face, the one that had so attracted Christopher to him in the first place.

"So, if not you, then who?"

"The Professor, Professor Jaheel-"

"That old duffer? An assassin? Oh Christopher, really!"

"He's not what he appears to be, Dominic. He's been involved in counter-intelligence for years, and his granddaughter is here-"

"Who?"

"The woman reporter, Jaheel, she...they have told him if he wants to save her..."

Weston leaned back in the chair and took a small sip of whisky, looking directly at Jennings who held his gaze without flinching. Christopher could see Dominic's mind working through things as he digested this new information. Finally Dominic nodded to himself and, draining the last of the whisky, he placed the glass gently onto the desk before looking back up at Jennings. His voice when he spoke was calm and matter of fact.

"So they believe that they can take me out! Yet surely they realise they can't control the release of the 6/707-unless of course they think I am bluffing? No, that isn't it either, so they must believe they can control the spread of the 6/707 and the only way they can do that is..." he looked up at the ceiling for a moment then smiled. "They plan to launch a strike on the estate, which would have to be big enough to vaporise the 6/707. And that means that it would be big enough to flatten everything within a half mile radius." He paused looking at Jennings for a denial. "But Mablethorpe would never go along with that. The ramifications would be massive. He'd have to step down; worse, he'd be indicted by the International Court." He paused again and stood up, turning his back on Jennings to look out of the window overlooking the square, and beyond it to the police and military vehicles surrounding the zone gate.

"Of course, "he said, with his back still to Jennings," that would assume that people actually discovered Mablethorpe had ordered the strike. If the sheep out there were told the subversive terrorists had decided to martyr themselves then of course they'd believe it. At least the people that mattered would believe it- the media moguls and the opinion shapers. Mablethorpe doesn't care what the great unwashed believe. And then," he carried on, turning back toward Jennings, placing his hands flat on the desktop and leaning toward him. "Then he could close down all the gated zones immediately, and with all necessary force, in the interests of protecting the nation. No-one will protest, given the fear and panic that would ensue after they had blown this place to kingdom come. In reality, at least for a short period while there was panic and hysteria, Mablethorpe could virtually get away with anything he wanted, and they'd probably proclaim him as a great leader for doing it."

Christopher had thought that Dominic would quickly grasp the nuances of Mablethorpe's position, though he had thought he would at least have had to lead him through the rationale. The speed with which he had worked it out was just further proof of Dominic's intellect. Now though would be the difficult part.
"So what's the old boy for, Christopher?"
"His job is to get you into a defined location, and then signal confirmation that you are where you are supposed to be."
Weston nodded, "Of course. They couldn't risk missing me, could they. I mean, what if I got out, what if I just jumped on a train and landed up in the centre of Manchester or London!" He stopped speaking for a long moment, smiling in that way he had. It was a weird vacant smile that used to creep Christopher out a little before; now he just found it frightening.
Dominic zoned back in and looked at him sharply, "How does he trigger the signal, Christopher?"
"He has some sort of device built into his pipe that allows him to send a direct signal. I'm not quite sure how it works but I know it has a GPS device inside it."
"If Jaheel is with me when he sends the signal, then he's committing suicide. That doesn't make any sense!"
Jennings nodded, "I know, except from what I understand it's a price he's willing to pay to save his granddaughter's life!"

It always amazed Dominic when he came across people who were prepared to sacrifice themselves for others; he just didn't get it. At the same time, he knew it was the case that some people were actually crazy enough to do such a thing. Wasn't he sat talking to one of those crazy people right now? He smiled at Jennings, "How much time do we have, Chrissie?"
"Four days. If he hasn't sent the signal by eleven am on the twenty fourth..."
"Then they do it anyway and take their chances?"
Jennings nodded, "Though obviously in that case it will be a much larger strike, so they will want to wait if they can!"

It seemed like an age since Dominic stopped speaking, but was probably only five minutes or so. He poured himself another whisky and sat at an angle on the beaten up chesterfield sofa, so he was close to Jenning's chair. He had been shocked when Christopher had suddenly appeared inside the estate, and it had panicked him for a brief moment. The yobs that he had recruited as his muscle wouldn't accept him if they thought that he had an intimate relationship with someone like Chrissie! They were throwbacks most of them, the thick headed dregs that people like him were always able to co-opt to a cause. The problem was he had brought them to his side by being the antithesis of the others on the committee- the free thinking, considerate, live and let live crew like Deveron and Sunny. Even the old cop Mallet, despite his reputation for being a tough old bastard, was just a typical soft liberal when push came to shove. A real cop, one who actually believed in justice that is, would have strung those three rapists from lampposts so everyone could watch them rot. Or even better, he thought now, would have been to castrate them while they were hanging there and let them die in their own blood. He smiled briefly as he envisioned the men's fear as he approached them with a sharp curved knife. No, not a sharp knife, he corrected himself, a bread knife would be better, one with a nice serrated blade that would saw and rag the flesh. He shook his head, aware how important it was now for him to remain completely focussed and not get distracted by idle fantasies. If he was honest, the decision not to execute the three men had actually helped him. It had been quite easy for him to tap into the simmering anger of the turnips and lump-heads, who thought that 'banishment' simply meant letting the three of them off.

No, his people definitely wouldn't understand about him and little Chrissie and, though the weapon of course was his real protection, he wouldn't feel comfortable now without the muscle- heads watching his back. He had seen how people looked at him lately, as if he was some kind of freak, and he had no doubt that at least some of them were stupid enough to try and restrain him. Maybe more than that, he thought remembering how the kid, Reeko, was barely able to restrain himself when he'd taken Christopher from them. On the way over to get Christopher, his mind had been running riot as he imagined Christopher spilling everything he knew to Mallet and his cronies. He could almost hear them shouting out his most intimate secrets to all and sundry. Still his good fortune, or more likely his fate, meant that Christopher hadn't had time to tell them anything, and now here he was in front of him, as pathetic and malleable as ever.

"Why did you come here, Chrissie?" he said, finally asking the question that he had been running over and over in his mind ever since he heard Christopher had arrived. "I mean, I understand the how, but that doesn't interest me as much as the why? Why put yourself so much at risk for me, especially after the way I used you to get in here?" He leaned back into the sofa, watching Jennings carefully as he spoke.
Christopher let out a long shuddering sigh, then looked directly at him as he spoke. "That day when I found out how you'd used me Dommie, it felt... well, it felt like someone had plunged a dagger in my heart. I felt so

betrayed by you that... well I was planning to take some pills and just be done with it, but then this policeman tracked me down. You know him- Shawcross."
Weston shook his head.
"That night at the gate he was the one who overruled the SSC man."
"Oh, right. I know who you mean now. Go on."
Christopher leaned forward and took a small sip of the whisky that up to now he had left untouched. "Well he, Shawcross, was so furious; he said that I had made him an accomplice and that, if I wanted to get out of the whole mess in one piece, I had to help him to get you back before anyone could find out how you managed to get in." He looked up briefly, then as quickly back down as Weston nodded for him to continue. "He, well it doesn't matter now, but he made it very clear that I was in great danger if I didn't cooperate. And then the woman was killed. They said it was an accident, but I didn't believe it then and I still don't."
"What woman?"
"The woman from your lab, Houghton..."
"Susan Houghton, she's dead?"
Jennings nodded, "They said it was a hit and run, but I heard she was trying to go to the press and well..."

With a huge amount of self control, Dominic managed to stop himself from laughing out loud. He bowed his head slightly and ran his hands through his hair.
"Look, Dommie, I know it's a shock but you aren't responsible; seriously her death wasn't your fault."
Weston looked up and shook his head, "That's nice of you, Chrissie, but- Oh hell" he put his head down again covering his face, "Go on with what you were saying, Chrissie I can't think about that now."
"I understand," Jennings said, placing his hand for a brief moment on Weston's' knee, before draining his glass empty. "Could I have another one, Dommie?"
Weston smiled, "Of course, but carry on talking while I freshen us both up." He walked over to the drinks cabinet, his back to Jennings so the insufferable weakling couldn't see how much he wanted to grab him by the shoulders and tell him to GET TO THE FUCKING POINT!
"I was scared Dominic; oh I know what you're thinking, no change there then! But everything was moving so fast and then, at the last security briefing the Chief Commissioner presented the plan..."
"What's it called- the plan to take me out?"
Jennings looked at him, bemused at the question, "Plucked Goose!"
Weston could feel his lip curling. Stupid fucking name, he thought, but didn't say anything, just nodded for Jennings to continue.

"Well, that's when I realised right there and then, when they were talking so calmly about killing everyone in Riverside, about killing you- that's when I knew that I couldn't just stand by and do nothing. I won't pretend that I'm not still hurt about how you used me, but I think I understand now why you had to do it. You were right about Mablethorpe, Dominic. Truthfully, I didn't really understand it before. I thought it was just some childish pique of yours left over from university."

He looked up quickly, checking he hadn't said the wrong thing. Weston gave his most winning smile that it was ok, he understood.

"Well, it made me realise when I saw how little Mablethorpe and the rest of them valued innocent lives. I realised that you had known all along that it would come to this, and that's why you would do whatever it took to stop them. I also know, or at least I think I do, that it hurt you just as much as me to do what you did."

Weston shook his head sadly, enjoying how Chrissie's eyes widened briefly as he feared he was going to tell him he was wrong.

"Ah, dear Chrissie, you know only you would see that! Only you would be able to look beyond your own pain and sorrow to see to the heart of the thing. You truly are a friend, and I can't tell you how much I have thought about what happened that night." He could see the tears beginning to brim in Jenning's eyes. "So is that why you are here, Chrissie? Is it simply to tell me you forgive me, or is there something else? Although in truth I should tell you that your forgiveness is more than enough."

He watched Jennings unconsciously straighten in the chair, a wave of confidence seeming to flood through him.

"More than that, Dominic. You see I have found us a way out of here!"

Chapter Twenty Two

Dominic was sitting in his usual spot in the far corner of Frankie's bar, with his crew surrounding him. Sally was pouting because Jennings was sitting in her usual place of honour on his right hand side. Christopher was playing his part well- that they were old 'comrades' from university and, Dominic was satisfied that none of the group suspected they had any other type of relationship. Deveron had been talking quietly to him for the last few minutes, telling him the official story that the old man Jaheel was here with a direct offer from the Government. If they gave up the weapon,

Mablethorpe would grant them all immunity and free passage out of the UK. Dominic forced himself to relax as he suppressed the anger he felt every time he thought about Michael, of all people, deciding to betray him. He had only come here to save Deveron and his idiotic cause, and he had been betrayed. The thing that frightened him most was that he would have bet his life...had bet his life, he reminded himself again, on trusting the one true friend he'd ever had. It was almost as if Deveron had finally shown his true colours after all these years and, in the end, Michael Deveron was just one more of Mablethorpe's Harrington boys.

He smiled and leaned forward slightly; keeping his voice quiet enough so only Deveron and Jennings could hear,
"I'm not sure I get it, Michael. Why would Mablethorpe suddenly concede this, and why now?"
Deveron nodded, looking at him with those beautifully sincere eyes, "I know, Dominic, and believe me I said exactly the same thing, exactly the same. But it's clear to me now that Mablethorpe has been put under huge pressure from the UN. They are demanding independent access to Riverside and clearly he can't allow that, so what other options does he have?"
"I suppose he could just assassinate us... me!" he said laughing, as he watched Deveron laughing right along with him at such an absurd notion.
"Oh, I'm sure he'd blow us both to hell if he could, but he can't!" Deveron said. "He knows you can release the 6/707 at the slightest sign of a threat; so, no, I don't think he would dare risk it," Deveron spoke as if even now he was still thinking it through. "He also can't afford word of the weapon to get out, so what else can he do."
Weston rubbed his hands together, smiling suddenly as he realised he was actually beginning to enjoy this charade.
"OK, so he lets us go and then what? What's to stop us just telling the whole world about the weapon's existence after we're safe?"
Deveron nodded, "Again, the exact same question I asked. The answer though is quite simple, and it does make sense. Jaheel says that, once we are out of the country, the whole thing becomes much easier to manage for them. Why? Because, if we leave the country they get the weapon back and if we keep our heads down, they'll leave us alone-"
"And if we don't?"
"If we don't, then as soon as we are gone from here, it becomes a straightforward black propaganda operation. They fabricate enough evidence that we created the weapon ourselves, in league with other international terrorist cells of course. After that, if we were assassinated, the suspect list would be so long given what we would have supposedly done, the UK would be able to deny any involvement in the assassination. The

other side of it is that of course most people would say we deserved what we got."
Weston stared down at the table for a long moment, as if thinking through what Deveron was telling him; when he looked up, he stared straight into Deveron's eyes as he spoke, "And you, Michael, you think that this, this offer is the best thing for us, for all of us I mean?"
Deveron didn't blink or look away when he replied, "I do, Dominic, I really do! I think we have beaten them, Dominic, Mablethorpe is a beaten man, thanks mostly to you!"
Weston smiled "OK, Michael, if you believe it then, so must I. So tell me then-what do we have to do?

*

Dominic had to admire how calm Deveron was as he outlined the plan which, on the surface, seemed straightforward and, of course, plausible. Deveron said that Dominic and Professor Jaheel would be secured in the old fridge to make sure no-one could interfere with the weapon, which remained their only real protection. Deveron said Danny had told him, that he had picked up two messages sent from inside the estate in the last twenty four hours, he'd now identified as having a Russian intelligence signature. Deveron said he thought that the Russians were trying to get the weapon for themselves, and would more than likely go all out for it once they realised the siege was about to be ended. They couldn't take the risk, Deveron said, of someone attacking him or trying to get the weapon from him. Deveron also said that he himself had insisted that Jaheel had to be inside the fridge room with Dominic, to make certain there was no double-cross by Mablethorpe.

The handover of the 6/707 would be done only after the estate was secured, and when Deveron personally confirmed to Dominic that everything was ok. As an added protection Deveron said they had got Mablethorpe to agree that they would be allowed to transmit a live stream of events to the outside world. They of course wouldn't mention the 6/707, but they would be able to tell the world that they had been guaranteed safe passage out of Riverside. They would be taken to the nearest small military airport, which was less than a mile and a half away. There they would be met by two French military transport planes and taken to France.

It all fit together very neatly, Dominic thought, The French government, which had been voluble in their support for the 'Riverside Revolution', had already agreed to give any of them who wanted it asylum. Deveron had said that before the operation which he told him was to be called 'Plucked Goose' which made them both laugh, that he personally would be speaking to the French President Jean Baptiste on a secure live link to confirm

everything was setup. Then and only then, Deveron had told him, would he signal to him that everything was ok.
It seemed a good plan, he told Deveron. He questioned him extensively of course, on the nuances and details of it. To not do so would be so out of character it would set Deveron's alarm bells ringing. At the end of the discussion, they had shook hands and then he had pulled Deveron into an embrace, Deveron hugging him back tightly and patting him on the back. He had only just seen it, there in Deveron's eyes for a brief moment just as they made physical contact. Deveron the pacifist was about to surface, maybe even confess to his betrayal, and tell him that the whole story was a sham, a crude trap to murder him. Too late, my friend, he had thought, pulling Deveron toward him so they couldn't see each other, stopping the confession that would now be meaningless. Deveron had betrayed him, and that couldn't ever be taken back. It didn't matter what guilt or regret Deveron was now experiencing, any friendship or warmth he had felt for Michael Deveron had gone, vanished and erased as if it had never existed in the first place. He was still able to smile and laugh with him, because it made the manipulation of him easier. It was a shame that he wouldn't be able to see first-hand Deveron's shock and bewilderment when he realised that Mablethorpe wasn't going to evacuate the rest of them, as they'd agreed as the price for their betrayal. In reality, Mablethorpe was going blow them all to pieces in the belief that the weapon was enclosed and secure. That wouldn't happen quite to plan now, of course, but Deveron was still marked for death and, just before it came, he would realise that he had been outwitted by a greater intellect and a greater man.

*

Professor Jaheel had explained to them how the old bakery fridge would need to be modified, so that it became, at the appropriate moment, an airtight cell that would seal Weston and, crucially, the 6/707 inside. He also laid out the materials that would be needed, and told them that they already had access to them within the estate. They were seriously alarmed at how the Professor had such an intimate knowledge of the inner layout of the bakery and other buildings. If they had a major security breach that could threaten their ability to broadcast a live stream, then they were sitting ducks. Nasri, for a brief time, had once again fallen under suspicion as a possible infiltrator, until Danny confirmed that the Professor's explanation was not only feasible, but highly likely. Jaheel had told them that the authorities had computer-modelled the whole estate. Some of that was based on evidence and information garnered from the people who had left on that first day, most of whom he told them had now been transferred to the New Towns. He also said that Mallet's former colleagues had been able to give further specific details of what was where, and the rest had been done with old town planning schematics and satellite thermal imaging from the helicopter sweeps.

Jaheel said the authorities believed that, if they could manage to get Weston inside the walk-in fridge and seal it up as he had described then it should last a sufficient time to allow them to come in and finish the job properly.

Chapter Twenty Three

Dominic had made Christopher go over the escape plan at least a dozen times, maybe more, as he probed and questioned him, looking for any inconsistencies or flaws. He hadn't found any though, and was now totally confident that, unless something went badly wrong on the estate within the next forty eight hours, he would be home and free. He had tried, truly he had, to feel some sense of warmth towards Christopher, but he couldn't. Even though without him he would most certainly not survive, he still despised that the man was so weak, so needy. He couldn't show it, of course, not until they were safe in the US, and he was certain that he was protected by the authorities. Only then would he feel safe enough to peel the man's cloying and suffocating neediness from him once and for all.

He was grateful, though; Christopher had shown levels of initiative that he hadn't thought him capable of. True, it was the Americans who had contacted Jennings but, once they had, Christopher had acted decisively in fleshing out their offer. It was a source of great amusement to him that it was Mablethorpe's own security operation that would lead to his salvation. Aden Walshaw, the CEO of the European arm of Safeworld Security Company, aka senior NSA operative for the United States of America, would be leading the operation to liberate him. Jennings said that the local SSC Chief, the one who had been overruled by the policeman the night Dominic had entered the estate, had come to his house a little over three weeks ago. The man, Pat Dixon, had insisted that Christopher accompany him, and had driven them both to a private residence in the City, that he later discovered was one of many ambassadorial properties owned by the US. They had known everything, Jennings told him. They knew about the 6/707, and about Christopher's own role in getting him into Riverside. They even knew of the various hotels where the two of them had infrequently met. He had wanted to punch Jennings then, hating the fact that other people would know about them; and he didn't doubt that these people would know all of it. It had taken huge self discipline for him to keep himself calm and steady whilst Jennings told him the rest. Walshaw had said that the US was extremely concerned about the instability in Europe, caused by the new axis between the Chinese and British governments. They had also recently received intelligence that Mablethorpe was countenancing an even greater synergy between the UK and the

People's Republic, a position that they were not prepared to tolerate. They were prepared to offer Jennings and himself political asylum in return for their cooperation, and of course for access to the 6/707 itself. Jennings said he believed Walshaw when he had told him that they just wanted to put it beyond harm's reach. Weston had smilingly agreed with him, knowing that the Americans would use the weapon as a tool to crash the Mablethorpe regime, and thereby end the Chinese threat. Dominic realised that, once again destiny had laid itself open to him like a golden pathway. Mablethorpe would be crushed, and in the end he would know that Dominic Weston was the man who had wrought his end.

*

The old bakery looked different to Dominic from all the times he had been inside it before when he'd assisted Danny with various 'techie stuff' as Danny liked to call it. He felt something was wrong or out of place, but couldn't identify it. Probably it was nothing, just his more than understandable paranoia, he decided. The room looked no different; the same tired and stained whitewashed brick walls lit by too few fluorescent lights. Danny's various banks of equipment were set out neatly on the stainless steel worktops, variously blinking or buzzing no differently than usual. But there was something about it that left him feeling chilled. He almost laughed as he finally realised what it was- no Danny! The man was always here and if he wasn't then, the place would normally be locked up tight as a drum. Today the door, though closed when he and Christopher had arrived, had been left unlocked as he had requested. He had told Deveron that he wanted to come and check everything over for himself.

His eyes moved across the room to the old confectionery fridge which filled three quarters of the back wall. The white paint had been chipped off it here and there, leaving dirty smears of rust that ran down the door and side panels, but it was still basically sound and still worked, its motor chirring softly in the background. He walked across the empty room, signalling to Christopher, who he still hadn't let out of his sight since his arrival in Riverside, to follow him.

He looked at his watch. Danny would be doing his anti bug sweeps at the old hardware store for at least another hour, which was why he had decided to come now. He knew they would be watching the building from outside, and he guessed that Danny would have rigged a couple of hidden spy cams to watch what he did. It was important that he played the role they expected of him, and if he hadn't come and checked the place out, they would immediately suspect he was behaving out of character. In any case, even though he wouldn't be following their plan, he still needed to make sure that the room and, most importantly the fridge itself, hadn't been tampered with.

His hand wrapped around the large pitted chrome handle and he pulled on it to open the door. He'd expected it to be stiff but it opened easily, without a sound. The fridge was probably twelve square feet inside, and was lined with stained latticed wooden shelving across its two sides. A large, overly bright fluorescent had switched on automatically as the door opened. The fridge had been cleaned out thoroughly by Danny, who used it to store some of his more temperature sensitive gear, though it was empty now. He could still smell faint traces of vanilla and something else, cinnamon maybe, that had impregnated the wooden shelves from its years of storing confectionery. He checked the outside handle, satisfying himself that there was no mechanism for locking the door from the outside, before he entered the fridge itself. The handle had not been tampered with, he could tell easily by the old skin of paint that covered the edge of the handle itself, and the screw heads which secured it to the door. Similarly, the hinges looked untouched. The inside door handle was a simple smooth push bar attached to a round Bakelite knob. It was designed so nobody could accidentally be locked in, and he tried it several times to ensure it was working ok. He took out a pen light and magnifying glass, and inspected the inner handle carefully, looking for any signs that it had been maintained recently, which would mean it had most likely been tampered with. It hadn't been touched though, as he could see the thin layer of old grease and food matter still impregnated on the sliding mechanism. It wouldn't matter in any case as the fridge, though sealed, wasn't airtight. It had a huge air extraction system on the rear wall which circulated the cold air through a heat exchanger on the roof of the fridge itself which, as well as returning the cooled air back into the closed system, also and crucially for him vented through an outside exhaust system. If he decided to release the 6/707 inside the fridge, even if they managed to block up the doorway, it would be no different than if he released it in the street outside. The result would be the same- death for a lot of people. There was a temperature gauge on the inner wall by the door, which was no longer working, though he guessed the temp to be around five degrees centigrade, which was normal. He sat down on one of the side shelves, took out a small powerful penlight and started to comb every inch of the place, looking for anything unusual on the stainless plated inner walls that Danny had relined recently. He removed several of the new panels but couldn't see anything that shouldn't be there. The motor canopy at the back was housed in a tin box, with mesh grills running around its sides. He took out a small tool case from his jacket pocket, climbing on one of the shelves, and started to unscrew the cowling.
"What are you doing?" Jennings asked.
He didn't look up from his crouching position as he spoke, "Just being

cautious, Christopher."
"Do you think something is wrong... do you think it's a trap?"
He gave Jennings a thunderous look. He had warned him not to speak when they came over, in case there were any listening devices. He let out a breath and smiled, realising that Jennings' question would just serve to convince them that he was behaving as they would expect.
He stood up and passed the grubby cowling to Jennings, who took it gingerly in his hands, holding it away from himself in an unsuccessful attempt to keep the old bearing grease off his clothes.
"Do I think it's a trap?" he said, enjoying Christopher's discomfort. "Actually I don't; still, I wouldn't be me if I didn't look at every possibility, would I?"
Jennings shook his head, still looking concerned.
He stood up and pulled the fridge door closed with the two of them inside, after ten seconds or so the light went out. He pressed down on the release knob opening the door, and the light switched on again. He reached up to the far side of the plastic housing covering the fluorescent tube and operated the switch he felt there, and then closed the door again. This time the light stayed on. He nodded to himself, satisfied.
"Don't worry, Christopher. I'm just being cautious, that's all! Really, don't worry," he said as Jennings looked alarmed, "there aren't any bugs in here, see!" He held out a small device that had a green ok on it. "This is one of our friend Danny's little snooping devices which I happened to have come across some weeks ago, and it tells me that we can talk quite safely without being overheard." He sat opposite Christopher on the shelf, and looked across at his pale and worried looking comrade.

"I've been thinking about the old boy, Professor Jaheel. He worked for the security services, we know that, and it occurs to me that if, they are going to launch a strike, they have to be certain I'm actually here, right?"
Jennings nodded.
"OK, so let's say he gets me in here as per their plan, and he sends the signal to launch? But... what happens if I then decide to leave, what then? He has to be able to stop me leaving and, for that, he either has to lock us both in, which won't work, because I could still release the agent into the atmosphere, or he has to have a weapon of some kind, a gun I presume?"
Jennings looked blankly at him.
"Think about it, Chrissie. He's an old man he can't overpower me, I'd flatten him with one punch."
"I guess... I mean, yes, you would."
"So, if he has a weapon, which we are now agreed he has, where did he get it from? We know he was strip searched when he came inside, so who in Riverside has given him a weapon or, more pertinently, who in Riverside

has a weapon?"
Jennings looked blank for a moment, then looked up quickly, "The young man, you mean-what's his name- the one with Mallet?"
Weston nodded, "That's right- young Mr Reeko- and now take that one stage further, Chrissie. If Mr Reeko, whom I have no doubt is the one who will provide the good Professor with a weapon, then that also means that Mr Reeko is the person that our friend Danny has been trying to track down!"
"Reeko, but he's-"
"Perfect, that's what he is, Christopher. It's always the one who you would least suspect who is the most likely candidate, remember that. But, put that aside for the moment, right now we have to be very clear about how we neutralise the good professor when it's time!"

*

This was Professor Alhim Jaheel's third day in Riverside and, though not exactly trusted, he was he believed seen as being of little threat to the estate's security. As such he had been allowed to stay with Nasri and, within limits, allowed to walk around unhindered. He was watched, of course, as he had expected to be. Usually it was by the nice young man, Bear, who he would pretend not to spot as the young giant suddenly darted back round a corner, as Jaheel would stop to light his pipe or to tie a shoelace. He chuckled to himself at the irony of his position. It had been many years since he had been in actual physical danger. Yet here he was, a heartbeat from death, feeling more alive than he had for years- foolish he knew, but still it was true. If it wasn't for Nasri also being in danger, he would even he believed actually be enjoying the experience. But so much of the plan was tenuous, not least because it depended not on his actions, but on someone else doing what they had committed and promised to do. If that person betrayed him, then likely as not they would all die. It was as simple as that. For himself of course, that was no longer of great concern; his end was approaching rapidly whatever happened. But Nasri, that was different. He had to save her at all costs and he would broker any deal, make any pact, and if necessary use deadly force to do so.

He stopped in front of the nightclub's side door and pressed the intercom, catching sight of as he did so his dedicated follower, who was just dashing behind the overgrown shrubbery and weeds lining one side of the cenotaph square.
The voice was metallic and full of static through the small wall speaker, "Who is it?"
"Are you a travelling man?" Jaheel said.
There was a long pause before Frankie answered, "I am a travelling man. I am on a never- ending quest for knowledge and insight."

"Yes, me too," Jaheel said, then finished the sign, "But we must always remember to be cautious!"
The door buzzed and clicked open, and Jaheel climbed the stairs.

*

Nasri and Dave had spent the last few days doing the final cuts to the segments of video they would splice into Nasri's live pieces to camera. It was good work they both knew that- probably the best that either of them had ever done. They had made a separate and complete documentary that would stand as an historical record of everything that had happened to date in Riverside. Neither of them said it aloud, but they understood that they were finishing it up now in case they didn't survive what was to come. Jo had been a godsend, filling in for their lack of a sound man. She had surprised them both with her ability to work Ian's equipment, and deal with the mixing desk. It turned out she had done a short course on sound management before she started working for her father in the club. Ian's gear was different, of course, but not so different that she didn't grasp it quickly.

Nasri had never worked like this, with so many non professionals involved. The committee people, minus Weston of course, came in and out of the room all the time. Most times they would just sit and watch the three of them splicing materials and recording pieces to camera. At first she had been annoyed that they still didn't trust her. But when she had talked to Gramps, he had made her see it differently. It wasn't that they didn't trust her, he said; he thought it was more likely that, by watching her explain the issues and events to camera, it gave them a sense of structure and perspective. Watching someone else describe dispassionately what had happened to them, in a way that only an outsider was able to do, somehow helped them to make better sense of what was happening around them.
Not that she was dispassionate any more, of course. She knew she had 'gone native'; a cardinal sin for a professional journalist, but it was the truth. She had found something in this place, something that she would find it difficult to explain even years later, when she would be interviewed about the Riverside Revolution.

Chapter Twenty Four

Mablethorpe sat in the Hawtrey room at Chequers. A muted television in the corner of the room was broadcasting the usual drivel of sanitised twenty-four hour news. He looked at his watch again, thirty minutes. In just thirty minutes, the whole thing would be over and he would be able to worry about something else for a change. Hawksworth had invited him to attend this morning's final briefing, but he had declined on the grounds that it wouldn't be possible to fly over to Manchester and be back here for his summit with the UN Secretary General. It was lie of course, and they both knew it; he had a Sea King helicopter parked on the Chequers' helipad which could take him there and back in less than an hour.

The truth was he didn't trust himself just now to remain calm in front of the security people, and he also wanted as much distance between himself and the specifics of the operation as possible. Ambassador Hunshai had made it very clear last night, over a strained dinner, that the Riverside issue would need to be satisfactorily resolved today, if the Chinese weren't to announce their permanent withdrawal from the United Kingdom. He also told him the decision to withdraw would happen in any case by the end of the week, if the operation for any reason didn't go ahead. Without the guarantor of China's economic and military might, they both knew the UK would be plunged into economic and political chaos. The currency speculators alone would strip the economy bare within one cycle of trading, and the UK's gold reserves had long since been plundered by himself and his predecessors. They would be at the mercy of markets which, of course were renowned for having none. The Europeans would relish the fact that the UK was finally reaping the rewards of its deliberate isolationism and its lack of solidarity with its own continent. He would have to resign; that would be the minimum demand made of him, though in truth that would be the least of his concerns if things did go wrong this morning. The simple and overwhelming fact was they had to neutralise and secure the weapon immediately. If it went wrong, and Deveron realised he had been double crossed, he would broadcast news of the weapon to the outside world. That would almost certainly result in the International Criminal Court indicting him and formally seeking his extradition. He had begun to hate more and more Hawksworth's smug assurances that everything was going to be fine, yet had no choice now but to rely on the bungling idiot. The moment this thing was sorted though, he would have the man's head on a platter. But, for now, he was a necessary irritant and he knew with his connections he would be a dangerous enemy if he tried to move against him too soon.

He looked at his watch again, twenty minutes. He got up and changed the channel from the BBC to the Free Press News channel, so he could be certain he was seeing an up-to-date picture. It galled him to do so as it was FPN more than any other media outlet that had kept Riverside in the international eye, and that had become even more the case since their reporter had gotten inside. He was still amazed that the woman Jaheel had not managed to send out any reports. They knew she was filming and interviewing the subversives inside, but not one minute of footage had so far been sent out for broadcast.
Reluctantly, he had to acknowledge that at least Deveron and his gang had stuck to that part of the bargain. Deveron had the means for, albeit a limited time, to speak to the outside world directly. The fact that he hadn't done so meant he had kept the terms of the agreement...so far. Today though would be the acid test on whether Michael Deveron would follow through with the rest of it. He had admired Deveron so much when they were contemporaries; out of the two of them, it would have been Deveron who their peers would have expected to achieve high office. The man had had everything- the right family, independent means, a great intellect. He still couldn't imagine how someone could betray their own class in such a way, and for no personal gain whatsoever. It just didn't make sense. Deveron had chosen to spend his life outside of the establishment that was his heritage. He had given up status, wealth and privilege, and for what? A life spent amongst the dregs of society, the unemployed, and the work-shy bottom of the barrel, the ones who weren't prepared to pull themselves out of the gutter. He pushed his fingers through his hair, knowing he would never understand people like Deveron, no matter how long he thought about it; the man must in the end be simply mentally flawed.

Dominic Weston, unlike Deveron, wasn't much of a puzzle as he simply seemed to be crazy. Security had informed him that they had been at Cambridge together, though at first he had no recollection of him. When they had shown him a picture of the man from his Cambridge days, he did have a vague recognition of the man's face but the name didn't ring any bells for him. Yet the briefing document said that a large part of Weston's actions were based on seeking to right the wrongs that he believed he had suffered at the hands of the Harrington Club and himself in particular. Even then though, he didn't remember him or what he was supposed to have done. There were a lot of pranks carried out in those heady, cocaine sniffing carefree days of course, so he supposed that this Weston had been caught up in one of those. And there were so many of them when he was at University, undergraduates who would try to become part of the inner circle of him and his chums. Those types were always devastated when they weren't accepted into the group; he even remembered one fellow, though he couldn't remember his name, that'd actually killed himself. He had read the eulogy out for the poor chap, he remembered that. But this Weston, he truly didn't remember him. It puzzled him that someone could feel so slighted that they would seek such an ultimate vengeance, and over something that, whatever it was, couldn't have been much of anything.

*

Doc had agreed with Weston that the committee would wait in the bistro whilst Weston, Jaheel, and Christopher went over to the bakery. They were all waiting for them now, as the three of them would have to walk past the bistro's window to get to the old bakery across the street.

John Mallet looked at his watch, "Fifteen minutes," he said, looking up at Reeko who was leaning against the counter, his arms folded.

"Everything is set, old man. Stop fretting."

Deveron lit a cheroot and looked around at them all, "Reeko's right, we've done all we can, this either works or it doesn't. In a little over two hours the authorities will enter the estate and, if Mablethorpe sticks to his side of the bargain, we will all be on our way to freedom."

The room stayed silent, everybody lost in their own thoughts.

"Maybe not!" Sunny said, draining the last of his Sprite then crushing the can in his fist and looking up at them.

"Sunny, what is it, what's wrong?" Jo asked, shocked at his haunted expression.

Sunny's shoulders sagged as if a large weight was pressing him down into the chair. He turned and looked behind him at Reeko, who as usual had his chrome-plated gun stuck into the front waistband of his jeans. He took a large breath and then exhaled before speaking, his voice soft but calm. "We aren't going to France, Doc; it isn't going to happen-"

"Sunny-"Doc started to interrupt him, then stopped as Sunny held his hand up.

"I know...the French are waiting at the airport. I know you've confirmed that, and it's true they are offering safe passage, but none of us...of you, that is... None of you will be allowed to live out the morning the moment that they know Weston is sealed up!"

"Oh God, Sunny, please say it isn't you?" Katy said, taking hold of Jo's hand as if worried she would faint.

Reeko moved fast, his gun digging into the back of Sunny's head, the sound of the safety clicking off echoing in the room. Sunny didn't flinch, as if he had been expecting it even wanting it to happen in truth.

Doc looked long and hard at Reeko to make sure his young protégé wouldn't do anything final. Satisfied with what he saw in Reeko's eyes, he looked back across the table at Sunny and waited.

Sunny squeezed his eyes tight shut for a moment, then began speaking in that quiet and mellow way he had. "You all know that I had trouble in Africa, that I worked for the World Bank and that they said I had embezzled monies from the assistance funds. I told you that it wasn't true, but I didn't tell you all of it-" he stumbled to a stop as he heard Jo starting to sob quietly, leaning her head on Katy's shoulder for support.
Sunny didn't look across at her, didn't take his eyes off Doc, knowing that if he did look at Jo he wouldn't be able to tell it all.
"It was the CIA who had been siphoning money from the assistance fund. They were feeding it into a local militia group who they wanted to use to organise a coup against Gamelia, and supplant him with a regime more sympathetic to US interests."
"And you found out about it?" Doc said.
Sunny nodded, picking up the sprite can and turning it over in his fingers for a moment before continuing. "I had a good relationship, or so I thought, with the Development Minister. We were... Well whatever. I was wrong about her; she was part of the whole US deal, whether from an ideological position or just personal ambition in the end, I never found out. She ended up getting killed during the attempted coup, which was ironic as she was the one in the Government that I had tipped off as to what was happening. Anyway, after it all kicked off, the mass killings, the riots, I tried to get out with the help of a French TV crew who'd agreed to help me leave, and also agreed to broadcast what I had discovered." He paused, watching as Doc leaned back and lit a cigar, his face impassive as he held it out. Sunny stared at it for a long moment as if it was an alien artefact, then took it, pulling the heavy smoke down in a long draw which made the cigar embers crackle before he handed it back.

"We were stopped near the Angola border by a pair of unmarked American gunships. They took me on one of the helicopters and then..." he took a deep breath before going on, "then they sent the TV crew on their way towards the border...but..." Sunny let out a sigh and looked straight at Deveron as he continued, "as we were lifting off, the second chopper fired on them and blew their van to pieces." He shook his head and started to stretch his neck muscles, then stopped as Reeko pressed the gun harder into the back of his neck.
"Anyway, long story short, Doc, they took me to the States, though first we had a little stopover in Guantánamo-"
"How long a stopover?" Doc asked, sliding his box of cigars across the table towards Sunny- who took one gratefully and lit it, blowing the smoke out of the side of his mouth, still not looking at anyone else in the room.
"Long enough to know I would never want to go back there, Doc. I mean there were people there who had no trials, no access to lawyers; they just

didn't exist in the system. There was an American guy there who I got to know a little bit. He'd reported his squadron commander for killing unarmed civilians in Afghanistan. He'd done it all officially through the proper channels and everything but... anyway, he'd been there ten years, and he told me he knew they were never going to let him out. He was an example to others you see, of what could happen to them. I checked him out once when I was back in the States; he was listed as MIA, presumed dead; they even had his picture and name on the wall of heroes!"

Doc looked across at John Mallet, who was tapping his wristwatch- time!

Doc twirled his hand at Sunny, who had also seen Mallet's gesture and nodded that he understood.

"Well, I didn't know till I got out, time is different in there, but afterwards I found out I'd been in there for just short of three years. Then they took me to the States and put me into the RODV programme, which took another fifteen months- that's the Reorientation of Democratic Values programme, he said to Doc's unspoken question. And then they sent me here to Riverside to spy for them. "

"No prison for drugs then, none of that?" Mallet asked from across the room.

"No, Sarge, that was all just part of the cover to make me more palatable to the people I had to infiltrate."

"So why now Sunny? Why are you telling us now, when it's too late?" Doc asked him.

"If..." Sunny began, holding his clenched hands in front of him, staring at them for a long moment before speaking again. "The things they did, the ritual humiliations, the sexual assaults, the beatings, the needles that they insert in you. Sometimes they strapped my hands flat on the table and inserted needles into the flesh under the fingernails." He said at Doc's puzzled look, "You piss yourself, I mean literally you really do, but the worst thing is they make you afraid that any minute, any hour, they might come for you- and they always do! And they don't just come with bad things, that would be too straight-forward for the mind to deal with; you kind of shut down to that, as strange as it seems. But sometimes they come for you and give you your favourite meal. Mine was egg and chips with tomato ketchup. And a shower, sometimes they'd let you have a hot shower before the meal. That was bliss. Then they'd tell you that it had all been a terrible mistake- that you're going home. One time near the end, I was sat in my old business suit, I mean actually sat in the military plane, a whisky in hand. I was going home. But it was just part of the bullshit. They dragged me off the plane, stripped me naked on the apron and...well they have these dog collars and if you've been a 'bad boy', they like to put you on a leash and make you walk around on all fours like a dog...they did that a lot!"

Katy walked across the room and placed her hand on Reeko's, the one holding the gun, and looked at him for a long moment. Reeko stared at their two hands, then looked up at her and nodded, stepping back and wiping the back of his hand across his eyes.
Katy turned to Sunny and put her hand on his shoulder, "So, answer Doc's question, Sunny. Why now, why tell us now when, if you had kept quiet, after today you would be safe?"
He shook his head, "I don't know really but I think it's Weston, watching him, the way he is with people- you know that cold disregard for others that he has. He reminds me of them, he reminded me of what they are capable of. And ... I can't do it! This sounds so stupid. I'm the one that's been spying on you all along. But you are...were my friends, and that wasn't fake, not any of it, except in the very beginning." He finally looked across at Jo, who quickly dropped her tear stained gaze to the floor. He smiled, "I know it doesn't count now, Jo, but I do love you, I need you to know that... none of that was pretending. To be honest I thought they would just get bored with Riverside, maybe even with me. None of you were a real threat after all, not to them, and sooner or later they would see that. But then there was D Day, and then Weston came inside and the stakes just went through the roof; everything just got fucking crazy."
"What about that first day? "Mallet said, "When they shot the kid?"
"I just got carried away I suppose. It's a weird thing you see, Sarge; sometimes I can just wipe all of that stuff out of my head. The whole thing, Africa, Guantánamo; it's like it happened to someone else, not to me. So that day, well, I just forgot what I was here for...went native, I suppose they would call it."
"What about now Sunny?" Doc asked.
"That night outside the club, Sarge, the night you tried to recruit me, remember? Course you do! Anyway, you said then that it couldn't be stopped, that they were coming for us all and we wouldn't be able to do anything about it. Remember?"
"Go on." Mallet said, folding his arms.
"That night you said that all you could do was to try and minimize how many people got hurt, or worse. That's what you wanted me to tell Doc and the others, right? Well, as it turned out, Sarge, that time you were wrong; we did do something. But this time, this time there is no chance. We can't stop them, but maybe we can stop some people, even maybe some of you, from getting too badly hurt. And that's why I'm telling you now. Because even though a part of me, and believe me it's a large part, is broken and beaten. Even though I can still feel that dog collar round my neck like it was yesterday... well for the first time since they took me, there is something more important than the fear they instilled in me, something that's more important than the panic attacks and the dread of going back- and that's all

of you."
"So what is it you think we should do, Sunny? You've already told us that they won't back off, that we are all as good as dead!" Doc asked him.
"But there is something you can do, Doc. You can make the live broadcast and you can make it the moment that Weston is secured. Tell the whole world in real time that you are surrendering. Announce that you are all going to walk out into the centre of the square with your hands up, and will offer no resistance. Do that and Mablethorpe wouldn't dare do-" Sunny stumbled to a stop as Doc shook his head at him.
"Doc, it's the only way out of this. I'm sorry, but it is. That's why I'm telling you now; there isn't anything else you can do, not this time!"
"If we did what you suggest, Sunny, and if it actually worked, then what happens? The New Towns?"
Sunny nodded.
"We both know that they won't let what has happened here stand. At the most, if we surrendered, it will buy us a few weeks reprieve in a detention cell. They'll lock us up just long enough for the media spotlight to fall away, and then what? Do you think our good friend Sergeant Mallet here, or any of us in this room, will be allowed to live and potentially expose what we know?"
Sunny sat looking across the table at Doc, unaware that he was crying. Doc leaned across and placed his hand over Sunny's, "This isn't your fault, Sunny- and I really mean that, "he added at Sunny's look of disbelief. "What you have been through, what you've experienced... I can't imagine it... Yet despite that, and knowing what it could mean for you, you have still shown the courage to try and help us. Don't be ashamed of that my friend."
Sunny bowed his head to hide his tears, his voice muffled as he spoke. "But it's still too late, Doc, there isn't any way out except to do what I say!"

Doc leaned back into his chair, looking first at Sunny, and then around the room at each of them in turn. He could see by their expressions they thought Sunny was right; surrender was the only way out for them now.
"Danny," he said finally, "Get Nasri over to the studio and warm everything up."
"You're sure about this?" Danny asked.
Doc blew a small smoke ring up into the air before replying. "Sunny is right; we have to make the broadcast if we are going to survive. How long will we have before they can shut it down?"
Danny didn't pause, "Thirty one minutes and twenty two seconds...approximately!"
Doc smiled, "OK, John. You and Reeko proceed as planned with Dominic; the rest of you start alerting people to assemble in the meeting hall. They can watch the broadcast from there."

Everybody started to get up, nobody speaking or looking at each other. Sunny walked across to Jo and tried to take her hand, which she snatched back as if his touch would burn her.
"Jo, listen, I-"
She pushed past him and out of the door. Katy put her hand on his chest, stopping him from following her.
"You need to give her time Sunny, she's in shock right now; give her time and..."
Sunny nodded miserably, watching as Jo headed across to the club, even from here he could see her shoulders shaking with uncontrolled sobbing.

Chapter Twenty Five

All three of them were silent as they entered the bakery room, the fridge seeming to dominate the space as they all unconsciously stared at it. The plan as outlined by Deveron was that Professor Jaheel would accompany Dominic inside the fridge and, when they were secure Jaheel would activate the signal that would launch their rescue by the UK authorities. Dominic made sure that Jaheel was in front of him when they entered the building, even though he knew the old man wouldn't make his play yet, it still did no harm to be cautious.
They stopped a metre away from the fridge door, Weston still making sure that he kept behind Jaheel. He nodded at Christopher to start checking the outer door lock and then the inside of the fridge as he had instructed him. Jennings looked terrified, something that in anyone else would have set his alarm bells ringing, but for Chrissie it was just par for the course. Jennings opened the door wide, and placed an old metal mixing paddle against it whilst he checked the inner and outer handles to make sure they hadn't been tampered with, while Dominic looked on. Jennings looked up at him, and Weston nodded for him to carry on as he'd instructed him this morning. Jennings took the pen light out of his jacket pocket and walked into the fridge, and began checking the seams around the ceiling and base. Dominic and Jaheel watched in silence as he bent down and checked that the bolts holding the fan cowling which Weston had marked with a felt pen earlier were still untouched. Jennings turned again and nodded to Weston that all was ok.

Jaheel chuckled to himself as Jennings exited the large fridge and stood to one side, "You are a cautious man, Professor Weston and quite right to be

so, of course!" He started to turn, "Shall we-"
He was cut off in mid sentence as the air whooshed out of him as Dominic pushed him hard against the side of the door and pressed the point of a sharp dagger into the base of the old man's neck. A small nick from the pressure of the blade dripped blood onto the collar of the Jaheel's shirt.
"Indeed I am, Professor Jaheel. I'm so cautious that if you do anything stupid at this moment, I will insert this blade upwards into your cerebellum. Now if I could ask you to please put your hands flat against the wall."
Jaheel did so, his voice was steady when he spoke, "This seems to be a diversion from our agreed plan, Professor Weston, I'm afraid I don't quite underst-"
"Oh I think you do, Professor. Now where is it?"
"It? I think you have to be a little more specif-" he grunted as the knife pressed a quarter inch into his neck."Inside jacket pocket," he said.
Weston smiled to himself as he heard the fight go out of the old man's voice; he turned to Jennings, "Get it!"
Jennings edged forward and removed two items from the professor's coat, a tobacco pouch and a briar pipe.
Jaheel tried to peer sideways at Jennings, "This is madness, Mr Jennings. You must realise I am your last hope?"
Dominic could hear the tremble in Christopher's voice as he spoke. "I'm afraid you're wrong about that, Professor-" he started to say, then gasped in mid-sentence as watched Dominic calmly push the knife upwards into Jaheel's neck. Jaheel grunted, then fell silent as blood began to suddenly spurt out of his mouth, his legs and arms twitching as if he was having an epileptic fit, before finally Dominic let his body slip to the floor, blood still pumping from the severed artery.
Jennings looked at Weston, his eyes wide, jaw hanging open.
Dominic kept his voice matter of fact, "Christopher, I know what you are going to say. I promised I wouldn't harm him... but think about it, Chrissie. If we'd left him outside, he would have been an enormous threat to us both. He doubtless has another backup system, people like him always do. No, I'm afraid it was just too risky. Anyway there is no point in worrying about it now, it's done." He looked at his watch. "In a little over an hour all hell is going to break loose when the Americans arrive and believe me, one more body won't be a problem. If anyone asks, all you have to say is that Jaheel was alive and well when we last saw him. The American's will just assume that the subversives did it when they realised he was planning to double cross them!"

Jennings squeezed his eyes tight shut for a brief moment. When he opened them his voice was calm. "You're right of course, Dominic. It had to be done."

Dominic stared hard at him. Christopher looked odd; probably the shock he realised, that's all it is. He was already counting the days when he could finally be rid of him, but for now Jennings was still his link to the Americans and freedom. He grinned, "Yes, it did have to be done my dear Christopher; now let's get inside before any of the trailer trash out there suddenly decides to start nosing around!" He placed his hand on Jenning's shoulder and guided him through the fridge door, pulling it closed behind them both, still grinning to himself.

Though the image from the hidden camera in the bakery was in black and white and quite grainy, there was no mistaking what was pooling out from under Jaheel's slumped body. Mallet had to physically yank Reeko back into his seat as they had watched Weston murder Jaheel.
"He's dead already, Reeko. There's nothing to be done."
Reeko smacked his fist onto his forehead, "I know that but, fucking hell, John..."
Mallet put his hand on his young friend's shoulder, "Come on, Reeko, we have a job of work to do. Our people are counting on us."
Reeko nodded three or four times in quick succession, clearing his head.

*

Mallet was unconsciously holding his breath as Reeko and Bear lowered the specially-shaped stainless steel bar into place. It had been cut so that as well as preventing the fridge handle from being opened, it would also wedge the door shut. Reeko had taped all the contact surfaces so it would make minimal noise but, even so Mallet let out a deep breath when it finally did slide into place without a sound.
The three of them then carried the three inch fire hose across the room and locked it into the tripod they had just assembled. Mallet looked at Bear and signalled with his thumb that he should go outside and start the pump. Bear grinned wolfishly and lumbered back down the stairs. Reeko drew his pistol and pointed it at the fridge door, holding it steady in both hands.
"If he gets out, we're finished anyway you know," Mallet said quietly, a half-smile on his face.
"Yeah, but the fucker will feel some pain first!"
The retardant foam was the main key to the plan, providing it worked of course. If it didn't then they were all dead the moment that Weston realised what was happening and he released the 6/707. They could just hear the muffled sound of the generator creeping up the stairwell; the soundproofing had been as good as they could make it, but not perfect, Mallet hoped that Weston couldn't hear it through the heavy fridge door. They both stepped back as the foam which was designed to immediately smother all oxygen from a hazardous chemical spill, and then set like

concrete, began to fizz up the pipe. The yellow foam erupted from the hose and began to spatter and cover the fridge, pouring down the sides immediately and starting to form a tentative skin on the still closed door. The two of them looked at each other and, without discussion, started to make their way outside to make sure Bear had managed to seal the plate over the fridge motor's exhaust outlet. He had. Mallet slumped down onto the pavement, the tension making him feel like he had run a marathon. Now all they could do was wait to see if it worked.

*

Christopher watched Dominic, who was sitting on the opposite bench of the fridge room. Dominic's eyes were closed as if in meditation, a slight smile on his face. The two of them had been sat like this ever since Christopher had sent the signal to the Americans via the scrambled handset. That had been ten minutes ago. Dominic had watched over his shoulder as he had carefully entered the numeric code, which came up on the screen as if it was a pizza order, as he punched in the numbers. They had both waited for what seemed an hour, but was actually less than a minute, when the message came up 'please confirm your mobile number'. He entered a further series of numbers which would confirm that Dominic and the 6/707 were secure, and pressed send. The reply was almost instantaneous, 'Delivery in 58 mins thx for your custom'.
Dominic spoke softly without opening his eyes, "It's stuffy in here, don't you think?"
"A little, yes." Christopher said softly.
Dominic leaned his head back against the wall and let out a long sigh, nodding. The fridge motor which had been purring almost unnoticed in the background suddenly coughed and then stopped altogether, leaving only silence. Dominic opened one eye, then the other, a bemused expression on his face as he cocked his head to one side, trying to identify what had changed. When he looked back at Christopher, his eyes widened in shock and he jumped up into a standing position, "They've done something to the motor," he said as he stepped toward the doorway, grabbing the door release. "Those stupid bastards, what are they playing-"
He stuttered to a halt, looking down at the emergency release knob which now sat in the palm of his hand and no longer connected to the door mechanism. He looked at it then tried to force it back into place, fumbling for several moments before he saw that its spindle had sheared off flush with the door.
He let out a garbled roar and charged the door with his shoulder, wincing with the resistance he found as the door didn't budge, "Aargh, you stupid bastards!" he shouted through the door, and then looked up at the ceiling. "What! Are you stupid?" He turned and looked at Christopher, looking for confirmation that they were idiots, but whatever he saw in Jennings

expression stopped him dead. His voice when he spoke was almost a whisper, "Christopher, what have you done?"
Christopher took in a huge breath, looking at him directly, "What I had to, Dominic. It's over now, there isn't any way out!"
Weston looked at him, then started to look around the room, his eyes darting across every seam and joint in the steel room. "Christopher this is stupid," he looked up at the ceiling shouting, "THIS IS STUPID! I KNOW YOU CAN HEAR ME! OPEN THIS FUCKING DOOR RIGHT NOW OR I RELEASE THE AGENT, THIS FRIDGE ISN'T AIRTIGHT YOU MORONS! YOU HAVE TEN SECONDS!" He started to count down from ten, shouting each number at the door. The spaces were becoming greater between each number as he realised nothing was happening. When he got to three, he suddenly stopped, his shoulders slumped down, his head pressed against the fridge door. Then he stood up straighter suddenly, his head cocked, listening to what sounded like soft rain.
"It's the foam, Dominic," Christopher said. "What you can hear, it sounds a bit like rain I know. It's some kind of sealant foam that they use in chemical spills. Apparently it-"
Dominic turned quickly and dragged Christopher onto his feet, pulling his face close to his own, "You knew about this? You knew!" He slammed Jennings back against the shelved walls, causing him to cry out as the wood cracked against his back. "You knew all the time didn't you, you stupid little shit? He held his wrist up so the pen and its trigger were just inches from Jenning's face. "This foam, whatever it is can't stop 6/707, you fucking moron!"
"They think it can, "Christopher said, his voice steady, "And, if it can't... well they've decided to do it anyway!"
Dominic suddenly dropped his hands away from Jenning's shirt and staggered backward, sitting down heavily onto the bench, "And the rest of it, the Americans, all of that, Christopher, it was lies? I thought we were going to be together, start a new life-"
Christopher pulled his shirt straight and sat down, "No you didn't, Dominic. You would have left me the moment you felt it was safe enough to do so."
Weston's eyes continued to flit around the room, looking for a way out. So, what then? Is this about revenge? Is that what this is about, Chrissie? I thought you understood why I had to do what I did. that I had to help Deveron and the rest of them. I thought you understood that?"
Christopher nodded, "I do, Dominic and it's ok because I understand completely now. Oh, at first I didn't, not for a long time; I thought it was all my fault as I usually do, but I understand you now a lot more."
"Christopher, I-"
"Don't, Dommie, this thing inside you that drives you, it's no more your

fault than if you had diabetes or cancer, it's in your genes."
"What is?" Weston said, his voice quavering slightly.
"I can't remember the exact term now, but basically you are sociopathic, and that can be treated though not cured, the worst symptoms can be alleviated by medication. But the type you have, which is some kind of psychopathic disorder, means you have no sense of morality, none! No sense of right or wrong, no ability to empathise or feel pity for those you hurt-"
"It's not true, they have brain-washed you. Don't you see that's what they've done?"
Christopher carried on speaking as if he hadn't been interrupted, "So once I fully understood what you were capable of, I couldn't allow you to continue. Not with the fate of hundreds of thousands of lives depending on it."
"And I suppose you think your precious Mablethorpe will give you a medal when they come to dig us out of here?"
"I told you before, Dommie, nobody is coming to dig us out; surely you see that by now? This place is the end...the end for both of us."
"But the plan? - The American rescue?"
Christopher shook his head, "It was all a fiction, Dominic, the Professor and I, you see, we planned it together; he was desperate to save his granddaughter-"
"But why you Christopher? Why would you do such a thing?"
"Because I realised that you had to be stopped, Dominic. I knew you see, that you would actually do it, release the agent I mean. If it got you what you wanted, you wouldn't think twice about it. Professor Jaheel explained to me that sometimes we have to conquer our fears, be prepared to sacrifice ourselves for something greater. He told me that you would do something unexpected, the Professor I mean; he warned me what you were capable of and... Well, he was right wasn't he?"

Dominic stared at him for a long time, his mouth hanging slightly open as he tried to rationalise what Christopher was telling him. He wanted to lean over and pummel the life out of the stupid little shit- how dare he do this, how dare he? He squeezed his hands into tight fists, trying to regulate his breathing, settle his thoughts so he could think himself out of this mess. He was angry at himself; he should have seen this coming a mile off it was so bloody obvious. He would have done, he realised, if it had come from anyone but Christopher- Christopher who would always do his bidding, Christopher who he controlled absolutely, Christopher who was in love with him, in awe of him. Christopher Jennings whose loyalty he would never even consider to question had lured him into this... this coffin!"

He felt the bile suddenly rise into his throat as if he was going to vomit. The air was becoming stifling; they had sealed them in to die and there wasn't a thing he could do about it. His eyes did yet another trawl of the room, and suddenly snapped onto the communication device that had been discarded on the shelf after Jennings had sent the message to the supposed rescue party.
Jennings followed his gaze and saw what he was looking at, shaking his head as he spoke. "Dominic, they won't let us out. You have to-"
"Oh, but they will Christopher. They will- look!" he said. His eyes were bright now, his face set in a fixed grin as he removed the pen out of the wrist holder and began to unscrew it.
"Dominic! Stop. What are you doing?"
Weston laughed, "What's wrong, Christopher? I thought you weren't afraid to die? Changed your mind?"
"No! I... what will it do to us though, I-"
Weston threw back his head and laughed as he unscrewed the inside of the pen, and began to pour the liquid inside onto the floor. The drops refracted the flickering light from the ceiling as they spattered outward on the painted floor before Jenning's startled eyes.

*

Gregory Mablethorpe suddenly realised that his mouth was hanging open, and he snapped it shut whilst continuing to stare at the television set. The normal Free Press News bulletin had disappeared into a snowy screen for approximately ten seconds, to be replaced by a live image of Professor Michael Deveron, who was sitting at an old desk and talking directly into camera. Behind him on the wall was a large banner proclaiming the banned internet site of Fringe Net, and below that the address.
https://en.fringenetlive.com/riversiderevolution#thetruth#

Mablethorpe grabbed the remote control off the desk and switched to the BBC, which was showing the same image. He shook his head as he scrolled through the various news channels, and then to various entertainment channels. The same Deveron broadcast was on them all. He started as the door behind him burst open, an aide's voice starting to tell him to 'turn on the television', then petering out as Deveron held up a hand to silence him as he turned up the volume.
The upper right hand corner of the screen was running footage of the first day of the siege, showing graphically the killing of the red-haired boy.

"...And so," Deveron was continuing, "we were faced with a simple choice. to either accept our forcible relocation to the work camps, or 'New Towns' as the Prime Minister likes to call them, or resist. We chose to resist. "
Mablethorpe turned back to the aide, "Get me Hawksworth, NOW!" he

shouted at the frozen aide, who blinked several times and then ran out of the room.

"I do not doubt that many will believe we are indeed a subversive group of terrorists, as the Government has tried to claim. But we also know that there are many in the country who will feel as we do- that it is right to resist the continued erosion and suppression of personal liberty, that it is right to defend an individual's right to freedom of expression, and that to do so is not an act of subversion or terrorism, but is in fact a true act of patriotism."
Deveron paused and turned to speak to someone off camera before turning back,
"We are asking today for your support in ensuring that we do not simply disappear like so many have before us. We ask that, by your very vigilance in monitoring the events that take place here today, you help ensure that the truth, the whole truth, comes out."

Mablethorpe had sat down some time ago as he watched Deveron tell it all, including a detailed account of the 6/707. Occasionally the broadcast would cut into various bits of footage including, to his horror, footage of the supposedly unrecorded meetings held in the square. One included close-up shots of Hawksworth as he ranted about the rebels having gained access to the 6/707. It was patently obvious from what Hawksworth was saying that he, Gregory Mablethorpe, was fully aware of its existence. He looked at his watch as his aide came in, his face flushed; the broadcast had been running for over ten minutes already,
"We can't find him sir, "the aide said The Chief Commissioner sir, no one seems to know where he is!"

*

Christopher couldn't look away from the tiny spots of liquid that Dominic had poured moments before onto the floor. He had held his breath for as long as he could, but in the end he had to take in a deep shuddering lungful of air as he held his hands to his throat, waiting for the thing to get inside him.
Dominic was laughing, not one of his crazy dangerous laughs, but a gentle chuckle.
Christopher looked up at him as he spoke.
"It's ok Chrissie. No, really, it's ok!"
Christopher lowered his hands and then clasped them together to stop the trembling. He shook his head in confusion.

"It isn't the 6/707, Christopher; it's just some water with a little food

colouring added in for dramatic effect! In the end you see, I decided it was too risky to carry it about with me!"
"But we... they tested it ... they tested the sample you gave them in the other pen."
"Yes, and of course that was the real stuff, had to be really, otherwise they would never have believed me. Anyway, the point is, this stuff," he waved at the spill on the floor, "it's harmless."
Christopher shook his head, still trying to absorb everything.
"The communication device you used earlier, Christopher... it's ok now, you can tell them it's safe. They'll believe it if you tell them, and then they'll let us out of here."

Christopher steepled his hands over his nose and mouth, shaking his head again before looking across at Dominic, who was leaning forward now smiling at him,
"Oh, I know I'll have to go to prison, Chrissie, probably for quite a while- I understand that- but they still need me."
"For what?"
"Why, for the antidote silly!" Dominic said, laughing, "The work I've been doing on the real 6/707 back at the lab; well, I haven't quite finalised it, but I have made quite a significant breakthrough which only needs working up, and it's only up here," he tapped his head." It isn't written down."
"It's a dummy!"
It was Weston's turn to shake his head and look confused.
"The communication device, I mean. It's a bit like your coloured water. It looks the part but it doesn't actually do anything!"
Weston grabbed hold of the device, holding it out towards him.
"It works, Christopher. I saw it work- the code, and the reply-"
"No, it really doesn't, Dommie. Try it and see for yourself; type in any random sequence of numbers, go on!"

Dominic looked at him, no longer smiling, and then pressed at random a series of numbers and pressed 'send'. After several moments, the device bleeped and the screen lit up with the message 'please confirm your mobile number'. Dominic looked up at Christopher, then punched another series of random numbers and waited. Again the phone bleeped and he read the message, already knowing what it would say, 'Delivery in 58 mins thx for your custom'. He looked up at Christopher and realised that the oxygen was already beginning to affect his breathing. He began to cry, softly at first, then in big racking sobs as he fell sideways against the wall of the fridge. Christopher moved across to him and pulled his head onto his shoulder.
"It's alright, Dommie. I'll take care of you; hush now, hush." he said gently as Dominic leaned his head against Christopher's chest, continuing to sob

but more quietly now.

*

Michael Deveron looked around the room at the upturned faces that were staring silently up at him, as they waited for him to begin.
When he spoke, his words would echo not just around the hall, but were being broadcast on live streams through Fringe Net, and via Fringe Net to most of Europe's live news networks. He had with Danny's help managed to keep secret from everyone, even the committee that they would be able to continue to broadcast a live stream even after the TV feed was cut. That had happened thirty four minutes into his broadcast, exactly as Danny had predicted, and as a consequence he had, at thirty three minutes precisely, informed the world that they could continue to follow live what was happening on the address written on the banner above his head.

He took the time to look at every face in the packed hall; many but by no means all held his gaze, many nodding or even smiling at him. He closed his eyes for a brief moment. When he spoke, his voice rang around the room.

"When this whole adventure began, I didn't know the vast majority of you, not your names, or the names of your kids. I was an outsider, someone who didn't grow up in this place and someone, if I am honest, who had little in common with most of you!"
A murmur rippled around the room, manifested by coughs and shuffling of chairs.
"I tell you this now, because it's important to understand what has happened here. This thing that we have created here the so called 'Riverside Revolution', that some call a subversive plot and others a justified revolt, is in reality something far simpler. What we, all of us in this room have made here has, at its heart, something that for many people seems an outdated and unachievable aim in our global society. Yes, the need to belong, to be part of something bigger, something greater than ourselves. That desire to do something that allows each of us to feel fulfilled, but not at the expense of someone else, is I believe the real future for humanity. We, all of us here in this room, achieved that, and we made something magical happen. We banded together in the face of overwhelming force and forged a community. This community hasn't been based on someone's lineage, or their social status, or on how much money they're paid. It's been built on a simple premise that everyone in society should have the chance to grow and thrive, that everyone should have access to education and opportunity. Somewhere where no man, woman or child is left behind who doesn't choose to be left. There will of course be those outside, maybe even here in

this room, that see what we have achieved here as merely an artificial construct- something only made possible because of outside assistance. They will say that we survived because we have carried out this experiment in a bubble, cosseted and shored up by supplies of food and power which we ransomed from the Mablethorpe regime. And I will admit that that is true in many respects. We have, could only in the end play the hand we were given; that's all any of us can do. But that isn't the sum of what we have here. Whatever happens today, however this turns out, in the end those of us who have been part of it know, beyond doubt, that we have discovered or more likely rediscovered a different and better way to live. We have made a community based on the simple principles of equity, of everybody contributing what they can to make things better, not only for themselves and their families, but for the betterment of our wider family, our community of Riverside. We haven't done that by suppressing people's individuality or by demanding conformity of beliefs. The people in this room are as diverse as any group you could meet. We have kept our individuality, have actually embraced and celebrated our differences and our diverse views on life, on religion and yes on politics. Our only rule has been that no member of this community should do anything that harms anyone else."

Doc paused to take a sip of water, the room remaining silent as they waited for him to continue. He looked at his watch as he placed the water glass back on the lectern, pleased and not a little surprised that his hand had remained steady. Still, that was the easy part, he thought, stopping himself from grimacing at the thought of what he was about to tell them.
"In a little over one hour, I intend to leave the Riverside Estate. I intend to leave, not to surrender as has been demanded of us, but to walk to freedom. You all know that exactly one mile from here, waiting on the runway at the New Barton Airport, are two fuelled and ready to go aircraft, sent by the French Government. Those planes are protected under international law by the authority of the United Nations-"

The sound of a kicked over chair suddenly shattered the quiet of the room, as George Beard got to his feet, his face bright red as he shouted from the back of the hall.
"Are people really going to sit here and listen to any more of this bullshit? Are you? Look out of the windows, people! Look at the gates, look at all those police and security people out there...What do you think is going to happen? Do you seriously believe that they are just going to let us, let you, walk out of here? Jesus H Christ."
He paused, breathing heavily as he looked around the room, clearly not liking what he saw in people's faces as he pointed his finger at Doc, and

then at the other committee members on the dais.
"They won't let a single one of them, any of them, leave here except in a prison van or a wooden box and, if any of you are stupid enough to follow them, you'll get the same treatment."
"So what do you suggest, George, just give up?" someone shouted across from the other side of the room.

George picked up his chair, setting it upright, then held his hands out wide.
"I'll tell you what I think- no not what I think, what I know- and that is that this little community is over, finished. It was finished the moment they sealed our one and only defence back in that fridge. And did he," he pointed at Doc, "or did any of them ask you if that's what you wanted? No, of course they didn't. The moment they decided to murder Dominic Weston was the moment this little community of ours was finished. Most of you know the whole thing was a load of bullshit from the outset anyway, despite what Lord Snooty there tried to make us believe."
"Suggestions, George, what are you saying we should do?" the same voice shouted.

George paused to look around the room, then nodded to himself.
"I'll tell you exactly what I'm gonna do. I'm gonna stand at one side of the square, and I'm going to put my hands on top of my head, and I'm gonna surrender peacefully, no resistance."
He looked up at the ceiling where the cameras had been placed,
"I'll tie a white rag round my arm and offer absolutely no resistance." He stared around the room again.
"And I suggest that anyone who wants to stay alive should seriously think about joining me, and leave Lord fucking Snooty and his merry band to it."
He stared up at the dais waiting for Doc to say something. When Doc continued to stay silent, he kicked over the chair and slammed out of the door. The room was eerily quiet for a few moments, before the silence was broken by the sound of scraping chairs as ten or fifteen people followed him outside. In unison, like a crowd following the ball at a tennis match, all the heads that had watched as people left the hall suddenly swung back to look at Doc, who unnoticed had lit one of his cheroots whilst old Gobby George had been talking. He took a long drag and then dropped it on the floor, crushing it with his boot heel.

*

His Excellency Hunshai Tan, Chinese Ambassador to the United Kingdom, watched his faithful nephew and bodyguard Shaitan Zhi duck under the door of their Lear jet, and walk down the aisle toward him. Zhi made his customary small bow before finally sinking into the expansive leather seat opposite him.

"It is done?" Hunshai asked, though he already knew the answer by Zhi's contented expression.
"It is."
"And did he leave this realm with quiet dignity, our glorious Chief Commissioner?"
"He died as you would expect a gweilo to die, like a squealing pig!" Zhi chuckled to himself. "Though maybe a pig would squeal a little less loudly!"
Hunshai nodded, his face remaining impassive, but inside he was satisfied knowing that the last person who could link them directly to any charge of conspiracy had been neutralised. Gregory Mablethorpe himself was of course of no import. The British Prime Minister was a small man leading a small nation, and he was also far too astute to risk his own neck. The silencing of the unpleasant and untrustworthy Hawksworth had been entirely necessary- and had the added benefit of reminding Prime Minister Mablethorpe, should he decide to forget, that there were worse things than political disgrace.

"What now, Hunshai? Are we in disgrace?" Zhi asked him.
Hunshai blinked, startled how Zhi had used the very phrase he was thinking of. He removed his glasses and began to meticulously polish the lenses as he spoke so, Zhi would not notice he had surprised him.
"Well, nephew, it is true that our benefactors are not entirely satisfied with the final outcome here, but disgrace? No, I think not. We will of course be sent home to Xinjiang for a period of...reflection. But we have too many allies for our exile from the centre of all things to be anything more than for a minor period. Besides, the failure here was in the end not of our making, as they will grow to understand in the coming days and weeks. The parts of this project that we controlled directly were successful, and our strategy remains sound, with only minor adjustments necessary. Very soon they will want to repeat the experiment and we, my loyal nephew, will be ready to serve." He leaned back and closed his eyes as the jet began to taxi down the runway.

All was well, Hunshai decided. Yes, he had made some errors but he had also learnt many lessons. The true sign of a great leader was not to make the same mistake twice, something he had never done. He would spend the next few months in study at his retreat in Xinjiang, which would not be unpleasant. He would need some time for himself in any case if he was to learn to speak and, more importantly understand the Greek language, which he had been advised was even more difficult than the barbarian tongue of English.

*

The square was noisier than they had ever known it, even on that first day when the young boy was killed- Schofield, was that his name? Doc was ashamed to admit to himself that for a moment he wasn't completely sure. The noise wasn't just from the estate's residents, who were all now congregated together in the square. The police vans and armoured personnel carriers on the other side of the gates all had their engines idling, and in addition there were at least three military helicopters that he could see circling around the perimeter of the estate.

He looked off to the right hand corner of the square at the other much smaller gathering of people, who were looking increasingly unsure and frightened. And why shouldn't they be, he thought, they should be frightened, we all should be. Strangely enough though, he himself felt extremely calm, despite the frantic activity of the people around him, who were still hurriedly stuffing the few belongings they would be able to take in carrier bags, and in some cases more sturdy holdalls.

He turned to John Mallet who, along with Reeko and Bear, had without being asked formed a circle around him and Katy.
"How many did we lose, John?"
Mallet rubbed the short stiff bristles on top of his head and grimaced,
"Last time I counted, there were sixty eight of them, though my guess is there will be a few more scurrying away when they think no one is looking."
Doc looked up at him, "Don't be too hard on them, John, Gobby George has a point. Surrendering may still be the most sensible option; maybe I should remind people that they still have time to change their minds?"
Reeko blew in to his clasped hands, though it wasn't that cold, as he shook his head,
"What! You think that you didn't lay it out clear enough the first half dozen times or so? Come on, Doc; people know what the choices are by now and, if they don't, then telling them another twenty times won't make any difference!"
Doc nodded, "I know, it's just-"
"Forget it, Doc, it's done. What's more important to everybody at the moment is how the hell we get out of here?" Reeko said.
"I told you we're going to walk out;" Doc said, looking at his watch, "In exactly four minutes to be precise."
"Through that lot?" Reeko said, nodding toward the massed ranks of SSC forces arraigned around the large gates, which had been opened wide earlier that morning. He shook his head again this time in disbelief.

Mallet put his hand on Reeko's shoulder.
"Oh, they'll let us through the gates, Reeko. That's the easy part. Think about it. They can't risk another death, or deaths, not when they know we

have cameras streaming out live footage of the square. No, they'll let us through alright. But the minute we are past the cordon, we become invisible to the outside world!"
"And then what?" Reeko said, looking at Doc.
"Then we have to hope I'm as good as I think I am," Doc said grinning, which Reeko thought was about the scariest thing he'd ever seen.
Doc lit a cigar and turned to John Mallet,
"It's time, John." he said taking Katy's hand in his as they all began to walk forward.

*

Gregory Mablethorpe sat in his favourite high-winged chair, the latest report still clasped tightly in his hand. The television was now set to mute, but was still showing the live streams from Manchester. The main shot was from a high-angled camera which showed the whole square as if it was a large chessboard. On the top right hand corner of the screen was a small inset picture, which showed scrolling close-up shots of the three main groups- the subversives, the security forces, and those who had chosen to surrender.

He knew he had to pull himself together before his meeting with the American Ambassador who was due to arrive any minute, but he was struggling to focus. Ambassador James Riley had been extremely insistent, and blunt to the point of rudeness, when he had said he had to meet with him immediately to deliver a message directly from the US President. At any other time, he would have had aides running around, attempting to find out before the meeting happened what it was going to be about. Jennings had been quite useful in that regard, but Jennings wasn't here- he was dead, along with Dominic Weston, the lunatic scientist who had caused all this chaos. And now Hawksworth too, he thought, still shocked as he looked back down at the briefing paper in his hand, in a vain attempt to fathom some sense out of it.

They had found Richard Hawksworth's body a little over an hour ago, from the tracking device in his car which was parked at the back of a derelict petrol station, approximately half a mile from the Riverside Estate. The report said that they could be reasonably certain, due to the blood spatter patterns, that he had still been alive when his arms and legs had been 'chopped off', and that the actual cause of death was due to massive blood loss, which would have occurred approximately five minutes after his limbs had been severed. It was the last line of the interim report that Mablethorpe seemed unable to stop himself from reading over and over. 'The murder weapon was left at the scene, buried in the deceased man's skull. Initial views are (again based on blood distribution patterns) that the victim was already dead before the axe was buried into his head. The weapon is similar to that used by the Chinese European Triad groups, leading to the initial view that one of those groups was responsible. This is also borne out by the type of dismemberment which took place, and which is known to be a traditional Chinese Triad gang execution method.' He started as his aide, standing in the doorway behind him, cleared his throat, "Sir, His Excellency Ambassador Riley is here!"

*

The SSC guards parted like water as the Riversiders got to within ten feet of them, and formed two lines either side of the roadway. Mallet thought there were close to five hundred guards, and the SSC personnel vastly outnumbered the few uniformed police officers, who he could see had been discreetly pushed to the back of the lines. He spotted Lewins at the back, and felt strangely moved when she gave him an almost invisible nod of acknowledgement. He didn't return it though, for fear he could compromise her.

It was obvious to them all that, once they were inside the phalanx of guards, they would be gathered up like discarded rubbish. Doc didn't pause though as he walked in between the ranks of security people. The guards were all wearing balaclavas, which left only their eyes showing with many in addition wearing mirrored sunglasses. Doc continued to walk purposefully through the avenue of black uniforms, staring straight ahead. On either side of him were Katy and Jo, and next to them Mallet, Reeko, Danny and Sunny.

The seven of them were walking abreast, almost filling the width of the space between the lines. Danny had kept with him a small seven inch tablet, so they would know when the final stream was cut off. He had kept the sound up at Doc's request, but had had to stop looking at the screen as it was just too disorientating trying to walk- whilst watching yourself walk, on a screen that showed a picture of you walking, via an overhead shot!

They could see as they got closer that the avenue had turned into a dead end, closed off by a three-deep line of SSC people in full riot gear, their clear full length shields held in front of them. From behind them they heard the rapid shuffle of boots moving, and knew without turning around the guards were moving to kettle the Riversiders into a secure box. Two men began to walk forward- Pat Dixon the SSC Chief, accompanied by the newly promoted Chief Superintendent Michael Shawcross. Dixon looked angry as he came toward them, finally stopping two feet away from Doc as he placed his hands on his hips.

He turned first to John Mallet, "John," he said nodding in recognition, then shook his head in disgust as Mallet ignored him. Dixon then turned to face Doc.

"It's over, Deveron; all you have to decide now is how easy or how difficult you want to make it."
Doc looked at Dixon for a moment and smiled.
"Do you know any Byron?"
Dixon screwed up his nose, "What?"
Doc spoke loud enough for everyone to hear him,
"Lord Byron, that is. He said something once, he said, 'Those who will not reason, are bigots, those who cannot, are fools, and those who dare not, are slaves.' "
Shawcross folded his arms and grinned, "Funny that, my old man used to say 'Son, if you find yourself in a shithole, stop digging!'"
"Enough!" Dixon said, his face beginning to go red, "Now here's what's going to happen, Deveron-"
He stopped speaking suddenly, and along with everyone else looked upwards.

*

Mablethorpe greeted the Ambassador as if it was just a normal day, offering the man and his guest, who to his dismay he saw was Aden Walshaw CEO of Safeworld Security, tea and biscuits, which both men declined.
He picked up the TV remote, "Excuse me, Ambassador," he said, going to switch the television off.
"No, please Prime Minister. Do leave the television set on. It's why we're all here after all;" Riley said unsmiling.
"Yes, yes, of course. It's a terrible business, as you know; still, the police, and Aden's people here as well of course, are well on top of the situation."
"It must be difficult though, Prime Minister, given the tragic news of the Chief Commissioner's murder this morning?" Ambassador Riley replied, an earnest expression on his face.
"Yes, yes, tragic news, tragic."
Mablethorpe turned to the drinks table and poured himself a glass of brandy, to cover his shock at how quickly the Americans had breached what was supposed to be a secure and closed incident site. "A drink, Ambassador, Aden?" he said, still with his back to them as he recovered his composure.
"A little early in the day for me, I'm afraid, but you go ahead. Aden?"
Walshaw shook his head as Mablethorpe turned back to face them.

"So, Ambassador, how can Her Majesty's Government help our most trusted ally this morning? As you can see, this Riverside nonsense as I say will be concluded shortly-"
"Well, we can start by cutting out all the bullshit."

"What? Just one minute, Ambassador-"
"6/707 Prime Minister. You must have heard about it; it's in the news, old chap! Just as well that it is, of course, as Her Majesty's Government seems to have forgotten to tell its most 'trusted ally'!"
"Oh come off it!" Mablethorpe said, his own voice growing louder in the face of the man's arrogance, "We both know there isn't much that goes on that your people don't already know about. Now what do you want? As you can see," he said gesturing towards the television, "I have a rather a lot on my plate this morning."

Riley stared at him for a long moment, his voice when he spoke back to its smoothest diplomatic best,
"At 07:15 hrs. this morning, Prime Minister, a Lear jet containing Hunshai Tan, the Peoples Republic of China's Ambassador to the United Kingdom, left the UK on a direct flight to Beijing. On board with the Ambassador was his faithful aide and nephew, Zhi Shaitan. Zhi we believe was the person who hacked the Chief Commissioner to pieces this morning, though that's of small import to us at this time. What is of importance, however, is where that leaves you, given-"
"Shit," Aden Walshaw burst out cutting off Riley in mid sentence.
All three of them stared at the television screen.
"Turn the sound up," Riley said.

*

The helicopter was low enough so that Danny's cameras, which were still streaming live, could actually see the pilot through the plexi-glass screen as it circled above. A number of SSC people raised their assault weapons, preparing to shoot, as they saw written across the front and both sides of the helicopter the words 'Free Press News'.
"Weapons hold! I said. Weapons hold goddammit," Pat Dixon roared out across the noise of the rotor blades.
The pilot, on seeing the number of weapons pointing at him, suddenly lifted upwards by twenty or thirty feet which allowed those below a clear view of the camera crew who were hanging out of the open canopy on one side of the helicopter, allowing them to film the scenes below. A metallic voice boomed from the speakers on either side of the helicopter's doors,
"This is Free Press News. I repeat this is Free Press News. We are no threat. I repeat we are no threat."

Danny's web stream from Riverside suddenly flickered and died, replaced in an instant by live footage from the FPN helicopter which took up half of his tablet's screen. The other half was filled with the reassuring presence of Seamus O'Donnell FPN's top news anchor, sitting in the familiar FPN studio as he spoke directly to camera.

"Good Morning, this is the Free Press News channel; we are live from here in our Paris News Studio, and we are also exclusively live from Manchester's Riverside Estate. The pictures you can see on your screens right now are live shots of what many are calling the Riverside Revolutionaries, and others refer to as simply Subversive Terrorists. As you can see, the people of Riverside are carrying out their declared intention to try and leave the estate. The world is waiting to see what will happen in this very tense situation and we here at FPN will, for as long as we are able, continue to be the World's eyes and ears. And now we are going over live to our top correspondent Nasri Jaheel, who is reporting directly and exclusively from inside the estate itself"

"Pat Dixon knew without looking at his phone's screen who was calling him; only two people had this phone number and he doubted it was his bookie.
"Pat, this is Aden Walshaw."
"Yes, sir."
Dixon's face went pale as he talked on the phone for several minutes, then his face tightened and he nodded stiffly before disconnecting.
"Please, no, not again?" Shawcross said, looking at the phone in Dixon's hand.
Dixon ignored him, and turned to the men behind him who were blocking the way through.
"Stand clear, men. Let them through."
The guards stood unmoving, clearly confused by the sudden change of plan, then quickly began to shuffle sideways as Dixon yelled,
"MOVE YOUR FUCKING ARSES!" at the top of his voice.

Pat Dixon looked up at the helicopter as if deciding something, then shook his head, turning back to face Michael Deveron, who continued to stare indifferently ahead.
"Well, Mr Deveron, it appears that I am to let you through!
"So it would appear, "Doc said still not bothering to look at him.
Dixon went to grab him by the jacket, then felt the iron hard grip of John Mallet holding his wrist.
"Don't do that Pat!" he said.
The sound of several hundred weapons being unslung could be heard even over the noise of the helicopter.

"Let me interrupt you, Nasri, as I think something is happening right now, if our cameraman can zoom in closer," Seamus O'Donnell's voice said, which they could all hear through the speakers on Danny's tablet.
Pat Dixon snorted as if amused, then relaxed his hand so Mallet would

release his wrist. Dixon shook his head then stepped to one side, bowing like a courtier, signalling that Deveron and his people could now leave.
As they started to move, Shawcross stepped forward, "Hold it. Not you!" he said, putting the palm of his hand on Sunny's chest.
Sunny dropped his head, his shoulders slumping in a gesture of weary resignation, almost as if he had been expecting something like this to happen.
"He's coming with us, "Reeko said, stepping forward.
"I think not, scumbag," Shawcross said, not bothering to look at him, "he has some explaining to do first, don't you Charles?"
Jo pushed past Reeko and put her hand on Shawcross's.
"You heard my friend here- whose name by the way is Reeko, you fuckwit! Now, either we all go or none of us do!"
"Jo, please don't do this, I-"
"You shut the fuck up!" she said to Sunny in a low voice. "I don't want to hear anything from you right now!"
Sunny stepped back, his eyes widening at the sheer venom in her voice.
Shawcross grabbed her wrist in his other hand as he spoke,
"I don't think you quite understand about Charles, Ms Johnson, otherwise you wouldn't-"
"Oh, we understand alright. We know exactly what happened, but the simple fact is that Sunny is still one of us despite what you bastards forced him to do. Now get out of our way."
"That isn't going to happen, Missy, so-"
"If we aren't gone from here in ten seconds, I'm going to fall over screaming!" she said moving closer to him, speaking quietly so only he could hear her,
"How's that going to look on camera?"
Dixon prised Shawcross's hand off her wrist,
"Leave it, Mike!"
Shawcross spun his head round towards Dixon, "What are you-"
"You need to trust me on this, Mike. I know what I'm doing!"
Shawcross glared at Sunny and Jo and the rest of them, and then stepped back.

*

As they reached the first corner after clearing the gates, Mallet moved closer to Doc's side.
"Well, that was a little too easy don't you think?" he said, looking quizzically at him.
Doc nodded.
"I assume you and Nasri cooked up that little fly-by?"
Doc nodded again. "I wasn't sure that she would keep it together, given what happened to her Grandfather, so I didn't want to say anything."

"Did you tell her that he knew he wouldn't be coming out of this alive?"
Doc shook his head, "I started to, but she had already worked it out for herself. Apparently he told her yesterday that he didn't have long to go, some sort of cancer, so she shouldn't worry..."

Mallet shook his head. He had liked the old boy even though he'd known him such a short time. He was a person of honour, just like his granddaughter.
"Well, she's bought us some time," he said finally, "but you and I both know that they will have already scrambled the choppers to force the FCN helicopter out of the area! What do you think, ten minutes?"
"Fifteen I believe," Doc said, looking at his watch, "Well, thirteen now!"
"And by then Danny's link will be out of range, right?"
"Yep, in fact it's already shut down."
"So?"
Doc looked at him and winked, "Well, you know you always say I'm a crap gambler?"
Mallet nodded, looking bemused.
"Well, let's hope this is one of those rare occasions when you're wrong!"

*

Mablethorpe was incandescent with rage as he ranted at Ambassador Riley, "You let them through! Are you out of your bloody mind? You are making us, making me a laughing stock, and I will not have it. Do you hear me, Ambassador Riley, I will not have it!"
He stopped, aware he was shouting but he didn't care. These damned arrogant Americans had gone too far this time.
Riley looked at him and shook his head in disdain,
"Aden, close the door and play this jackass the tape?"
Walshaw nodded, walking past an opened mouthed Mablethorpe to close the door, whilst pressing play on the small tape recorder he had taken from his jacket pocket.

The sound of Hunshai Tan's clipped voice sounded in distinct contrast to Mablethorpe's exaggerated manner of speaking, as the two men discussed the next phase in dealing with the 6/707 situation in Riverside, and the planned strike.

*

"Explain it to me, Pat?" Shawcross said to Dixon as they watched the last of the subversives leave through the security gates.
Dixon folded his arms, genuinely smiling for the first time today as he replied
"In fifteen minutes or so, the FCN helicopter will be forced from this area. They'll squeal and complain of course, but we received a credible threat to

their safety, so of course we had no choice."
"What threat?"
"Well, it turns out that one of the subversives has a WMD strapped to his chest and he's probably going to detonate it. My guess is, it's most likely to go off as they walk under the M62 flyover. Unfortunately, an explosion of such magnitude- well its most likely going to result in the deaths of most, if not all of them...tragic, of course!"
"Jesus!" Shawcross said, "They're prepared to do that? Kill all of them...Christ!"
Dixon nodded, "Our friends are serious people, Mike, as you'll come to realise as you get to know them better; and they take it very badly when they feel threatened!"
He looked over at Shawcross, who was still staring at the diminishing group who were already a quarter of a mile from the gates.
"Don't worry though, Chief inspector, they like you and they like the fact you're prepared to put the extra effort in when it's needed."

*

Nearly six thousand miles away, sitting in his Hong Kong apartment, Michael Chen keyed in Danny's last instruction. He had just received and verified the authenticated encryption key known only to the two of them. His eyes widened as he realised that Danny had somehow managed to get direct access to Fringe Net, which was now broadcasting a live satellite feed. As he looked at one of his TV monitors, Michael Deveron's face suddenly filled the screen. Chen burst out laughing as he imagined Danny's expression when he saw Chen had piggybacked onto the code, so his own personal avatar of a spinning sword in a golden circle appeared in the bottom corner.
"Boy, we hackers really are competitive!" he said aloud and laughed again, then quieted himself, as Deveron's pre-recorded message began to broadcast live around the world.

"Friends, I apologize for once again interrupting your chosen viewing this morning. The reason I do so is that, despite our best efforts to resolve matters peacefully, there are other darker and more powerful forces that are intent on stopping us. In a little over ten minutes, the live feed from the FCN news helicopter will be silenced as UK government helicopters force them to move away, under threat of being shot down. It is our information that, shortly after that, there will be an incident which will, if it is not prevented, result in the deaths of all of us. It is not clear in what form the attack on us will be, only that there will be one. We have decided to make this broadcast, in the vain hope that by doing so we can prevent it, though in truth we have little belief that we can do so.

We ask, then, that the citizens of this great nation, and indeed the citizens of all nations who value freedom, monitor and record what happens here today, and later hold to account those such as Gregory Mablethorpe who perpetrate such criminal actions."

*

Mablethorpe looked at Riley, "He knows what you are planning to do, Ambassador Riley. You have to call it off."
Riley shrugged
"Call what off, Prime Minister? As you just reminded me, the United States of America has no jurisdiction here-"
"I heard Walshaw on the phone, you bloody fool, he told your man down there what was about to-"
"What you heard, Prime Minister was Aden telling one of our people that we have learned of a potential threat from one of your domestic terrorists who plans to make martyrs of them all. Unfortunately the information we received came too late for anyone to prevent the atrocity. Now, as the British Prime Minister, you can if you wish it instruct Aden here to ask your police officers on the ground to try and intercept the subversives before they can detonate the device. " He paused and looked at his watch, "I'd say you have at least five minutes to get that organised, though I'm sure Aden can help expedite matters for you, should you wish him too.?"

Mablethorpe sat down heavily on the chesterfield sofa, feeling the by now all too familiar panic beginning to close around him. If he tried to stop them, the likelihood was a lot of police officers would be killed alongside Deveron and his people. There would be no doubt that he would have to resign in those circumstances and, without the protection of his office, he would be highly accessible to the vultures at the ICC. His successor would probably just give him up anyway, as a way of deflecting blame from the rest of the Government. And if he was extradited, he had no doubt the whole 6/707 fiasco would be laid directly at his door.

Riley had just set out the President's request- demand he corrected himself, call it what it is Gregory; it's a demand. He had almost, not quite, but almost, burst out laughing as Riley laid out what they expected from him, and through him the UK government. It was so similar to the subjugation that the Chinese wanted. Oh, it was couched in more diplomatic terms of course, but essentially it amounted to the same thing. And he would give it to them, of course he would, there was no other choice. The tape of him and Hunshy talking was damning enough that it would lead to his indictment internationally. It would also, he felt certain, mean he would be charged with treason here at home. The irony that he had so passionately campaigned for the return of capital punishment, which he could now be subject to, wasn't lost on him.

So, just like with Hunshai, he had little or no choice, and in any case there was little difference in being a Chinese puppet or an American one. He would be able to hold onto power, which meant he would still be in the game. He would bide his time, and take the opportunities when they were laid before him. Let the Americans kill Deveron and the rest, in the end it was probably the safest option. The US, despite its lessening of power, was still the world's master when it came to sowing mistruth and creating false realities. It would be their mess; and they could clean it up for him, and he would survive!"

"Shall we have that drink now, gentlemen?" he said feeling suddenly calmer and more centred than he had felt in weeks.

*

The M62 flyover had been originally built in the early seventies, and had been repaired extensively on several occasions over the years. It was seen as a noisy eyesore by locals, but had made a lot of construction companies pots of money as each government-funded refurbishment grew ever more expensive, whilst the repairs seemed to last for a shorter period each time it was fixed.

The main road leading toward Barton Aerodrome had been closed off by the police, who had parked cars and vans across every intersection, turning what was normally a congested route into an eerie tarmac strip where they could hear their own footsteps as they walked along.

They had listened to around a third of Doc's recorded broadcast before it started breaking up and stuttering, as Danny's tablet finally lost its signal. Probably as well, Doc thought, as he walked along at the head of the nearly two hundred remaining Riversiders. He was still flanked on either side by the committee, and the chill was palpable as they had listened to the recording of him outlining what they were now being threatened with.

"You ok, Babes?" Katy asked, squeezing his hand.

Doc nodded and looked at her, "I love you, Katy Marsh," he said unsmiling, "Did I tell you that?"

She felt the tears prick the back of her eyes and squeezed them away, "You just did," she said smiling at him.

He could see the road beginning to curve as it led under the flyover, and knew instinctively that was where it would happen. Once they passed underneath they would be out of sight of satellite cameras and the windows of the high rise flats that were dotted along either side of the road. He still felt quite calm, to his surprise, but he was also filled with a deep gut-wrenching sadness, knowing now that they had probably come as far as they could. He knew, as he supposed most of the others walking with him knew, that it was highly unlikely they would reach the airfield. Yet still we go on. The human condition is, he thought not for the first time, amazing- to hope even when all hope is lost. He had also and finally become a leader; he accepted the truth of that now, though he had shied away from it for all of his life.

He'd never been comfortable with the thought of leadership which, in his view, invariably accrued to men of greed and ambition, and to men who had certainty in their own judgement. Yet he accepted now that he was these people's leader. For better or worse, he'd done everything he could, and that at least was something.

Every step he took now as they were only twenty yards from the bridge, he could hear the voice in his head shouting at him, 'Stop you fool. They will kill you all of you.'
"Too late!" he said aloud, causing Katy to look strangely at him as they passed under the shadow of the graffiti covered concrete. Everyone looked up as they heard the sound of running boots coming toward them from around the bend of the tunnel. Behind them they could hear the engines of the police vehicles moving up the road, closing off any hope of retreat.

*

The FCN newsroom was still in uproar as they received word that not only had their helicopter been forced to make an emergency landing, but that the crew and equipment had been seized. Tony Ferrin, the show's producer, yelled at everybody who was in the gallery with him to 'quiet the fuck down' as he tried to speak to Seamus O'Donnell through the news anchor's earpiece.

"No, we're totally blind right now, Seamus. Our road crews can't get past the roadblocks!"
"OK, Tony, we are back on in what?" Seamus replied his voice steady and calm.
"One minute!"
"OK. I want live streams of anything we get on my monitor whilst I recap to the audience where we are. The minute I see anything useful I want you to patch it into the broadcast."
"We haven't got anything, Seamus. The helicopter's down, I told you; the road crew is stuck, and Nasri is-"
"Listen to me now, Tony; I want to see every social media vehicle from that area tripping across the bottom of my monitor. I mean it- anything I-"
"Got you, Seamus I'm on it!" he said.

This was why O'Donnell got paid so much, he suddenly remembered. Forget all the other bullshit baggage that O'Donnell carried with him, the man was a talent. He turned and looked at everyone, Seamus had reminded them all, and reminded him, what they were really here for. Tony took a breath and started to count Seamus in.
"OK, in five, four, three..."

"Good afternoon, ladies & gentlemen. We are live from Paris with breaking news from the City of Manchester, where FPN's news crews have had to make an emergency landing. Our news helicopter has been forced down by heavily armed military helicopters, in an unprecedented attack on freedom of speech by the UK authorities. Our reporter on the ground, Nasri Jaheel, is telling us that the authorities even now are attempting to break down the door to the room she is broadcasting from. Stay with us as long as you can, Nasri; the whole world is listening to you live right now."

*

The Riversiders had closed up together without anyone suggesting it, so that they were roughly twenty abreast now. It meant the column was only half the length it was when they had left the gates of Riverside behind, and suddenly it felt like there were very few of them. Without comment, the children had been moved along with their mothers into the centre of the group. All their eyes were turned toward the approaching sound of the running footsteps, a small gasp coming from someone near the front of their group as the distended shadow of the first person about to reach them rounded the bend.

It's a kid! Doc thought, blinking rapidly to make sure he wasn't hallucinating; a kid maybe twelve or thirteen at the most, and he was holding his phone above his head and in front of him. The kid had stopped suddenly, and was breathing heavily as he stared at them, his mouth hanging open whether from being out of breath at running or at seeing them, Doc wasn't sure. Others started to arrive behind him- some younger, some a little older, all of them holding their phones, the screens glowing like little night lights as they were pointing towards Doc and the rest of them. Doc started to walk forward slowly and felt the others following after him.
The kids moved back against the walls of the tunnel to let them pass, tracking them with their phones as they went past. As they began to round the bend, there were more and more people, hundreds of people, Doc guessed, lined up on either side of the road. Still more of them were coming out of the high rises and the run down estates and running across the open ground towards them. Most of them were holding aloft mobile phones, all

of which were pointed their way as Doc and the others carried on walking toward them.

Doc stopped at the side of a group of three boys who were smiling at him.
"Hello, Doc!" the smallest one said.
Doc shook his head, bemused, till Katy nudged him in the ribs. "Hello!" he said, "What are you all doing here?"
"Well-"the boy began, till someone further under the bridge shouted.
"We're all Riversiders now Doc!"

*

"Seamus O'Donnell cut off in mid sentence the sociology pundit who was earnestly if a little woodenly trying to trash the notion of the undeserving poor,
"Excuse me, Professor, but I think we have some more breaking news over in Manchester. I'm going to ask our Producer to put up on the screen behind me the live streams that I am seeing on my monitor."
Tony Ferrin looked down at monitor seven to see a live view, from under the flyover that Deveron and the others had been due to enter, just before they lost their live feed. The images were clearly coming from a mobile phone, as they were shaky and didn't have great resolution, but they showed Michael Deveron and the woman (Katy, he thought her name was), staring at whoever was filming them. It was strictly against FPN policy to broadcast unfiltered footage from unknown sources which could be used by any unhinged group or faction. Seamus knew that as well as he the Senior Producer did; he paused for a brief moment to consider getting clearance.
"Fuck it," he said aloud, thinking of Nazzy and Dave, who had gone silent several minutes ago.
"Put Monitor seven up on the big screen, and pull up every other stream that's coming out from that area by the bridge, and put it up behind Seamus."

Chapter Twenty Six

Aden Walshaw finished giving the 'stand down' order to the strike team by secure communication, and turned back to Riley and Mablethorpe.
"It's done. They're on their way back."
Riley nodded. He was still sorely tempted to launch a strike on the airport, as he watched the ragtag band of locals who were effectively escorting the terrorists to the airport. There would just be time, as it would be another ten minutes before Deveron and the rest of them made it to the waiting

French air planes. The trouble was that there were now more locals with phone cameras than there were terrorists from Riverside, and they were lining the road in numbers that were far too great for the police to clear them away. Wherever they did try to disperse some of them, it quickly descended into a brawl which was instantly broadcast by FCN, and now even some of the UK news outlets were beginning to surface from their foxholes, and starting to show at least some of the footage.

The three of them watched the TV screen from which Seamus O'Donnell was now spouting about 'the people' having voiced their support for the Riverside Revolutionaries. Riley determined that one of the first things he would do when all this quietened down was remind that smug Bastard O'Donnell who he was supposed to be working for.

He looked across the room. Mablethorpe was sitting in the big chair, a glass of brandy as usual in his hand. He was staring morosely up at some old yellowed oil paintings which Riley thought looked vaguely familiar. He looked at Walshaw, who was still waiting for him to sanction some kind of last minute action. He shook his head as he spoke,
"Too late, Aden old friend. They got away from us!"
"Only for now!" Walshaw said.
"Yes, only for now." Riley agreed.

EPILOGUE

It was two days since Doc and the others, including his own darling daughter Jo, had left for France, something Frankie still found it hard to believe. Francis 'Frankie' Johnson, who was also a Secret Master of the Provincial Grand lodge of Cheshire, sat waiting patiently as His Royal Highness the Duke of Kent and the Grand Master of the United Grand Lodge finished reading the letter that Frankie had insisted he had to deliver personally

.

The Duke lowered the letter and removed his glasses, looking up at the vaulted ceiling above him as he spoke.
"You have read the contents, Brother?"
"I have Grand Master."
"Yet, having read it, you still insisted on delivering it here?"
"It was a solemn duty placed on me by one of our own Brethren, Grand Master. How therefore could I refuse?"

The man was right of course, the Duke acknowledged to himself, a request

from a fellow Mason could only be refused on the grounds that it would cause he who had received the request, his family, or a fellow Mason to suffer injuriously in some manner. If the man before him wasn't so stupid, he would have known that that particular order was written in such a way as to always allow one to decline any request in myriad ways.
"Of course, the fact that Brother Jaheel would be instrumental in assisting your own daughter to escape from justice didn't spur you on at all?"
Frankie said nothing, continuing to stare at the letter in the Grand Master's hand.

The Duke felt a great need to stamp and rage a little, which unfortunately would clearly be unseemly and unforgivable in front of someone from the lower orders.
"You may go now," he said without looking up at Frankie.
He watched the vulgar little man, who besmirched the title of Secret Master, give the sign and leave as quickly as his dignity would allow.
He looked at the letter from Jaheel again.

Dear Grand Master,
As I write this brief note, it is still unclear on whether I will succeed in dealing with the threat posed by Dr Weston, but I am hopeful and confident that this will indeed be the case. In any event, the fact that you are now reading this means I am now with the One True God, Insha'Allah, and have sacrificed my life in striving to complete the task which in part you set out for me.

When we made our bargain, Grand Master, we agreed by our sacred oaths that the life and liberty of my beloved Nasri would be protected.
At one time I would never have doubted that such a sacred oath could be broken, but alas over many years I have realised, indeed have personally witnessed, the betrayal and duplicity that exists within our order and, to my eternal shame, have even on occasion played some small part in such duplicitous schemes myself. This has led me therefore to underwrite our bargain with some additional sureties.

.

If then, at any time, however far into the future, Nasri, her future progeny or her extended family are killed, injured, or are caused to suffer personal or financial loss, or indeed defamed in any manner by the Brotherhood or those they control, the full extent of my knowledge of all matters pertaining to our Brotherhood and the Royal Household will with irrefutable evidence be disseminated instantly around the globe.
It will not be necessary nor prudent for me to set out these matters here, as we are both aware of their import and consequence should they ever become public. I am also confident that you will know I am capable of making the arrangements I outline above in a competent and undiscoverable manner.

Finally, Grand Master, I come to the brother who has carried this missive to you today, whom I also place under the same protections as those for my granddaughter. Like me, this fellow traveller has made no betrayal against the word, but has merely sought to protect his family as is set out and demanded of us in THE WORD OF THE LAW.

Yours in the light

Professor Alim Jaheel Knight of the Sword and of the East

*

Doc cupped his hand around his cheroot and tried to get the Zippo to light, with no more success than his previous three attempts.

"Come here, husband of mine," Katy said, laughing as she opened her coat wide to block off the gusting winds that were blowing across the ship's deck. He grinned at her and ducked behind the impromptu shelter, finally managing to light his small cigar. They smiled at each other like a pair of daft kids, and then both burst out laughing. They were below the bridge deck, but still high enough that they could see most of the container ship as its bow ploughed deep into the blue sea, before rising up easily again in a dazzle of white spray.

"You know I still can't get over that I haven't been seasick!"

"Yes, dear, you've already said, on several occasions!" Katy said, looking sideways at him.

She had not been able to stop retching and vomiting, along with most of the others for the first three days out of port.

"Maybe it's because my family's line had so many Captains and quite a few Admirals down the centuries?"

"Or maybe it's because you're such an insensitive jerk that you don't get affected the way us plebs do?"

"Well," he said, seeming to consider it. "That's possible as well I suppose!" and burst out laughing again.

She realised that, for as long as she had known him, other than for the intimate moments they had spent together, she had never seen him like this. It was as if the moment that they were all safely boarded on the French plane on that crazy day, which she realis*ed with* a shock was still only a fortnight ago, that he had been able to cast off all his worries and concerns for everyone else and actually relax.

She knew it wouldn't last, of course. She knew that, after some rest and some time, he would miss it all too much; that he would immerse himself once again back into his world and start the fight again. He was, she knew, too important to the movement for change, especially now after Riverside had become such an international phenomenon.

Yes, the New Towns had been shut down, and the American's now had a foothold back in Europe courtesy of the UK; but injustice and oppression had not gone away, merely 'the boss' had changed into a new suit of clothes. People still cried out for better lives, both for themselves and for their families. Riverside had become a symbol to people. True it was a small symbol, but it burned brightly and signalled the hope of a new beginning, and Doc would be a major part of that- how could he not be?
Professor Jaheel had given Doc the key to accessing Fringe Net, because he recognised that Michael Deveron was someone who wouldn't stop fighting for what he believed to be right. He hadn't told her any of that, but she had known a lot of it anyway without him having to tell her. When they had took their vows in stuttering French the day before they left for Guyana, she had known that all of this was part of him, part of what made him what he was. And, in truth, it had now become a part of her. Still, for now and for at least the year he had promised her, they would live their lives by helping to build the community they had first begun at Riverside.
French Guyana would be a lot different than her home of rainy Manchester, she knew that. They had been given grants and assistance to create the infrastructure on the land that had been bequeathed to them by the French State, but the Riversiders would all have to become self reliant in a way that they hadn't had to be back home.

Doc took out the small tin from his jacket pocket and carefully extinguished the cigar inside, snapping the lid shut. That first day on board ship, the Petty Officer had given him a dressing-down in front of all the other Riversiders, or at least the ninety six who had decided to accept the French Governments offer. It had been a long dressing-down that reminded all of them that, for the next five weeks, they were under maritime law and that drinking, messing about, and most definitely 'throwing manky old fucking cigar butts on the deck of my fucking ship' would have serious consequences. Doc had stood and taken it in good part- largely, Katy thought, as he had spotted how much the Riversiders were all enjoying the bollocking he was getting. He put the tin back in his jacket, looking at her to see if she would make yet another crack about having to walk the plank. When she didn't, he nodded at the thirty or so Riversiders who were strolling around the cargo vessel's top deck.

"We lost some good people," he said. "I'm going to miss Danny and Reeko- especially Reeko!"
Katy nodded. In the end, there had been one hundred and ninety three of them made it to France. Out of that number, fifty four had elected to stay in France, among them Reeko, Danny, Bear, and Sally Smith's daughter

Caitlin.
She took his hand in hers, "They are doing what's right for them, Mike."
He nodded, "I know, I guess I knew it was inevitable." He pointed across the deck, changing the subject. "Still, I never would have seen that coming!"
Katy looked at John Mallet who was leaning against the starboard railing his arm around Sally Smith Caitlin's mother who had her head leaning on John Mallet's chest her long auburn hair blowing back in the wind.
"You didn't? Pretty obvious I would have thought!"
Doc gave her a look of disgust,
"Well, what about those two then, oh Oracle of mine? Do you think she'll ever forgive him?"
She looked where he indicated. Sunny was sat on a bulkhead talking animatedly, whilst Jo leaned against the wall listening.
"Oh, she's forgiven him already; in fact she forgave him almost as soon as she found out what had happened. But I guess she'll make him work a bit more for it before she tells him that."

He shook his head. "You know, since I met you, Katy Deveron, I have begun to challenge my lifelong commitment to the principles of feminism and equity between our two species."
"That right, Mr Deveron?"
"It is, Mrs Deveron! But you know I love you right?"
"How could you not!" she said laughing.

*

Alitheia's engine rumbled quietly to itself, the prop turning just enough to charge her batteries without straining the mooring ropes, which Nasri had made certain were still firmly tied to the mooring rings.
She was sat cross-legged on the saloon floor, an empty microwave meal and half- drunk bottle of Gramps finest red next to her. The letter that Frankie Johnson had brought her was sealed and was brief.
My Darling Nasri,
Always hold to the 'Truth'. Look into her heart and she will ever be your guide!
Your loving Grandfather
She had left earlier that afternoon for the long drive down, and just managed to start the boats engine and get the wood burner going before it went fully dark, which was about an hour ago. She hadn't tried to search the boat, but had let her eyes drift around the walls and surfaces. Alitheia, *'The Truth' 'Look into her heart'*. All at once it came back to her, a crystal clear memory that transported her back instantly to almost twenty years ago.

Gramps was in his crusty old boiler suit, insisting she witness first-hand the laying of the ballast before the boat was fitted out. She had been mightily unimpressed at the layers of grey engineering bricks that would serve as ballast in the old boat. But Gramps had insisted that she understand that these simple bricks were the heart of Alitheia, they were what gave her balance and centred her in the water. Without them, he had told her Alitheia would just roll over on her back like a dying tortoise. She had humoured him as they both wrote prayers for Alitheia's safety and wrapped them in plastic, and placed them inside an old tin box which Gramps placed in the keel covering it over with two of the ballast bricks.

She managed to pry up a corner of the glued-down carpet, which smelled of old diesel oil and canal water, with an old screwdriver and began to peel it back relatively easily, only breaking two nails in the process. After several minutes, she had unscrewed the wooden service hatch and removed the old tin, and taken out the letter.

My clever girl!

In this box is a key to a lock that, should you decide to open and act upon its contents, will send you on a journey, though to what final destination I cannot say!

It is, though, a journey that strives for justice and truth, and demands a better world for all peoples of this earth, irrespective of race, creed or nationality.

I have walked its path, and it is not without its perils or dangers but, as Gandhi said 'You must be the change you want to see in the world', and I have found that to be true.

Be at peace, my beloved Granddaughter, for I will see you again.

Insha'Allah

Nasri wiped her eyes with the back of her sleeve and placed the letter carefully to one side, removing the data stick which sat at the bottom of the box. She plugged it into her tablet, then watched wide-eyed as the worldwide logo of Freenet flashed onto the screen, which turned red after an instant and flashed up a password demand.

She looked around the boat and saw Gramps battered old coat and hat hanging on a hook next to the stove. She shook her head and smiled through her tears, and typed one word into the box.

'Alitheia'!

The End

ABOUT THE AUTHOR

Steve Grieves was born in Manchester in the United Kingdom which is the setting for his novel The Gates of Sedition. The Novel was previously published under the title Alithiea.
Among many other jobs he was for ten years a Senior Trade Union Official for the TGWU, which later became the Unite Trade Union.
His work is heavily influenced by his socialist principles and commitment to equality & social justice.

'The Gates of Sedition is set just a few years into the future. It is about the daily struggle of ordinary men & women who neo-conservatives would describe as the 'undeserving poor'. Much more it is about the grace and dignity with which they choose to resist the power of the State.

Steve currently spends his time between the UK & Greece where he plays in local bands for a free beer (or two) .

23907213R00148

Printed in Poland
by Amazon Fulfillment
Poland Sp. z o.o., Wrocław